Cavern

CAVERN

JAKE PAGE

University of New Mexico Press Albuquerque

First paperback edition, 2003

Library of Congress Cataloging-in-Publication Data

Page, Jake

Cavern:a novel/by Jake Page.—1st ed.

cm.

ISBN 0-8263-2227-1 (alk. paper)

1. Caving—New Mexico—Carlsbad Region—Fiction.

2. Radioactive waste disposal—Fiction.

3. Carlsbad Region (N.M.)—Fiction.

4. Spelunkers—Fiction.

I. Title

PS3566.A333   C38   2000

813'.54—dc21

99-050965

ACKNOWLEDGMENTS

I am grateful to many people who helped in material and other ways with the writing of this story, and to no one more than Zack and Tyson Barrett, who conjured up nameless monsters and elemental fears while standing in the utter dark eight hundred feet below the surface of the earth. Ford Stone, Roy and Barbara Carey, and Tom and Joyce Summers provided wonderful forms of hospitality in Carlsbad, New Mexico, as well as information and some yarns the swiping of which is hereby thankfully acknowledged. Another Stone—Nat—provided technical advice and encouragement at the outset, Jim Whittaker (no relation to Jack) provided an irresistible one-liner, and several people at the Department of Energy (who would all, I am sure, prefer to remain nameless) provided details and insight. Sara Voorhees applied a sensitive tuning fork and yet another Stone—Nancy—supplied a crucial insight along the way as well as encouragement. No matter what gets said about the creative flame, etc., etc., nobody doing this stuff can go long without encouragement. Another thing every writer needs is a sensitive and eagle-eyed copy editor and this book benefitted greatly by falling into the hands of Karen Taschek.

None of this would have taken place without the generosity of Kathleen Maynard Page, Brooke Pacy, and Kathy Willis. And you wouldn't have this book in your hand if it were not for Elizabeth

Hadas and her capacious definition of the role of the University of New Mexico Press.

It is typically at this point that authors pay obeisance to their long-suffering, patient spouses who never complain even once when the authors vanish into their lonely caves but instead divert children and clean up after the dog and . . . and all that sort of thing, meaning that the spouses played no role in the writing of the book and probably thought it was another damn fool gamble, jeopardizing the family's future. I cannot do that. My spouse, Susanne, was in every way part of this enterprise, including telling me that I should do this in the first place . . . and over a few initial and churlish refusals. Thereafter she plotted with me, schemed, read every word like a benign terrier, improved what she found, and might well have been listed as coauthor, but she seems to want me to take the heat on this one. God bless her.

Jake Page

PART ONE

The female slowly awakens from the long sleep of hibernation and finds herself in the presence of two new beings. She is unaware of how they got there, and the question of who they are does not trouble her mind. She does not recall licking them clean or hearing their high pitched squeaks as they fumbled around her.

As she slept, she was unaware of them suckling her, depleting her.

It makes little difference, for she follows urges that are so ancient, they are unidentifiable as to beginnings. She cares for these newcomers in the dark as vibrancy returns to her body, and she is aware again of a world around her and of a great hunger inside her—all part of a perpetual and mysterious cycle.

She growls with the irritation that arises from a cavernous hunger and stands up. Her long limbs tingle with the renewed flow of blood. In the utter dark, she makes her way through familiar ground, picking her way among the rock, down to where the stench assaults her nose, the smell of rot, of damp, the place where she knows she can gorge herself.

She stops, sniffing deeply. Something is different. Irritation turns to anger, and she rises up on her back legs, threatening the new.

ONE

Salt crunched under Dale Jenkins's feet, the endless, omnipresent, dead salt. White walls, white floor. All salt. Salt overhead, and about two thousand feet of rock. At first, it gave him the creeps, but he was used to it now, after six months working here. If he'd listened to his mother ten years ago and at least put in a couple of years at a community college, he might have gone on to be something else, maybe an accountant or something, somewhere else besides Carlsbad—maybe in Santa Fe doing taxes for all the stars. But here he was a cop. Well, yeah, a rent-a-cop, but he still had a big responsibility that went with his green uniform and the big thick leather belt and the weapon. Dale Jenkins liked being a cop, liked the responsibility, the image. Like, don't frig around with me.

Behind him he could hear the clatter of men and machines, guys whizzing around in electric carts, guys scraping loose salt off the walls, guys like him, underpaid, overworked undervalued . . . interchangeable parts. But still, it was a job, and it had authority.

Okay, he thought, here it is, S10249. The new tunnel, the one they closed down a few hours ago. Some technical glitch. No one was supposed to be here now. He'd walk on down into the gloom to the far end, make sure nobody had snuck down here to smoke some weed or whatever. And if someone had, he'd give 'im a warning, shoo his ass out, do the guy a favor, and maybe he'd behave. That was Dale Jenkins's style. A good guy.

But tough. Cross him twice and it was curtains, baby, curtains.

He made his way along the tunnel, salt crunching under his regulation steel-toed boots, and he saw the huge mining machine at the end, shadowy, a spooky-looking damn thing with its big-toothed cylinder raised on iron arms like some kind of steel monster out of a horror movie. As he approached it, he became aware of a smell, a musty stink, something way different than the smell of oil from the machine. He drew up beside the big mining machine, hand over his nose against the rank smell, wondering what the hell could it be.

He turned and looked back up the tunnel to the pool of ugly yellow light cast on the floor by a naked overhead bulb. Then he turned back to the machine and saw the teeth. Saw the red eyes, way up toward the ceiling. White face, immense white fangs . . . Blood roared in his head and he stood frozen as the bear, enormous, slashed at him with its paw . . . excruciating pain . . . and he blacked out, sensing in the recesses of a dying brain that he was being dragged.

Jack Whittaker was probably the only person in the crowd sweltering in the sun who didn't give much of a damn one way or the other about radioactive wastes. He wasn't really sure, even, why he was here, standing in the glare of the sun in a parking lot outside a chain-link fence, the dry air redolent of human sweat. Above him, sunlight glittered from sensuous coils of razor wire that snaked along the top of the fence.

Jack watched twenty-four figures, like monks, faces invisible, deep in shadow under gray hoods, as they proceeded toward the fence single file. A hush fell over the crowd, which parted as the procession approached. At the fence, the lead monk turned, cradling a gray metal canister in his arms. The others formed a semicircle behind him. Between the semicircle and the fence, a row of a dozen security guards in green uniforms stood alert but without expression, arms behind their backs, eyes unseen behind mirrored sunglasses. In the eerie silence, broken only by the whisper of a breeze that blew across the land from the southern horizon, the lead monk stepped to the center of the semicircle, raised the canister to the level of his shadowed face, and, abruptly, tossed his head backward. The gray hood fell away, and the sunlight gleamed from a white skull, hideously smiling. Like a wave, the hoods fell away from the other monks' heads, and twenty-three more skulls grinned in the sun.

Something exploded, like the sound of a far-distant firearm. The uniformed guards crouched down, hands on their shiny black holsters, as a metal plug from the bottom of the monk's canister hit the ground with the clank of a hubcap and green liquid gushed forth, splattering in the dust. An acrid, sickening stench filled the air, a poisonous miasma, and the monks swayed. A low moan rose in unison from their grinning mouths and their vacant eye sockets, and they all sank down, gray hoods and cloaks fluttering to the sand like funereal confetti at a parade of the dead.

Jack Whittaker recoiled from the stink. These people are lunatics, he thought, and decided to leave.

The uniformed guards relaxed and stood up while the crowd broke into applause, and several shouts began to meld into one loud cry, the throng all voicing their single command:

"No nuclear waste!

"No nuclear waste!

"No nuclear waste!"

Only moments after the monks' morality play in the desert had ended, and as if on cue from the rulers of universe, a semi rig appeared, rolling down the access road. It was the first of a caravan of four specially built tractor trailers completing their journey from the green-carpeted mountains to the north that cradled the haunted ground called Los Alamos National Laboratory. Each of the four semis bore two immense canisters with double titanium steel walls separated by a layer of a fireproofing material.

Within each canister were eight oil-drum-sized containers packed with tools and white suits and gloves, all of which bore traces of the most long-lasting lethal substance on the earth—plutonium.

5

"Here they come!" someone in the crowd shouted, and Jack Whittaker's head, along with all the others in the crowd, turned south toward the approaching caravan. A TV cameraman swiveled around and held the trucks in his viewfinder for the long minutes while they rolled along the access road at thirty miles an hour. Below him, the crowd began to move, surging with a rumble of voices toward the point along the chain-link fence where yet more green-uniformed guards stood by to open the gate.

This was the first shipment of materials contaminated with transuranic waste to reach what was called the Waste Isolation Pilot Plant, located some twenty miles out in the desert east of Carlsbad, New Mexico. It was known by its acronym, WIPP, and people had been protesting it, harassing it, taking it to court, calling their senators and representatives about it, damning it, heaping upon it every possible delay for nearly twenty years. But finally the great grindstone of federal intent had milled all complaints, all the people's stratagems, into dust, and the nuclear wastes were at last this side of the horizon. Here, in a man-made cavern that almost rivaled Carlsbad Caverns in size and depth, was a place of huge hallways, mined deep in a deposit of ancient salt, and here these most lethal wastes known to the world were to rest secure and unmolested for ten thousand years—a period at least three times that of any known civilization that has graced the planet. Ten thousand years backward in time, Canada was covered by a thick sheet of glacial ice, and in its cold shadow mastodons and immense bison and vultures with twelve-foot wingspans filled the landscape. Who was to say what would be plying this land ten thousand years into the future?

But the nuclear wizards guaranteed that here, a half mile down in a thick layer of salt, there would be no earthquake, not the slightest tremor, no disturbance for ten millennia. Here no water would ever seep. Here, once the mammoth cemetery was full and closed and the salt had obligingly flowed around the thousands of fifty-five-gallon drums, sealing them tight, somehow people would always remember to stay away, never to probe this particular part of Mother Earth's flesh.

WIPP wasn't the only industrial installation out in this god-forsaken desert, a place of thorny acacia bushes, greasewood, and mesquite. Elsewhere around the landscape were potash mines, oil pumps nodding like great insects, and several salt-processing plants. These were engaged in scooping up salt from the vast brine lakes that lay in the lowland depressions of the desert. The lakes looked for all the world like sparkling snow fields, and they were growing. Critics of WIPP would point to the expanding lakes of salt and suggest that the region wasn't as inert as the scientists thought.

The demonstrators now moving toward the gate—what they called the Gate of Hell—all knew their protest here in the desert was a hopeless mission, like a few fragile palm trees standing on a beach in lone opposition to an onrushing tsunami. But they required in their hearts that their views be heard, that they be counted however anonymously when, at some future time, Armageddon arrived and the world looked back and said, "If only . . . if only . . ."

Jack Whittaker watched the monks play out their stark reminder of the nuclear future with mixed feelings. He didn't normally think about such things, didn't hold particularly strong opinions about anything he thought of as political. Nor did he think very much of man-made holes in the ground—mines, for example, or this monstrous excavation in the salt beds below. The only way to get the hang of the subterranean world, as far as Jack was concerned, was to crawl around its natural nooks and crannies in the dark and the wet like a bacterium creeping through an intestine. Jack felt this way because he himself did just that—crawled around in the bowels of the earth. It was his avocation and his vocation. He was a spelunker, an explorer of caves who hired out as a guide. Two thousand caves—from small to immense—had been discovered in this one large area of southern New Mexico, and a lot of people, awestruck by their first visit to the bizarre cathedral-like formations of Carlsbad Caverns, thirsted for more. Well, maybe not a lot of people. *Some* people . . . enough for Jack to eke out a bit of a living and pursue his peculiar star.

His was a carefree life—no foreign entanglements, as he had taken to saying now that he was unmarried.

Typically, one does not start out with an inherent ambition to explore the dark passages under the earth's surface. Any miner's son hopes to make a career of doing something—anything—else. Jack was born in Colorado, in the mountains, and had come to know miners and their complaints. He had studiously avoided summer jobs in such places as he went through high school and then the University of Colorado at Boulder. He had studied as much as he had to in order to get by and spent most of his free time hiking around the high country. One time he joined some New Mexican students at the university on a trip during spring break to the cave country of the Guadalupe Mountains. And he was hooked, as quickly and as thoroughly as some people get hooked on cocaine. He had never left, never finished up at the university. He became a caver, a spelunker.

Like others of the odd spelunker ilk, Jack would drop anything to go "push" a new cave. And since the big fire in the eighties that had literally denuded the Guadalupe Mountains of trees and brush, leaving that ragged range naked, nothing but sharp craggy peninsulas of rock and scree rising vertiginously above precipitous canyons, they'd been discovering caves—some just shallow wind caves and some bona fide caverns—almost faster than they could name them.

Like all cave pushers around the world, Jack lived on the dream of finding a new cave, a mighty cavern. He yearned to be the first to enter a vast and utterly unknown, unspoiled underground phantasmagoria. Compared to such a dream, the salt cavern below him, scraped out by giant machines with the boring geometry of the engineer, was a major yawn. A rabbit warren of tunnels sitting there, passive and dead.

Many people—like all those around him in this mob of protesters—thought the place was surely full of leaks and subject to earthquakes, and radioactive goop was going to ooze out someday and an invisible lethality would spread across the landscape and the world would glow in the dark until life fizzled out except for cockroaches, maybe. But Jack figured that the big layer of salt about half a mile down probably was pretty inert, the whole region free of seismic activity—tremors, quakes, or anything else that would cause trouble—again, not that he thought much about it.

The salt, of course, was the result of the evaporation of a vast ancient inland sea. Off to the south and west—mostly within the crags of the Guadalupe Mountains but extending north in an arc around the city of Carlsbad—was the gargantuan reef that had grown up along the ancient sea's shoreline. That was where the action was, Jack thought. That was the happening place. The place where acidic water dripping down through the limestone had etched out caverns like Carlsbad, now a national park and lodestar to a zillion tourists . . . and the one called Lechuguilla they found in the eighties, bigger and deeper than Carlsbad and still off-limits except to experts . . . and others Jack had helped push during the last fifteen years since he had arrived here . . . *and* the cavern Jack Whittaker himself had found only a month ago in the shadows of the Quahada Hills, where no one thought such a cavern could exist.

So far, no one but Jack knew of its existence.

Jack had agreed to come with some flaky friends to the protest. Why not? He was idle that day. His friends were now somewhere in the middle of the crowd, and Jack stood off to the side, near the gate at the end of the road down which the trucks were coming.

The monks were coming his way too, leading the protesters. Behind him, a bunch of cops were shifting their feet nervously, and the wind was beginning to blow harder, kicking up little dust devils from the parking lot outside the fence. Overhead, a few clouds were materializing in the enormous sky. Behind the chain-link gate, the huge, light brown industrial-type buildings of the plant rose up in functional ugliness among a little city of trailers. WIPP had an odd look of impermanence.

Jack watched the monks approach, now a disorderly array of bobbing, livid death's heads, and was surprised when, as one, they reached up and removed their rubber skull masks. All twenty-four of the monks were women, mostly in their thirties and forties,

Jack guessed. The lead monk—monkess?—turned and spoke in a loud voice.

"We are the Mothers Against Poisoning the Living Earth. We will stand vigil here every day, every week, every month. . . ."

Jack tuned out as the woman continued her oration. He worked out the acronym. Mothers Against Poisoning the Living Earth. MAPLE. Wow, he said to himself, and was shoved violently from behind. A green-uniformed guard with a white cop helmet and a thick brown neck elbowed past and stood between him and the oncoming crowd.

"Okay, you people!" the officer barked. "That's far enough. Anyone who blocks the roadway will be forcibly removed." The female monks surged forward, as if pushed by a great pulse from within the crowd, and two of them fell against the officer, shoving him backward. His helmet struck Jack's right eye socket full force, and reflexively he shoved the cop away from behind.

"Watch out, for chrissake," he said, and the cop turned just as several more of the Mothers Against Poisoning the Living Earth crashed into him. Jack found himself lying on his back, the smell of dust and sweat in his nostrils, with about two hundred pounds of infuriated security cop struggling to get off him while more Mothers piled on, apparently helpless before the surging crowd. There was a lot of shouting, and Jack shoved the cop off to the side, saying, "Look, look, I'm not . . . ," when the light turned red and a pain exploded in his skull and shot down his neck like an ice pick through cheese, and it was all black everywhere.

Anna Maria Gonzales sat in the office of the director, Waste Isolation Pilot Plant, U.S. Department of Energy. She was a career federal bureaucrat who had been born to a poor couple from the little mountain town of Truchas, New Mexico, forty-three years ago. Immaculate in a blue business suit and a peach-colored silk blouse, she wore her jet black hair in short, carefully coifed curls, the picture of the American woman executive. Now she glowered at the TV screen and watched the crowd of demonstrators surging toward the gate. She saw a billy club flash in the melee, almost reflexively thumbed the button on her radio, and shouted into the static, "O'Connor! O'Connor! No violence! I said we would have no violence."

A voice came back through the little loudspeaker.

"Some guy slugged Moreno and . . ."

"No *violence,* I said. Handle it, O'Connor. There are women out there, and I don't want some Tiananmen Square scene on my . . ."

"Yes, *sir,*" the voice crackled, and Anna Maria's full black eyebrows lowered menacingly over her eyes as the static stopped and the radio connection clicked off.

"Insubordinate gringo *bastardo,*" the director said through her teeth, damning the policy that set the Department of Energy security section apart from all of the other employees of this plant and beyond her immediate control since they reported through a separate chain of command to the director of security in Washington. WIPP was, in fact, an administrative nightmare. Over each of WIPP's several departments was a Department of Energy chief, but the day-to-day management of the entire plant had been contracted out to a private corporation, Westinghouse. Among the day-to-day concerns that Westinghouse managers saw to was plant security—all the tighter now that nuclear waste was arriving for the first time. But as a cost-saving measure, Westinghouse had subcontracted the security guard function to a private local concern. So the WIPP site was guarded from terrorists or vandals or whoever might interfere with it, including demonstrators, by what some people sourly referred to as rent-a-cops.

Anna Maria watched the TV screen as the insubordinate gringo bastard O'Connor appeared, pulling the women in the gray monks' habits—a sacrilege, these people imitating the brothers!—away from the pile and pushing one of the security cops away. Moreno, she supposed. The lead truck was now nosing into the crowd, which began slowly moving back, begrudging it passage.

She heard a knuckle rap on the door and one of the techs, a young engineer named Feldman, stuck his head in, his face screwed up with concern. His job was to watch the console in the outer office, checking the flashing green lights—one for each hundred-yard sec-

11

tion of the fifty-two tunnels and connecting passageways a half mile below them in the salt. Each motion detector there lit up its own light on the console so WIPP's central nervous system would know if the workers below were where they belonged—or where they didn't belong.

It was a new installation, the expensive idea of someone in Washington, D.C., that had been imposed in the general paranoia as the opening day approached. Until recently, the standard mine safety practices had been sufficient. Chief of these was that everyone going underground took a small brass coin with a number on it down with them and brought it back up and replaced it on a large board in the waste-handling area. One always knew, then, if someone was still down below after the shift was over, and the mine safety people would go find him. It was simple, but it worked. In addition, gongs, sirens, and so forth all had particular meanings, such as "man down." But now the place was strung with all manner of super-high-tech electronic devices.

Anna Maria waved the tech in and said, "What is it?"

"Someone in S10249," Feldman said. He had a slight lisp.

Anna Maria looked at her watch, a gold Tag Heuer that said one thirty-six. "So?" she said.

"S10249 was closed an hour ago," Feldman said. "A one-oh-five."

A one-oh-five was a routine closing off of an area to permit other sensors in the tunnel to perform an exhaustive chemical analysis of the air whenever they detected a minimal trace of something improper. Yet another innovation. The sensors were sensitive in the realm of a few parts per billion, just a few molecules in a space the size of a bathtub. Oversensitive, Anna Maria thought, sending work crews scurrying off for two and sometimes three hours of dead time, money wasted, while the little machine digested the sample and decided what it might be. The damned little electronic busybodies hadn't found anything to worry about in six months, but they had rung the alarm eleven times in the same interval.

"Mine safety?" Anna Maria said. "You called?"

"They're on the way," the tech said, "But no one's supposed to be there. The brasses are all accounted for. This is weird."

When Jack Whittaker returned to consciousness, the sun had moved more than halfway down the western sky, where it was perfectly positioned to beam painfully into his eyes once he opened them.

His head throbbed already—what the hell had happened?—and now the sun was tying an ugly knot of pain behind each eye—where the hell was he? In a room with white walls, the sun pouring through the window. That much was clear. Lying on a cot. But where? He closed his eyes, and the sun was red inside his eyelids.

Sit up, sit up. Ouch.

He touched the egg-sized knot throbbing just above and behind his left ear. It began to come back to him—the female monks tumbling into the cop, the cop tumbling . . . pushing the cop off . . . then *whammo.* From somewhere. One of the other cops.

Jack pulled himself slowly to his feet, grunting, and took in his surroundings. The room was small, maybe eight by eight, with no furniture but the cot. On the floor, which was made of gray linoleum tiles covered with the ubiquitous pale dust of the desert, a pile of magazines lay in the corner—devoted to guns, knives, hunting. He saw an issue of *Soldier of Fortune* with a photo on the cover of a mean-looking white guy in camouflage, his face blackened to match the soldiers he apparently was leading into some awful jungle in Africa. Jack turned and saw an open doorway, leading to another room. He went through the door and saw one of the rent-a-cops sitting on a stool next to an open window. He realized he was in the guardhouse at the plant's main gate.

The cop turned and looked at him without apparent interest. He had a brightly sunburned face, except it was dead white around his eyes from sunglasses. It gave him the look of a slab of raw meat.

"You can go," the cop said.

"I need permission?"

"Don't be a smart-ass. You assaulted an officer. We could shovel your butt into a jail cell if we wanted. So beat it, Whittaker."

Jack reached for his wallet. It was still there in the back pocket of his jeans.

"Yeah," the cop said. "We peeked. We know all about you. Got you on our list now." The cop grinned, showing a row of large yellow teeth so even, they looked false. "Whittaker's Cavern Tours. Member of the American Spee-lee-oh-logical Society. One of them spee-lunker crazies. You live in a trailer over near Rocky Arroyo, and you drive a six year-old Isuzu Trooper that's in the shop to get a new transmission. So you're gonna have a long walk home. Better get started, Whittaker. It'll be dark before you get halfway back to Carlsbad."

Jack stepped out onto the top stair of three wooden steps that led down to the dusty ground outside the main gate. From behind him, he heard the cop chuckle, a phlegmy rasp.

"Protest is over, Whittaker. All the loonies and queers went home. It's called progress, boy. You can't stop it—don't make any difference how many women you throw in front of it."

The grounds outside the fence were deserted. His friends, every-one—gone, as the slab of raw meat had said. Jack turned and stepped back inside the guardhouse.

"I guess you're right, " he said, attempting a winning smile, but the effort made his knot throb, and he winced. "Well, you know, everybody plays their hand out till the game is over, right? No hard feelings."

The cop stared at him. Jack noticed the little green plastic name badge on his shirt—it said Wingo in white capital letters.

"Sergeant Wingo, you don't suppose I could make a local call on that phone, do you? I'm still a bit shaky here, and maybe I can get a ride." Jack had no idea what the man's rank was, but he thought he'd heard that sergeant was a big deal in police forces—a bigger deal than in the army.

Sergeant Wingo flipped a thick red hand toward the phone that sat on a shelf under the window. "Help yourself. Prob'ly ought to check in at the hospital. You look like shit."

Still not sated, the female bear returns to the place, forcing her way back in, and slowly her eyes adjust to the light. Merely the act of seeing is so new an experience that she is confused. Neither she nor any of her kind have ever experienced fear, the flight response. Quite the opposite. There is the salty taste still in her mouth, and she yearns for more. She will be patient in this new world of unfamiliar images and new prey. She stands between the strange cold rock with its beckoning smell and the side of the cave, listening.

TWO

Earlier, Anna Maria Gonzales had listened while the head of security, the crew-cut old marine, Chuck O'Connor, barked into the
radio, "What do you mean, there's no one there? The lights were
flashing."

The voice of the mine safety chief came back through the static.
"There's no one here. The place is empty. Just us."

"Someone else was there when you got there."

"Maybe the sensors are screwed up."

Madre de Dios, Anna Maria swore to herself. If anything can go
wrong, it will.

"Okay," O'Connor said. "We'll send a tech down there." He
glanced at Anna Maria. "Okay?"

The director nodded.

Since then, the mine safety team had come up the elevator from
the depths of WIPP and a tech had gone down. Staring at the console, the director and O'Connor had watched the lights flash on
and off, tracking the tech into S10249, one of the new tunnels, still
incomplete, and one where work had now been stopped for almost
five hours. Sometimes it struck Anna Maria more forcefully than
others that it was an enormous waste of time and money, hollowing
out all these tunnels long before they were needed, scraping the
walls and ceiling over and over.

But WIPP was now open, under way. On her watch. And now

one of the sensors devised by the geniuses at Los Alamos to help guarantee the security of this place was acting up, blinking like an idiot when no one was there. Another headache, another snafu. She would have to wait until it was resolved, which meant another long evening spent in this office.

Now the tech, a sour little man named Holmein, was talking again over the radio, explaining that the sensors in S10249 were all in perfect working order.

"Then get the hell up here," O'Connor said, and thumbed off the radio. "I'm gonna close the whole plant," he said. "Maybe one of them goddamn enviros got in somehow."

"Is that really necessary?" Anna Maria asked.

"Look, someone was down there before the mine safety guys got there, and he's nowhere to be seen. Now, don't that just chill your bones, Madame Director?"

"Judging from just the length, I'd have to say this is *Bison antiquus antiquus.*"

The woman in the white lab coat wore her blond hair arranged behind her head with a silver-and-turquoise clip. She put the fossilized leg bone back into a large cardboard carton. Removing a pair of half glasses that had slipped down toward the end of her nose, she turned to face her visitor, a smallish man who stood anxiously beside her. Several inches taller than he, she looked down at him from large, dark brown eyes, and smiled. The man reddened slightly and looked away. He had something of a crush on this graceful woman with long legs and a smile that was like a sudden burst of sunlight.

"Overall front leg length for this guy," she said, "would be about nine hundred centimeters plus a bit, maybe. That's a hundred centimeters less than *latifrans,* the old guys from the Ice Age. So this is pretty recent, maybe two, three thousand years. Sorry to disappoint you."

The man clearly was disappointed. He was an amateur bone hunter who often brought his finds into the museum, always with high hopes that he'd found something truly ancient. He was smart

17

enough to know the difference between a bison femur and that of a cow and to know the difference between something fossilized and something recent. But that's about how far his knowledge went, and Cassie Roberts couldn't remember how many times she had sent him off with that same look of disappointment on his face.

The man's shoulders slumped, and he picked up his carton. "That's okay, Dr. Roberts. I'll just keep on looking," he said. He looked longingly at the shelves that lined the walls on either side of the large table where Dr. Cassandra Roberts had measured his bison femur and dashed his dreams yet one more time. The shelves were laden with old bones, old fossils, a library of Ice Age mammals. He was a retired dentist from Iowa City, had moved to Carlsbad about a decade earlier, and found some old teeth in his backyard (it turned out they were camel teeth from the time around the Civil War when the Confederates tried out camels as beasts of burden, finally letting the cranky beasts go wild). Thus began the ex-dentist's passion.

"Bye, Dr. Roberts," the man said, turning to go.

"You take care, Dr. Holloran," Cassie said sympathetically to the man's narrow back as he made his way down the aisle to the door. She turned back to her table and glanced up at the huge poster hanging over it, an elaborate and considerably romanticized painting of the La Brea Tar Pits in Los Angeles. It showed a mammoth up to its belly in the tar, struggling in its final agony. Surrounding it on firmer ground were a saber-toothed cat with its jaws ferociously agape and several huge vultures lurking like hunchbacked messengers of death. Beyond, here and there in the landscape, were several utterly unconcerned herds of Ice Age grazers, including, at the horizon, a herd of *Bison latifrans,* immense but relatively short-legged and clumsy-looking versions of the bison of today. This was Cassie Roberts's world, her specialty—the great beasts that once roamed the North American continent, almost all of which were extinct by eleven thousand years ago, shortly after the great glaciers had begun to recede back into the north country. The bison, of course, had survived, as had pronghorns, elk, and moose, but over the millennia the bison had become smaller, longer of leg, and fleeter of foot.

When asked how she had become a paleontologist, she would point to her childhood summers at her grandparents' beach cottage on the Delaware shore, where for about a week each summer the beach was filled with horseshoe crabs, females come ashore to lay their eggs. Cassie had learned early on that these creatures weren't really crabs but descendants of trilobites and that they didn't bite or pinch like crabs. She also learned that the horseshoe crabs had been doing exactly the same thing every year for hundreds of millions of years—far longer than a child or anyone else could really imagine. Some would become stranded when the tide went out, littering the beach with what looked like abandoned helmets, and Cassie made a practice of tossing them back into the sea.

So it seemed almost instinctive to her, once she had finished four years at an eastern women's college, to apply for graduate school at the University of Pennsylvania in paleontology. There she focused on the great mammal populations of the Ice Age. She had made a name for herself in her field quite soon out of graduate school by proving to everyone's satisfaction that most of the great Ice Age creatures had gone extinct on their own, without the help of early hunters. This put an end to the theory that they had been wiped out by overzealous ancestors of the American Indians, a theory the Indians resented deeply, of course, and so she had received a special award of merit from the Congress of Indigenous Peoples, a Washington-based lobbying group that apparently spent most of its time trying to get the Washington Redskins to change their name. She had then been offered the job of curator of vertebrate paleontology at the Carlsbad Museum, hardly the Smithsonian or the Carnegie Institute, but positions were few and far between in her narrow field. She had taken the post with enthusiasm and had worked here for eight years now.

In those eight years, she had built the museum's collections with great skill, obtained more than her fair share of grant money, and married. He was a lunatic and, she still thought, a wonderful lunatic in some ways, but she didn't have to remind herself that he was hopeless too. It simply hadn't worked out, so she was single again. Had been single for two and a half years now. Carlsbad wasn't exactly overrun by eligible men, so Cassie Roberts kept her nose to her particular grindstone and tried not to think very often about how lonely she was.

The shrill electronic sound of the telephone jarred her out of her reverie. It was a wall phone, mounted next to the tar pit poster with a twenty-foot cord now all tangled up. She reached out and plucked the receiver off the wall.

"Roberts," she said.

"Cassie."

Oh no. It was Jack. The hopeless lunatic of an ex.

"Cassie, it's me. I'm really sorry to bother you, but I'm stuck out here. I need a ride. Is there . . . ?"

"Stuck where?" Cassie said, noting that her voice sounded icily neutral.

"WIPP. I was out at the demonstration."

"That disgusting old Trooper break down again?"

"Yeah. Two days ago. It's in the shop. I came out here with friends, but things got rough, and everybody left."

"Rough?"

"I got slugged by a security cop. Just standing there and . . . Look, can you come and get me? I'm really sorry. . . ."

Cassie Roberts rolled her dark brown eyes heavenward and sighed.

"Okay, okay," she said. "It'll take me about forty minutes."

"Cool. Thanks, Cassie. I really mean it. I'll walk out to seven-ninety-four."

"You're okay for that?"

"It's just my head they hit."

They had parted in friendly enough fashion given that they were getting divorced, which is—no matter how you rationalize it—a major rejection, a major *no*, leaving both parties wondering, if only secretly, if they were even more blameworthy than they thought, never mind how intolerable the situation the other side had produced. Now, still, after two and a half years, Cassie thought with a kind of bittersweet fondness of the man who had made her life so miserable for four years but also so unpredictably, irresponsibly—well, yes—fun.

The ups and downs had looked like a Japanese seismic chart, and finally it was simply too much for Cassie. She was on her way to a distinguished career, she had an orderly scientific mind, responsibilities, complicated worlds to conquer, and she had grown up with a timid mother and an alcoholic father from whom she had learned to fear the unpredictable and to keep her own counsel. Zany Jack's whimsical approach to the world had finally left her exhausted, confused, and—eventually more often than not—pissed off. Particularly the times he'd disappear. Following some lunatic spoor, searching for his Holy Grail out in the crags and canyons, some cavern yet unknown, some major new feature of the earth he could put his name on, like a fortune hunter, like a treasure seeker, like those gold prospectors in the old days. Madmen, stuck at the mental—or was it emotional?—age of a fourteen-year-old. Jack and his spelunker buddies—all of them hoping to be the next James White, the legendary discoverer of Carlsbad Caverns in 1901, who'd then spent twenty years mining bat guano from the cavern before he managed to persuade people to look at the place. Some hero.

And after these sudden disappearances, Jack would come back days later, looking like death warmed over, his lips all chapped, covered with dust, with a stupid shit-eating grin on his face, and say, "Well, that sure didn't work out like I thought," and go to sleep for two days while all the scrapes on his arms and his belly turned to scabs.

Even thinking about it—visualizing him with his broad shoulders and sunburned neck, his shock of black hair all greasy and tangled, standing there in his cruddy old hat with the *brim*, even, stained with sweat and grease and God knows what else, looking straight into her eyes as innocent as a dog, his legs slightly bowed, legs that seemed a little too short—she felt the old rage rise up in her gorge.

Cassie turned onto Route 794 and headed east across the flat desert scrub toward the WIPP site while the sun, in its own fury and disappointment at a day gone by, turned the world behind her a violent vermilion.

Ten minutes later, she saw him on the side of the road about a half mile ahead on the edge of a brine lake that glowed pink. He was sitting on his haunches, the lowering sun turning his T-shirt a bright orange and casting a long shadow that tracked maybe a hundred feet across the desert. He was the only living thing in sight except for the scrubby sage and acacia sprinkled thirstily on the land, each casting its own elongate shadow. He didn't move as she approached, but squatted still as a rock. He was asleep, she knew. He could sleep standing on his head or hanging from a rope over a precipice in the pitch dark. She slowed down, and as she passed him at about ten miles an hour, he looked up, blinked, and smiled. The shit-eating grin.

She threw the car into a U-turn, throwing gravel and dust into the air, and pulled up beside him, heading west. Or at least where she guessed he was, since he hadn't stood up and she couldn't see him out the passenger-side window.

"Jack!" she called. "Let's go!" She realized she was furious. Again. Still.

"Come on!"

His head appeared in the window. He grinned again and pointed with one finger at the lock button, which was down. Cassie leaned over and pulled it up, noting that his face, beneath the bronze of the sun and the dust of the day, was pale, dead looking. His nearly black eyes seemed to be covered with a film of confusion. He opened the door, moving in slow motion, and got in.

"Cassie," he said, looking out the front. "You look beautiful."

She put the car in gear and pulled out onto the road.

"You *are* beautiful," he said. "You don't just look beautiful."

She shifted into second, and the engine roared under her too heavy, pissed-off, no, infuriated foot.

"You've always been beautiful."

She shifted into third. The speedometer read fifty.

"Inside, too, I mean. In your soul, you know?"

She hit sixty-eight, the engine screaming, and shifted into high.

"We're going to the hospital," she said.

"Oh," he said agreeably. "Okay."

From the corner of her eye, she saw his head fall forward.

"Wake up! You've got a concussion, you asshole," she said, even though she knew he couldn't hear her.

Phil Holmein didn't like working at WIPP. Not at all. He was a security expert, meaning he was a techie in the esoteric realm of providing security devices of astounding cleverness. He was officially employed by Sandia National Laboratories in Albuquerque, the sister lab to Los Alamos, where his department worked on developing and perfecting the equipment used by the Department of Energy to keep terrorists from getting into the nation's scattered stores of nuclear material like plutonium, with which a terrorist with a brain or two could build an atomic "device" and blow New York City or Los Angeles off the map in about three seconds, thus bringing to an end the cultural life of the United States. The Sandia engineers had also been asked to provide a better way for airports to detect weapons and what have you before they got on airliners full of people, and even simple devices for sniffing out drugs and guns on the Mexican border and in the nation's elementary schools. They had taken a Los Alamos design for sensors that could be used at the WIPP site and had turned it into something practical.

Phil Holmein was no great inventor, nor did he have an actual advanced engineering degree, but he was handy as hell when it came to the delicate sort of security machinery that had been installed in WIPP. So, much to his dismay, he had been loaned to WIPP for an unspecified period, his task being something like the Maytag repairman on the TV—available to fix things that didn't ever, or only rarely, need fixing.

Phil, who was now thirty-one years old and single, was a man of neither great imagination nor cultural ambition, but even for him, life in Carlsbad, New Mexico, on the edge of the vast and flat plains, seemed pretty tame on a good day and utterly, devastatingly barren on bad ones. In short, Phil found himself in a permanent state of boredom resulting from underutilization of both his talents and his senses. At least Albuquerque had its "Loin," its strip on Central Avenue, where a single cool dude could find a little action. Carlsbad, on the other hand, might as well have been an Amish Bible camp. So many God-fearing people in the same place gave Phil Holmein's rather nasty little soul a case of claustrophobia. And these damned caverns a half mile down in the earth were even worse.

The tunnels all looked alike, long and wide, wide enough to make the fifteen-foot ceilings seem low, ominous, threatening. The walls were all covered with circular ridges, scraped out by the toothed, whirling cylinder that was the business end of a huge machine called a Marietta Miner. The walls glistened and sparkled in the light, but the tunnels were all lit with only the occasional bulb, providing pools of sickly yellow light amid long stretches of gloom. He couldn't describe the smell—that much salt is like nothing else in the world—but it was cloying, a kind of helpless smell. It made him feel embalmed. And, of course, knowing that the salt moved, however slowly, just moved on its own by some sort of geophysics he neither knew nor cared to know—it gave him the willies. They had to prop up the ceilings with long steel bolts and chain-link fencing to keep them from collapsing from the weight of a half mile of rock and earth above the salt layer, but the salt still moved here and there, and they scraped it clean every now and then, nice and geometrical, and he still knew the salt was creeping, and it always made the hair on his neck stand up when he was down here.

The sensors in this tunnel—S10249—all checked out. They always checked out, didn't they? He had no idea what it was that had got the director's tits in a wringer, sending him down here, but whatever it was, it wasn't any malfunction of his equipment. And so all he had to do now was walk down this creepy tunnel about two hundred feet to the elevator, which was open, waiting for him, and get sealed up in it like some kind of capsule and be shot up to the surface of the earth. And then he would be off duty. He had an irrational state of nerves about elevators—always had since he was a little kid, a toddler, and he and his grandmother got caught in one for seven hours in an old apartment building on New York City's Lower East Side, where she lived by herself with a cat. But elevators were nothing compared to the willies these damn tunnels down here gave him. Maybe it was because they were so utterly otherworldly and so utterly silent. And maybe it was because he always wondered if the lights might fail and he'd be down here enveloped in the pitch-dark silence. He fondled his radio, hanging from his techie tool belt.

Phil set off for the elevator, relieved that his task was over, and bowed elaborately to the first motion detector he passed (Phil wasn't without a sense of humor, after all). But something then impinged on his nervous system, something he couldn't quite place. He walked on, eyes staring straight in front, his other senses tingling with alertness. It came again, and he identified it as a scratching sound, like a bit of static. He thumbed his radio button to reassure himself that he had turned it off after reporting Upstairs. It was off.

He heard the sound again and spun around, and his eyes widened and his throat closed off, choking the scream that had risen up from the depths of his being into a gurgle.

Tracer Dunn glowered at the pattern of horizontal stripes that vibrated behind the picture on his TV. It was on old TV, color'd gone thin, and the reception was enough to give a man a headache. Tracer Dunn didn't really want to see all those hippies carrying on over at the WIPP site, just the sight of people like that made him angry, but he watched anyway. The picture cut to a close-up of that fellow Tom, the Channel Four newscaster, kind of a pretty boy, talking at the camera, explaining that after twenty years the great trucks bearing radioactive waste were rolling toward the WIPP site after driving in a caravan of four down from Los Alamos. They were right there on the horizon. Over the years, he explained, the opposition had tried every avenue to put off this fateful day forever, but finally all the lawsuits, all the injunctions and delays, all the protests, had come to naught, and the trucks were coming. The TV showed the trucks approaching. An era was over, the an-

25

nouncer was saying, and a new one was beginning, and only time—a lot of time—would tell who was right. The camera now showed all the protesters milling around the gate and the Energy Department cops standing there, looking self-conscious.

Tracer Dunn wished a pox on the whole bunch. Hippies and government thugs.

A clatter of pots being put away in the kitchen drowned out the announcer's next words, and Tracer Dunn shouted, "Will ya be quiet in there? I'm listenin' to the TV." The clatter subsided. He hated these cramped quarters, this trailer he and the woman had needed to move into when the old ranch house roof had given in. It wasn't much of a place, the old ranch house, never had been, but it had hardwood floors and five rooms, counting a kitchen, giving a man a little room to spread out. He'd bought the trailer from a displaced Texan who wanted to go home—for six thousand dollars—and hauled it out here. That was two, no, three years ago.

He'd bought the ranch ten years ago—in all, fifteen thousand acres if you counted the leased ten thousand Bureau of Land Reclamation acres that came with the place. Between running three hundred head on the long since overgrazed land and stints as a hunting guide in the Guadalupe Mountains, he had been eking out an existence here all these years. But not enough to put a new roof on that damned ruin of a house.

The Mexican woman in the kitchen had been with him eight of those years, which he guessed made her his common-law wife, though he didn't really think about her that way. Didn't really think about her at all, truth to say. Tracer Dunn was sixty-three years old, gaunt as a stick, with not much on his bones but sinew. He had grown up here in southeastern New Mexico, on the staked plains, and had run through at least three different lives before he fetched up here on this deteriorating ranch just east of the Quahada Hills almost in sight of that damned WIPP site.

In fact, the WIPP site was his closest neighbor, which made him uneasy because he had a deep-seated suspicion of the feds, no matter what form they came in. The Energy Department mafia. Forest rangers in the Guadalupes. Bureau of Land Management busybodies. Park Service people over at the caverns. Fish and Wildlife goody-goodies prowling around, trying to seal off what was left of God's own country so nobody would harm the last two living, transparent, two-inch, useless, inedible pupfish in some creek. And the environmentalists, Sierra Club pantywaists like those hippies over at WIPP today, cow haters, want to take a man's living away from him so they can hike around in their special little walking shoes in a great, open, manureless West . . . Now look at that, Tracer Dunn thought, a bunch of them in cloaks like the old friars, walking around in skull masks, if that don't beat all.

"Hey, Lucia! Get in here. They're wearin' death masks. Just like you people on the Day of the Dead."

"No, thank you," Lucia said in Spanish from the kitchen.

Tracer Dunn laughed out loud and watched one of the green-uniformed cops being pushed by a bunch of women and a billy club go through the air, and then Tom again mumbling something, and Tracer Dunn's mind switched over from the melee to his cattle, which were now mostly grazing the parched grass over near the WIPP site. He'd moved them over there from the Quahada Hills side after he found one of them dead, a carcass all torn to pieces, and one other missing, just plumb disappeared. Poachers, probably. He wouldn't put it past those enviros either, to run off with his cattle. And here was a bunch of them sure as hell going to be thrown out of the WIPP site—no telling what they'd do.

He stood up, flicked off the TV, watching the pretty boy announcer's face implode in a field of electric blue-green and vanish with a click, and stumped stiffly across the room to where his old Winchester 30.30 stood in the corner.

"I'm goin' out," he said. "See if I can catch me a vandal."

In the kitchen, the woman called Lucia listened to the trailer door slam and raised her eyes to the ceiling. Lucia was much given to prayer, but this gesture of the eyes was no prayer. It was despair. Her man, never easy, was now slowly going mad.

THREE

"Anytime you think someone may have a concussion, you keep them awake," the young doctor said, and Cassie Roberts bristled inwardly. It was the U.S. Government who'd knocked him cold for a couple of hours. And he'd dozed for only ten minutes in her car. And furthermore, she wasn't his keeper anymore. And she didn't like being preached to by this didactic little man who was probably no more than a year out of medical school. He had entered the waiting room, looking at his clipboard, and without even glancing at her, said, "You're the one who brought Mr. Whittaker in?" And then launched into his lesson for the day.

"Does he?" Cassie said, interrupting the beginning of what sounded like a further lesson on head injuries.

"Does he what?"

"Have a concussion?"

"In fact, no. Just a big egg behind his ear and a disorienting head-ache. We've given him an analgesic and told him to rest for a day or two till the headache goes away. He'll be along in a moment." With that, the little doctor turned and marched off, his white coat flap-ping around his knees, thick sponge-rubber soles squeaking on the polished linoleum tile floor. Cassie noted that the officious little man walked with his toes pointed outward, like a duck. Quack, quack, she thought, and smirked at the pun.

Beyond the doctor's receding figure, down the hall, Jack Whittaker emerged from a side corridor and began walking toward her. He was a six footer, a couple of inches taller than Cassie, with broad shoulders and a thick chest, long in the torso or, as the cliché had it, tall in the saddle. His black hair was usually a bit independent, but now it looked positively disheveled. Small stature was an obvious advantage for a caver, and many she had met during their marriage were quite small. But Jack made up for his size with strength and suppleness. He was, even at a casual glance, an athlete of some sort, but he didn't look like one now. He moved slowly on his slightly bowed legs, like someone balancing a teacup on his head. In the waiting room, he smiled weakly.

"You have some shades I could borrow?" he asked. "Mine got lost."

"They're prescription."

"That's okay; I'm already blurry."

"The sun's gone down," Cassie said.

"Okay, *okay*," he said testily.

"Now, look . . ."

Jack threw up his hands and winced. "Ouch. Okay, I apologize. I'm very grateful to you. Do you think you could give me a lift to my place?"

"I wasn't planning on having you walk."

"I'm okay."

"Come on, let's go."

"Maybe you could stop in for a moment?" he said, following her into the lobby. She turned her head and looked at him severely. "I've got something to show you."

"I've seen it," she said.

"No, no, I've got something you need to see. A photograph. Maybe you can identify it."

She pushed open the glass door and held it for him as he walked out into the dusk.

"A photograph of what?"

"That's what I need you to tell me."

"Touché," she said, and struck out across the parking lot.

Twenty minutes later, Cassie pulled off Route 185 onto the paved road that led across the desert west to Rocky Arroyo and, beyond, to Sitting Bull Falls.

"It's near Rocky Arroyo," Jack said.

"How's your head?"

"Better. They gave me two Tylenol, and I took three more when they weren't looking. My ears are ringing, but my headache's better." Cassie shook her head.

When they reached the place called Rocky Arroyo—which consisted of a few fieldstone homes—Cassie slowed to a crawl, and Jack pointed to a dirt track that led through some low trees and brush. The headlights soon picked up the dead-white siding of his trailer.

"There it is. Home, sweet home."

Presently Jack bent over the lock on the trailer door and fumbled his key into it. He opened the door, reached in around the doorway, and flicked on a light. Cassie walked in past him and stood in the middle of a living room. What she guessed was a kitchen was beyond a doorway at the far end to her right, and to her left was a door into what had to be a bedroom. On the wall opposite the entrance was a homemade bookcase of unfinished pine lumber, floor to ceiling, filled with books and reports, some of which she remembered. Jack's extensive library of caverns, spelunking, and geology. To the right of the bookcase was a table built from a door and two-by-fours, which was covered with a scatter of U.S. Geological Survey maps and other paper. Next to the table was an aged easy chair with a seedy green slipcover. On the walls were posters showing caverns, all beautifully lit to show off the bizarre formations, like enormous cathedrals designed by trolls or hobbits. And in the corner, up against the kitchen wall, was a vast heap of ropes and carabiners, pulleys and other gear, hard hats, carbide lights, electric ones, masks, aluminum Halliburton cases. Spelunking gear, the finest. A little ways off was a neatly stacked pile of shoe boxes—maybe a dozen in all.

"What's in the shoe boxes?" Cassie asked.

"Shoes."

Cassie looked at him.

"Vietnam army boots. They're hard to find nowadays. A lot of people I take out, you know, newbies, they have the wrong footwear. So I keep a supply here, different sizes. Just one of the benefits available to clients of Whittaker's Cavern Tours. You want a beer?"

"No."

"You look uncomfortable."

"I am uncomfortable."

"I used to be a better housekeeper, huh? I don't have much of a reason now."

"Let's not . . . ," Cassie began, and Jack's face brightened.

"Okay," he said. "The photograph." He crossed over to the map-strewn table and began rustling around in the mess. "Actually, I have a set of photographs here, different angles on something I came across in my travels, my quest for the Holy Grail you never thought all that much of. Sit down in that chair there. Go ahead, it's not as bad as it looks. Here," he said, whisking a set of eight-by-ten black-and-white prints from the cluttered table. "Sit down."

Cassie sat down, sinking into the deep stuffing of the chair, and took the photographs in her hand.

"It's a footprint," she said, looking at the photograph on top.

"Right. A bear."

She looked through two more, different angles of a bear's footprint in some white sandy-type soil, shadows from a flash putting the print into sharp relief. The five similar toes with the claw marks showed sharp and deep in the dirt beyond the toes, and the large, pear-shaped footpad pressed deeply and clearly into the ground.

"So, it's a bear," she said.

"What kind of bear?"

"It was around here?"

Jack nodded.

"So it's a black bear. That's the only kind around here."

Jack shook his head. "After I took those three, I remembered you need something for scale. So look at the water bottle in the next photos. I did the whole sequence over with the bottle beside it." He spun around and began groveling around in his heap of equipment. "Here. Here's the very bottle." He put it on the floor next to her feet.

Cassie looked at the photograph, and her eyes widened. She looked down at the clear plastic bottle, picked it up, put it down, and looked back at the photograph.

"Jesus!" she said.

"Yeah. And hallelujah too. So what is it, Cassie?"

"It's the biggest bear print I've ever seen. A grizzly? The last grizzly here in New Mexico was killed in the 1920s. You mean there's still . . ."

Jack snatched a paperback book off the cluttered table, a brand-new copy of the Peterson *Field Guide to Animal Tracks*. It fell open in his hand to a page showing a series of footprints—three types of bear tracks.

"Look here, see? A grizzly print is ten inches long from heel to claw and five across. This one in the photo, it's like fifteen inches long. That's no griz. It's more than an inch deep there in the rock."

"Rock?"

"Limestone."

"Like . . . ?"

"Like old, Cassie. Old. One of your guys, maybe. That's what I thought. All those old animals were big, right? Giant sloths, giant beavers. Were there any really big bears back then?"

"My God," Cassie said. "My God." She was having trouble breathing.

"Your eyes are rolling around, Cassie. What is it? Was, I mean."

"This could be the first footprint anyone's ever seen of a . . . Where did you find it? In a cave, right?"

"Not just any cave. I'll tell you. No one else knows about this cavern. No one." Cassie looked up at Jack's face. It was glowing as if there were a light shining from within. His black eyes were boring into her like laser beams.

"I think maybe I'll take that beer you offered," Cassie said.

In a weak moment, Tracer Dunn might have admitted that it was an act driven more by paranoia than good sense. Every time cattle were moved in this unforgiving land, they lost a bit of whatever weight they had gained scuffing around among the scrub for a few bites of dried-up, sun-bleached bunchgrass. And the ranching business was so tight that a few pounds off a steer meant the difference between profit and loss. But Tracer Dunn was, this night, possessed by his distaste for environmentalists and DOE goons and decided to move his cattle away from the WIPP site and back to the western side of the ranch, even though that's where one had been killed and one had gone missing.

The cattle moved along amiably enough ahead of Tracer's horse, a pinto called Chico, who knew exactly how to do all the work of moving cattle. Tracer was, in a sense, along for the ride in the moonlight. This was the only part of ranching that he enjoyed anymore—being out on his horse, moving cattle across the land. The rest was tedium and hard labor and worry. And he was just plain getting too old for all that. He was getting fed up with it all, especially all the rules and regulators, and he was damn tired of being a poor man.

They were almost there now. Afterward, he decided, he'd go into town and look for a little society.

The Stand Pipe Saloon, which is locally known simply as Ma's, sits back about a hundred feet off Canal Street, the main drag of Carlsbad, surrounded by a dusty lot where several generations of pickups and other vehicles have hollowed out large and small depressions in the underlying caliche, which is the cementlike substance the earth often turns into in these parts. When it rains, which is not very often, the depressions quickly fill up with water, and on several occasions patrons of Ma's, their carelessness augmented by too many long necks, have stumbled into these miniponds, fallen, passed out, and nearly drowned.

No fool, Ma watches such a patron leave the premises and listens for an engine to start up. If one doesn't, she waits a few moments and then sends one of her four sons out into the lot to rescue the drunk. No one, not even her sons, knows how old Ma is. She could easily be in her late sixties, seventies, or even early eighties, but her hearing is astonishingly acute for any age, and she can unfailingly hear an engine start outside in the lot (or not start), even over the wailing of country singers who carry on about loves lost and loneliness from one o'clock in the afternoon, when Ma's opens six days a week, till two o'clock in the morning, when, out of respect for the neighborhood, she closes.

Despite saving some of her patrons from death by drowning and other kindnesses that Ma is properly admired for, the nice people of Carlsbad don't go there often—or at all. It is, well, a little bit grungy. Besides the normal offerings of the bar, Ma can be induced to produce any one of two dishes—steak and french fries, or a hamburger and fries. Ma holds that french fries constitute an adequate vegetable dish. None of these dishes are looked after by the "chef" (one of her sons) with much care while they cook, and practically no one orders the food there. The seriously hungry go elsewhere, to one or another of Carlsbad's few non-fast-food restaurants, or stay home.

Derby Catlin considered himself one of the nice people of Carlsbad. He was the editor of the city's second newspaper, a weekly called *The Intelligencer,* a free handout that survived on a thin trickle of advertising dollars from the local merchants. He was also something of a self-styled local historian. But Derby Catlin was also something of a regular at Ma's, it being to his professional advantage, he thought, to keep his finger on the pulse of the common folk of Carlsbad, those whose opinions were often overlooked if heard at all. Which is to say, Ma's was not only about the only place where there was much anyone would call nightlife, except for a few similar places that catered to a Mexican clientele, but also a first-class rumor mill. Nice people, Catlin had learned long ago growing up in a ritzy suburb of Chicago and later as a stringer for *People* magazine, rarely realize how much of their own lives are scrutinized and discussed by house workers, yard men, gas station attendants, grocery clerks, ranch hands—all those day laborers who attend them.

So at about eight o'clock, Derby Catlin, having finished up his work at *The Intelligencer,* pushed open the swinging doors at Ma's. (The doors themselves were antiques, Ma claimed, that once swung

34

open "on easy hinges" at a saloon in rough-and-tumble Seven Rivers in the late nineteenth century, permitting them to be used, when needed, as stretchers.) Five minutes later, Catlin was sitting with two other men at the bar, engaged in yet another discussion of the Waste Isolation Pilot Plant, the largest employer in the area by far and a godsend particularly since the Arabs had practically killed off oil as a viable enterprise in southern New Mexico.

It was a quiet night at Ma's. Only four other men, sitting at a table in the corner, were in attendance.

"Well," said the man at the bar sitting to Catlin's right, "I'll sure as hell be interested to see what the chamber of commerce says now the place is open. Jobs, yeah, but I think them motel people are nuts. A whole lot a people are scared half to the grave by the word *nuclear*. I mean, up north, you remember? They had that outbreak of virus, that Navajo virus...."

"It wasn't a *Navajo* virus," Catlin said. "It's just that it got started there. Lot of white people got it too."

"That's egg-zactly what I'm sayin.' Some Navajos caught this thing, and then some white people, and then everybody from all over the damn world heard about it and started cancelin' their reservations in every hotel and motel and campground in New Mexico. Wasn't but twelve people died from it, but the whole world got in a panic—you'd a thought it was the black plague. Now just how do you think the Carlsbad New Mexico Chamber of Commerce, never mind those twenty-watt bulbs in Santa Fe, gonna persuade people who're scared of a virus that radioactive waste ain't a bigger hazard? I mean, how you gonna persuade people that bone-ignorant that Carlsbad Caverns itself ain't a waste dump? That's what I'm sayin', and I've been a-sayin' it for thirteen years and nobody's ever given me a satisfactory answer yet."

The man took a long swig on his long neck—a Bud Light. At the end of the bar, sitting on her stool from which she kept track of things, Ma rolled her eyes. Everyone had heard much the same thing from this man for almost the entire thirteen years.

"Well, Ollie," the man on Catlin's left said. "I guess we'll just have to see."

35

"Say," Ollie said. "Derby? Did you see them women dressed up like dead monks on the TV tonight? You know, at WIPP with their skull masks and all? In my book they were the best yet. Get my annual award for the most oh-riginal way to make a damn fool of yourself.... Hey, look. There's old Tracer Dunn comin' in."

"I heard his truck," Ma muttered.

The gaunt old rancher walked slowly across the floor to the bar and put his hands on it. They were large hands, gnarled and muscular, and they looked far too big for his wrists. Ma's son, languishing behind the bar, opened him a Bud Light and put it before him.

"You found any poachers yet?" Ollie asked.

"Not yet, Ollie," Dunn said.

"But when you do . . ."

"Ollie, I'm not in any mood for you tonight."

"Reason you can't find them poachers," Ollie said, "is they're Satanists. You know, go around cuttin' up cattle and doin' unspeakable things and then—*poof*—they vanish into the night. The devil's own, Tracer. They don't leave no tracks."

Tracer Dunn turned his head and stared at the man called Ollie from blue eyes that looked like dry ice. "I'm not the only one around here missing head," he said. "Hendrix, over near Seven Rivers, he's lost three or four."

Ollie looked away. "Yeah, I heard. And a couple of others too. Say, did any of them environmentalists straggle onto your place? Like the women in them skull masks? Probably a bunch of lady queers, you know.. . . Now where do *those* demonstrators go at night?"

"Well, Ollie," Dunn said, "I believe they all stay out at the campgrounds near your place. Those women'll probably come by your trailer tonight when you're passed out and turn you into a horny toad. Maybe Derby here'll run a picture of you in his paper, though I don't guess most folks'd see a big change."

"What do you mean, he's gone? Gone? Where the hell could he go?" O'Connor was shouting, and Anna Maria Gonzales bolted out of her office into the room beyond, where O'Connor and four Westinghouse managers were fixated on the console with its blinking green lights.

"What, what?" Anna Maria demanded.

"The tech," O'Connor snapped. "Holmein. He's gone. He didn't come up in the elevator."

"So he's still down there. Why would he stay down?" Anna Maria said.

"No, he's *not* down there, and he's not in the elevator, and he's not anywhere else. I've got three men down there in S10249 and he's not there, I'm telling you." O'Connor's face was dangerously crimson. He ran his hand through his graying brush cut.

"Let's be reasonable. People can't just vanish in this plant," Anna Maria said calmly. "He's somewhere. You just have to find him." She looked at the console lights dedicated to that portion of the plant. They were blinking frantically. "It looks like your men are running around like chickens," she said. "Tell them to calm down, slow down, and look around carefully. Holmein could have fallen. A few small fissures have opened up in that tunnel. They should look there. He may be hurt, unconscious. There's no need for a general alarm. Let's keep this quiet till we find him."

She turned and walked back into her office, hoping her words had brought about a calm, hoping her words were prophetic and would make what she had said come true. But she couldn't breathe. She stood by her desk and put one hand on the back of her chair, the other over her chest, and tried to breathe.

Anna Maria Gonzales traced her ancestry directly back to the days of conquistadores, those men of Castilian blood who had first entered these lands four hundred and fifty years earlier. And still, in her veins, some of that Castilian blood ran and with it the enduring sense of fate, of the need for a penitential approach to the world and its vicissitudes. She was far more educated than her poor, beloved parents who had so long eked out a living in the thin soil of the Sangre de Cristo Mountains north of Santa Fe. She had lived in a far more sophisticated world for all her adult life, a world where one didn't call for the intercession of angels and saints.

Anna Maria was accustomed to taking matters into her own

37

hands, solving problems. Yet still, some of the old and honored Castilian preoccupation with fate and death clung to her, and never more than now had she felt its icy finger touch her shoulder. In her bones and in the deepest regions of her heart, she believed her calming, reassuring words were just that—words. And if her premonition was correct, this would be the first time anyone had been lost at the Waste Isolation Pilot Plant during her watch.

She tried to recall what the man, Holmein, looked like, tried to place him, but his face refused to come forward from the sea of seven hundred WIPP employees, the people whom she had assured, when she was appointed to the position of director, she would consider as important as family.

It was a little after ten o'clock. Probably she'd wind up sleeping on the sofa, the only amenity her government-issue office held.

FOUR

Cassie Roberts sipped her beer in Jack's ratty green easy chair, thinking that she knew a good deal about the seeking of new caves. Many times she had sat listening to Jack and his fellow cavers talking about such things into the night, the long necks accumulating around them.

Finding an undiscovered cavern, they all agreed, is a combination of skill, patience, timing, and luck. To begin with, you have to know what you're looking for—the telltale signs of a cave entrance. Almost never do you see a big black hole in the side of a canyon or ridge, staring out at you invitingly. The entrance to Lechuguilla, for example, was small and also about seventy feet down in a narrow pit that people once mined for bat guano. The narrow, subterranean entrance had gotten covered by rubble, but then some people had heard a whistling sound coming from the pit, figured it was a cave, and over time dug away the rubble. Caves like that tend to breathe, the difference in barometric pressure causing what can be a steady breeze to blow out—or in—the cave entrance. They blow, in caver talk.

The extra humidity a cave exhales may also promote the growth around the cave entrance of trees or other plant life. A piñon pine growing at too low an elevation might be a sign of a cave entrance. Or the branches of a tree that are moving slightly—or better yet, wildly. The wind from a cave can reach sixty miles an hour or more.

Up in the Guadalupes, cave seekers clamber out onto one of the high ridges and stand there for minutes, even hours, inspecting the canyon wall across from them. If the angle of the sun is just right, they may see something over there that *could* say "cave," so they descend from the ridge, maybe a thousand feet, and climb up the one opposite to the point where they think they saw whatever it was—a particular shadow, an actual opening, a telltale bush—that might be a cave. Usually it isn't.

As a natural scientist with a generally sunny view, Cassie found all the natural world awesome, but she had never thought much about caverns until she moved to Carlsbad and then met Jack. Of course, she had taken the tour of Carlsbad Caverns with their tasteful lighting and straightforward walking paths. It was, to be sure, an amazing place, but it was lifeless too. And she regarded caving with considerable distaste, having tried it once to please Jack, who naturally enough wanted her to see his special world. On her one venture, she had found herself in the total dark on her belly, trussed up with a harness of webbing, squeezing through an endless, greasy-feeling tunnel barely big enough around to let her hips pass. She had become so claustrophobic that she seized up in terror and couldn't move. She was stiff as a board, making it impossible for Jack and the others to pull her out. Fortunately, her panic then built up to such a pitch that she fainted, rendering her body supple enough for Jack to pull her through the tunnel. Having suffered such fear, not to mention humiliation, she had vowed never to go again.

She sat now while Jack paced the narrow confines of the trailer, making large, sweeping gestures with his hands, describing the curves and flows of great draperies of limestone, orange, red, tan . . . gypsum crystal chandeliers bedecking the ceiling of enormous chambers . . . intricate white crystals of argonite, as thin as horsehair in grand tangles, growing every which way from the wall . . . moonmilk and soda straws and balloons . . . multicolored flowstone undulating across the floors . . . cave pearls like cue balls . . . lagoons of crystal clear water under rims of stone . . . strands of orange and red crystals hanging from the rims under the water . . .

beards of calcite . . . strings . . . webs . . . masses of blue clay . . . walls of white jelly beans.. . .

Cassie listened with what she had to admit was fascination to the peculiar poetry of the deep, and also, again she would have to admit, entranced by watching her former husband, this addict, now aglow with the thrill of his own personal discovery. He was humbled by the awesome nature of the cavern itself, seeking with an intensity she had never seen to make clear and visible the beauty he saw. She was caught up more in the dance than in the lyrics . . . almost physically sensing the fire within him. She had never seen him so wired. Words and gestures rippled out of him, flowed like rushing streams, tributaries to a great river he had seen, a grand torrent he had conquered.

And with yet another part of her mind, she forcefully tried to blank out the phrases about sixty-foot-deep holes, low, winding tunnels, suddenly precipitous drop-offs into an abyss of sheer blackness . . . the terrifying details that meant challenge to him, fulfillment, but terror to her . . . wrenching, shuddering reflexes of panic, walls closing in like a ghastly tale from Edgar Allan Poe.

"You're shaking," Jack said, breaking off in midsentence and midgesture. "Are you okay?"

"Claustrophobia," she said.

"Here?" Jack said, a look of bewilderment on his face. "It's just a trailer, but . . ."

"No, not that. I'm going to have to go into that damn cave with you. I hate caves. I've never had a worse time than in . . . Well, you remember."

"When you fainted."

Cassie nodded. "But I've got to see that footprint. Tell me exactly where you found it. In English." She grinned up at him.

"No cave speak?"

"No cave speak."

"Okay. I'm down fourteen hundred feet in a big room below another big room. The two are connected by a big vertical river of red flowstone coming through the ceiling. I came down the flowstone on a rope. At the far end of the big room I'm in, I see what looks like another vertical passage down. I've been down two days already, and I figure I better start thinking about leaving, but . . . I'm like, I'll just take one more peek. So I go over to the edge, and I'm looking down about ten feet at a pool, clear as glass. It's all rimmed with flat stone, you know, it grew out when the water level was higher, like lily pads. The pool is real clear. I could see the bottom. There's a faint funny smell, and I guess it's sulfur. You know, there are caves that . . . well, never mind. I'm lying there looking over the edge at this pool, just looking around, and a couple of feet back from the edge of the water I see this shape in the limestone. It's that footprint. So I photographed it, then lowered the bottle down on a string next to it and photographed it again. Then I came up."

"You didn't go down?"

"Well, no. Like I said, it was really time to leave. I'd already stretched my supplies and—"

"But you could find it again?"

"Of course," he said, bristling.

Cassie ducked her head. "Sorry. Of course you could find it again. A dumb question for the Dan'l Boone of the underworld. When can we go?"

"You're serious," Jack said, a big smile spreading unbidden across his face. "So what is it? The footprint."

"That's what we have to go there for."

"Come on, Cassie. I showed you mine. You got to show me yours. What do you think it is?"

"Arctodus simus."

"In English, " he said.

Cassie uncoiled her legs from beneath her and sat forward. "If I'm not mistaken—and I'm pretty sure I'm not—that's the footprint of a short-faced bear." She let the name drop as if it were that of a major celebrity who had just walked in unexpectedly, like Robert Redford or Charles Darwin. She stared down at the stack of photographs now lying on the floor in front of her.

Jack was silent for a moment, trying not to smirk. Presently he said, "I've never heard of the short-faced bear."

"They went extinct about twelve thousand years ago," Cassie

said. "No reason why you would have. It's known only from about ten specimens. None of them complete."

"And it had a short face? What, like one of those pug dogs?"

"It had a disproportionately short snout. That put all its teeth in a fairly straight row. It had a lot of teeth. It was probably the most ferocious predator that ever lived on this continent. It was huge, stood about as tall as a moose at the shoulder."

Jack said nothing.

"That's about six feet at the shoulder," Cassie went on. "When it reared up on its hind legs, it would've been about ten, eleven feet tall. The males anyway. Females were a little smaller. In comparison, the saber-toothed cats were like pussycats. It was pretty closely coupled, long legs. The Carnegie Institute has a biomechanician working on the staff, a guy named Morton; he says that both males and females probably could run as fast as a horse. In spurts anyway. At least as fast as a lion." Cassie's eyes focused elsewhere, and Jack assumed she was seeing one of those giants lumbering, no hurtling, across some Pleistocene landscape.

"What did they eat?" Jack asked, trying to glimpse the scene.

Cassie grinned again, looking straight into Jack's face. "Whatever they damn well pleased."

"So what happened to them?"

"They went extinct, like most of the other big mammals. The climate changed. The ice was going north. It was a mess, weather conditions haywire. Every ecosystem changed; things got hotter and drier here, wetter there. The kind of arctic world all those big guys were used to ran out. Horses, camels, all those—their habitat got smaller and smaller, they became fewer and fewer, lived in isolated pockets, not ranging all over the place. The big carnivores, like the cats and our buddy here, the short-faced bear . . . they ate a helluva lot. If the herds they preyed on got too small and too isolated, then there wasn't enough meat on the hoof to sustain them. The bison adapted by getting smaller. Same with bears. And bears became omnivorous. You know, berries and stuff like that, as well as fish. Like grizzlies eat a lot of fish. You don't have to be all that fast a runner if you're a fisherman. Anyway," Cassie said, and yawned. "All we've got are partial skeletons of these bears, in some cases just a few leg bones, foot bones, a handful of skulls. No one's ever seen a footprint."

"I have," Jack said. "Maybe you guys should rename it. For me. You could call it *Ursus Jackerooney* or something."

"Can I borrow these photographs?" Cassie asked, unamused.

"They're yours."

Cassie scooped them up from the floor and stood. "I'm going back to the museum."

"Now?" Jack glanced at his watch. "It's ten-thirty."

"I need to make some detailed measurements, comparisons with the literature. Can I borrow the bottle too?"

"Sure."

She leaned over, scooped it up off the floor, and turned to face him.

"Thanks," she said. "I mean, really, thanks a lot. This is awesome stuff." Her hand rested for a moment on his forearm and fluttered away.

"You really want to go down there?"

"For sure."

"Tomorrow, then. We should leave about nine. At night."

"Why at night? Why not earlier?"

"There are reasons," Jack said, folding his arms across his chest.

She grimaced. "Okay, tomorrow at nine." Maybe he had some kind of date. Of course, he'd have a girlfriend. Or two.

"I'll pick you up. Your place. I'll bring all the gear. Size ten B foot, right?"

She nodded and stepped out of the trailer into the night. Jack stood still until he heard her drive off down the dirt track and realized that his heart was pounding in his chest the way it did when he was surprised in a cavern by coming on a sudden drop-off, a precipitous hole into the unknown abyss.

Maybe, he thought . . .

Maybe *what*, asshole? he replied.

44

Maybe I should get a haircut tomorrow, he thought. His headache was gone. He made a fist.

"Yes!"

The divorce had been her idea.

Tracer Dunn arrived back at his ranch at midnight, having reached another momentous decision in his life. In all, Tracer Dunn had made four such decisions. He plucked the old Winchester off the gun rack mounted over the back window of his pickup, an old Ford 250 that had seen better days and needed, among other things, another valve job—which meant another three hundred and fifty dollars he didn't have right then. With the fine old rifle in one big hand, he stumped across the dusty yard toward the door of his trailer, now dark in every window. She was long asleep by now, Lucia, probably lying on her back as she usually did, snoring ever so lightly through her partly open lips, the blessed sleep of the innocent and devout. Well, not so devout that she hectored him anymore about getting married, but pious. A God-fearing woman. Tracer stood on the upper step, a sagging wooden board, with his hand on the door handle, thinking back over the other momentous decisions he had made in his life.

The last one had been ten years ago, buying this place with his last few thousand dollars as the down payment, ever the optimist that he could make this godforsaken piece of land productive enough to pay off the debt that loomed every year as a bigger, more ominous burden on his shoulders what with the second loan, and the third, that had become necessary.

His first big decision had been to quit the ranching life he'd grown up with over near Clovis. After ten years working as a hired hand since high school, he still didn't have more than three hundred dollars in the bank, and the fun of rodeoing didn't make up for being broke all the time. So he went to work in the mines over in Arizona, where they paid a man a union wage anyway.

He lasted in the mines—mostly open-pit mining of copper in Bisbee and then Morenci—for almost twelve years before deciding to move on. In the process, he had to dump his first wife, a Colorado girl with big tits and a sharp tongue on her. He never thought of marriage as a momentous decision—just something a man did till it got inconvenient. And then, at age forty-four, he found a cabin up in the Black Mountains of Arizona and let it be known he was a mountain lion hunter. Again he got married—to a seventeen-year-old mountain girl who was slow of mind but an obliging cook—and they lived in the boonies for eight years until she took off with the man who ran the Coca-Cola delivery truck in the two underpopulated counties.

Tracer had already decided that taking people on hunting trips was getting to be too much of a hassle, what with the U.S. Fish and Wildlife busybodies always asking him questions. Whenever he did come across some critter that might be an endangered species, he followed the local wisdom in such matters: shoot, shovel, and shut up. Otherwise the feds would declare the area critical habitat and kick everyone out. The Fish and Wildlife snoops never could prove anything on him, but they were always trying. So he sold his dogs—all twelve of them, the finest hounds, by God, sold for bargain rates at three thousand dollars apiece—and used the proceeds to go back to ranching.

And now, he didn't know what the hell he would do next, but he was sick of pouring his labor and his soul into this rat hole of a ranch, running a few scraggly cows, being hounded by the banks, cheated by the Department of Agriculture, ordered around by the Nazis at the Bureau of Land Management, who owned most of his rangeland, and yelled at by every damn eastern transplant and Sierra Club carpetbagger for raping the land—who the hell could rape *this* land? And getting further and further into debt.

Tracer Dunn had decided to sell the place. Standing there in Ma's, listening to that bone-stupid loudmouth Ollie running off at the mouth about whatever came into his skull, listening to that prissy-assed newspaper editor from Michigan or wherever back east talk as though he knew more about the area and its wonderful, wild, shoot-'em-up history than anyone else—suddenly it had come to him. He didn't want to spend another ten minutes in this godforsaken, hot, dusty, pointless part of the world. He'd put the ranch up for sale, clear what he could, and take off. Maybe Brazil or one of those Spanish countries, where Lucia could translate for him and he could die eating fruit off the trees on some beach in the shade.

If she wanted to come.

If she didn't, well . . . it wouldn't be the first time Tracer Dunn had lit out on his own.

He opened the door, set his rifle in the corner, and walked as silently as he could over to the chair where he sat when he was watching the TV. He sat there in the dark for almost two hours, listening to the coyotes yipping off in the distance in the moonlight, hearing the feathery snoring of the Mexican woman in the bedroom, and feeling profoundly sorry for himself.

FIVE

The phone rang at three thirty-two in the morning, eastern daylight time, and on the third ring, T. L. Smith reached out a hand and picked up the flimsy plastic instrument that lay on his bed table next to his lamp, his shoulder holster, and the Walther .38 he had asked the manufacturer to make personally for him. He was a left-hander with two fingers missing from his left hand, and he had worked out his own design for the grip, modeling it in clay. Smith always wore his Walther, even at a White House reception once, even though he hadn't used it for hostile purposes for eleven years. It was, however, what he thought of as a badge of office, a well-earned badge of merit. He made sure his tailor emphasized, rather than obscured, the bulge it made under his jacket so everyone would know that T. L. Smith, director of security, United States Department of Energy, was never really off duty but always ready for trouble of any kind whenever it reared its head.

As director of security during the course of three successive administrations, responsible for such matters as the safety of the nation's storehouse of nuclear material, he held a position that was well out of the public eye but almost as independent as that of the director of the FBI and far more independent these days than the much harassed, even hen-pecked director of CIA. On the organization charts so beloved of government, he reported to the assistant secretary for administration, who reported to the secretary of energy, but were he to punch into his phone a certain eleven numbers only he and a few others knew, he could speak directly to the president. And were T. L. Smith to make such a phone call, it would most likely mean that a terrorist group had run off with enough plutonium to make a nuclear device, and every law enforcement officer in the land, not to mention the nation's agents abroad, would suddenly find themselves reporting to T. L. Smith.

"This is T. L. Smith," he said pleasantly into the phone.

The woman lying next to him in the dark said, "Oh, shit. Not again," and rolled over, turning her back. "Don't they ever let you sleep?" she mumbled.

He patted her bottom under the sheet and flicked on the light.

"This is Chuck O'Connor, out at WIPP," the voice on the phone said. "Sorry to disturb you, sir."

"What's up?"

"We got two men missing out here. A guard and a tech. They were both down in S10249; that's the latest tunnel they're workin' on. The guard seems to have disappeared, and the tech went down to check out the motion sensors. So the tech reported the sensors were okay, and he hasn't showed up. We've been—"

"When was that?"

"Uh—when was what, sir?"

T. L. Smith took a deep breath and said, "How long have the men been missing?"

"Since seven. Nine your time. We scoured the place. Still at it. The men are missing. You know, tho salt walls and the ceilings and all down there, they move, creep. Sometimes you get a crevice open up. But they aren't in any of those. And that means we may have a . . ."

"Oh, shit," T. L. Smith said.

"I thought you'd better know."

"Good, O'Connor. Good. I'm on my way. I should be there in, let's see"—he looked at his watch—"by six your time. What's the name of the director out there? Garcia?"

"Gonzales."

"Yeah, tell her I'll want a list of everyone who knows that men

49

are missing in the tunnel. I assume you put a red flag on this, so that list better be short as a Doberman's tail. Tell her not to say a word to anyone—*anyone*—about any of this till I get there. Keep that part of the plant closed off; say it's closed for an EPA inspection. Business as usual everywhere else. O'Connor? Not a word about this. If it leaks, I'll feed your ass to the tigers in the zoo."

T. L. Smith hung up and sat up, swinging his feet over the edge of the bed.

"You make yourself comfortable, darlin'," he said, patting the woman on the bottom again. "I'm off to the goddamn desert."

"What, what?" the woman asked without much interest.

"Don't worry. The world isn't coming to an end. I promised I'd tell you if that was happening, didn't I? Wouldn't want the apocalypse to catch you without your makeup on, huh?"

"Screw you," the woman mumbled, and T. L. Smith punched a few numbers into the flimsy plastic phone.

"I'll be flyin' out in forty-five minutes, Sam. Get 'er warmed up. We're goin' to Carlsbad, New Mexico, of all the goddamned godforsaken places in the whole world."

At 4.21 A.M. eastern daylight time, a white Cessna Citation bearing the blue seal of the Department of Energy, its two engines emitting red flame like a rocket, shot off the runway at Andrews Air Force Base outside Washington, D.C., and set a course that would take it just south of Nashville, Tennessee; Little Rock, Arkansas; and Lubbock, Texas. It was scheduled to land on the airstrip recently built for visiting bigwigs a half mile out in the desert east of the Waste Isolation Pilot Plant at 7:12 A.M. mountain time, just before the beginning of the workday.

As the Citation swooped in for its landing, a van rolled up to the western end of the airstrip and waited, its motor idling. The plane touched down with a squeal of rubber at 7:11, slowed, turned, and taxied to within fifty feet of the van. From a small building made of sheet metal with a large air-conditioning system already hard at work, dripping water onto the tarmac that surrounded it, a man with earphones emerged and approached the plane. The door of the

50

plane swung open and, ducking his head, T. L. Smith stepped down the metal steps onto the tarmac. He wore a blue pin-striped suit and carried a large suit bag in one hand, slung over his shoulder, and an ancient black valise in the other. The man with the earphones averted his eyes from the shoulder holster visible under Smith's jacket and offered to take the valise, but Smith shrugged him off. Behind Smith, down the steps, came a stocky man in sharply pressed tan gabardine pants and a white shirt, the cuffs rolled perfectly evenly in two folds, exposing thick wrists covered with golden hair like fur. He flipped a set of keys to the man with the earphones and followed Smith to the van, where the side door slid open.

The director of security stood for a moment, looking out at the horizon, at the distant row of the Guadalupes lit yellow in the first sunlight. The stocky man drew up to him, and Smith said, "Jesus Christ, it must be ninety-five degrees here already." He ducked his head and stepped into the van.

"Mr. Smith," Anna Maria Gonzales said. The seats in the van ran from front to back along the sides like an airport bus, and the director of WIPP was seated opposite the sliding door. "Good morning," she added. "I am Anna Maria Gonzales."

"Glad to meet you," Smith said. His voice was both sharp and a bit gravelly. "This here is Sam Blood. He's what we call my administrative assistant."

Anna Maria nodded at the man, who nodded back and sat across from her, calmly looking at her legs. Anna Maria was dressed in a gray rayon suit over a white silk blouse with wide lapels. Around her neck she wore a gold chain with a small gold cross resting against her skin and an ugly WIPP ID card in plastic on a chain. Her shiny black hair was, as always, perfectly coifed, the ebony curls framing her slightly copper-colored face.

"Sam's great-great-grandfather was a pirate, right, Sam?" The van began to roll quietly, and the powerful air-conditioning rid it of the heat that had entered with the men.

"Yeah," the stocky man said, his high, soft voice a surprising contrast to that of his boss. "Off Cape Cod."

Anna Maria smiled, unperturbed by this odd, macho line of introductory chatter. "My great-grandfather was a soldier with Pancho Villa when he invaded the United States," she said. "In 1912. And yours, Mr. Smith?"

T. L. Smith laughed, a kind of bark. "He was a Cherokee."

"And that," Anna Maria said, "leaves nine great-grandfathers unaccounted for, doesn't it?"

"Huh?" Smith said. "Oh. Yeah."

"Is this your first visit to WIPP, Mr. Smith?"

"Two years ago. In June, about the same time of year as this time. You came on a year ago, from Rocky Flats, wasn't it? I'm surprised we haven't met before."

"We have," Anna Maria said. "Only briefly, though. At headquarters three years ago. I'm not surprised you don't remember. As I recall, you were very distracted." The van slowed and passed through the gate with a wave of the guard's hand.

Smith cleared his throat. "Well, Ms. Gonzales, as you know, in this kind of emergency situation, the director of security takes effective command of the installation until the situation is neutralized. So I . . ."

"I'm aware of the regulations in that regard," Anna Maria said pleasantly. "We, the DOE people, have already taken over from Westinghouse. I'm at your service, of course, as are all the others in my administration. This is a very disquieting matter, and we are very glad to have your personal attention to it."

T. L. Smith smiled—a wolfish smile, Anna Maria thought, from a man who clearly had the self-confidence of a large predatory animal. More like a jaguar, she thought, correcting herself, not a wolf. With dark green eyes like a jaguar. And the other man, Sam Blood. He had pale blue eyes that seemed to peer at the world with an underlying humor or maybe skepticism. He had thick wrists and capable-looking hands. Glancing back at T. L. Smith, Anna Maria noted that he had lost the first knuckle of two fingers on his left hand.

She took a thin sheaf of papers from her leather case and held them out across the narrow aisle to Smith. "These are the names of the people you requested," she said as the van halted next to the bare tan walls of the WIPP administrative building. Smith glanced at the list. There were two lists, altogether comprising abut thirty names. "The B list," Anna Maria explained, "are security people."

Smith handed the papers back to Anna Maria and stood up, reaching for his suit bag. "I want 'em all out of here in one hour. Except O'Connor. I've arranged to have them all attend a departmental retreat in Pittsburgh. Two weeks of sensitivity training. You know, diversity, multicultural understanding. All that good stuff. They get to act out all their deepest hostilities. I'm told it does wonders for morale." He smirked and stepped out of the van. "Jesus. It's hot. I know, I know. It's a dry heat you people have out here."

Ten minutes later, Smith and his assistant, wearing their own ugly WIPP ID badges around their necks, were walking down a long corridor of light-green-painted cinder block toward an elevator. The Gonzales woman was walking about twenty feet ahead of them, talking to her own assistant. Smith leaned over to Sam Blood and said, "That woman has what her people call *cojones,* Sam."

"What are ko-ho-nees?"

"Balls, Sam. Balls. That may not make any of this any easier."

"That's not all she's got," Sam Blood said.

Up ahead, Anna Maria Gonzales stopped before the elevator doors and smiled. Her hearing was exceptionally acute.

Cassie Roberts woke up, and her eyes came to rest on the window next to her bed. The window looked out over North Halaguena Street, not far from the Carlsbad Museum in a residential neighborhood thought of as Carlsbad's historic district since several of the homes dated back to late Victorian times and several of these had been restored to the modest glory of their early days. Cassie's house was one of these, smallish and trim with a pleasant front porch that harked back to the days when people sat on front porches and nodded as their neighbors promenaded on the sidewalk in the cool of the evenings.

From where Cassie lay, all she could see through the window was the sky, bright with the early sun, and a few strands of her hair formed a glinting gold blur over her left eye. Languid with sleep, she pushed away the hair and turned onto her back. She had been dreaming, but it had already vanished from her mind, leaving her only with a sense that she had been working her way frustratingly through interruptions—interruptions of interruptions, an endless series of interruptions. She stretched luxuriously as the sense of frustration also vanished, and she thought back to the night before.

Oh, God, she would indeed have to go with Jack into his cavern.

After leaving his trailer, she had driven straight to the museum, let herself in through the rear door where deliveries were made, and, in her office, turned on her computer. Within minutes, the printer was gaily issuing a report from *The Annals of North American Paleontology,* dated 1991, by E. Morton, the biomechanician at the Carnegie Institute. In all, the report was sixteen pages, in which he argued that the leg length and articulation of the short-faced bear were that of a fleet animal, capable, he asserted based on various formulas, of long bursts of speed up to at least fifty-eight kilometers an hour. This translated into sprints of more than thirty-five miles per hour over a distance of at least a couple of hundred yards, the distance having been estimated from the likely heart size and other features of metabolism that could be inferred.

More to the point, however, were the detailed drawings of the legs and feet of the creature, reconstructed from the fossilized skeletal material. Matching the photographs to the drawings, Cassie confirmed to her satisfaction that the footprint was without much doubt that of a short-faced bear. The biomechanician's reconstruction of the fleshy part of the foot was an exact fit with the impression in the limestone.

So, sometime long ago, a male short-faced bear had stepped in some soft, limy material somewhere down in Jack's cavern, and over time the substrate had hardened, preserving the print perfectly. What was it doing down there? How did it get there? How old was the print? When had that part of the floor been deposited, and how long would it take to harden, and under what circumstances? She was not at all familiar with the geophysical processes involved in cave formation except in the most general way, but she assumed that such things were known—at least by the small handful of geologists who specialized in such things.

She still felt the exhilaration of the night's events: she would be the first scientist to lay eyes on the actual footprint of the continent's most appallingly efficient predator. She doubted that the footprint would add much to the scientific understanding of these creatures except to show that they could make their way into the complex world of an underground cavern. Hardly what the popular press liked to call a scientific breakthrough, but an exciting discovery nonetheless and—she let herself dwell on it briefly—a nice feather in her cap.

But . . .

But it meant she'd have to go down into that damned cave, and she hated that, knowing full well that she would suffer agonies of claustrophobia, panic, probably make a fool of herself again, in front of her ex with the twinkle in his eye, knowing that he had to think less of her in spite of being excessively polite about it and not mentioning it.. . .

She sat up in her bed. She knew she was as safe as anyone could be in one of those caverns if she was with Jack. He was totally expert, one of the best if not *the* best, and he had participated in God knew how many rescues and evacuations. He was something of a hero among cavers and had produced an illustrated manual of rescue techniques—all kinds of special knots and pulleys for lifting litters either vertically or horizontally out of awful places. It was the official booklet of the American Speleological Association. He'd left a box of them—pamphlets printed on yellow paper—in her garage when he left.

Still . . .

She began to sense a familiar tightening of her chest, so she leapt out of bed, strode into the bathroom, and turned on the shower. As she stepped into the shower stall, she glimpsed her image in the mirror and paused. Not bad, she thought. Not bad for a thirty-four-year old.

Standing under the lukewarm spray as it began to grow hot, she asked herself why she was thinking about that.

At eight o'clock, she arrived in her office, down a short hall from the room that held the vertebrate collections, only seven hours after she had left it the night before. She would busy herself for most of the day with writing a grant application and try to keep her mind off the footprint, the cavern, and her irresponsible, impossible ex.

In southern New Mexico, the sun bursts upon the day, leaping white hot above the horizon as if it is eager to get to work turning the world into a furnace. Later on, it sets reluctantly, slowly, with an emotional display like a spoiled child, and, without its direct heat, the dry air will soon drop in temperature as much as forty degrees. But within an hour of its arrival on a summer morning, the temperature begins to soar, and by nine o'clock it can be back in the high nineties or higher.

By four minutes past nine, when Seth Baker emerged into Carls-bad's Canal Street, the mercury had risen to ninety-two in the hour during which he had lingered over breakfast around the block at the Court Café. Breakfast in the Court Café was a daily affair for a group of men who were, in a sense, movers and shakers in Carls-bad. The regulars included three lawyers, the owner of the city's largest car dealership, the Episcopalian priest, the county clerk, a retired oilman, and Seth Baker, a realtor. Others who attended less regularly were the publisher of the city's main newspaper, the owner of Carlsbad's largest furniture store, and, when he was in town, the state senator. Every now and then, on a basis that was clearly provisional, Derby Catlin, editor and publisher of the Other Paper, *The Intelligencer,* was informally invited. This morning he had been present, and Seth Baker had kidded him about what was clearly a major hangover.

The talk and the good-natured but pointed ribbing had leapt from one thing to another, hovering briefly on the minor outbreak of cattle disappearances. The man who owned the car dealership, who was now in his midseventies, mentioned that he recalled something similar back in the forties, right after the war. They had then gone on to discuss a current trial of a politician from nearby Loving and other matters.

Out on Canal Street, Baker, a short, stout man in a straw cowboy hat and a lightweight tan suit, glanced up at the sky and set out toward the offices of Eddy County Real Estate ("Specializing in Ranches and Country Properties"), of which he was sole proprietor and sole employee. With one of the Court Café toothpicks at a jaunty angle in the corner of his mouth, he strolled along the sidewalk, convinced as always, until it was proven otherwise, that a new day could be better than the last. He patted his ample belly optimistically. It was going to be a scorcher, but then, what else was new?

A half block from the office, a pickup slowed to a stop beside him and a figure leapt out of the back into the street and shouted, "Thanks a lot!" It was that Whittaker boy, the spelunker, and he dusted himself off with his straw cowboy hat, which looked like it had been stepped on by a horse a few times, and said, "Mornin', Seth," as the pickup pulled back into the center lane.

"Mornin', Jack. What you doin' hitchin' a ride? Don't tell me that Japanese vehicle broke down again."

Jack grinned pleasantly. "Old Man Cobos is giving it a brand-new transmission."

"You suppose he knows they fit sideways? Just like them Oriental women have—"

"Right. See you later, Seth." Jack turned and strode off in the opposite direction from Seth's course. A little farther on, Seth saw that a tall man in jeans bleached almost white, a denim vest, and a wide-brimmed hat was leaning against the wall of his office. It was Tracer Dunn, grumpy old son of a gun, who kept to himself over there on that broken-down ranch near the WIPP site. Man's strange as a snake with three ends, Seth thought. I wonder what he wants.

"Well, if it ain't Tracer Dunn," Seth said. "Best lion hunter in New Mexico."

"I got some business I want to talk to you about," Dunn said.

"Come on in," Seth said, pulling his keys from his pocket. "I got me one of them Mr. Coffee machines, works on a clock. I'd say the coffee's just about done." He opened the door, sniffed, and said, "Yep, come on in here. What can I do for you this mornin', Tracer?"

Seth noticed that the lanky rancher wouldn't look him in the eye, and to himself he said, This old boy's gonna sell out. He fixed two mugs of coffee, sat down behind his desk, and watched Tracer Dunn fold himself into the wooden chair on the other side of it, observing with part of his mind that Dunn was the sort of man that nothing fit right—not clothes, not furniture, probably not life itself. With the other part of his mind, he was running rapidly through some calculations. He knew what the mortgage was on Dunn's place and what the other outstanding loans were. He didn't know how much Dunn had in the place himself by now, but he guessed it couldn't be more than forty-five thousand dollars, probably thirty. He also knew about what he could sell the place for, so Seth had been right. This was going to be a better day than yesterday. He'd explain to Tracer how hard it was to sell property out there next to WIPP, which it was, but he thought he could find a buyer for the place before too long. Seth was looking at a commission of at least ten thousand for Eddy Real Estate, which would, he thought happily, buy a few groceries, now, wouldn't it?

He beamed at Tracer Dunn, who glanced his way and said, "Feller up in Colorado, owns a big old ranch, several he's put together. Over near Glenwood Springs. He wants me to manage the place for him. He's runnin' it more like a wildlife park than a ranch."

Seth knew this was all bullshit. "Well, now," he said, "that sounds pretty good."

"So I guess I'll sell my spread and move on out of here."

Bingo, Seth said to himself. Yes, Lord, I got bingo right here on my card.

By noon, everyone in Carlsbad who amounted to anything knew that Tracer Dunn was selling. It was the sort of news that would provide many splendid long nights of speculation and gossip at Ma's. Everyone knew that Tracer Dunn was one strange duck.

By noon, in Anna Maria Gonzales's office at WIPP, the four people sitting there uncomfortably knew there was good reason to think the tech, Phil Holmein, was dead—and probably the security cop, Jenkins. All four stared at Anna Maria's desk—she herself, T. L. Smith, the stocky man, Sam Blood, and Chuck O'Connor, the one-time marine who headed the security unit at WIPP. Some of the Westinghouse managers had been sent to Pittsburgh to hone their social skills; the rest had been told to spend a week working up wholly unnecessary reports on trivial matters. Matters at WIPP were firmly in DOE hands.

On Anna Maria's desk, in a plastic bag, sat the tech's portable radio. It had been found in a three-inch-wide crack that had developed near the side wall at the far end of the tunnel called S10249. It was badly scratched, as if it had been thrown against something metal, maybe the giant Marietta Miner that was still extending the tunnel its final forty feet. And down in the tunnel, on the other side of the machine in the shadows, was a spatter of blood, unquestionably Holmein's (though that would need confirming). But the body of the tech was nowhere to be found.

"It's just damn impossible," O'Connor said. "I'm telling you, from the time he went down till the time my men went down there to look, no one came out. Not a damn soul. And no one but my men ever came out afterward. I've checked and rechecked."

"And let me tell you, Chuck," T. L. Smith said. "You're gonna check again and find out where the other entrance is."

"There is no other entrance," O'Connor said. "Just the main elevator for heavy equipment, the smaller one, and the two air shafts. Those elevators're monitored closer than fleas on a dog."

"Well, if nobody came out and nobody is there now, there's got to be another entrance. That's just plain logic." He stared at O'Connor. "Unless your rent-a-cops are responsible for whatever happened to that man."

They all turned to the door as Anna Maria's administrative assistant rapped on it. He stuck in his head and said, "Sorry to interrupt. I thought you might want to know—the protesters are back. About fifty so far, and they say a whole bunch more are on the way."

The face of T. L. Smith lit up.

"Excellent!" he said. "Let 'em come. Chuck, you have your boys give 'em just a hard enough time to keep them steamed up. Sam, you go on out there and see what you can do. Be a protester. Give those hippies some courage. You know what I mean? We need all the distractions we can get till we get this figured out. Press gets ahold of this, you'll all wish you had a one-way ticket to Mars. Okay, meetin's adjourned."

SIX

Familiar smells envelop the mother's senses, ever stronger as she approaches the dry place that emanates warmth, the warmth itself insistent, compelling. She is satisfied, belly full, at ease now after the long sleep. She is getting drowsy with surfeit. The smell fills her brain, and the little sounds now added to the quiet, distant *drip-drip-drip* of the world. Slowly she settles down, settles in, and feels the insistent mouths on her, the hot, frantic lips. She flows. She licks her own lips and tastes the new, exciting, salty taste again. She has found a new kind of food, new prey, in her world, just beyond where the nauseating smell is. She senses that her world is changing. But here, it is as always, the cubs' mouths on her, suckling. She dozes, fulfilled for now.

Shortly after noon, Jack Whittaker pulled up outside Estella's Café on Canal Street, just south of where Dark Canyon goes beneath the road. The new transmission in his white Isuzu Trooper was smooth as silk, and Old Man Cobos had found a few other minor glitches—a couple of oil leaks—that he had repaired. In honor of the new transmission, Jack had run the Trooper through the Octopus car wash, explaining that he wanted The Works but without the scent. Damned if he wanted his vehicle to smell like gladiolas or lilacs or whatever. And, Jack told himself, his second mission that morning was also in honor of the Trooper's spiffy new incarnation—the exterior sparkled, and the little swarm of car wash folk had vacuumed every particle of dust from its interior. Jack had helped himself to his first professional haircut in two and a half years.

Estella's consisted of seven small tables, each presumably garnered at different times from the swap meet, and a six-person counter where Estella herself occasionally paused between duties in the kitchen to chat with the customers on the stools. The dingy light green walls were decorated with a few Mexican bullfight posters and a handful of signed black-and-white glossies of rodeo riders from the professional circuit. Estella served a thoroughly western American breakfast full of cholesterol and pure traditional Mexican food at other times. Her clientele was mostly local, with the occasional tourist or retiree showing up to ogle the local color.

Jack swung onto a stool at the end of the counter, and, when Estella emerged from the kitchen in a nondescript, blue-flowered smocklike dress, he smiled and said, "Afternoon, Estella. Anything new on the menu today?"

"I made the salsa fresh today," she said. "What happened to your hair?"

"You like it?" Two men perched at the other end of the counter turned their heads.

"Makes you look twelve years old."

Jack ordered three beef burritos and began wolfing them down when they arrived. Estella stood behind the counter, arms folded across her chest, watching him eat.

"So Estella," he said between mouthfuls. "Besides the salsa, what else is new today?" Since most people who knew much about the doings of Carlsbad ended up eating at Estella's at least once a week, she tended to be an excellent source of local news and gossip.

"Tracer Dunn is selling his ranch."

"What?"

"Tracer Dunn is selling. They say he's got an incurable cancer and is going up to some sanitarium in Colorado to die."

"Jeez."

"They also say that his woman, Lucia, is demanding that he get married to her, so he's gonna sell the ranch and escape."

"Oh."

"And they also say that the Fish and Wildlife people caught him tryin' to sell some endangered rattlesnake he caught, so he made a deal that he'd sell out and leave if they'd hold off charging him."

"Oh, right. What do you think?" Jack asked.

"I think it's none of the above. But he is gonna sell." She turned and went back into the kitchen. Jack swallowed the last bite of his third burrito, put a five and two ones on the counter, and left, breaking into a run when he got outside, sprinting all the way to the courthouse, where the records of Eddy County land sales were kept.

The security cops at WIPP were halting buses and cars about a mile from the plant, forcing the protesters to walk through the heat—now just under a hundred but far worse on the tarmac road. All around, the landscape shimmered in the heat, as if it had become liquid. In all, about two hundred people had arrived at the plant's gate or were straggling toward it, carrying their handmade signs and their canteens of water. At the campground that morning, the experienced locals had provided yet another seminar, explaining how to avoid dehydration, heat stroke, and other desert maladies awaiting the unwary. The first trucks of the day were expected at two-thirty, and the protesters waited patiently, sweating like pigs and singing folk songs.

When Sam Blood, newly transformed into a ragged protester, joined the plodding stream on the tarmac access road, he went largely unnoticed. He was decked out in a pair of cutoff jeans, black Teva sandals, a green baseball cap that said Greenpeace in turquoise blue, a black T-shirt proclaiming his membership in Amnesty International in white italics, and a fanny pack. He swayed slightly in rhythm with the folk songs but didn't sing. Instead he peered around him from behind dark glasses, seeing if he could pick out the leaders, assuming there were any.

At two o'clock, one of the protesters, a frizzy-haired woman of about thirty, wearing a pair of workman's overalls over a running bra of some sort, stood up on a crate and, through a bullhorn, began reminding people why they were here. She went on and on, and the protesters began to talk among themselves and fidget. Someone shouted, "It's too fuckin' hot, man—I'm leaving."

The woman with the bullhorn shouted, "Hot? *Hot?* Think how hot this poison is they're pouring into the earth. . . ." But it was obvious to Sam Blood that she was losing her audience and the demonstration was in some danger of disintegrating. He made his way through the crowd and, stopping next to the crate and the woman in overalls, reached up, grabbed the bullhorn, and took her hand, gently but firmly forcing her off the crate, which he mounted.

"Excuse *me,*" the woman said, but Sam ignored her.

"Excuse me," he said into the bullhorn, and the fidgeting in the audience ceased. "I don't think you people are serious enough about this."

There were a few boos. The security guards at the gate looked at each other and smirked.

"I'm not kidding. This isn't just another demonstration. This is life or death. I know. I used to work for the Department of Energy."

A great buzz arose.

"That's right. I was a safety engineer at Rocky Flats, that sink of radioactive leaks up in Colorado. Let me be blunt here. I know these people. They don't give a rat's ass about human beings. They couldn't care less if your grandchildren grow up with thyroid cancer. I saw the corruption up there in Rocky Flats. Corrupted canisters and corrupted officials. I saw radioactive wastes leaking into the ground. Into the water table below. Into the water they drink in the suburbs of Denver. I saw all that, and I blew the whistle."

Some people cheered tentatively and clapped.

"So I got fired, thrown out. They threatened to take me to court for some trumped-up charges, breaching security, all that crap. So here I am, to tell you that we have to do more here than be counted. Of course we're all against this shit. Anyone with the sense God gave a jackrabbit would be against it. But we have to do more. We have to stop it! We have to sacrifice ourselves, take a little heat!"

From the pocket of his jeans, he pulled a pair of handcuffs and held them up toward the sun. "I got three more pairs!" he shouted. "I'm gonna chain my ass to that gate over there. Who's gonna join me? Who here has the balls to throw themselves in the path of these fascists and take the consequences? Who?"

The crowd surged forward toward this new and daring hero, some of them with their hands outstretched, crying, "Me, me."

Over by the gate, the security cop named Moreno leaned over to his partner and said, "This guy is cool, huh, mon?"

On the monitor in Anna Maria's office, she and T. L. Smith watched the four protesters cuffing themselves to the gate while the others applauded and cheered.

"Whew!" Smith said, smiling broadly. "Old Sam really let 'em have it, didn't he? I didn't know he was *that* good an actor. Why, it sounded as though he really believes we don't care about humans and grandchildren and all." T. L. Smith laughed, a sharp bark.

"That man," Anna Maria said, looking at the screen, "has real *cojones*."

She looked up at Smith innocently. His eyes widened, then narrowed.

"You don't miss much, do you?" he said. He laughed again and walked out of the office.

Anna Maria knew what she missed. The cliché was true. It was lonely at the top. And for a woman, long since divorced, it was lonely in Carlsbad. She watched the monitor fixedly, deciding things. With the ominous and still mysterious events of the past days, it was clear to her that she—her career, her future—was now largely in the hands of T. L. Smith, a man whose very job description called for deviousness and a man who fit his job description well. She couldn't trust him, and she would never know what he had in mind that could be dangerous for her.

But his assistant, Sam Blood, with the thick wrists covered with golden blond hairs and, she noted from the monitor, strong-looking legs—he would know.

By three o' clock that afternoon, the ambient air temperature outside the WIPP site reached one hundred and two, but for the protesters standing in the burning sun on the bare, dusty heat sink of the parking lot, it was closer to a hundred and ten. The big semis loaded with more nuclear waste appeared to have been delayed. There was no shade, only the glare of the sun—everywhere the glare, filling the sky, reflected from the sun-bleached asphalt, glinting from the razor wire coiled along the top of the fence. For an hour, an uneasy stasis had prevailed. Four protesters, including the former DOE safety engineer from Rocky Flats, sat handcuffed to the gate. The rent-a-cops stood along the chain-link fence without visible expressions behind their motorcycle-style black sunglasses and sweated profusely. The rest of the mob sat on the ground in a sullen and exhausted state of near paralysis and approaching heat stroke. Every so often, one of the faithful would approach the four heroes chained to the gate and give them a drink from a canteen, eyed by the cops in the manner of a frog watching a fly.

Into this strange and nearly motionless tableau a van arrived at three-fifteen, having been listlessly observed by the protesters while it drove up the long entrance road through the rippling heat mirages. As it slowed to a crawl a hundred feet from the bedraggled crowd, one of the protesters noticed the writing on the van's door: UNITED STATES GOVERNMENT ENVIRONMENTAL PROTECTION AGENCY.

"Hey," he shouted. "It's the EPA!"

A ripple of life stirred the crowd. "Shut the bastards down! It's not too late!" someone shouted.

"Yeah," another yelled. "Do your duty for once, huh?"

As the van came to a stop, each of four guards produced a fencing tool from his belt and approached the protesters chained to the gate.

Inside the van, the man sitting next to the driver turned around toward his three colleagues in the back.

"Did you see that? The guy in the cutoff jeans they cut loose from the gate? That was Sam Blood."

"You mean our Sam Blood? Smith's goon? A protester?"

"Yeah, him. What the hell do you suppose is going on here?"

"I guess we'll find out soon enough."

When the van pulled up near the main entrance of the administration building, the four men—each bearing two large aluminum suitcases labeled EPA in bright green letters—stepped out and were ushered into the building. They were, in fact, employees of the Department of Energy, not the EPA. They had been flown in from Washington on T. L. Smith's order, landing at the airport outside Las Cruces and hustled into a commandeered EPA van, where each put his specialized equipment into EPA cases. The four men represented the closest thing in the DOE's security division to a full-scale crime-scene team. T. L. Smith had no intention of inviting outsiders—local cops or, worse, the Feebs—into any situation where he wanted the answers and wanted them first. So he had created his own crime-scene department, on call day or night. It was rarely employed but ever ready—*semper paratus,* Smith liked to say—and technically up-to-the-minute.

A half hour later, clad in green government-issue overalls and yellow hard hats, the four men, accompanied by Chuck O'Connor and one of his cops, stepped into a small, cramped elevator that looked like little more than an open cage. It began to move and quickly gathered speed, and all four of the Department of Energy's special forensic team watched in near terror as the dead white walls, less than a foot from the cage, became a nightmarish blur. They all felt their stomachs rising alarmingly—gravity and fear—as the elevator plummeted down through the earth to the level 1,980 feet underground, coming to a gravity-filled, thank-you-ma'am stop. The doors purred open, and the men followed O'Connor's bulky form into the salt wilderness.

"You're just about at sea level down here," O'Connor said. "So you ought to feel right at home." His voice came back to the forensic team amid its own muffled echoes.

"Hey," one of the team, a tall and bulky man named Fred, said in a quiet voice. "Officer Krumpke's a wit."

"Christ," the man next to him said. He was short, with black kinky hair, and wore large, dark-rimmed spectacles. "I've been in some shit holes, but this place takes the cake. It's like a big coffin."

"Don't be morbid."

"Don't tell me don't be morbid, Fred. It's my job to be morbid. Yours too. What's this don't-be-morbid crap?"

After several minutes plodding along through tunnels that all looked alike, they turned right into yet another one. The tunnel stretched away, lit with a sickening yellowish light every two hundred feet or so. The far end was lost in murk.

"Okay, this is S10249 we're in," O'Connor said, stopping. "It's about eight hundred feet to the end. They're still extending the drift down there. Now, see that doohickey on the right-hand wall about two and a half feet from the floor? Every hundred feet there's one of them—motion detectors. Each time anything goes by, a light blinks upstairs. So we watched this guy Holmein walk along right where we're going. When he was done, he started back this way and . . ."

"And," said the man called Fred, "your guys came down here and scoured the place, looking for him."

"Yeah."

"So the place is basically trashed," Fred said.

"My men are careful. They're trained in—"

"Sure, Chuck-o, sure." Fred began humming the tune of an old song, "Second Hand Rose." "Well," he added, "it won't be the first time we've been stuck with sloppy seconds."

"We'll be lucky if we get out of here tomorrow sometime," said his morbid companion, setting down his aluminum cases and staring glumly at his surroundings.

The painfully methodical business of collecting forensic material was soon under way, O'Connor and his guard having returned to ground level, leaving the four white-gloved men poking around, plucking up specks and bits here and there and putting them in carefully marked plastic bags, shining ultraviolet light over every inch of the floor and partway up the walls, looking for signs of human tissue.

In another hour, the man called Fred was standing for a moment in the half-light at the far end of the tunnel, staring at the great machine. Its base was squat, like a mammoth turtle or crab, with a huge and lethally toothed cylinder suspended up near the ceiling on powerful steel arms. It was the cylinder, spinning as it moved up and down, that ground tons of salt from the walls to be scooped backward by frantically sweeping crablike arms near the base, passing through the machine's innards to vehicles that hauled away the salt. Before the descent in that insane elevator, the WIPP people had showed him and the others a photograph of this monster and explained how it worked. But he was unprepared for the real thing. It almost filled the tunnel. The dim light glinted dully from the fangs on the enormous cylinder, which pointed dumbly at the wall like a beast frozen in time, something prehistoric and mammoth. The wall itself was a crumbly mass of salt, piles of it littering the ground, yet to be swept up by the machine's giant crab legs.

Fred began his patient and methodical inspection of the giant machine, starting with the cracked leather seat. Anything they found would have to be differentiated from the machine operator, the guy who would have left all kinds of stuff around—hair, bits of dandruff, dry skin. Considered from the standpoint of a microscope, humans were pretty disgusting, Fred thought, not for the first time. The nearly absolute dryness of the air was making his throat sore.

SEVEN

The workday at WIPP ends at four in the afternoon. Shortly afterward, the workforce drives away like maniacs at half again the speed limit, a huge caravan of high-speed tailgaters racing down the highway that is locally known as the "WIPP 500." Thereafter, the plant is manned by a night manager, an emergency medical person, and a few security guards. It goes silent; the lights underground go off. And nothing moves. This night, of course, the lights remained on in the tunnel called S10249 while the forensic men toiled. Usually this great man-made cavern falls utterly silent, completely dark, like a natural cavern. It goes dead.

But who knows what goes on, really, in so alien a place? Nothing goes on there, the engineers had averred. And nothing will, except that the salt will soon creep around the tonnages of radioactive waste and seal it off forever. Others of course doubted this, based not so much on any intimate knowledge of the underground scene but on the hunch that the great earth still held secrets that little men with little instruments might not recognize or completely understand.

Until a few decades ago, for example, no one thought that life could exist in the ferociously high temperatures—up to 250 degrees—where gases and lava erupt from the deep ocean floors at long ridges. Here is the earthly embodiment of man's worst fears; namely, hell. A place that never feels the radiation of the sun, a place, though, of intense heat, red-hot, searing heat, a world of sulfur and sulfuric acid. And yet . . .

A host of creatures live in this hell on earth, the most plentiful being certain strains of bacteria that need no sun, just sulfur. And other creatures feed on those bacteria—worms and other lowly forms, to be sure, but they form the beginning of a food chain—a wholly different evolutionary path based on sulfur.

Where else could hell exist?

Again a place of total dark, a velvet blackness where the energy of the sun is absent, where the temperature is constant, where there is plenty of sulfur to consume. Such places have been found in the solid earth as well as the ocean deeps. One is a newly discovered cave in southern Mexico called Cueva de Villa Luz, the Cave of the Lighted House, named for a few skylights that let light into a few of its upper passages. But in its lightless, inhospitable depths some fifteen hundred feet down, it is perpetually dark, and it stinks. The air is suffused with the reek of rotten eggs, the smell of a cave that is becoming. The smell of hydrogen sulfide.

This foul gas arrives in these depths from oil fields many miles off, dissolved in groundwater seeking out its secret passages under the earth, flowing through the rock. Arriving in the soft beds of limestone, the hydrogen sulfide reaches water that seeped down from above, water that contains oxygen. Like lovers, the two waters mix and their offspring is sulfuric acid, which attacks the limestone, forming dark sulfuric mud, eating away rock, forming skins of gypsum over some of the rock, leaving otherworldly shapes in the utter black.

And like a plague arising from some unknown source, bacteria arrive that can eat sulfur, combining the hydrogen sulfide gas with oxygen from the air, making more sulfuric acid, etching the caves into yet greater dimension. The bacteria live in the very limestone they are destroying, forming great spongy excrescences with the consistency of phlegm, and coat the walls with gelatinous wallpaper.

And again—from somewhere, somehow, other creatures have arrived and have come to feed on the clever bacteria. Spiders. Midges so profuse, they form clouds that literally roar. So many tiny fish live in ancient pools and lagoons in the stygian dark that they can be scooped up by the handful.

Only a few other caves of this kind have been found—caves aborning—and the cavers and scientists have only just begun to fathom the astonishing processes that carve out these niches for such alien life-forms. None of them, for example, has thought much further about the infinitely plentiful fish—a form of molly that appears red in a caver's light because their blood shows through their transparent flesh and organs. Stunned by the spectacularly plentiful life in a place where life should be impossible, it has not occurred to them to ask if all those fish represent the top of the food chain . . . or if they are instead a plentiful rung in the food chain, fodder for something the cavers have yet to see. Something perhaps that likes the dark and prefers not to be seen or sensed.

None of this speleological lore was known to T. L. Smith or Anna Maria Gonzales or the other officials at WIPP when a routine printout from the sensors in S10249—the ones that had caused the tunnel to be closed for further analysis of the air—was routinely circulated that afternoon. The printout showed the normal, relatively harmless substances in the air and, for a short period, hardly more than an instant, the suggestion of two parts per billion of hydrogen sulfide gas. Even though this was within the margin of error for the sensor—meaning it could be a total misreading—it had been enough to sound the electronic alarm. But since the tiny trace almost immediately vanished, there was no reason to give it much thought. It was dismissed as just another operating error arising from the sensor's supersensitivity.

Nothing particularly to worry about, especially when management had something more pressing on its mind: two probable homicides.

When Jack Whittaker turned his Trooper southeast toward Loving and away from Carlsbad Caverns and the Guadalupe Mountains that lay to the southwest, Cassie stared at him. The Trooper's headlights and the glow of the dashboard lit his face. He was looking intently, resolutely forward, eyes shining. He had barely looked at her since they left her house.

"Where are you going?" she asked.

"To the promised land," he said.

"But . . ."

"I know, I know. That's what's so amazing. No one would have thought the old reef came this far east."

"But—"

"I know, all the geological surveys and all. My experience is that scientists find what they're looking for and not—"

"That's just bullshit, Jack."

"*Some* scientists, I mean. Like the guys checking out the salt deposit for WIPP. They found what they wanted and didn't go any farther. Anyway, the reef definitely extended as far as the Quahada Hills, 'cause that's where the entrance is. Just east of 'em."

"Isn't that Bureau of Land Management land out there?"

"Most of it. But not the entrance."

Cassie sighed. "You're telling me the entrance is on private land?"

"Well, yeah."

"Which explains why we're starting out at night, huh?"

"Right. It's a tiny bit—"

"Illegal," Cassie said. "You haven't told the owner? Who is the owner?"

"A guy named Tracer Dunn. An old rancher. Part of his place stretches across the road up near Quahada Ridge. The guy's kind of a loner, lives in a trailer with some Mexican woman. I've seen him around, but I never met him."

"So we're going to sneak onto this guy's property. You know, I think this sucks."

The Trooper suddenly began to decelerate. Looking straight ahead with his jaw set like concrete, Jack pulled off the road onto the shoulder and stopped. Dust swirled in and out of the beams of the headlights.

"Look, Cassie," he said, his nearly black eyes flashing as he turned toward her. "Listen to me. Finding this cavern is the biggest thing that's ever happened to me. Ever. It's my dream come true. This is an enormous cavern—it could take months, maybe years to explore its full extent. Like Lechuguilla. They still don't know where Lech goes after fifteen years. Now I found this cave, no one else. And this guy Dunn is selling his ranch—I just found that out today. You've always given me a hard time about pushing caves and all—"

Cassie opened her mouth to say something, but Jack cut her off.

"Don't deny it, Cassie. You were on my case all the time. 'Get serious.' 'Grow up.' All that. Well, this is it, babe. This is it. This is worth a damned fortune. And if you want to see this footprint *I* found, and *I* photographed, and *I* showed *you* the photographs and not anyone else, though sure as hell you're not the only paleontologist in the world who'd be interested . . . Anyway, you want to see that footprint, then you've got to sneak on Tracer Dunn's ranch and sneak down the entrance, which is in a place he never goes 'cause he doesn't take his cattle across the road. I've done it maybe four times already, and there's no problem. And now he's gonna sell the place, and I'm gonna buy it. And that means *I'm* gonna own your short-faced bear's footprint, among other things. So get off your high horse and be nice."

Cassie sat, looking forward, her arms crossed over her chest. Her chin was jutted forward ready to do battle, and twice she began to lash back but twice thought better of it.

"How," she said finally, "are *you* going to buy a ranch?"

"I don't know yet. But I'll figure a way. A business partner, maybe."

"Isn't there some kind of federal law about caverns, even ones on private land?"

"So I'll get a lawyer, too," Jack said. "Do you want to do this or not?"

"You know I do," Cassie said. "Don't get so hot under the collar." He tromped on the gas and the Trooper peeled onto the highway, engine screaming in protest over too low a gear, and Cassie grabbed at the door to keep from crashing into it.

"The other day," she said, "you told me you thought I was beautiful. Inside. So why are you so hostile?"

"I had a concussion when I said that."

"That's not what the doctor said."

"That little twit . . ."

"He was a twit," Cassie agreed. "A little duck-footed twit with wonky sponge-rubber soles. Walks like a duck, quacks like a duck . . ."

"Must be a quack," Jack finished as he slowed down and turned left on Route 31. "Just a couple more miles," he said.

Cassie watched the landscape go by, lit silver by the newish moon, every feature of the land casting strange shadows.

"Too bad it's not overcast," she said. "Awful lot of light out there."

"Don't worry. It's way off any beaten track."

Three miles later, Jack slowed and pulled the Trooper off the left-hand side of the road, bouncing along the shoulder for about fifty yards, peering intently out the side window.

"There," he said, apparently seeing some landmark among the scrub. He stopped, clicked off the headlights, pushed the four-wheel-drive gear into four, and proceeded into the scrub. The vehicle lurched over the terrain, and Cassie noted that all the equipment in the back remained motionless. Nothing fell loose. Jack was as meticulous about his equipment as he was carefree, even sloppy, about everything else. Like an idiot savant, Cassie thought, then decided that the thought was unkind. Thank God, she thought he *was* so meticulous about all this stuff. She was beginning to dread the moment when the Trooper stopped and they piled out and hooked her up with all that gear and they went down into some awful black hole where there wouldn't even be moonlight. . . . She shuddered.

They climbed a slight rise, and then the hood of the Trooper tipped precipitously downward into what seemed like an abyss.

Cassie chewed her lower lip as the Trooper crept down a slope at what seemed an impossible angle, lurching over solid rock.

"How did you ever find this place?" she asked.

"Car broke down out there a month ago. I had to take a leak, so I came over here before I called Old Man Cobos on the car phone. And when I saw this canyon, I decided what the hell. I didn't expect anything, of course. Not over here. But it just looked like an interesting place. Then," he said, slowing even more, "I saw that side canyon. Over there." He pointed off to the right.

"I don't see it."

"No. But it's there. And first, when I got almost even with it, I felt a breeze, you know, a light breeze had come up. But then when I turned in, like we're doing now, it seemed like it was too humid a breeze, and it was coming out of this side canyon, and I knew right away I'd found one. It took me an hour to find the entrance. Up ahead, there's kind of a ledge, a bench, maybe ten feet above the canyon floor. It's up there, the entrance, hidden in some boulders, stuff that fell off the side of the canyon."

He turned to face her, and she could dimly see he was smiling with an almost childish elation. She looked away. The walls of the side canyon they had entered rose up about twenty feet on either side. The Trooper came to a halt deep in shadow, and above, the moon was no longer in sight.

"We're here," he said.

Five minutes later, Jack finished transferring his gear from the Trooper to the rocky bench, which was high enough to catch the moonlight. It didn't amount to much, Cassie thought nervously. She could make out two backpacks already loaded, no doubt with what Cassie recalled was the standard array of stuff—drinking water in plastic bottles, a rubber-cased flashlight, extra batteries, a candle, a few plastic packets of food like PowerBar Harvest, a disgusting chocolate concoction, a few tools, a first aid kit, plastic bags, and a sweater. Two coils of braided rope—Jack always used the most expensive, and Cassie thought she remembered its brand, something like Eldridge Pearl. A clattering collection of carabiners—D rings with hinged clasps—pulleys, and ratcheting devices called Jumars, along with what looked like bicycle locks with six little tubular bars—for rappelling down cliffs. Cassie shuddered at the thought. Various straps to make harnesses out of. Two hard hats with electric lamps attached to them and to a battery pack on a three-foot cord. Two tightly furled inflatable air mattresses. Cassie looked glumly at all this gear, most of it lightweight enough but all of it suggesting a continuous string of problems, a night and a day of discomfort.

"I've got a couple of thousand feet of rope already down there," Jack said. "Every passage we need is roped or marked with little strips of tinfoil. Now, slip out of those jeans and your shirt. I've got a webbed shirt for you, boots, overalls."

He handed her a bundle of clothing, and she turned her back to him as she removed her clothes down to her underwear and put on the unfamiliar shirt and overalls. Two and a half years had passed since their divorce, and she felt a flush of embarrassed modesty on her throat and face in spite of the darkness. Once dressed, she turned, and he handed her a brimless helmet that looked black in the dark but was, she guessed, red. The electric lantern was strapped to it, and when she put it on, Jack busied himself stringing the battery cord through a hole in the back of her overalls collar and back out through an opening above her hip. This he attached to the battery pack, which slipped onto her belt.

"Don't want the damn cord hanging up on anything," he explained. "Okay, now your harness."

She blinked and felt his hands bumping around her waist.

"I can do it," she said a bit too quickly, and buckled on the harness of tubular webbing as Jack hovered beside her in the gloom. "Hey!" she said when she felt his hand poking around her fanny. "You don't get to do that anymore."

"Tighten it," he said. "The harness."

She did so.

Then he handed her the brake bars, a ladderlike array of bars on a rack that resembled a bicycle lock. "Here, run this line through." She was aware of Jack peering closely at her as she accomplished this surprisingly complicated task.

He spent a few minutes securing the rope with carabiners and webbing to two boulders and paid it out into the hole.

"Okay," he said. "You first. Over you go."

"You mean . . . ?"

"It's about ten feet down rappelling, then you're hanging free for about forty feet, then you'll hit a slope. Just let yourself down the slope and you'll hit bottom after maybe another thirty feet. Piece of cake."

Clutching the line in one hand and the brake bar in the other in the approved manner, Cassie backed out over the abyss and began the descent. He'd gotten her in the entrance on the rope so fast, she hadn't had time to work up a debilitating dread. Even so, she swallowed hard as the harness took her weight, and her dry throat constricted in the process. Stop that, she commanded herself. She sucked some saliva into her mouth and swallowed again. I hate this, she said to herself over and over as the blackness began to surround her and pebbles rattled off the rock under her boots. She looked up, and through the entrance hole the sky was a deep blue-black. She saw a single star, inert in the clear air, and she heard an inner voice—hers—intoning words she hadn't said since childhood: "Starlight, star bright, first star I see tonight, I wish it may . . ."

Fred Fontaine was on his knees not far from the huge Marietta Miner, peering at the salt floor from about a foot away. He was wearing a pair of standard magnifying goggles and shining a powerful flashlight at the floor, moving it slowly back and forth.

"Jesus," he said. "My fucking back." He put the flashlight down precisely where it had last shone and slowly raised his torso so that he was kneeling upright. The familiar ache, centered on the third vertebra from the bottom, where he had suffered a compression fracture twenty years earlier on a football field, now felt like a knife in his back. He looked at his watch. Ten-thirty, about. How long had they been down here? And so far, nothing interesting besides the blood, of course, which he had scraped up and bagged. And he knew that a blond guy with what could be a case of psoriasis ran the big mining machine. Big deal.

He put his white-gloved hands down on the soft, salty floor and had begun to push himself up off his knees when he felt the tremor.

A shaking, like a silent rumble.

Only for a millisecond.

In the stillness, he wondered if it had been his imagination. Maybe it was him, his body shaking. Or something.

He stood up and ever so slowly bent his pelvis forward, straightening out his spine, and felt the pain diffuse over a larger area, lessening until it took on the almost pleasant sensation of an old bruise. Maybe, he thought, I should get one of those operations. He looked down the tunnel. The other three were crawling around in the shadows maybe seventy yards away. Again he bent his pelvis forward, tracked the pain . . .

Another tremor.

Shit, he said to himself. I thought this place was inert. No earthquakes for ten thousand years. What the hell? He thumbed the button on the radio hanging from his belt.

"Did any of you guys feel that?"

"Feel what?"

"Like shaking. A tremor."

"Fred, maybe you should sit down awhile. Take a rest. Have a snort of that bourbon."

"You guys didn't feel anything."

"No, Fred."

"No, Fred."

"No, Fred."

Fred shrugged. He fished an expensive silver flask from under his overalls, screwed off the cap, and took an utterly illegal snort from its narrow mouth. Then he took another and screwed the cap back on and put the flask under his overalls.

And me, he thought, an officer of the law. He leaned over to pick up the flashlight from where he left it on the floor, and his eye idly followed its beam to the wall of salt at the end of the tunnel about five feet away. Something on the wall moved. Bits of salt were falling. He had stood up and taken two steps toward the wall when, all at once, the world went mad, fell off the track. At the same time that something like a huge white arm thrust out of the salt, a torrent of air blasted into Fred's face like a dust devil, hurling him back toward the monster mining machine. His head filled with an overwhelming putrid smell. As he was hurled backward, his light flashed over the wall, and for an instant he was looking into two crimson eyes that squinched shut in the light, a cavernous maw with huge fangs . . . when his brain shut down.

EIGHT

The descent seemed endless, especially dangling in the open for forty feet before her feet struck the slope. In that wide part of the chimneylike entrance, Cassie's light showed a dull gray-brown rock all around, wherever it struck the walls. Ugly. Not until her feet hit the slope did her light reach the bottom. But by the time she reached the bottom, her hands had grown familiar with the action of the brake bars and she felt a flush of achievement. She disengaged the bars and shouted up: "I'm off the rope."

Immediately the orange rope began to sway before her like a cobra responding to a swami's flute, and she knew Jack was on his way down and at a far greater rate of speed than anything Cassie would ever be comfortable trying. She knew that cave protocol suggested she turn off her light to conserve the batteries, but it was just too early for her to permit herself to be enveloped in the blackness of even this early point in the cave with the entrance hole only seventy feet above her, outside of which the world was lit by the moon and at least one star. Around her, beyond the slope she had descended, the cave was shaped something like a clamshell, the six-foot ceiling sloping down to a point some ten feet away, where a horizontal crevice led off into the pitch blackness. She heard pebbles rattling down the slope, realized she was standing too close, and felt one strike her helmet with a loud *click*. She ducked her head and stepped rapidly away from the slope, only to bang her helmet against the lowering ceiling.

"Ow, dammit!" she said, feeling clumsy and thinking that sooner or later down here, she was going to knock into some priceless, never-seen-before formation of crystals growing out of the floor or somewhere and shatter it, thus breaking the first and last commandment of the caver—Don't break anything. She couldn't remember the name—something-ites—for the delicate little crystals that grew every which way, looking like crazed white worms, or Medusa's perm, tiny, delicate strands of crystalline hairs that would snap off and crumble into smithereens if you even breathed on them. Break one of those and your name was crap with a capital *S* and you'd be kicked out of your grotto, which is what cavers called their little clubs, and shunned forever like an Amish girl who gets caught in the barn with her bloomers at half-mast.

To Cassie, one of those something-ites wasn't all that different from any other something-ite, and why everyone felt they had to pussyfoot around in what was just a geological formation was beyond her. There were thousands of caves and how many something-ites, so who cared? It's not as if there was anything alive or even anything fossilized. Just rocks. Just geology. Just endless, lifeless geophysics. Water dripping, full of minerals. Drip. Drip. Drip. World without end.

She was feeling too grumpy, she realized. She didn't share the caver's manifest belief that these creepy places were God's underground temples to herself, but she understood the need for conservation and care. The public, the careless, could wreck anything and usually did. Happily, her train of thought was interrupted by Jack's soft landing at the bottom of the slope. He was like a cat in these caverns, and for a moment, Cassie felt even more clumsy.

"Why," she asked, "did I go first?"

"Ladies first," Jack said.

"Don't give me that. You thought if I had to wait up there, I'd—"

"I knew you'd do it. It's just easier if you don't have to wait around, wondering what's down there. Now, we need to crawl through that crevice there for about twenty feet. At one point it's too low for crawling, and you'll have to go on your stomach. Maybe about the length of your body. Then we're in the clear for a while. Here," he said, holding out a pair of black household knee pads. "They're a bit clumsy, but you can take 'em off when you don't need 'em."

Cassie stooped and strapped on the knee pads.

"After you," she said, looking glumly at the crevice. "Is it wet in there?"

"Not right ahead. There are some wet spots later on, but we can get around most of 'em." He scrabbled into the horizontal crevice, which she could see by his light narrowed down into a tunnel. She scrabbled after him, crawling on the lumpy knee pads, keeping her head unnecessarily low, which meant she needed to crane her neck upward to keep her light shining directly on Jack's receding posterior. Then he removed his pack, tied it to his ankle, and began slithering through the tight spot. Cassie followed hurriedly, a bit of panic settling over her as she felt the walls close in, rough surfaces scraping at her belly and her shoulders, inching along by pushing with the toes of her boots and pulling with her fingers. She imagined the top of the tunnel—only inches from the back of her neck—dripping with large spiders all infuriated by the destruction of their webs, and her neck began to itch violently. She kept her eyes fixed on Jack's pack three feet in front of her and audibly sighed in relief when she noticed that he was up on his knees again. Soon she was crawling through a widening tunnel and then—as if visited by a silent chorus of angels—she was standing up.

They were standing on a rocky balcony near the ceiling of a vast chamber, too vast for the puny electric lamps on their helmets to illuminate. Cassie had the sense that this "room" was endless. The ground before them dropped off in a slope full of automobile-sized boulders of limestone, dead-looking rubble. Shrine, hell. This place was God's trash dump. Dimly she could make out some large columns in the gloom, and she realized with some chagrin that she was thinking in religious terms, or maybe sacrilegious terms, neither of which she was accustomed to.

They began to clamber down over the boulders, and the columns ahead grew clearer. Some reached up from the floor, others hung from above, and a few were joined. Most of them were fluted in flowing patterns.

"Which are which?" Cassie said. "I forget. Stalactites and stalagmites."

Jack paused on a large, flat boulder and looked back at her with a cheerful grin. "When the mites go up, the tights go down."

"Well, that's graphic enough," Cassie said. "I'll keep it in mind."

They picked their way across the rock-strewn floor, the lights casting vast shadows that moved as if they were alarmingly alive. Cassie began to feel disembodied, disoriented, and realized it was her light doing it to her. Each time she moved her head slightly to one side or another, the world before her simply vanished, went dark, while a new world beside her burst into existence. The light glistened from crystals embedded in the columns, then winked out; shapes loomed and disappeared. For all the tonnage of rock around her and over her, the cavern seemed insubstantial. She concentrated on moving her head, and therefore the lamp on her helmet, as little and as slowly as possible, and the strange sense of virtual reality left her.

At the far end of the room, the walls were hung with huge masses of stone draperies, reddish, like a great arras from behind which Polonius might emerge, saying something hypocritical. Off to their left, flowstone like caramel had flowed from a dark place partway up—about ten feet over their heads. An orange rope snaked down the flowstone from a black hole, and she watched Jack deftly hitch himself to it, rapidly and easily ascending. His torso disappeared into the hole, and he began to wriggle into it, legs and then feet disappearing, leaving her standing alone below.

No, no, she thought, I don't want to be alone in here. She hitched her harness to the rope and began an inelegant scrabble up the flowstone.

"Take your time," Jack's voice said, and as she approached the hole, she saw his hand reach out to her.

"I've got it," she said, and heaved herself into the hole without help, wriggling over the ledge, and found herself lying on her stomach in another tunnel. The ceiling was too low to stand but high enough for her to walk stooped over for at least twenty feet.

"Let's catch our breath," Jack said, his own breathing regular and calm. He flicked the switch on his light and part of the tunnel vanished.

"What's ahead?" Cassie asked.

"This goes about a hundred feet with a long curve to the right, south, and then there's another big room. Fantastic place. All kinds of decorations." Cassie was pleased to know that her sense of direction seemed intact. She had assumed that they were headed east, and they were.

"Don't you cavers always name these places, like the Crystal Snowman or the Palace of the Gnomes?"

Jack laughed. "I've been thinking about names. Like this tunnel up here. Maybe I'll call it the Alimentary Canal. Ready?" He flicked on his light and, stooped over, began to walk into the gloom on his slightly short legs, arms hanging down like a chimp. Cassie followed and smiled when Jack absently scratched his ribs, completing the apelike illusion.

When the tunnel veered south, it also narrowed and descended at a gentle angle, and they crawled for what seemed like a half hour but was far less, only ten minutes, finally emerging into another spacious room where white decorations hung from the ceiling, glowing against reddish brown walls. Thin white stalactites hung like clusters of pencils, glistening with what looked like dampness.

"Soda straws," Jack said.

Beyond, the ceiling apparently swept upward. A large white column rose from the floor, disappearing into the gloom. Reddish crystals sparkled from the column.

"Listen," Jack said, and breathed silently through his mouth. The silence was immense, oceanic, dizzying. Cassie breathed through her mouth and could hear only the rhythmic pumping of her heart. Then she heard the sound of a distant gong from somewhere up ahead.

"What's that?"

"A drop of water. This cave is still happening. One drop every ten or fifteen seconds. Come on, I'll show you."

They climbed over another heap of rubble, giant blocks that had fallen from the ceiling at some point in the ancient past, and came upon a small forest of dull gray stalagmites, standing at attention like soldiers in the Confederate army. Looking up, Cassie saw that each sentinel had its counterpart descending from the ceiling, their ends about ten feet above. Jack approached one of the stalagmites and put his hand on the top.

"Put your hand up here."

Cassie did, and yanked it back reflexively when a drop of water splattered on her fingers. She felt jumpy, nerve ends jangling, and she wondered how just a drop of water falling from above like a leaky faucet could have set her off. She clamped her jaw against the tingle of panic she felt in her chest, part of her watching the other her in irritation. She swung her headlamp slowly to and fro, lighting up the gray sentinels, which now struck her more as stones in a cemetery than a battalion of Rebs, and shadows jumped and vanished. Suddenly she had the sensation she was drowning, water filling her chest, green water, salty in her mouth, and she needed to clutch something, reach out to the wooden hull now upside down . . . and she shook her head violently, shattering the moment, the memory, as a voice called out to her from a great distance. . . .

It was Jack, his light shining obliquely at her. He was looking at her from the corners of his eyes, his head turned slightly to the side. Cave courtesy, Cassie thought, suddenly relieved—you don't look directly at others lest you blind them momentarily with your light.

"How about a drink?" he was saying, and the iron grip that had clamped over her body eased. She took the plastic bottle Jack held out to her and squeezed a stream against the back of her mouth. It tasted ever so faintly of chlorine—city water. Not salt. She took another gulp and handed the bottle back to him. She had panicked, hadn't she? And she found herself wondering how obvious it had been. The old sense of humiliation embraced her, and she summoned up her courage and said, "*Some*thing got me there."

"Yeah, you looked a little pale there for a moment." He shrugged and smiled. "It happens."

Cassie found herself holding this simple reassurance, the calm smile in his eyes, as tightly as a little girl clutches a stuffed animal, and soon the two Cassies, the observer and the observed, melded back into her familiar sense of herself.

"Where now?" she said, eyeing what seemed to be the end of the cavern, a great wall of ragged, broken rock, mostly gray and dull. More spillage from above sometime long ago. The thought crossed her mind that ceilings in these subterranean grottos could fall at any time, the luck of the draw. A little too much of this or that, some straw working on the camel's back, and *whammo,* it's all over for the cavers who happened to be in the wrong place at exactly the single moment in millions of years that . . . Would it make a noise if no one was around to hear it? A dumb question. She knew enough physics to know that sound waves don't need ears to happen. She attempted a calculation in her mind of the odds of being hit by a falling ceiling in a cave that was, say, fifty million years old, but the numbers escaped her, and she gave up, convinced in her soul that she was safer in this godforsaken hole in the ground than she was stepping off the sidewalk in front of her house.

"We've got about another thousand feet to go," Jack said.

"That seems pretty good," Cassie replied.

"A thousand feet down," he said.

"Oh. How far down are we now?"

"About four hundred. The last three or four hundred feet will be the fastest."

"Do I like the sound of that?" Cassie asked.

"You're doing great," Jack said, evading the question. "We'll go on for about another hour and then get some rest. In a beautiful place."

Another long tunnel like a wormhole led to a huge cavern the shape of an enormous kidney. The floor of the kidney-shaped cavern was filled entirely with water as still as a mirror, pure green and transparent in the light of their headlamps, but inky black down below where no light had ever shone. Jack pointed out that the water level had once been higher, evidenced by the flat rocks, like white lily pads, that extended out from the edge about a foot above the water. They had to cross the cavern on ropes that Jack had earlier strung along the dank curving wall about twenty feet above the water.

"We could swim it," Jack said, "but even without clothes we'd get it dirty." Cassie noted that his face was streaked with dust and sweat, a gray sheen over his deeply tanned cheeks. She assumed she looked just as grimy. And the thought of getting naked with her ex-husband struck her as unpleasant. It was as if they had never been intimate, as if he was someone different now. And so, of course, was she. We retreat, don't we, she thought, like hermit crabs into their shells. We try life on the open beach for a while, then we back into ourselves, tumble around in the waves for a while and reemerge onto a beach that's been rearranged by the tides, never again the same. She watched Jack fussing over the ropes with a bittersweet mixture of gratitude for his technical prowess and puzzlement over who exactly they had each become. She realized that she had been veering around emotionally since eight o'clock that night—or was it last night?—like a roller coaster or like a seismograph recording earth tremors.

Later she methodically pulled herself along the wall, attached with carabiners to the rope. Every twenty feet or so, Jack had rigged belaying ropes, hitched to outcrops and stalagmites up the sloping wall near the ceiling. When she reached each of these belaying ropes, she had to unhook her carabiners and put them back beyond the belaying rope, which left her suspended by only one until the maneuver was complete. She was relieved to find that she suffered no acrophobia and escaped with her self-esteem intact and with only a few bruises from banging into the rock. The next tunnel was another stoop-walking exercise, soon over.

"And here," Jack announced as he stood up straight and held his arms out wide, "is the first pièce de résistance."

Cassie emerged from the tunnel and stood beside him. Their headlamps lit up the middle of a large room that struck her eyes for a second or two as an ornate banquet room hung with dozens of sparkling crystal chandeliers, a sumptuous place where people might appear any moment in long silk gowns and dinner jackets. The room was mostly white, ivory, the one wall she could make out lined with ribbonlike furls of draperies. Overhead, clusters of white crystals hung from the ceiling, dozens of clusters, each crystal element growing straight down like pencils only to go berserk, curling upward, outward, forming an impossible tracery of loops and dangles and twists.

She turned her head slightly to the right, and her lamp lit up a group of five pencil-thin white stalactites hanging delicately from the ceiling ten feet above her head. At the base of each was a brilliant array of needle-sharp red crystals, as if a huge garnet had exploded and was caught in a stop-action photograph. That they could hang there at the end of such slender white reeds of support seemed to defy the laws of nature. The light gleamed from the red needles, and Cassie found that moving her head ever so slightly up and down made each array dazzle and dance.

"My God," Cassie said, almost breathless. "It's beautiful."

"Damn straight," Jack said. "I've never been in a place that was so perfect. Look, nothing is out of place. It's perfect. Even the floor— flat as a ballroom." He stepped out onto the white limestone floor and looked obliquely back in Cassie's direction with a wide, cheek-stretching smile, presenting her with his magnificent chamber the way a cat proudly presents its owner with a mouse it has caught.

"There's more," he said, "but that's for later. We can grab some z's here. Let me have your flashlight for a minute." She slung her pack off her back, opened it, and fished out the red-rubber-encased flashlight. He took it from her and said, "Wait here." Weaving and bobbing to avoid coming near any of the elegant decorations, he pointed to one of the chandeliers above his head and said, "Helictite. The most amazing damn helictites the human eye has ever seen." He pointed to one of the garnet explosions. "Aragonite crystals," he said. "You don't want to get any closer than ten feet. Just the air currents could snap 'em off." And then he was gone.

She heard his voice calling from around a great sweeping fold of white drapery. "Close your eyes for about two minutes, okay?"

She did and heard him moving around.

"Okay, open."

The chamber was the same but different. To her right she noticed a glow rising from nowhere, illuminating the wall of drapery with highlights of soft gold and sensuous shadows of darker gold. Overhead, light gleamed from the helictites, glancing this way and that, like star clusters winking in the sky. To her left, a light glowed from the inside of a niche, a small, self-contained grotto, filled with miniature stalactites and stalagmites, a tiny fairyland, a forest for elves.

Jack stood in the middle of the chamber, glorying in his light show. "I came in here out of that tunnel the first time, and I'm like, this is *magic.* This place is *enchanted.* This is the queen of queens!" He spoke with a nearly ferocious vehemence. "This is the Hope *diamond,* Cassie. The Taj Mahal. I can hardly believe I found it. You're the second person in the history of humanity to ever see it. Think of it. There are six billion people alive right now who've never seen this place."

NINE

"So, Sam Blood, tell me. I'm curious. How did you know?"

"Easy. A woman doesn't look at a man that way unless she's got one thing on her mind."

"So you arranged to stay here at the plant tonight."

"Sure. In case the foreunion came up with anything. How did you know?"

"A man doesn't look back at a woman that way if he doesn't understand what she has on her mind. Tell me, was your great-grandfather really a pirate?"

"No. He was a fisherman. Was yours one of Pancho Villa's soldiers?"

"No, no. The soldiers were Mexicans, mestizo. My family are all descendants of the conquistadores. Well, mostly. They make a big thing of that to this day. Your hands are very gentle, Sam Blood."

"Your skin is very soft, Anna Maria Gonzales."

"And you . . . ready again so soon? My, my. *Cojones* indeed."

The young male bear fears nothing, but over the generations since they took to the dark, his kind has learned caution. Particularly when venturing out into the place where there is light. Light hurts. Yet some vestigial ancestral urge impels him out to prowl the world where his forebears ruled in colder times.

Hunger, yes, ravening hunger after the sleep, but something perhaps stronger than that—the surging, haunting male urge to roam, to move, to find new territory, to be alone.

And so he approaches the entrance to the open world and sees no light. He proceeds, squeezing his bulk through the walls of rock and out where the air is different, alive and rich with tantalizing odors. He moves more slowly, and the pungent scent of the large prey is very strong. In his dim vision, he perceives one source of silvery light overhead, but it does not hurt his eyes. He follows the strong scent of prey, slowly making his way across the rocky ground that is familiar to him now that several such hunts have proved so successful.

He stops, hearing a sound that is new to him, a kind of roar. Dimly he sees a glow of light moving across the horizon. The sound grows louder and the glow brighter, and he stands, swinging his head back and forth, listening as the glow and the sound diminish into the dark. A new scent, an acrid, unpleasant scent, comes to him and then disappears on the wind.

Slowly he follows the promising scent of the prey through the night, his memory of meat and salty warm blood refreshed.

A half hour after his three forensic colleagues found Fred Fontaine lying on the floor at the far end of S10249, the medical staffer on duty that night concluded that he had suffered a stroke. He reported this to the director, who answered her phone on the fourth ring with the irritated sound of someone whose sleep has been interrupted.

Fontaine was awake, eyes open, staring blankly. The milky blue pupils minimally followed anything within a few feet of his face that moved. But that was his only reaction to the world around him. He had no reflexes, no evident feeling in his feet, hands, or elsewhere in his body. The flesh on his face had lost elasticity, as if it had been subjected to an enormous gravity field. Without a brain scan, there was no way of telling how much of his brain still functioned. That would be done in due course, once the mine safety people moved his inert body onto a stretcher, loaded it on one of the electric carts that served as silent people movers in the WIPP drifts, and brought it up in the elevator to where a helicopter was waiting to whisk him to the hospital in Carlsbad.

It would, it turned out, take far longer for the doctors in Carlsbad, Fontaine's forensic colleagues, and an observant member of the mine safety team to get the slightest inkling of what had really occurred in the shadows at the far end of S10249.

Shortly after midnight, T. L. Smith sat at Anna Maria Gonzales's desk, the phone receiver clamped to his ear. Alerted in his motel room in Carlsbad by Anna Maria, he had arrived on the helicopter sent for the downed man. She now stood near the one window in her office, looking out at the greenish light in which the yard outside was bathed. She was, as usual, immaculately turned out. Sam Blood had arrived in her office five minutes after his boss and sat silently on the sofa, looking idly at the floor.

T. L. Smith was nodding with what looked like impatience, listening intently to the voice on the phone. It was the young neurosurgeon at the Carlsbad hospital. Smith had draped his jacket over the back of her desk chair, and his weapon rested with quiet lethality in the black leather of his shoulder holster.

"Okay, Doctor," Smith barked in his raspy voice. "You're gonna have to put that into plainer English. . . . Yeah, I'd be obliged."

He listened for a minute, nodding, and said, "Okay, thanks. You'll let me know. . . . Good. Thanks. Right now, this is a security matter, you understand. . . . Excellent." He hung up without saying good-bye and swiveled around toward Anna Maria.

"Well, Christ almighty," he said. "This beats all." He shook his head.

Anna Maria turned to face him, arms folded across her chest. The man simply had marched into her office and taken over. She knew the regulations, and she knew the reasons for them, but she couldn't help resenting him, sitting at her desk, using her phone, without so much as a word of thanks or what? Empathy? He was macho, but without the gallantry of the truly macho. She didn't trust him to do this right. Whatever *this* turned out to be.

"They don't think it was a stroke," Smith said. "There's no sign of a stroke in the scan. No region of the brain that's gone kaput. Everything in there is just buzzing along uniformly but at a rate that's just enough to keep him breathing and all, and maybe even thinking. But not like real thinking, not like regular brain activity. They say it's the worst case of shock they've ever seen, if that's what it is."

Anna Maria sucked in a breath, a long, sibilant hiss.

"What the hell could do that to a man?" T. L. Smith demanded, not so much of Anna Maria or Sam Blood, but of the universe at large.

She shook her head. First Jenkins the guard, then Holmein the tech missing, presumed dead . . . somehow. Now this.

Abruptly Smith stood up and smacked the top of the desk with his open hand. "Sam, go get those guys, will you? And then go on to the hospital. If Fred comes to, I want you there to hear what he has to say before anybody else does. The world is full of busybodies."

Presently the three remaining forensic specialists were seated in uncomfortable straight-backed chairs while Anna Maria was again turned to the window and Smith sat one haunch on the corner of the desk, the expensively shod foot swinging to and fro a bit like the irritable lashing of a cat's tail.

"Now, what's this stuff about Fontaine and the . . . what did he call it? A tremor?"

The man with the glasses and curly hair seemed to have been appointed spokesman for the three.

"Yeah, he called on the radio from down there; we were maybe a hundred yards away. He asked if we felt anything, and we said no, maybe he should sit down. And then he felt another, asked us if we felt that, and we hadn't. Then maybe a minute later, I don't know, maybe a little more than that, we heard something like an explosion, but softer, like. And a bump. So we went down there, you know, calling him. There he was, lying in a heap."

"What do you mean, a heap?"

"Well, curled up sort of, but with one of his arms, his left one, out to the side. Like he passed out and then fell down. Sideways. His eyes were open, and we could tell he was breathing but only barely. But nothing moved, not his eyes, nothing. His head was only about a foot from that big fuckin' machine—excuse me, ma'am. His head was exactly fourteen inches from the machine's base, and so we figured he'd hit it somehow, knocked himself out. But that's not what happened. No sign of anything on the base of the machine or on that big cylinder with all the teeth, which are the only places his head could've hit except the ground, of course. No hairs. Nothin'. And no contusions on his skull, not a bump. He was lying with his feet six and a half feet from the end of the tunnel, where there's all that loose salt. It's on the map we did. It looks like he had a stroke, and that's what that EMT guy said when he looked at him."

Anna Maria opened her mouth to speak, but T. L. Smith glanced up at her, brows furrowed, and she said nothing.

"You felt nothing. Nothing like a tremor, the ground shaking, anything?"

"No. I figure it was something inside him, like the beginning of the stroke, you know? But what do I know about that stuff? The docs would know."

T. L. Smith frowned at the man.

"Anything else?" he asked, looking from man to man. They all shook their heads. But then one of the men opened his mouth.

"Uh, I thought I smelled something when we got there, like Fred had . . . you know, evacuated, soiled himself. But there was more to it, something like rotten eggs but worse. Putrid. Don't you remember?" he said, looking at his two colleagues. "I said, what's that stink? And you said, it's shit. And I said, yeah, but what's the matter with it? Remember?"

"Yeah," the spokesman said. "I remember that, but I didn't smell anything unusual."

"Me neither."

"And then I didn't smell anything strange anymore either. So I forgot about it."

T. L. Smith fixed a stare on each of his forensic team, one by one, and then looked at the window, staring through Anna Maria. The room was silent. Presently Smith yawned and said, "All right, I want you boys to get some sleep. Then I want you on your knees, crawling over every damned inch. We're still looking for anything that'd help." He turned to Anna Maria. "There's a place here where they can bunk in for a few hours?"

She gave them directions to a small dormitory room with six cots in it, and after they left, she turned to T. L. Smith.

"You let them think it was a stroke. Why?"

"Because that's just what it was. Officially. Until I find out what it was. You got that? No one but you and me know it wasn't a stroke. And the doctors. I told them to keep it to themselves, and the one on the phone said they could do that. I feel better, though, with Sam goin' there." He leaned back in Anna Maria's chair, and she thought she noticed a grim flicker of a smile cross his face.

"Anyone can have a stroke, at any time," he went on. "They're the great mystery. Folks just drop with 'em. Every day. Nothing remarkable about it. Well, except to the victim and his family, but Fontaine doesn't have any family. We'll have to let people know, like the press, that an EPA man from Washington on a routine inspection tour had a stroke. Most unfortunate and all. Try and keep the rumor mills from spinnin' out."

Anna Maria saw the wisdom of this approach. The long history of WIPP was so fraught with controversy that none of its directors over the years had needed to be told to keep unpleasant details quiet. The public simply couldn't handle what they thought were the mysteries of radioactivity—never could. The slightest problem—something that would go completely unnoticed in any other industry—brought out the worrywarts from every cranny in society. On the other hand, to those who dealt with radioactive material on a regular, daily basis, there was no mystery about it at all. It was just another toxic waste one dealt with prudently. You couldn't get this across to a nation of scientific illiterates.

In any event, if you worked at DOE, you kept information that would cause unnecessary fretting to yourself and emphasized the positive. Over the years, WIPP made a big deal of its safety record, for example. The mine safety team was regularly cited as the most effective in the nation, and WIPP made as much PR hay as it could from its record of one and a half million man-days without a day being lost because of accidents.

As if he was reading Anna Maria's mind, T. L. Smith said, "Fontaine wasn't a WIPP employee, so your record is still intact."

"No," Anna Maria said, bridling, "The other two were employees. That record is gone."

Smith smiled his wolfish smile.

"And nobody knows what happened there. In fact, no one outside of us and a handful of other people here even know that those two are missing. And for all we know, they snapped and took off. That ain't an industrial accident. It's just flipped-out rednecks takin' a powder. And that's how it's going to be till we get this all straightened out."

"What about the blood they found down there? It's going to turn out to be Holmein's. Then what?"

"I guess a man could get cut down there and then get pissed off and leave."

"And that's an industrial accident," Anna Maria said.

Smith stood up from Anna Maria's chair. "It could be, Anna Maria. You don't mind if I call you Anna Maria, do you? But it could be any number of other things too. Anyway, we aren't obliged to explain this to anyone till we find some reason to think the man is dead. And for that, we need a corpse, right? And what's more important is that I'm the head of law enforcement on DOE property, so we are making our own investigation of these matters. And if we find anything that needs the services of other law enforcement agencies, we'll certainly call 'em in. So for now, it's us. Just you and me, Anna Maria. You and me. Okay? Now let's talk to the mine safety guy. What's his name again?"

"Yazzie," Anna Maria said, and when Smith looked puzzled, she added, "He's a Navajo. Used to work in the coal mines on the reservation."

A couple of minutes later, Albert Yazzie sat in one of the wooden chairs, looking uncomfortable. He was a large man with extra-large shoulders and chest, with a face that was pure Mongol. He kept shifting his weight in the little chair as he spoke in a soft, almost womanish voice with a curious lilt.

". . . the salt looked kinda soft, you know. More than just the

97

usual flaking, crumbling. Me and Jones, we were too busy with the patient to really look. Gettin' him on the stretcher and the cart and up here."

"Soft?" Anna Maria said.

"Yeah." Yazzie moved again in the chair. "Be a real good idea to have someone go down and inspect it. One of the engineers. Do a seismic test or something. If they're runnin' into an air pocket down there, it could be real dangerous. You know, a big burst of air. Maybe even worse."

Smith glanced over at Anna Maria.

"Okay," he said. "Have someone go down tomorrow morning . . . but with the forensics. I don't want people stomping on whatever evidence is still there." Yazzie looked crushed. "No, don't worry," Smith said. "You were doin' your job, takin' care of the man. Thank you, Mr. Yazzie."

The big Navajo rose out of the chair, a look of relief flickering over his features, and left.

"Does that add up to anything?" he asked.

"Not to me," Anna Maria said. "We'll get a report from the engineer tomorrow. Maybe . . ." Her mind filled with calamitous scenarios. Air pockets were bad enough, but if they had drilled into an area where the salt was compromised in some way . . . She shook her head.

Smith stood up, plucked his jacket from the back of her chair, and strode toward the door, stopping to look at her again with a smile that was both ingratiating and conspiratorial.

"This is a dangerous game we've got to play here," he said. "But what else is new in this business? Now, I'm going to go find one of those beds. We're going to need our wits, and mine, such as they are, don't get out of first gear unless I get some rest."

Anna Maria watched him disappear through the door, knowing that he had been trying to soften, to turn on what he supposed was charm. He was, after all, all-male, forceful, determined, crazy. A walking, breathing stick of dynamite. She wasn't sure if she was pleased to be included in his high-stakes scheme or nervous at being part of so clearly illegal a conspiracy. She had no choice, of course, but she did have a hole card now.

The man, Fred Fontaine, lies on his back on the hard mattress of the hospital bed. He is attached to various monitors that gauge the amount of life in what appears to be mostly husk. All the little green lines move along the screens nicely, bip, bip, bip.

Occasionally there is a flickering image in the void of his mind, images too faint to register on the cathode-ray tubes to which he is wired. The images make no sense, of course, since he has no means of making sense. Only an infinitely fragile and dim awareness exists in his mind, his eyes reacting to certain kinds of motion, shapes moving. His eyes act on their own, sending optic signals that are denied entry by the rest of his brain, which crouches in his skull like a fawn lying in deep grass, instinct rendering it still as stone and barely breathing in the presence of a lethal hunter.

But the images come, materializing out of the man's mental abyss—flickering images that mercifully wink out as quickly as they arise.

The most complicated and least understood device in the known universe, a human brain, is protecting itself, burying the images of white wind, white arm against white, crumbling white, white fangs . . . instantaneous, an appalling stink. . . .

Derby Catlin, editor and publisher of *The Intelligencer*, had spent the last hours of the afternoon in the library, looking through microfiche copies of what he called the Other Paper, the *Carlsbad Current-Argus*, from 1950 back to the summer of 1947, when he hit pay dirt. The antiquarian impulse had come that morning from old man Vandergrift, the auto dealer, at breakfast at the Court Café. He'd mentioned some die-off of cattle sometime after World War II, touching off Derby's curiosity as an amateur historian.

Well, maybe more than an amateur, Derby believed. After all, he had studied history as an undergraduate at the University of Michigan, and only last year he had published a thirty-six-page pamphlet—almost a book—on the early days of oil exploration in Eddy

County and had sold more than four hundred copies locally. It had been favorably noted by the *New Mexico Historical Review.*

Semi-pro.

Now, he sat in a leather chair in his bachelor household in the most modest house in a quiet, upscale neighborhood along River Edge Road, looking at the articles he'd printed up from the micro-fiche machine. The Carlsbad library simply didn't have the funds to put all the old records on computer so a man could sit at home and manipulate the electronic world and deliver unto himself, whenever he wanted, the entire contents of the library. So Derby had done his research the old-fashioned way, and he was pleased with what he had found. Deeply pleased. Four stories—one in the last week of June 1947 and three in the following month.

The first, barely more than a brief notice in the June 24 issue of 1947, said that a rancher whose spread was east of the Pecos River up near Seven Rivers had found one of his herd badly mutilated, probably by a mountain lion, in an arroyo in Seven Rivers Hills. This was the third time in a week the lion had hit his herd. The rancher was mounting a hunt for the varmint and welcomed any-one who wanted to join up.

The other three stories came after the famous UFO sighting of July 2 outside of Roswell, a couple of hours north of Carlsbad. Thereafter for months the Carlsbad paper, along with every other one in New Mexico and many nationally, was breathlessly full of conflicting stories—of those who had sighted the object in the night sky, of the sheep rancher who found metal foil-like remains scat-tered over the ground, and of the air force, which said something was real about all this, something abnormal, but then recanted, saying it was just a weather-research device gone astray. Then what about the dead alien they'd found out near the wreckage, others complained, the corpse spirited off by the navy? And so on.

But amid the continuing excitement, the claims and counter-claims about alien aircraft that also began to be seen in many parts of the country, the Carlsbad paper reported, albeit briefly, on three more incidents of livestock loss. Cattle and one horse were vio-lently ripped open, carcasses left mostly eaten, and some cattle just plain missing. The other three incidents occurred east of the Pecos River as well, on two different ranches, one of them north of the city, the other due east. The ranchers were up in arms, and much of July was evidently spent in a concerted effort to kill every mountain lion in the region in hopes of getting the one or ones that had given up on hunting deer and pronghorn or whatever and had developed a taste for beef and horse meat.

Sitting in the comfort of his leather chair, with a glass of Jack Daniels black over ice on the table beside him, Derby now reread the four articles, noting something he'd overlooked in his first excited glance. One of the afflicted ranchers, an old-timer then in 1947, recalled a similar outbreak sometime before the turn of the century, when he was in his twenties. He wasn't quite sure of the exact year, but it was before the Spanish-American War in 1898, and the old-timer knew this because he had joined Teddy Roosevelt's Rough Riders as a sergeant and fought in Cuba *after* the rash of cattle killings that had led to a month-long mountain lion hunt in which about fifty locals had participated with great effect, killing twelve lions altogether, most of them in the Guadalupe Mountains.

Ranchers actually didn't know much about mountain lions in those days, just that they were dangerous, profit-threatening varmints. A few men knew how to track them, but whether a mountain lion would come all the way from the Guadalupes to the vicinity of Carlsbad was just conjecture. Ranchers still didn't know much about mountain lions, Derby mused, except that they were profit-threatening varmints no better than wolves.

That fellow Tracer Dunn, the rancher out near WIPP—word was he'd been a professional mountain lion hunter for some years over in Arizona somewhere. Maybe the locals ought to hire him. He was losing cattle too.

Anyway, Derby thought, this looked like an interesting trail to follow. A mountain lion outbreak every fifty-odd years. An interesting pattern. How would you explain that? One of Derby's hobbies was cycles—he was convinced that the world operated on distinct cycles, like the stock market, the weather, El Niños, the incidence of madness, sunspots, and all that. He'd pursue this approximately half-century cycle of the crazed, beef-eating mountain lions further. But for now, he had plenty for a few column inches he would put on the front page. It would be a scramble, and the printer would hate him, but it was worth it. A scoop. He took out a yellow pad and began to write. Ten minutes later he finished off his Jack Daniels and went to bed, happy as a kid in a candy store with a fistful of money in his pocket.

TEN

"Are you awake?"

Jack couldn't believe it. He'd been lying quietly for five minutes in the lovely dark, drifting closer and closer to unconsciousness. He was in that state when you have the delicious feeling that sleep isn't just coming but quietly surrounding you in its velvet, fondling grasp. It hardly ever took more than seven minutes for him to be off with the sandman.

He knew where they were. They were in the magical room that Jack, with a sentimental bit of Irish in his genes, had considered naming Cassie's Ballroom or maybe Cassie's Banquet Hall. It had now returned to its original and primeval state—invisibility—and they were lying on its smooth floor under unseen helictites of supernal beauty and almost perfect privacy—caves were the scene of eternities of privacy—which made it all the more important to respect them.

Cassie was about five feet to his left on the inflated mattress, probably lying on her right side with her left leg drawn up. She had taken off her Vietnam jungle boots before stretching out.

"Probably I stink," she had said as he clicked off the flashlight.

"No problem," he had replied. "Everybody does after a while in a cave. No one notices."

She laughed.

"I notice," she said. "I can't help thinking about a shower. Shampoo. A manicure. Pretty stuff from Nordstrom's, Neiman Marcus."

"You'll get over it."

"Brooks Brothers," she went on.

"Oh," Jack said, getting it. "Sorry. I like to think of it as the camaraderie of St. Pigpen. A state of odorific holiness, like the Essenes or whatever, the monks who . . ."

"Never mind," Cassie said, and evidently fell asleep, leaving Jack to his momentary thoughts before he began to fade into the delicious and delicate enfolding . . .

And now she had said, "Are you awake?"

A moment flashed through his mind, several moments, when he would be lying in bed next to her toward the end of their marriage, feeling stupid and inarticulate, knowing he was guilty of some transgression or another and had failed to satisfy her request that he explain himself and his actions and the foundations of his belief system and worldview, as well as what in his upbringing might have led to such a catastrophic excuse for an adult, and despite his failure, he was done for the night and was planning to fall asleep, hoping the entire matter would go away by dawn, and was slipping toward sleep and she would say, "Are you awake?"

She's not my wife anymore, he told himself. I don't have to put up with this. I don't have to tell her anything except how to keep from falling on her ass as we go through this cave to show her the footprint that *I,* in my unbounded generosity, brought to her attention . . . and why did I do that? I don't love her anymore. She de-married me. Divorce. Okay, she *divorced* me. The dreaded *d* word. Oh, you're divorced, they say, wondering what the poor woman had to put up with. I suppose I deserved it, but, well, hell . . . I don't need *this.*

"Yeah," he said. "I'm awake."

Christ, how he loved her. She could light up the world with the expression on her face. Eyes dancing like live coals. Wonderful long body, languid but strong. Enormous, capacious mind connecting things with lightning speed, things he had no idea were connected—ideas, processes, bones, evolution, Shakespearean sonnets . . . What a world she lived in, they had both lived in. Now? Was she still the same person? Did two and half years change everything? Probably.

Yeah, probably.

He longed to reach out, put his hand in that valley where her rib cage ducked down and her hip rose up.

That would still be the same, even if she was a different person now.

"I can't believe how dark it is in here," she said. "Total, utter, complete lack of everything. I mean, up in the world, there's always *some* light. Just from a star or two. Here, it's like you almost don't exist anymore."

"It gives some people the creeps," Jack said. "On the other hand, I took a blind guy down into Gunsight Cave once. Last year it was. He'd climbed Mount Rainier or some damned thing and he wanted to go in a cave, you know, showing that guys with handicaps are up to any challenge. So I took him and, like, he never noticed the difference. If you don't know dark and light, one of these places can't really mean anything."

"I remember I had an English teacher in college named Vaughan, Professor Vaughan. He said *dark* and *light* were the two most overused words in all of American fiction."

"Probably had a streetlight outside his bedroom all his life. Sure as hell never pushed a cave. I mean, how many words are there to describe the presence or absence of light? I never met an English professor who didn't have problems with the real world."

"Ah, the Jack Whittaker holier-than-thou anti-intellectual pose."

"We've been through this, Cassie. I don't pose. I do things."

Cassie was breathing ever so lightly. Otherwise the world was completely silent.

"Oh, Jack," she said presently, her voice coming from what seemed a great distance. "You had so many poses, I could never figure out who you were."

Here it comes, Jack said to himself. Here it comes.

"Like my father," she said.

Her father, the drunk, Jack thought. He remembered all this. "I

105

know, I know. The disappearance act. Presto, and the charming genie disappeared back into his bottle. The vanishing act. Like me going caving. We've been through this. I never meant to disappear; I was just . . ."

"Following your addiction," she said. "I used to think it was something like going off with a mistress, a lover. I was jealous, of course. Then? Then I woke up. You weren't being unfaithful. You just had something more important than me. So how could I care? It doesn't matter now." She fell silent for a long moment and said, "I'm very grateful to you for showing me that photograph and for bringing me down here. I feel perfectly safe down here with you. You're so . . . proficient . . . down here."

Jack didn't move. He felt a bit like a yo-yo.

"And you were sweet about my panic attack back there. Thank you."

Jack remained silent, then he said quietly, "Maybe we better get some sleep." But Cassie was already asleep.

Bewildering, he thought. Absolutely bewildering.

When Cassie opened her eyes, they were greeted by the dazzling starbursts of the helictite chandeliers overhead. Jack had set his lamp on the floor, pointing upward, and a large part of the ceiling was lit with a white-gold glow. She stretched luxuriously, forcing the little aches out of her back muscles, and sat up, aware of a soft breeze blowing across her.

"Coffee?" Jack said, and held out a shiny titanium cup. "Feel that breeze? Barometric pressure outside must have dropped. The cave is blowing."

Cassie sipped the coffee from the almost weightless cup. "You know," she said, "I've been thinking. I thought you cavers always insisted on at least three in a party. Never alone. Wasn't there some famous case of a guy alone in one of these caverns who got stuck? Buried alive or something?"

"That's right."

"But you've been coming down here alone. You're Mr. Safety, the big rescue man."

Jack shrugged. "I know at least five other guys who'd've done the same thing if they found something like this. It's a risk, but you can minimize the risk. And the more people who know about this place, the sooner it'll leak out. That's the big risk. Here," he said, handing her a breakfast bar and a sandwich bag full of cashews. "Breakfast. We should get going."

"What time is it?" Cassie asked.

"Five-thirty. We'll be there in a couple of hours. There's two ways to get there, but the longer way is easier. Otherwise you've got to go up a chimney for about forty feet. This probably isn't the time for you to learn how to do that. It takes a bit of practice."

It took longer than two hours. Climbing up an incline of loose rock and scree in a large room filled with dull gray columns connecting the ceiling sixty feet above with the floor, Cassie lost her footing, fell sideways, and began to tumble down the slope. Her helmet crashed against a rock, knocking her head sideways, and for an instant she was blind, the terrifying thought leaping to her mind that her headlamp was out, broken, but the blindness vanished, her light was working, and somehow, instinctively, she righted herself, and slid the rest of the way down on her bottom, throwing up a cloud of gray dust, her left foot catching on a rock and twisting painfully.

"Shit," she said.

Jack was beside her in an instant, kicking up another swirl of dust that danced in the light from their headlamps. Cassie was holding her ankle, her face pinched with pain.

"Bad?" he said.

"Jee-sus, that hurts." She was filled with dismay.

"Sprained?"

"I hope not."

"The best thing is to walk on it," Jack said. "We can see . . ."

"I know that," she said irritably, and started to get to her feet. "Ow!"

"How about the rest of you?" Jack asked.

"Both my pride and my butt are terminally bruised," she said, and took a halting step. Then another. "Besides all that, I'm fine. Just fine." She hobbled around among the stone columns for several minutes, muttering to herself and limping less as the minutes passed. "Okay," she said, limping over to where Jack squatted on his haunches. "Let's go. It's not sprained. Just twisted. It's better."

Jack had her lead the way up the scree to a wide opening, another great intestine but large enough to walk upright most of the way. When it narrowed down, making it necessary to crawl, Cassie found it easier on her ankle. But they had lost some time, and after the allotted two hours, they were standing on a ledge in a huge cavern, looking at a frozen Niagara of nearly vertical, reddish flowstone that disappeared into the stygian murk below. There was a faint new smell in her nose, the dank odor of ancient rocks and water.

"It's down there," Jack said. "About three hundred feet." He busied himself checking an orange line, fastening it to a loop of black tape that he had previously wrapped around a boulder the size of a compact car. "Piece of cake. Just like an elevator ride."

Cassie felt the world closing in on her and at the same time falling away from beneath her feet. This is stupid, she said. Not now. She gritted her teeth and willed the gathering panic to leave. Go, go, go, she said to herself, and watched Jack deftly hooking up the rigging, listened to the carabiners click against rock. She couldn't get the image out of her mind of the yawning abyss awaiting her while she dangled on a skinny piece of rope that was all there would be between her and a catastrophic plunge into the center of the earth, where it would be wet, not hot, an icy pool of black water that would close over her head. . . .

It's the best rope money can buy, she told herself, braided, no twisting in the dark. Her ankle began to throb. Don't lose it now, she commanded. She tried to bring into mental focus the photographs Jack had made of the footprint down below in the black hole— *Arctodus simus.* She repeated the Latinate phrase like a mantra and saw in her mind's eye the footprint, black and white, shadow and light delineating the five toes, the trapezoidal pad in the white limestone, and the panic dissipated. Jack, who was squatting on his heels, checking the line, looked up at her.

"Okay?" he said.

Cassie nodded.

"I'll go down first," he said. "You'll be okay up here for about five minutes?"

She nodded again. He stood up, rigged his brake bars and hooked on, and backed out over the precipice and disappeared. Cassie felt her eyes squinch up with oncoming tears.

Stop that! she told herself. And suddenly a phrase popped into her mind, a phrase she hadn't thought of since she had been forced to take Latin in the tenth grade. It was the beginning of a rule her Latin teacher, a little man with a nasal voice, had said she would never forget.

All verbs meaning . . .

All verbs meaning . . . *favor!* That was it.

All verbs meaning *favor, help, please, trust,* something . . . *believe!* . . . *persuade, command, obey, serve, resist, envy, threaten, pardon, spare, indulge,* and *involve* . . . take the dative with the exception of *iuvo, adiuvo, iubeo,* and *delecto.*

The rule had been permanently etched in her brain, as if she had been hypnotized by the little man's nasal voice. She repeated it over and over until she heard Jack call from somewhere way down: "I'm off the rope!"

Grasping the brake bar in her left hand and the rope with her right, she backed out over the edge and began the descent.

Iuvo, adiuvo, iubeo, and *delecto.*

Delecto: to delight or charm.

Sure.

By eight o' clock in the morning, an engineer had spent fifteen minutes examining the salt at the end of S10249 and returned to ground level, reluctantly leaving the three forensic specialists behind. He sat in Anna Maria's office with a mug of coffee, running his hand through a shock of blond hair that was evidently modeled on Robert Redford. There the resemblance stopped. He was an unnaturally thin man, about six foot four, all angles. Even his face was all angles, which were emphasized by the pallor common to people who spent most of their time indoors or underground. His hard hat was beside him on the floor.

"It's like Yazzie said," the engineer was saying. "It's gone soft. Crumbled, like. It's hard to tell how much. It could be just a patch, like we had in N10444 two years ago. You can't just probe it manually. If a big air pocket's in there, it could blow. Now, I didn't get anything like that on my readings and no moisture. Dry as dust. But . . ." He shrugged. "I'd feel a lot better if we got Sandia down here. And to be honest, I'd feel a lot better if those guys weren't down there. I mean, I don't see any reason for a code red or anything, but . . ."

He paused again, and Anna Maria guessed that he was giving her an opening to explain who those "guys" were. He obviously didn't believe they were EPA inspectors. She chose not to take the opening.

"Get the Sandia people down here," she said. "And keep this absolutely quiet until we know more about the situation." She stood up, signaling that the meeting was over. "Understood? Not a word to anyone."

"Yes, ma'am," the engineer said, and unfolded himself from the chair. Need to know was as much a byword at WIPP as at the Central Intelligence Agency, and this wasn't the first little secret the engineer had been in on. He had a twelve-year record of loyal team playing—a man with a good future.

ELEVEN

"Here," Jack said, going down on his knees and crawling forward. "Come over here."

They were at the far end of an immense room, if that was the word for it. It was the size of at least five football fields, with an immensely high vaulted ceiling, much of it beyond the reach of their puny headlamps. They had picked their way across from the bottom of the enormous cascade of flowstone, through fields of columns and other gigantic formations. The floor was damp in places, littered with chunks of limestone, large and small. At one point, they had both stopped, hearing a sound that wasn't water dripping or the crunch of their boots on rock.

"What was that?" Cassie asked, an icicle of fear materializing in her innards.

"A little rockfall," Jack said. "Just pebbles. Sometimes it happens. You know, wherever these caves are still happening."

The idea wasn't reassuring, but Cassie pressed on. Her reason for making this awful journey into the earth—the footprint—lay just ahead, and her mind focused on it as eagerly as a bird dog on grouse.

Before them now, the floor fell abruptly away, and a large black maw, nearly circular and maybe fifty feet across, gaped at them. Cassie listened to the occasional *plink* of water dripping from the ceiling somewhere behind them. No doubt, aeons from now, another stalagmite would have arisen.

Jack had reached the edge of the hole, and Cassie crawled up to his right. About ten feet below them, the mirrorlike pool gleamed in their lights. The water was clear, every detail of the white limestone bottom sharply focused. Huge white lily pads of limestone extended from the edge out into the water. The air felt clammy, and Cassie shivered. By now, she had grown accustomed to the stillness, the motionlessness of this world, its utter emptiness but for rock—the stillness punctuated only by the occasional gleam of water oozing downward, the sound of drops falling somewhere in the unseen beyond, or, now she added, a few pebbles dislodged by water. But there was something almost ominous about this silent jewel of water, its surface as smooth as polished glass, set in the white limestone floor, which itself was particularly smooth. In the real world, no body of water, not even a puddle on a windless day, could be this still. Water meant motion, change, but this pool had every appearance of something eternal.

"There," Jack said, pointing. "Over there just under the overhang. See it?"

She followed the direction of his hand. To the right of the pool, the white limestone floor vanished into a long and deep horizontal cleft. And there, on the narrow strip of stone, as clearly defined as if it had been molded in plaster of paris, was the footprint. Light and shadow limned the toes and the large heel pad in sharp relief. Feeling an odd nausea, Cassie realized she hadn't been breathing for some moments. She gulped in the damp air.

"Oh, wow," she said, almost a prayer. Fourteen thousand years ago, maybe longer, *Arctodus simus* had stepped here, its fifteen hundred pounds pressing its foot in a soft place, a damp place, and left its perfect print behind to solidify. An array of questions flooded her mind, questions she had already asked herself a hundred times since seeing Jack's photographs—it seemed like weeks since she had seen them in Jack's depressing trailer, though it was only two nights ago that he had snatched them from among the pile of maps and held them out to her with such studied nonchalance.

What had it been doing down here? The short-faced bear was a land mammal, possibly nocturnal, though probably not. It was fleet, probably rarely experiencing failure whenever it set out to hunt—though possibly at the end, as it neared extinction, it might have had to search farther for prey. But down here? In this lifeless wilderness of rock? They had found remains of the saber-toothed cats in shallow caves where they evidently sometimes dragged their prey, maybe to keep their dinner out of the jaws of short-faced bears. Maybe this one simply strayed in, got lost. Getting lost in this place, even for a bear, was pretty easy to imagine. But it was an immense animal, long-legged, with a slender body unlike the chunky bodies of grizzlies and black bears.

It had cave-dwelling counterparts. In Florida, they had often found remains of an equally large cave bear, much like the cave bears of Europe and Asia that earnest woman had made famous in her silly romances like *Clan of the Cave Bear*. But cave bears in Europe and Florida had the wide, flat molars of a vegetarian. They were huge, about the same size as the short-faced bear, and they evidently hibernated in caves, but not anything like the depths of this cavern. And, Cassie wondered now, how could a bear that was bigger than a horse have gotten in here? There was hardly room in some of those wormholes for a hundred-and-thirty-pound woman to pass.

It was totally awesome. Cassie didn't like the overused words, the wonky mantras of inarticulate youth, but here, in the presence of this beautifully preserved and utterly unique piece of the Pleistocene, the words popped unbidden into her head, clad in their real and original meaning. Cassie had never experienced a rush like this, not in years of field work, uncovering the fossilized remains of the strange and wonderful fauna of the Ice Age. Here was a record of flesh and blood, matched only by a few discoveries of intact mastodons in the glacial ice of Siberia.

"I've got to get down there," Cassie said.

"No problem," Jack said. "I would've gone down there, but I didn't have much time. Neither do we, as a matter of fact, if we want to get out of here before dawn tomorrow." He busied himself stringing a line, attaching it to one of the columns behind them that disappeared into the blackness of the ceiling. Distantly more pebbles rattled down some slope, but Cassie and Jack paid no attention.

Within five minutes, they were standing beside the clear, still pool, a pale emerald, shucking their backpacks. Cassie pulled out her camera, a small, automatic Rollei Prego with a zoom lens.

"You'll want to stay off the lily pads there," Jack said. " Some of 'em could probably take your weight. Others . . . they could snap off and you'd be in the drink."

Cassie shrugged. "It's pretty shallow."

"It *looks* pretty shallow. I'd guess it's over your head, easy."

Cassie methodically began to photograph the scene with the wide-angle setting—28 mm—the pool and its environs exploding with light with each flash. After four frames, she approached the footprint, stealthy as a cat, putting her feet down carefully. When she was within a pace of it, she bent over and peered at it, remaining still for nearly a full minute, during which Jack watched her intently.

"Jesus," she said. "It's huge, isn't it? Fifteen inches. Well, we knew that already, but *seeing* it, seeing the real thing—it's entirely different." She looked back at Jack, a broad smile straining her cheeks.

"Thanks," she said, and put the camera to her eye, then looked suspiciously at the rock of the crevice that was only a few inches from her head. Then the camera went back to her face. "I need something for scale. Oh, one of these'll do." She unhooked a carabiner from her belt. Slowly, as if she were fearful that something, maybe the footprint itself, might vanish, nothing more than a dream—ever so slowly, she placed the shiny metal carabiner, the shape of a D, a few inches from the footprint—and pulled her hand back as if bitten by a snake.

"What?" Cassie shrieked.

"What, what?" Jack said, stepping toward her.

"It's wet!" she said, reaching out with her forefinger. She touched the rock an inch from the heel print. "The ground is *wet,* for Christ's sake! It's wet sand."

"It can't be."

"It is, it is. And look—I didn't see this before. This little indentation. This is where you put your canteen. See?"

Jack was too far away to see. He began to step along the rock floor toward her.

"It's fake!" she said, her voice rising into the shrillness of outrage. "I can't believe it. You faked this thing and got me down here—what are you, insane? Why? Why do this?"

"It's not fake," Jack shouted. "I promise. Goddammit, I found it here just like it is. From up there. I've never been down here before."

On her knees now beside the footprint, Cassie ripped at the Velcro fastener on her helmet, tore it off, wrenching it free of the battery cord, and hurled it at him. "You bastard!"

The helmet bounced off Jack's knee and, before he could grab it, bounced on the edge of a lily pad and toppled into the pool. Taken by surprise, he saw it begin to sink and finally lunged for it, but too late. As it sank beyond his reach, the water rippled outward, disturbed for perhaps the first time in thousands of years.

Misinterpreting Jack's lunge, Cassie backed away as she stood up, and her head smashed into the rocky ledge.

"Ow!" she cried, and crumpled to the ground under the overhang. The little black Rollei clattered on a lily pad. "Oh, Christ," she moaned, her hand clutching the side of her head.

"Are you . . . ?"

"Stay away from me. Leave me alone. Oh, Jesus. I just want to lie here for a minute." She felt something hard under her shoulder, pressing into her flesh. Pain flooding through her head and a surge of nausea spreading through her gut, she reached under her to move the offending rock.

Jack was crouched just outside the overhang, staring at her, when she held up the bone, a big bone, like a femur, and gaped at it.

"Hey," Jack said. "You found the bear." A footprint *and* a bone, he thought. The jackpot.

Cassie was gasping for breath.

"It's not a bear," she said in a hoarse whisper.

"Huh?"

"It's a human femur." She gulped air again and dropped the bone. "And it's still *wet*. It's still wet. There's still some gobs of rotten . . ." The whites of her eyes were enormous, gleaming in the light from Jack's headlamp.

Abruptly she scrabbled out from under the overhang, stood up, lost her footing, and fell against Jack's leg. He reached for her arm, felt her shuddering, a violent wrenching of her entire body. He pulled her to her feet. Blood ran through her matted blond hair, emerging in a gleaming trickle below her right temple.

"It could be out there," she said. "Anywhere. Those rockfalls . . ."

"What could be out there?"

"Don't you see? Whatever left that footprint, whatever brought that bone in here." Her voice was rising from a whisper on its way to shriek or a howl. Jack pulled her against his chest, feeling the tremors racking her body. The words poured out of her. "It couldn't be more than two or three days old, the bone. I mean, it would've dried out if it was here longer than that. Something, some kind of bear, *ate* someone."

Jack put his arm around her shoulders and herded her over to the rope hanging down from above. "Let's go, let's go," he said, not as calmly as he would have wished, and squatted down in front of the orange rope. "Put your feet on my shoulders and hold on to the rope." Cassie did as she was told and soon felt herself being precariously lifted as Jack stood up. "Okay, now lift up your feet, one at a time." He put a hand under each raised foot and slowly pushed her farther up until she could hoist herself over the edge.

"Please hurry," she said. "It's dark."

Jack picked up the two backpacks and hurled them up into the void, hearing them land on the rock above. "Get your flashlight," he said, and pulled himself up the rope, hand over hand, feet stepping up the vertical face as easily as crossing the street, and hauled himself onto the flat surface of the enormous cavern. Cassie had her flashlight on and was shining it back and forth through the gloom. Its beam skittered over the formations.

"Shit," Jack said.

"What?"

"Your camera. I'll go back and get it."

"Not on your life. Forget it. We've got to get the hell out of here. I mean, that creature could be . . ." She waved the flashlight again, its beam flashing over columns and boulders. "What if those rockfalls were it?"

The hair was standing up on the nape of Jack's neck, the skin crawling as they hoisted their packs. "We've got one advantage," he said. "Lights. Animals that spend a lot of time in the dark don't like bright lights."

He started moving across the cavern at a quick pace, and Cassie made a point of keeping only a step or two behind him.

"Most animals that spend their lives in caves are blind," she said. "Don't try conning me. I'm scared to death."

"This thing can't live down here all the time. There's nothing to eat."

"It ate the first guy to discover this cave, it looks like," Cassie said sourly.

"The other thing is," Jack said, "most of the way we're going, a bear big enough to make that print couldn't get through. It must have another way of getting in here."

"Great. But it got in that hole back there, and it could get in this place. I can go faster, you know. My ankle's fine."

All signs, or even thoughts, of claustrophobia left Cassie, overwhelmed by the cold, implacable fear that at any minute, around any stalagmite, a huge bear might appear out of the dark and turn them into brunch. As the hours passed, she found herself relieved and not at all claustrophobic in the narrowest places, inching along where she knew no bear could pass. It was the large passageways, the big chambers they quick-marched through, that were now the enemy.

Her legs ached from the effort and the pace until they felt almost numb. Her feet hurt; her back was feeling the strain of the pack, which seemed to grow heavier with each passing moment. The bleeding from her head had quickly stopped of its own accord, but her head ached as well, and the muscles in her neck were as taut as piano wire. Without her helmet and her headlamp, she felt naked and vulnerable, the flashlight seeming an inadequate toy, its beam thin and feeble.

But amid the fear and exhaustion—and the multiple aches and pains—she felt a slight tinge of pride. She had gotten the hang of ascending a rope—a technique Jack called prusiking. It was a complicated process involving two loops of webbing, one for each foot, a metal device called a Jumar attached to the rope at the level of her navel, and a lot of other hookups. The rigging permitted her to literally walk up the rope. It was exhausting, and at first she despaired that she could make it work, but by the time she had risen halfway up the first great cataract of flowstone in the great room full of giant formations, she got the rhythm. You used the big muscles of thighs and haunches, not your arms and shoulders. And, of course, when she was dangling from a rope God knows how far up in the air, she knew she was at least safe from the bear.

Not since childhood had Cassie felt such fear of the dark. Like many little kids, she suffered through a period when she would become convinced that something shapeless and hungry lurked under her bed, possibly even between the sides of the mattress and the sheet. One didn't put one's foot down there. The closet in her room also harbored malevolent nocturnal creatures. Her mother knew about such things, though she never said anything about it, and always saw that the closet door was firmly closed before she kissed Cassie good night and left the room. Now the shadows in the chambers they crossed, shadows leaping and crouching in the motion of their lights, made her inwardly cringe, inwardly try to keep her feet away from . . .

No, she thought. I have good reason to be terrified. She tried to keep her mind from dwelling on the stories of people being attacked and eaten by grizzlies in Yellowstone Park—a couple of women once, one of whom had started her period, the odor bringing in the bear like a moth to light. Hustling across one chamber— it looked utterly unfamiliar to her, seeing it now from the other direction—she asked Jack if they shouldn't go slower, more cautiously through these relatively open places.

"The best thing we can do," Jack said, "is get out of here as soon as possible. If one of them is in here, it's got to be going by another route. It can't follow us through the wormholes. And if it gets into one of these rooms—and at the same time we do, which isn't real likely—it won't do us much good to try and sneak through. We have to count on our lights to repel it. And whatever noise we can make."

"But . . . ," Cassie began, then thought better of it.

"Did you smell anything back there? At the pool?"

"Yeah," Cassie said. "Rotten flesh on that bone." She shuddered.

"Nothing before that?"

"No."

Later, much later, she said, "Aren't you, well, scared?" She was two paces behind him, her eyes fixed on his shoulders as he strode along, snaking his way past the endless formations.

"Shitless," Jack said.

"Could've fooled me," she muttered.

"When you're up to your ass in alligators," Jack said, "the wise general calls for an orderly retreat. I read that in some book on the art of war by a Chinese general. I'm just trying to be orderly."

It struck Cassie again how topsy-turvy things had become in this damned cavern. Places that had given her the heebie-jeebies on the way down were now the only places she felt safe. And she had spent most of the journey down and practically all of the journey out on the verge of losing it. She had lost it, in fact, twice. Once when a drop of water surprised her, for God's sake, and then at the footprint . . . Earlier in their life together, she had been the one who was steady, reliable, while Jack was unpredictable, a flake. Down here, he was in his element, precise and attentive to every detail. He knew where he was going and just how to get there, and every move he made reminded her of an artisan at work, like a cabinet-maker, maybe. Or a general. Everything was thought out in his mind before it came up. Well, almost everything. He hadn't, of course, known the footprint was fresh, that the cavern was inhabited, at least used, by the huge creature that had left its mark there, along with the remains of a meal.

"I'm sorry, Jack," she said.

"What about?"

"Losing it back there. At the footprint. Accusing you of . . ."

"No problem," Jack said. "I just feel dumb as hell, not having taken a few minutes to go down and check that thing in the first place."

As the hours passed, the sheer physical effort and pain of keeping up began to displace the fear that had gripped her like icicles in her chest. Finally all she could think of was the effort of the next step, of putting a foot down so it wouldn't slip, so she wouldn't stumble. When, as happened more often the farther they went, she lagged behind Jack three, four paces, then more, he would stop, wait for her to catch up, and urge her on until they reached a place that seemed safe, where they rested. They drank water from their plastic bottles, and Jack would fish blue Aleve tablets from his pack for her. They sat or crouched for a few minutes in silence, the only sound that of their own breathing and the occasional *plink* of water hitting stone. It occurred to Cassie that the farther they got—without meeting up with the nemesis of the cavern—the farther fear receded. She was no longer in the throes of truly heart-pounding terror like a knife in her chest. Instead her mind was filled with a generalized sense of dread, like a bruise.

But when at one such stop Jack said, "We're almost there. Another fifteen minutes and up we go," the terror returned, full-blown, howling in her being. What if the creature was waiting there for them, arrived by some other route that it knew, standing there at the bottom of the long climb up? After all this effort, all this time, to be intercepted at the end of the journey, mauled, dismembered, devoured in hideous jaws . . . She shuddered and flicked on her flashlight, hoping its weakening beam would drive the demons away. She couldn't stop the shaking, and the pallid beam of light was a wobbling extension of her tremors.

She heard Jack rustling around in his pack. He reached out, took her hand in his, and with the other placed three batteries in her palm.

"I'll carry the old ones out," he said, flicking on his light.

When she finished the exchange, she said, "That's okay. I'll take them."

She knew it was ridiculous. She wanted to keep the old batteries at hand. The notion was ludicrous—winging Duracell D-size batteries into the face of a ravening, fifteen-hundred-pound bear, towering up on its hind legs, ten feet tall, in hopes that it would cower and slink back into its black world.

Even so . . .

She put two of the batteries in her pack and kept the third clutched tightly in her hand as they set out on the last leg out of hell.

TWELVE

With what she was sure was the last surge of strength she would ever again experience, Cassie dragged her torso over the edge. On her stomach, with her legs still dangling in the hole, her eye fell on a chunk of limestone lit silver by the moon. It was the most beautiful thing she had ever seen, a piece of rock—with light on it. Real light. The blessed natural light of night, moon, stars, a silver glow.

She pulled herself out of the black hole and onto her knees, unhitched her gear from the rope, and looked up into the blue-black vault overhead. The open sky, a vista that stretched away without an intervening ceiling of rock formations, crystals, stalactites—just a magnificent void that conferred upon the earth its most precious attribute: light. Among the scattering of stars, she made out two familiar constellations, Orion and the Pleiades. Orion the Hunter, huge and bold. She had heard somewhere that the Pleiades reminded some of the Indian tribes of the spots on a fawn—the hunted. She too had been the hunted—or had she?

To the south, near the horizon, the sky was almost totally black—clouds sweeping in from Texas and Mexico on a front of damp air, part of the ever changing, ever fresh circulatory system of the earth's surface.

Reminding herself of her duty, she crawled over to the edge of the entrance hole and shouted, "Off-line!" The cave was breathing out slightly, expelling air that smelled of dead rock, old dirt, the odors of a lightless world.

She sank onto her back on the hard rock, looking at the pinpricks of light in the firmament. Some of the light striking her eyes at this moment had started out on its journey long before water and gravity had begun carving out the cavern she had just escaped, perhaps even before the earth itself was born. She found herself crying, tears pinching out from her eyelids, in relief and appreciation.

Luxuriating in the sumptuous gift of moonlight, she knew she would have to begin to think—rationally, scientifically—about what had happened down there. Obvious questions rose to the surface and flickered in front of her, the questions she had asked but avoided as she and Jack made their hurried way out of the cavern.

What exactly was it that had made that footprint? A bear, certainly a bear. Bigger than a grizzly by half.

But that was impossible. Not just implausible. Impossible. No bear that big had existed for thousands of years. The only bears that big were long extinct, cut down by radical changes to their world as the continent was slowly relieved of its burden of ice. All hell had broken loose—the land rising, the sea level rising, river systems gouging out new paths, joining—and the great creatures of the Pleistocene had died out with what amounted to a whimper. They were gone.

She was repeating the word *gone* in her mind and realized she wasn't thinking at all, just gibbering in relief at being out of the cave. Tomorrow would be time enough to interpret all this. Or was it tomorrow already? Never mind.

The sound of Jack's boots on rock preceded him. Cassie remained on her back and saw him emerge into the moonlight and flick off his light. The whites of his eyes shone against his face, black with grime. He unhitched the webbing that enfolded him, removed his hard hat, and stood for a moment, breathing deeply. Cassie almost giggled. With his grubby overalls and begrimed face, he looked more like an auto mechanic than the cool, proficient general who had led an orderly retreat from the edge of doom.

"You did great down there," he said, and began coiling up the line, withdrawing it from the entrance hole. "We made incredible time. It's just two o'clock. You'll be in bed in an hour."

Slowly she sat up and began to unhitch her harness.

"What are we gonna do about that down there?" she asked. "I mean, aren't we supposed to report a homicide? Aren't we supposed to let someone like BLM or Fish and Wildlife know about that . . . creature?"

"What is it? All we saw was a footprint—"

"And a human femur, mostly picked clean—"

"But no creature, no animal. No bear."

Jack continued with his methodical collecting of gear.

"Sure," he said. "We're gonna go to the feds and say we think there's a giant bear in a cave on private property, where we just happened to be trespassing the other day, and wouldn't they go on down there and catch it? Chances are they'd think we're lunatics or hoaxers and run our butts off the premises. And do you think the county sheriff's gonna send a team of people down there because we say we saw a recently defleshed human leg bone fourteen hundred feet down in a cave no one has never seen before?"

"Bones happen to be my business."

"Right. And tell me, Dr. Roberts, where is that bone?" Jack asked in a Texas-style drawl. "You picked it up. How come you didn't bring it with you? You dropped it? Because you figured it was part of the dinner of a what? A bear that's half again as big as a grizzly. Right, Dr. Roberts. And you and your nutty friend, that no-account cave pusher, fled from this bear? This bear you never saw but believe to be alive and well in a cave that—oh yeah, ma'am—that just happens to be on private property where you wasn't invited to go in the first place."

Cassie began to bristle again. They were trapped. Jack had trapped them. "So what do you think we ought to do?"

"Get some sleep. Think about it tomorrow. Try and figure out what could have left that print. We're both too wiped out to think straight."

Five minutes later, the Trooper was packed and Cassie had

exchanged the filthy overalls for her own clothes. The vehicle bounced and swayed along the bottom of the canyon, then up onto the rimrock, and made its way toward the highway. Most of the sky was now obscured by clouds. The desert was deeply shadowed, vague shapes in the dark, and Jack kept the headlights off until he reached the road.

It made no difference to the man who watched them from a rise two hundred yards off, peering down the nightscope of a rifle.

He'd been looking for a mountain lion up in the higher ground across the highway. Or a vandal. Another of his herd had been torn up that afternoon, and he couldn't sleep anyway these days. Might as well just hang out and see if he got lucky.

Like many hunters, Tracer Dunn felt a certain empathy with his prey. He understood what lions were doing down here, out of the Guadalupe Mountains. It was simple. If the state decides to put some half-baked, arbitrary limit on how many mountain lions—or anything else, mule deer, pronghorn—you can shoot, that population is going to rise. And as soon as there are more mountain lions than they got territory, they're going to spread out into places they wouldn't normally want to go. Mountain lions simply couldn't put up with overcrowding, and Tracer knew all about that.

So the younger lions go off looking for a territory of their own and find the country's now taken up by people, people with cattle, or even dogs, and the lions are just bound by their natural heritage to stay there and try to make a living. Then people get up in arms about lions eating their critters and posing a threat to their children, so they complain to the same government that put the limit on the lions in the first place, and those idiots have to try to do something about it. In fact, those idiots get to do the hunting, leaving out the people who make a specialty of it and would have kept the population under control if they'd been left alone in the first place. Well, Tracer Dunn wasn't about to put up with a bunch of clumsy officials tromping around his place with rifles. He'd get the lion himself. If that was what was doing this.

He had been resting in the moonlight on a pretty little escarpment of limestone that looked almost like someone had set out to build a staircase when he heard an engine start up in the canyon below him and about two hundred yards north.

Poachers? Enviros? Satanists? Tracer Dunn trained the night-scope on his rifle on the white vehicle, one of those Troopers, when it came into sight. The faces of the two people were bright enough in the scope, appearing through the windshield black and white like an old TV. A man and a woman—at least it looked like a woman. Hard to tell. They were both covered with grime, like those blackface minstrel people in the old days, like the movie they made about Al Jolson.

The man behind the wheel was vaguely familiar. Probably Tracer had seen him around in Carlsbad, but he had no idea who he was. But from what he could see of the gear in the back—coils of that orange rope, all those ratchet-type things—the two trespassers were cavers. Maybe that Whittaker guy.

When the vehicle bucked out onto the highway and headed south, its headlights flicked on. Tracer Dunn lowered the rifle and spat into the dirt, listening to the gears change, second, third, fourth, and then a hum that was soon lost in the night. He looked up at the sky, noting that the low clouds had obscured most of the sky overhead. The moon was now gone, and the few remaining stars to the north left it too dark to poke around in that damned canyon. He'd come back in the morning, follow the tracks. He took the reins of his horse, the pinto named Chico, and began to walk it over the rough ground toward the highway.

Cavers.

Tracer Dunn had never done any of that, but he'd listened to those crazies talk about it often enough. He reckoned that just to get as dirty as those two looked, you'd have to spend a fair amount of time underground.

This could be a sight more interesting than a lion, he thought. All but a quarter mile of that canyon was on his property.

A few hundred yards on the other side of the highway, he stopped in a slight depression on a slight rise, where he unfurled his bedroll, hobbled Chico, and lay down. Somewhere off in the night, a coyote yipped, but Tracer didn't hear it. As soon as he was horizontal, he fell asleep, looking forward to the dawn and a new day for the first time since he could remember.

Four hours later, Tracer Dunn's eyes opened and he looked up at an overcast sky, tatters of clouds to the south twitching nervously like a horse's tail in a swarm of flies. In the east, the sun was a yellow disk, just up over the horizon in the pale blue sky over the high plains that stretched halfway to the Atlantic Ocean. During the night a new front had blown in from the northwest, clearing out the clouds, but the wind had shifted again to the south, and the weather was going to change again, like it usually did. The new front, another low up from Mexico, would bring in more clouds, another humid day. Maybe even some rain. God knows, a little rain would be a blessing.

He got painfully to his feet and stretched, forcing out the aches of oncoming arthritis and too many hours of inactivity, lying on the ground. It was the price of too many years doing a man's work. Some people liked to quote old Winston Churchill, who said that nothing was better for the inside of a man than the outside of a horse, and Tracer was inclined to agree. But he also knew what Churchill didn't at the time—too much of the outside of a horse eventually made your bones seize up like an iron machine left out in the rain too long.

"Come on, Chico," he said to the horse, who was standing nearby. He stooped to remove the hobble, and Chico placed his forefeet together out in front of him and sank back in a long and seemingly luxurious stretch.

"Two arthritic old has-beens," Tracer said, and briefly smiled. The pinto stood expectantly, awaiting the saddle, and moments later Tracer was mounted and turned the horse west across the highway, picking up the tracks of the white Isuzu Trooper. He followed them—both the coming and the going—even though he knew where they were headed. The tracks disappeared when he got to the rimrock where the canyon descended, and he picked them up again a little ways ahead where the rock and caliche gave way to hard sand littered with limestone chunks in the old stream-bed. He followed them, appearing and then disappearing for a stretch, to where they turned into the side canyon and, after about a hundred yards, stopped. He could see where the vehicle had come in, sat for a time, then turned around. Around the spot were the imprints of boots with deep treads, and he followed them up till they petered out, headed for what appeared to be a ledge about ten feet up the slope of the canyon wall.

Tracer Dunn had been in this canyon years before, walking his land on this same horse, but he hadn't had an occasion to come here since. And he hadn't taken the time to climb up to the ledge. It was just like any other ledge in any other canyon. Just another place where some prickly pear cacti had gotten a toehold and sat stolidly growing in the heat and the stillness. But now he heard a whistling sound, a low, continuous whoosh of air that was something else than the wind blowing from the south. A bigger sound.

He scrambled up the loose dirt and over a small field of loose rock and boulders, achieving the ledge, where he stopped, out of breath. The whooshing sound was louder. It was coming from the far end of the ledge, where some big chunks of limestone had fallen. He crossed the rocky ground and climbed over the big white chunks. Before him, the ground was flat, a little clearing among the rubble. Dust was swirling over a black hole in the ground, what looked like a little crevice. He crossed the clearing and squatted down on aching knees a few feet from the hole.

So here was the entrance. He looked up and saw that low clouds now filled the southern half of the sky, swarming northward. A raven swooped overhead, veered off, neatly avoiding the column of upward-flowing air, and disappeared over the canyon wall.

Tracer fished a packet of cigarette papers from his shirt pocket, took three out of the packet, and balled them up into a little clump. Still squatting, he lobbed the clump of cigarette paper into the hole and watched in awe as it was whisked six feet up in the air above him.

That was one hell of a big wind coming out of the cave. And that surely did mean it was a hell of a big cave.

He would have to get his old bones down there, have a look. That meant he'd need some equipment, ropes and all. Mainly ropes. He didn't know anything about how to use all those little ratchety things, and it wouldn't be a good idea to go buy some at that outfitter store, Guadalupe Mountain Outfitters, in Carlsbad. The gossip would get to the entire population that old Tracer Dunn was going to do some caving, and the busybodies would be swarming. No, he'd better just improvise with the things he was familiar with. After all, he thought, that fellow White who found Carlsbad Caverns back around the turn of the century—he was a cowboy out in the foothills of the Guadalupes and saw the bats swarming up like a cloud of smoke. Went down there with nothing but some water, some kerosene, a hand ax, and a few coils of rope. Made himself a ladder out of rope and sticks. All this fancy stuff was new, probably invented by prissy little Europeans for climbing around in the Alps. What was good enough for Jim White was good enough for him.

He tossed a little chunk of limestone into the hole and listened for it, but what with the whooshing and all, he didn't hear it hit.

He guessed he'd need a hell of a lot of rope.

While he was back at the trailer, he'd call that fat little realtor, Seth Baker, and take the ranch off the market. And he'd get Lucia to rustle up a big, big breakfast. Steak and three eggs. He hadn't felt this hungry since he could remember.

PART TWO

THIRTEEN

No one has ever invented an association of people larger than a nuclear family where rumor is not the chief form of communication. No business, no small town, no military unit has ever been able to quash it. Even in the most democratic and humane organizations, in which the feelings of all hands however lowly are deemed paramount and frequently aired in public get-togethers, retreats and workshops, and all decision making occurs in the light of open scrutiny and comment, rumor rules.

The Waste Isolation Pilot Plant outside Carlsbad was the opposite of such benign institutions. It was administered, as are so many government organizations but especially those that deal with sensitive matters, under what amounted to a cloak of secrecy and, as needed, not excessively veiled threat. It was management by confrontation. Orders were typically shouted, explanations few. Some blamed this style for the uniformly high blood pressure of the managers. The others, the laborers and technicians, took it in fatalistic stride, merely grumbling about the lousy pay, doing what they were told, and spreading rumor in a place where information of all kinds was as closely held as in a nation at war. Elaborate precautions were in place that one might expect where every employee was a potential James Bond working for the other side. No file cabinet was without an elaborate lock. And no office. The number of keys to such places one possessed was the clearest mark of one's power, a substance as eagerly sought and jealously husbanded as one's salary.

Official policy—and unofficial policy—was that the loose lipped were shipped off to the Department of Energy's version of Siberia, if not sacked outright for violating the rules about classified data. Almost everything was classified. Well-paid scientific consultants quickly discovered that it wouldn't do to research questions that might result in a wrong answer.

In such a situation, rumor cannot be prevented any more than the earth can be halted in its orbit. Every cubicle at WIPP, every office in the trailers out in the yard, every guard post and lavatory was awash in rumor within minutes of the beginning of the workday.

Something was up in S10249, the latest tunnel to be gouged out of the salt. The official story was that someone—an EPA engineer on a routine inspection—had a stroke and was carried out in what amounted to a coma and taken to the hospital. He was one of the four people who had arrived the day before. Some said he had died in the hospital, others that he was dead before the elevator reached the surface. Others argued darkly that it was no stroke but something else that no one was supposed to know anything about. Probably never would.

A good deal of speculation revolved around the fact that S10249 had been closed before the "inspectors" arrived. They had encountered a noxious gas (the fallen inspector was gassed). Or an air pocket (and he was blown to pieces by the rush of air).

Water, some said, they hit water is what I heard.

No, it was a column of broken salt and rock; what do they call them? Yeah, breccia columns. A sure sign that the salt layer is breached.

Nah. Those things don't happen here.

What, are you some kind of scientist?

Others scoffed at such ominous possibilities. No, it was just all those damn fool sensors the Sandia people stuck down there last month, standard DOE paranoia but all the worse now that the waste was actually rolling in. The sensors had snafued; that kind of super-high-tech stuff always does. Lookit all the duds we fired in the Gulf War—those Patriot missiles.

Okay, then, where was that little geek, the Sandia guy, Holmein?

A bunch of people were shipped off last week to some workshop on manners or whatever. In Pittsburgh. Him too, maybe.

Why would they do that? With the sensors on the fritz that he's supposed to maintain? That doesn't make any sense.

So what else is new around here, huh?

Your name just gets put on a list, you know, some computer in Pittsburgh, and off you go. It doesn't have to make sense. We're all just interchangeable parts, right?

Maybe Holmein was a plant, put in here by the Sierra Club or that band of anti-nuke pantywaists up in Santa Fe. Yeah, they caught a mole. . . .

And so it swirled.

Some wiser heads discounted much of this kind of detail as the usual bullshit speculation but sagely said that *some*thing was up and it had to be bad because that guy T. L. Smith was here. The director of security for the whole damn DOE. He wouldn't be here if something big hadn't gone wrong.

Not necessarily. They're bringing in the nuclear waste, and the protesters are hanging around, and it was a big fucking deal—after twenty years of work, remember—and it made sense that the director of security would be here just in case . . . What if some of these terrorists tried to . . .

So where are the Westinghouse people, the managers? What are they doing? It looks like Chiquita Banana is actually running things.

I'll tell you what one of them Westinghouse nerds is doing. I was talkin' to that nurse, Flora Fallows, this morning. She said one of the Westinghouse guys—she wouldn't say who—came in with one of his eyes all red and running. Would she look and see what was wrong. So she looks at him and says, Do you wear contact lenses? And he says no. And she says there's something in there, like a circle. So she calls in the other nurse and they start looking, and one of them takes one of those swabs or whatever and touches his eyeball and . . . *plink* . . . out pops a little curly hair. A pubic hair. So the guy walks out, never says a word. Just walks out. Can you imagine?

Do you suppose it was Chiquita's?

What was Chiquita's?

The hair, stupid.

I hear that Smith character has taken over the place, not the Banana. Him and that goon he's got with him.

Who is that guy anyway?

I hear Smith's gay and that guy is . . . you know, his wife. . . .

He don't look like a fag.

Come on, they got football players, friggin' tight ends, who're fags. . . .

Hey, hey, don't talk like that. Didn't you get anything from that diversity seminar? You're supposed to honor different lifestyles.

Honor my ass.

Look, if they don't open up S10249 pretty soon, like today, then you can bet your ass something's really gone wrong down there. . . .

Well, we'll be the last to hear about that, huh?

T. L. Smith arrived at the WIPP site at eight o'clock, after the morning race on the WIPP 500 was over. He was refreshed from eight hours of deep sleep, and he pulled the bland white sedan that had been requisitioned for his use into the space next to that earmarked The Director. A trim white Chrysler convertible was in the space, covered by a thin coat of dust. So, he thought, the director spent the night on-site.

Standing outside his car, he stretched mightily and looked off to the east, where the sun was lighting up an immense and flat accumulation of salt, an artificial mesa brooding outside the fence. It had all been dug out of the ground and lifted through a shaft drilled especially for that purpose. It made T. L. Smith think of ants. Another shaft was designed for taking the radioactive waste down into the tunnels. In addition, two other large shafts were for air intake and for exhaust. Several years ago, Smith had been down in the tunnels when he was inspecting the operation for security purposes—more of a show than a necessity. He had a perfect map of the underground labyrinth in his mind.

T. L. Smith shook his head. "My God," he said. "If this isn't the ugliest place on earth, I don't know what is."

Minutes later, he strode into Anna Maria Gonzales's office in an expansive mood. His forensic team was due to deliver their report this morning, and he had high hopes that they would get to the bottom of at least one of the tragedies that had taken place in S10249. At last, he would have information. Good or bad, information was the bone and blood of action.

He had spent most of the previous day in a state of exasperating inaction, except for dealing by telephone with departmental security matters around the nation and the world. He had spoken to the secretary of energy once, the man now visiting Singapore, Maylasia, and Indonesia on departmental business. He had said little about the troubles at WIPP, explaining that it was a relatively trivial matter that had taken him there. Mostly administrative. Hopefully he would resolve the matter in the next day or two and return to Washington.

When he entered the office, Anna Maria was seated behind her desk, signing requisitions for materials and equipment—everything from a new van to replace the old one that served as a commuter bus for employees not up to the WIPP 500 to replenishing the supply of analgesics in the on-site clinic. As Smith entered, she stood up.

"Mornin,' Anna Maria. Stay put." He flopped down on the sofa at the far end of the office. On the wall above it hung a four-by-six-foot color photograph of a Marietta Miner, its great cylinder studded with dragon teeth raised high, the machine dwarfing the men in white hard hats and overalls who stood and knelt between it and the wall of salt. The machine filled the salt cavern, and its circular scrape marks on the walls glowed bronze in the photographer's lights. Anna Maria was wearing the same suit as the day before but a different blouse, this one hot pink.

"Where's Sam?" he asked. "He spent the night out here, waiting on the forensics."

137

Anna Maria kept her eyes on the papers in front of her, and Smith noticed that she reddened ever so slightly.

"I haven't seen him," she said, and looked at her watch. "Maybe he's in the commissary. Did you have breakfast at the motel?"

"Did you know that Sam was in the special forces? U.S. Army. After his own stint, he wound up training those people. Think of it, training people in every technique known to man for, uh, eliminating enemies. He did that for ten years before I found him. Licensed pilot, you name it. A man for all occasions." T. L. Smith grinned.

"All I know is that his great-grandfather was a pirate. Off Cape Cod." Anna Maria smiled back. She felt a tingle ripple through her torso at the thought of a killer of men bucking and plunging atop her.

"And there he is," Smith said as Sam Blood entered the office, carrying a mug of coffee.

"Mornin,' Sam. Those boys done yet?"

"They're on their way." Sam nodded to Anna Maria and sat down on one of the wooden chairs.

"Have we heard anything more about Fontaine?"

"I called this morning," Sam said. "Condition's unchanged. They're flying in a specialist from Albuquerque, a big shot neurologist named Voorhees. One of the docs called last night, right after you left. Said they found something curious about Fontaine's overalls. So we went and got 'em. The forensics will tell you if it amounted to anything."

It was a long speech from a man who T. L. Smith considered as cool as a block of lake ice and, on a normal day, just about as talkative.

Within five minutes, the three forensic experts and Chuck O'Connor, the ex-marine in charge of plant security, were sitting in straight-back chairs around the desk. Anna Maria had given it up to Smith and stood near the window, arms folded over her chest.

T. L. Smith and the others listened to the long preamble, recounting procedures followed and other esoterica the forensics always felt it necessary to review whenever presenting their findings. The man droned on until Smith could stand no more.

"Goddammit, Jimmy, I'm not a damn review board. I know you follow all the proper procedures and all. Did you find anything that's going to help us with this mess? What about Fontaine's overalls? Sam here said . . ."

"Yes, sir. The doctors called. You know, those guys just cut people's clothes off with scissors in a big hurry? Well, someone noticed later that there was also a tear in them. Not a scissors cut. So we went and got 'em and confirmed that there was a tear, from near the left armpit about nine inches to just above the waist."

"What could've done that?" Smith said. He looked back at the couch at the other end of the room. "Maybe he got hung up on that machine. Those big teeth. That possible?"

"Well, yes sir, it is. That's what we thought too. Until we found this. Over near the end of the tunnel."

He leaned down and opened the attaché case on the floor by his feet. From its innards, he plucked a clear plastic envelope the size of a sandwich bag and held it up.

The light coming in the window reflected off the bag. He handed it across the desk, and T. L. Smith held it up in his left hand.

"Hairs," he said. "White hairs. Almost white anyway. Four inches long. Like a couple of tufts and then some singletons." He put the bag down on the desk. "All right, Jimmy," he said, smiling, showing a lot of teeth. "I do know that you like to put a little drama into your presentations, but I am not gonna sit here in front of all these people while you try to get me to guess whose hair this is. So get on with it."

"Well, sir, it doesn't make any sense. Not to us. Those aren't human hairs."

"Oh, for chrissake," T. L. Smith said. Anna Maria unfolded her arms and stepped over to the desk, leaning over to peer at the bag.

"Then what the hell are they?" Smith barked.

"Some kind of mammal. Beyond that?" Jimmy shrugged.

Smith stared at him and then at Chuck O'Connor, whose jaw was clamped so tight that large knots had appeared on the sides of his jaw. T. L. Smith was an accomplished duck hunter, but the only mammals he had ever hunted were human ones.

"What've you got here, Chuck? You got somebody's dog runnin' around down there? A zoo? A fucking wildlife refuge you're running on the side? What *is* this?"

O'Connor was speechless, perplexity rendering him dumb. His face reddened as T. L. Smith continued his harangue.

"I know you got that environmental department here, keeps anyone from killing a jackrabbit or whatever the hell, trying to show the Sierra Club that WIPP cares. Well, that's a lot of bullshit, as we all know, but maybe our own enviros are sneakin' *mammals* into the plant. C'mon, Chuck, what the hell is this?"

He turned on Jimmy, the forensic.

"What *kind* of mammal?"

"We don't know yet."

"Who would?"

"Fish and Wildlife. The Smithsonian. The FBI."

"Look, Jimmy, I got you people on board so I don't have to have the Feebs in my patch. And too many of those Smithsonian weirdos do contract work for the Feebs. And if the Fish and Wildlife people get wind of some critter in the WIPP site, they'll probably declare it a threatened species and try to close the damn place down. Can't trust those people, and they take forever anyway. There's gotta be someone local who can tell what this is just by lookin' at it. I mean, we're not takin' this deal to court. I just want to know what the hell it is."

"Maybe the museum in Carlsbad," Anna Maria said. "There's a woman there who studies prehistoric animals. She probably knows a lot of zoology."

"Maybe a local hunter," Chuck O'Connor said. "Those guys know what's around here."

T. L. Smith turned to Sam Blood. "Sam?"

"A hunter," he said. "There can't be too many animals around here with whitish hair that long. With claws big enough to make a tear like that in Fontaine's overalls."

140

"Maybe a mountain lion?" O'Connor said. "A badger? It just doesn't make sense."

T. L. Smith stood up and plucked the plastic bag off the desk. He walked around the desk to where Sam Blood sat.

"Sam? Tell me what this is by noon today." He dropped the bag in Sam's lap and turned to Chuck O'Connor. "Between now and when Sam comes back, you are going to show me every inch of every place where some damn *mammal* could get into this plant. Maybe, Madame Director, you'd want to come along."

"Absolutely," Anna Maria said.

"So," Sam Blood said, rising from his chair. "Are we thinking now that Fred Fontaine was scared comatose by some mammal he saw down there?"

"Until we get some information," Smith said, "facts, some goddamned *data,* then thinkin' won't do us any more good than a case of the clap."

At eight-thirty that morning, Sam Blood drove out of the WIPP parking lot in the nondescript sedan that had been assigned to T. L. Smith. About two miles out on the WIPP 500, he slowed down and peered at the wrought-iron gate twenty feet back from the road that marked the entrance to the ranch now owned by Tracer Dunn. The gate was replete with wrought-iron figures: a cowboy on a horse driving three head of cattle. The name in wrought-iron read Harwell and there was some sort of brand next to it. Beyond the gate, snaking out into the scrubland, was a dirt road that appeared to end at an old ranch house that was clearly sagging back to the earth. Down the dirt track, no one was in sight.

Chuck O'Connor had told Sam that Tracer Dunn, whose ranch ("the old Harwell spread") abutted the WIPP site, was also known as a hunter. Professional hunter once. Specially mountain lions. If anyone would know what animal the coarse whitish hairs in the plastic bag had come from, he would.

Sam sped up and drove on by, proceeding past a succession of brine lakes sparkling in the morning sun, until he reached a large industrial installation with a sign that said Diamond Salt Company. He pulled into a white driveway that led into a white parking lot full of trucks and aged automobiles between the buildings and some heavy machinery on one side and a massive pile of discolored, brownish salt on the other. There he turned around, wondering what on earth the brown stuff was in the big salt pile and wondering further if the Diamond Salt Company got all of it, whatever it was, out of the salt before he sprinkled it on his fried eggs. Out on the road again, he headed back for WIPP, pulling off the road at the old Harwell spread and coming to a stop at the gate.

He stepped out of the air-conditioned sedan into a wall of heat and opened the gate. He drove through, closed the gate, and proceeded slowly down the dirt track over land that undulated gently off to the horizons through an expanse of black twiggy shrubs, gray leafier shrubs, and the occasional prickly pear cactus, also looking gray with thirst. Passing the collapsing ranch house, he saw the trailer. Some clothes were strung up on a clothesline, looking inert, even morose, in the still air, and behind them was a red-and-white pickup of early vintage. Beyond the pickup he could see some of what evidently was a series of corrals built, rebuilt, and patched with the silvering trunks of twisted trees. In one corral, a brown-and-white horse lifted its head and looked at him across the distance. Somewhere Sam had come across the fact that one of every six people in the West live in trailers.

He sat in the sedan with the engine running for a moment, reluctantly turned the ignition key, and stepped back out into the heat.

He knocked at the trailer's door, and presently it was opened by a stout woman with black glossy hair and a coppery face. She was wearing a blue dress under a yellow apron.

"Yes?" she said, glancing at Sam with large, dark brown eyes.

"I'm looking for Tracer Dunn, ma'am. Is this where he lives?"

"*Sí.* Yes."

Silence.

"Well, ma'am," Sam said slowly and in the slightly too loud voice most people use when speaking to someone who may not understand English with great clarity, "I'm new in the area, and someone told me that Mr. Dunn was a hunter. I'd like to talk with him."

The woman nodded as if pondering this puzzling information.

"Back there," she said finally, gesturing toward the rear of the trailer. "By the corral," she added, and shut the door.

Sam found the rancher on the other side of the corrals, where he had evidently been digging a new posthole in the rocky soil. Now he was standing, leaning on the posthole digger, and watching Sam approach.

"Mr. Dunn?" Sam stopped about twenty feet from the tall, gaunt man. He had pale eyes in a tanned, lined face that was mostly in shadow under a straw cowboy hat stained with sweat and tattered from long use.

"Yeah," he said, staring at his visitor with what appeared to be indifference.

"My name is Sam Blood. I'm the new assistant production manager over at Diamond Salt." He gestured with his head in the direction he had come from. The rancher continued to stare at him.

"I rented a house over near Loving, and the other night I heard something out in the yard. Looked out there, but I didn't see anything. So in the morning I went out and looked around. Found this." Sam pulled the plastic bag from his shirt pocket. "They tell me that you're a professional hunter, the best there is around here. So I thought maybe you could tell me what these hairs come from." He smiled ingratiatingly. "I'm from Virginia, and I just don't know the local game out here."

From the other end of the corrals, the brown-and-white horse nickered impatiently. Tracer Dunn stuck out his hand, a big brown hand with long thick fingers.

"Take a look," he said, and waited for Sam to cross the rocky soil between them and put the plastic bag in his hand.

"You can take 'em out," Sam said, and the rancher glanced up at him, then back to the bag. He held the bag up between himself and the sun and squinted at it. Then he handed it back.

"Nothin' from around here," he said.

Sam looked puzzled. "Gee, I found these in my backyard—"

"A prank, maybe."

"Oh," Sam said, a big smile spreading over his jaw. "I get it. Scare the dudes, the greenhorns." He laughed. "Well, even so, I'd sure be interested to know what these hairs might've come from. Any idea?"

"If they wasn't white like that, I'd say they come from a bear. Only white bear I know of is a polar bear. And the nearest one o' them is in the zoo up in Albuquerque."

"A bear," Sam said.

"That's what it looks like. No pronghorn's got white hairs that long. No lion neither. Looks to be a bear. Guess someone's tryin' to get your goat." A hint of a smile flickered over the man's face. He thinks it's a pretty good joke, Sam thought.

"Well, much obliged, Mr. Dunn. Thanks for your time. It's nice to meet you."

He turned and walked back to his car. A polar bear? Jesus Christ.

FOURTEEN

My God, Cassie Roberts thought. It was like mainlining adrenaline. How many hours was it they were down there? How many flight-or-fight responses? She wondered if that kind of prolonged chemical assault on her body, her organs, her muscles could have a permanent effect. The way marathoners are usually depressive from OD-ing on stress. Certainly she was so exhausted even after eight hours of slumber that it seemed like exhaustion would from now on be a permanent condition. Her head was sore where she'd hit the rock, and earlier this morning, when she began brushing her hair, she absently scraped the bristles across the wound and jumped, shouting "Ow!" to the empty bathroom. Her ankle had swollen up during the night in spite of the ice pack she'd put on it (and kicked off in her sleep). It throbbed now, and she leaned back in her desk chair and put her foot up on the desk. Every muscle ached. Under the soft and loose-fitting tan rayon slacks she wore, both knees bore ugly round scrapes she hadn't had since she was eleven years old, raw red skin now dry and taut, turning to scab. Her belly felt like it had been sandpapered. In spite of the heat of Carlsbad summer, she wore a long-sleeved white blouse to cover the scrapes on her elbows and forearms.

She sat staring at the poster of the La Brea Tar Pits and the last agony of the mammoth being sucked down into the oily depths, the gaping, snarling mouth of the saber-toothed cats threatening it with dismemberment even as it drowned in the tar while distant herds of herbivores paid not the slightest attention to the tragedy unfolding—an everyday tragedy of the Ice Age. She empathized with the mammoth and shivered.

The artist had not included, in his almost ridiculously crowded landscape, any short-faced bears. No *Arctodus simus.*

She had to think about that. She desperately wanted to think about that. She wanted to train all her understanding of evolution and extinction and physiology and anatomy onto *Arctodus simus.* The scientific implications were immense, almost unimaginable. If a huge predatory creature thought long extinct had somehow managed to survive for twelve thousand years *without anyone knowing of its existence,* it was surely the most amazing zoological discovery of the century—any century.

It suddenly struck her that all her professional life had been devoted to studying the past, things that had died, gone extinct. Sure, some had left direct descendants, but the grandeur she could see and almost feel that had been the Pleistocene landscape . . . that was no more. But now that wasn't so. Some direct descendent of the largest and most ferocious carnivore that had ever lived on this continent, an animal probably more efficient even than the dinosaurian predators like *T. rex* . . . a descendent of *Arctodus simus* as gigantic as its ancestral stock *still lived!*

How could it still exist? She found that each time she began to focus on any of the cascade of questions pouring through her forebrain, she began to shake, reliving fragments of the terror that had whipped her like a hurricane wind during the hours of flight after she found—held in her hand—the human femur, still greasy with decomposing gobs of flesh clinging to it, stinking of death and decay. She couldn't concentrate.

"Damn it!" she said out loud, and stood up. She had to pull herself together. Jack would be arriving anytime now.

Last night, he had walked her up to the porch in front of her house and flicked on a flashlight when she fumbled with the key and the lock.

"You going to be okay?" he asked in a soft voice.

"Oh yeah," she had said. "Nothing to fear but nightmares."

"I can stay here if you want. You know, sofa. Just for . . ."

She paused, tempted, but said, "No, no. I'm fine. But we're going to need to talk about this. Soon. You can't just flake out for two days like you used to."

"In the morning. I'll come by maybe around ten, ten-fifteen?"

"At the museum," she said.

He had stood silently as she opened and closed the front door and only then turned to go. She watched him until he got in the Trooper and turned on the ignition, then dragged herself upstairs, exhausted, sore, and for the first time in years wondering how she was going to bear being alone.

Now she leaned on two hands on her desk, angry with herself. She simply had to concentrate. Surely she didn't need another mug of coffee. She was struck by an urge, an inner yearning she hadn't felt since her first year of graduate school, when she gave up smoking. Nicotine. A cigarette. For several days after she had cold-turkeyed the weed, she had been restless and unable to concentrate, not to mention irritable to the point of elevating bitchiness to an art. But . . .

"Damn it!" she said again. From under a pile of books and reports on her desk, she snatched a large paperback book called *Before the Indians.* It was by a deceased paleontologist named Bjorn Kurten, and the other night she had marked a page that showed *Arctodus simus,* two of them, in fact, snarling at each other over the carcass of a species of horse. In size, she knew, the carcass was somewhere between that of a pony and a small horse like an Arab, and the two bears loomed above the twisted corpse, immense. The artist had given them relatively slender bodies raised high off the ground on long, gracile legs. While the lips were pulled back in ferocity, revealing large and apparently very sharp teeth, their very gracefulness made them look less fearsome here on the page than they clearly had been in real life.

And still were?

Her mind began to focus on the impossible notion that a Pleisto-cene predator that had probably always helped itself to whatever it wanted hadn't led its prey into extinction but had somehow man-aged to take up a different existence, in a totally different world. Such a thing couldn't have happened overnight.

Every biologist knows and admires the succinct phrase that a great Yale ecologist, G. Evelyn Hutchinson, used to describe the processes of life on earth: It is, he said, an evolutionary play in an ecological theater. And Cassie began to realize that she might be, in a sense, witnessing a whole new act in that play. And how would it have gone? What lines had been written? What would *Arctodus simus* have become since making the astounding adaptation to life lived (mostly? entirely?) underground in caves? Would it first have gradually changed from a daytime hunter to a nocturnal one? Why? What would it have found in caves that it couldn't find above-ground? In fact, there isn't anything to eat in caves. A few insects, maybe? But . . .

This bear—or something down there—ate some person in the last few days. Who? How did he (probably a he, judging from the size of the femur) get there? Dragged in by the bear? Who's missing? Why drag a meal so far before finishing it?

Would it have become blind, like moles?

Without pigment, transparent? Some cave creatures like spiders are transparent.

Grizzly bears overlapped the short-faced bear for a few thousand years (and maybe still do!). Grizzlies are omnivorous: they eat plants and animals, do a lot of fishing. She had heard that some caves have a few transparent little fish in pools of water—but how could something half again as big as a grizzly survive on a few pathetic little minnows? Impossible. It had to come out of the cave to find food. But what? Six thousand years ago there were still bison herds here, but now? A few pronghorns scattered around and livestock. If this creature were eating livestock, we sure as hell would hear about it.

Whatever was down there, of course, wasn't *Arctodus simus*. It had evolved into something else. A different species. Just as big, judging from the footprint. And still a carnivore, a meat eater—at least given the chance. And of course, there was more than one, more than a pair—how many would it take to sustain a population for ten or twelve thousand years? Small populations of animals can lead to inbreeding, which can lead to big-time problems in reproducing and then extinction. But inbreeding can also lead to relatively sudden changes—albinism, for example? What else?

She sat down, turned on her computer, and, once it had settled down to business, she began systematically making lists of facts (few) and questions (many categories of questions), imposing at least that much order on the chaos. With her mind utterly engrossed, the aches and pains, the nerve-racking recollection of fear, even horror, disappeared, along with any sense of time passing. She was now the hunter, the trained tracker of biological possibilities, and she felt a quiet tingle in her soul that arose from doing what she did best—and also from the knowledge that she was engaged in a truly momentous scientific quest. In a world where virtually everyplace had been tramped over, where satellites spied on every ecosystem, finding a new species—even of bird—was a big deal. Finding new mammal species was far rarer. They'd found the giraffe relative called the okapi in Africa in the 1920s and the pygmy chimp around the same time. But that was the last she knew of.

But to discover a *bear* species—a descendant of a bear long thought extinct, what was called a *relict!* That was huge. Huge! The answers to the questions she was organizing on the screen before her would change the natural history of the North American continent.

When the phone on her desk sounded its electronic whines, she winced and in disgust said, "Aggh."

"Roberts," she said into the receiver.

"There's a gentleman out here who asked to see you."

Jack. Jack was going to come in this morning. She looked at her watch. It was ten-thirty. She sighed.

"Send him in, Martha," she said. "Thanks."

She saved the questions on her screen in a file she named, whimsically for now, *Arctodus cassandra,* and turned to the door across the room, pushing a few strands of hair away from her cheek and back on her head. She owed the damned kook a lot, and she smiled an anticipatory greeting.

When a figure appeared in the doorway, her smile vanished. It wasn't Jack. It was a man in a perfectly pressed white shirt with the sleeves folded up in two precise folds, gabardine pants with a razor-sharp crease, and polished city-type shoes with dust on the tips. He had close-cropped light brown hair and blue eyes that looked on the world with what could be a mild mirthfulness from a face that looked somehow hardened even though the individual features were smooth, unremarkable.

"Dr. Roberts?" the man said from the doorway. "I'm sorry to bother you, but I was told you might be able to help me out. I'm new here in Carlsbad."

"Come in," Cassie said, and stood up.

"My name is Sam Blood," he said, approaching her desk and putting out a big hand that extended from a thick wrist covered with fine blond hairs. She shook it and sat down, gesturing to a chair. He sat down and smiled, revealing a row of small, even teeth.

"I've just come on as an assistant production manager at the Diamond Salt plant. I'm renting a place over near Loving—you know, get the wife and kids out here, and then we'll look around for a good place to buy. . . ."

"Welcome to Carlsbad," Cassie said. "Where in the East did you come from?"

"Oh," Sam Blood said. "Accent, huh? New Jersey. This sure is a different world out here. Well, I don't want to waste any of your time. What I'm curious about is this. Last night I heard something moving around outside my place, like an animal of some kind. So I looked out and didn't see anything. I guessed maybe it was a coyote or something."

"It probably wasn't," Cassie said "You wouldn't have heard it if it was a coyote. Unless it yipped."

"Oh. Okay. Anyway, this morning I went out to see if I could see anything, like tracks? And I found this." He pulled a plastic Ziplock bag from his shirt pocket and put it on her desk. "I'm just wondering what these could have come from."

Cassie looked down at the bag, seeing a few clusters of long, whitish hairs. She felt a tingle of sweat breaking out on her forehead. She held up the bag.

"You can take 'em out if you want," Sam Blood said.

"Okay," Cassie said. "Mr. Blood, I don't know if they told you, but I'm a paleontologist. My specialty is bones, fossil bones." She gestured at the wall of shelves filled with fossil skulls, bones, and bone fragments. "I'm not exactly a zoologist, so all I can do here is guess."

Sam Blood nodded eagerly.

"First of all, it's a mammal, of course. Mammals have fur. Next, you'd guess it's a pretty big mammal. These hairs are what? Four inches long? Maybe a pronghorn. They have white in their pelage. Probably too long for a skunk. Or a badger." She smiled at the man, who sat looking intently at her, and wondered if he could hear her heart pounding in her chest.

"I'm really out of my league here," she said. She opened the bag, plucked a little cluster of hairs out, and rolled them between her thumb and forefinger. "They're pretty coarse, aren't they? I just don't know. Where was it you said you rented?"

"It's a little place, you know, temporary, between Loving and, what's that little town to the south? Malaga." He smiled sheepishly. "I actually don't know the street names yet. I just know how to get there."

Cassie fumbled a bit as she put the hairs back in the bag and leaned back in her chair. "I have a colleague in Albuquerque who can identify these for you. He's at the natural history museum there and has all the analytic equipment for checking these things. Fur and feathers. Sometimes the FAA sends him a bunch of feathers they've dug out of a jet engine to see what bird flew in and caused it to crash. Isn't that amazing? Anyway, I'd be glad to send these to him. It would take a few days."

Sam Blood had begun to shift uncomfortably in his chair. "I don't think that's necessary. I mean, he's probably busy and all. It's just a matter of curiosity." He stood up and retrieved his plastic bag. "Not all that important."

"He'd be interested, I know. And he's quick. And if I ask him, he's free."

The phone buzzed again, and Cassie picked it up.

"There's another gentleman out here to see you, Cassie."

"Tell him I won't be a minute," she said. Sam Blood was already on his way across the room. He turned and smiled, showing his row of little teeth, and said, "Really, it's not important. Thanks for your time, Dr. Roberts."

She smiled and waved. "Good-bye, then." She watched this Sam Blood stop in the doorway, confronting the slightly larger figure of her ex, Jack Whittaker. The two men sidestepped, each the same way and through three attempts until Jack stepped back out of sight, laughing. Sam Blood disappeared down the hall, and Jack entered. Cassie noticed for the first time that he had managed to get a haircut.

"Who's that guy?" Jack asked.

"His name is Sam Blood."

"And . . . ?"

"He wanted some help identifying some fur he found in his yard."

"Oh. I guess you get a lot of that." He sat down in the chair Sam Blood had vacated. "Why are you grinning like that? You look like you ate the canary."

From the cuff of her left sleeve, Cassie plucked a couple of hairs and held them up. "These are some of the hairs he was asking about."

"So? I don't . . ."

"They're long, white, and coarse. What is there around here that has long, white, and coarse hair?"

"Pronghorns? I don't know. How the hell would I know? You're the naturalist."

"Nothing around here has hair like this."

"How about a dog? Like one of those big white German shepherds?"

152

"No way. Jack, I'll bet the ranch that this is a bear."

"Shit. You mean, our . . . ?"

"Yes. He says he found it in his yard in a place he rents over between Loving and Malaga."

"That's a long way from the cavern. Fifteen, twenty miles."

"I'm going to send this hair up to Albuquerque," Cassie said, carefully placing it in a small plastic envelope she fetched from a drawer in her desk. "You remember Ferrell? Ferrell O'Hara?"

"The geeky guy."

Cassie frowned. "And what do you suppose he thinks of you?"

"Hey, I'm sorry. I just think a guy with no chin and . . . Okay, he's a genius. He's the one who knows all about feathers."

"And fur."

"Cool," Jack said.

Cassie stood up and walked over to the fossil-laden shelves. "This thing is huge, Jack. Huge."

"Yeah, a big bear, that's for sure."

"No, the scientific implications of this It's a really explosive discovery." She shook her head in wonderment.

"I think we better buy Dunn's ranch, pronto," Jack said. "Before anything leaks out about the cavern."

"We? You think I want . . . You think I have . . . ?"

"I know you've got enough money squirreled away for a down payment on that place. All it'll take is twenty-five thousand, max. You've got that, right?"

"That is none of your business, Jack. But it's not the money I was talking about. What makes you think I have any interest in being some kind of partner of yours? We already tried that, remember?"

Jack's dark eyes flashed at her.

"That was different, Cassie, for chrissake. That was husband and wife, loving, honoring, sickness and health, sex, all that. This is business. Just business."

"Business? Just business? Are you kidding? What're you thinking about? Catching the bear and putting it in a cage for people to gawk at when they get down in your cavern? Will you charge extra for that? Jesus, Jack."

He pushed his chair back, stood up, and carefully replaced the chair.

"Cassie, I need you for money, for getting ahold of that cavern," he said quietly. "You need me to help you do whatever it is you have to do about that bear for science. Just for starters, I'm the only person who can find that footprint again."

Cassie pondered that for a moment.

"Now, I've got an idea," Jack said. "Suppose you and I get out of here and go have some breakfast. You didn't have breakfast, did you? No, I didn't think so. We can go to Estella's, work all this stuff out. It's like neutral ground." He looked around the room. "All these dead things give me the creeps."

They decided to walk to Estella's. Cassie was revved, talking rapidly as they strolled eastward along a tree-lined residential street toward the main drag. She made large gestures with her hands, and her smile, Jack thought, was wide enough to give her cheeks cramps.

"See," she was saying as they turned onto Canal Street, "the first humans on this continent came sixteen, seventeen thousand years ago, when there were still plenty of the big mammals here. Mastodons, mammoths. And this short-faced bear. Those guys could kill the elephants. But probably the big cats and this bear were nothing but terrifying problems for them. So some people've wondered why there aren't a lot of stories, you know, myths about them in the Indian tribes. Like a tribal memory.

"Well, I think there is. Up in Nova Scotia or one of those places, the Indians had a myth about a monster with a long nose that reached the ground—it had to be killed to make the world safe. A mastodon, right? Why not? And the Iroquois have their monster of the forest, Windigo. It kills and eats people who get lost. A huge, hairy thing. Now, that could be a tribal memory, like a poetic or mythic version of . . . what, Jack?"

"Let me guess. A bear?"

"Right," Cassie went on, paying Jack's wiseass attitude no heed.

"Bears have a long and ambivalent role in all the tribes. They're always part of a tribe's myths. Good some places, bad others. Like shamans are both good and dangerous. But even grizzlies aren't that lethal. I mean, they're not that hard to avoid. But a bear that could run like a horse, that was as tall at the shoulder as a man? What a nightmare. And get this. The Apaches and the Navajos and the Hopis and I guess all the Indians around this part of the world? They have this story about how, soon after people were put on the earth, they were threatened by monsters. So two brothers, hero twins, fought the great battles and cleared the place of monsters. One of the twins is always called Monster Slayer. Now—"

"*Arctodus whittakerensis,* undoubtedly," Jack said.

Cassie laughed, a light tinkling sound.

"That's *Arctodus cassandra,* buster."

"How come? I found the footprint."

"Because I can write for the scientific journals, and you can't. You're just a layman." She laughed again, and Jack had never seen her so happy

FIFTEEN

From time to time, Derby Catlin believed he'd made a major career mistake starting *The Intelligencer* four years ago. It was a one-man show still, and it looked like it would never develop enough advertising revenue to permit Derby an employee or two. Charging for it rather than having it be a freebie appeared out of the question. So, until he got a real break, a tremendous scoop, or some other miracle rare in journalism—a Pulitzer?—it would probably remain a one-man show. The story on page one of this week's issue about the fifty-year cycle of cattle predation was terrific—the Other Paper was soundly scooped—but it was, he had to admit, not the sort of thing to bring people rushing into the local stores with money in their hand, demanding their copy of that dynamic protector of the public weal, that searchlight on corruption and hypocrisy . . . in short, that version of *The Intelligencer* that Derby had dreamed of.

So he was stuck with the mule work as well. Distribution, it was called.

Every Thursday morning throughout the year, Derby picked up the baled stacks of his newspaper from the printer, loaded them in his pickup, and dropped them off at the thirty-one stores and twelve motels in Carlsbad that carried it. This was the part of newspapering that he thought of as The Pits. In fact, he hated to be seen by friends while he was doing it so he typically kept his head down while unloading some papers into a store and leaving, hoping that no one would notice him.

At a few minutes before eleven, Derby stopped in front of Estella's and took a stack of papers in the front door, depositing them on a table near the entrance next to a short stack of the National Parks' infrequently published rag for tourists, *The Capitan Reef,* which was mainly announcements about tours at Carlsbad Caverns and a bit of local natural history. No competition.

Once back on the sidewalk, he heard a man's voice.

"Hey, Derby."

It was Jack Whittaker, the caver. He was walking toward Estella's with a pretty blond woman who Derby didn't recognize at first. Then he realized it was Cassandra Roberts, the paleontologist, Jack's ex-wife. Jack was smiling broadly, and the couple stopped.

"You got your new issue out, Derby?"

"Hot off the press," Derby said.

"Dug up any dirt on the mayor yet?"

"I hear the mayor is dating a sheep."

"Why would she do that?" Jack asked. It was a stale joke, but one that was repeated something like a mantra in certain social realms of the town.

Derby watched Jack usher his ex into Estella's, and he wondered what the couple was doing together again. In Derby's experience, exes put as much distance between each other as they could and kept it that way. At least, that was his strategy. He had left his ex, a fire-breathing dragon, in Michigan years ago, thank God. Last he'd heard, she'd married and was no doubt tormenting her new husband, a local sales rep at one of those athletic shoe companies.

Derby had several times considered making up the name of a gossip columnist and running tidbits. "The Ear took note of one of Carlsbad's most exciting couples together again, after crashing and burning three years ago. Yes, Jack Whittaker, Cavern City's spelunking hero, was seen arm in arm outside fashionable Estella's with none other than his zaftig (and still wonderfully slender, dears) ex, Cassie Roberts—Dr. Cassandra Roberts to you! Tongues are abuzz!"

"Cute," Cassie said, sitting down at one of Estella's six tables. "The sheep joke. This town is still stuck in the 1950s. At least the men in this town."

"When in Rome," Jack said. "How would you like your cholesterol? Breakfast or lunch?"

"Green chili stew and Dos Equis. Every meal."

Jack went over to the counter to pass along the order. Moments later he returned with two uncapped bottles of Dos Equis beer and a copy of the new issue of *The Intelligencer*. He sat down, placed the two bottles equidistant from each other, and put down the paper, turning it so Cassie could read it.

"Look at that story," he said.

Cassie read the headline.

Cattle Deaths Part of Fifty-Year Cycle?

"What cattle deaths?"

"Read it," Jack said.

Cassie slipped on a pair of reading glasses and bent over the paper, scanning the article. Then she read it more slowly.

"My God."

"Sounds more like your bear than God," Jack said.

Cassie looked up at him. Her eyes were wide, whites showing all around her dark brown irises. "That's how it could have happened."

"How what could have happened?"

"It would mean a completely unheard-of change in metabolism," Cassie said.

"Excuse me?"

"At least in mammals."

"Please go on, Professor," Jack said. "This is riveting."

"More like an insect. Seventeen-year locusts. Or spadefoot toad eggs."

Estella appeared and put two bowls on the table with a clatter. "You want eggs too?" she said.

Cassie looked up, as if waking from a trance. "Eggs? Oh, no thank you, Estella."

"We got eggs. Fresh. Today."

"No, no, this is wonderful, Estella. Thanks." She turned back to Jack and said, "You know how some toads in the desert lay their eggs and the eggs just sit there in the dust for years until it happens to rain right there? So they hatch and go through the whole life cycle in just a few days while a puddle is there. Then more eggs, waiting for the next rain."

Cassie's eyes went out of focus as if she were staring off at a distant horizon.

"You won't believe this," Jack said, "but I am just a little bit lost here."

"Hibernation," Cassie said. "Bears hibernate. It's not like suspended animation or anything sci-fi like that. It's like things slow down, the body processes go into slow motion. It's real complicated. Body temperature drops, the whole metabolism goes into low gear. Hummingbirds do something like it every night; their temperature drops from a hundred and twenty to seventy, something like that. It gets 'em through the night. Bears go through the whole winter that way. What if a bear—like the short-faced bear—developed a longer hibernation time? Not to avoid the cold like other bears today, but to avoid the heat that was melting the glaciers? A longer and longer period of time when they were inactive, resting in caves where it was cooler, a constant coolness. See what I'm getting at?"

Jack spooned some green chili stew into his mouth, chewed thoughtfully, and swallowed.

"You're beautiful when you think," he said.

"See?" she went on, not hearing him. "The hibernation period gets longer over the generations. It's like *Brigadoon!* They're awake, you know, hunting, eating, mating, all that for less time compared to the time they're out. Hibernation times get longer and longer between periods of activity. They would live longer, way longer. *Centuries,* maybe. So you don't have to have so many of them. Just a small number could . . . survive. It's crazy, *crazy,* but it might work."

"Well, something worked," Jack said.

"I mean, theoretically."

"Cassie, goddammit, that was no theory in there."

She turned her attention to Jack and put a hand on his forearm, which was lying flat on the table between them.

"Jack, anything that can't be explained by evolutionary processes doesn't exist."

159

"Look," Jack said. "I think that's fine. But we've got more practical problems here. What if word gets out about that cave?"

"How? It's just you and me who know about it. I'm not going to tell anyone."

"What if that rancher, Tracer Dunn, stumbles onto the cave? Or onto the bear? The article said he's one of the ranchers whose cattle have been taken. And he's some kind of hunter."

"Okay," Cassie said, leaning back in her chair and smiling benignly. "Let's buy the place."

"That photograph doesn't really tell you how big that monster is."

T. L. Smith stood before the huge photograph in Anna Maria Gonzales's office. He was still wearing the white coveralls and hard hat required, along with other gear, for any visit underground. The photographer had used a wide-angle lens, and the machine's toothed cylinder loomed outward on its steel arms, dwarfing the men in coveralls and hard hats who were crowded together between the machine and the wall.

"It's like someone crossed a hammerhead shark with *Tyrannosaurus rex*."

Smith and Anna Maria had spent two hours in the tunnel called S10249, peering at every corner and crevice, also examining the four shafts that connected the tunnels to the surface, looking for any way any creature of any size greater than a rat could achieve an unauthorized entry into the underground complex. They had stood between the Marietta Miner and the end of S10249, staring at the salt, probing it with their fingers and with the scraping tool that all employees carried when underground.

"What's beyond it?" Smith had asked.

"More salt," Anna Maria said. "The geologists' seismic testing says the salt goes another half mile in this direction."

"Let me ask you this. Just how often do those boys do this seismic testing?"

"The entire grid was laid out more than ten years ago, based on

160

seismic observations made over the previous years, starting back in the seventies."

"Nothing since then?"

"Not really. Nothing extensive. They established the extent of the salt layer. You don't have to establish it over and over."

Smith reached out and scratched some loose salt off the tunnel wall. "Unless it ain't as inert as they thought."

"Meaning what?" Anna Maria asked, bristling. That the salt beds might not be inert was so catastrophic a notion that mentioning such a possibility out loud was the same as shrieking a blasphemy in St. Peter's in Rome, the Holy See. She was perfectly aware of all the objections, the caveats, the independent studies by busybody environmental groups that raised such a possibility. And she had recently, of course, had some reason to wonder if at least some of those studies might be right. But hearing it out loud from the lips of a DOE employee . . . It was a shock.

Anna Maria had found herself shaking. The disappearance of the guard and the tech, and the collapse (from shock?) of the forensic man Fontaine, and the mysterious hairs—all this had undermined her confidence in the grand system of WIPP. Something was breaching the system somewhere in this tunnel; something was awry and on her watch. She couldn't shake the lurking sense of Fate, a personal shadowy figure about to snip a vital thread. . . .

Now, in her office, she watched T. L. Smith warily as he stood facing the photograph of the Marietta Miner.

"Those people from Sandia," he said.

"Yes, they're due in an hour or so. They'll be able to—"

"Tell 'em to turn around and go home," Smith said.

"What?

"I said tell 'em to go home. Don't let 'em in. Tell 'em that we had a false report and we have now ascertained that there is no problem. Everything is fine, hunky-dory. Smooth as a baby's bottom. We just don't need anyone from anywhere else poking around this place."

"But—"

"Anna Maria." T. L. Smith turned to face her. "Listen up. We've got ourselves what could be a five-billion-dollar problem on our hands, and until we get a better idea of what the hell is going on in your plant here, then it is to the advantage of the entire U.S. Department of Energy if we keep it to ourselves. We don't need a bunch of alarmists around here, especially now. You get my point?"

Anna Maria glowered at him. "Now, you listen—"

"Let me make it even more clear to you, Madame Director. It's your career on the line here. If I have to shut this fucker down for reasons of security, I'm just doin' my job. And if it has to be shut down, there's not a man jack in the entire nuclear enterprise who's gonna vote against strippin' the director of WIPP naked and paintin' her with a coat of tar and feathers and runnin' her fanny out of town on a goddamn rail." T. L. Smith smiled his predator smile.

"You do get the point," he added unnecessarily.

When Sam Blood entered Anna Maria Gonzales's office at quarter to noon, the tension in the room was as palpable as the metallic smell of ozone after a lightning storm. His boss, T. L. Smith, sat slumped on the couch at the far end of the room beneath the giant machine in the photograph. He was in shirtsleeves, talking animatedly on the phone, his left ankle resting on his right knee, for all the world the picture of a man at ease. He lifted a finger at Sam, as if saying, "I'll be right with you." Calm and casual as could be. The tip-off for Sam was Smith's left foot, twitching up and down. And at her desk, Anna Maria was leaning forward, also talking into a phone, the receiver clutched tightly in her hand. Her back was ramrod straight and, under the gray rayon jacket of her suit, her shoulders were hunched. Sam could almost see the electricity crackling back and forth between the two people, like anode and diode in a lousy monster movie; Frankenstein, maybe.

Sam felt a bit sorry for the woman. Smith could be a real meat grinder.

She looked up, glowered at Sam, and turned away from him, murmuring in the phone.

Across the room, T. L. Smith said, "Of course, I'm responsible for it!" and slammed the receiver down onto the flimsy plastic carriage.

"Goddamn cover-my-ass mentality of your government-issue bureaucrat," Smith said. "So, Sam, what'd you find out?"

Anna Maria said, "*Sí,* yes," into her phone, hung up, and swiveled around toward him in her chair. With studied deliberation, Sam's eyes moved up her legs to her lap, from there to her chest, and then to her face. He winked. She gazed back at him expressionlessly.

"Close as anyone can say, it's a bear," Sam said. "Local rancher named Dunn, Tracer Dunn, he's also a mountain lion hunter, says it's a bear but not like anything around here. He said the only white bear it could be is a polar bear. The Roberts woman, the paleontologist at the museum, has no idea. Not her field. She has a guy in Albuquerque who can identify it, expert in fur and all. Can you imagine? I guess they do DNA analysis, all that."

"We don't have time for—"

"That's what I told her. How does it get in? You find anything?"

"There is no way in," Smith said. "There's no way anything big as a bear, hell, big as a dachshund, can get in there by any of those shafts. There's no cracks or crevices or holes big enough. There's just salt, Sam. Salt. Wall after wall of salt."

"Maybe it doesn't make that much difference how it gets in—"

"Of course it does—"

"If we kill it," Sam finished. "It's just some kind of animal. What's the big deal? So far, best we can tell, it's been there in the late afternoon and at night, like about ten. We could just go down there and wait for it."

"But we don't know what it is," Anna Maria said.

"It's a mammal," Sam said. "Mammals bleed when they're shot, and then they die."

"So what we need," T. L. Smith said, "is a hunter."

"I could just—," Sam started to say, but both Smith and Anna Maria cut him off.

"No," Anna Maria said reflexively.

"Sam, huntin' bears is different than snipin' at gooks. We need a hunter. A professional. You're too valuable to be set loose down there with a ferocious beast. Ain't that right, Anna Maria?"

Anna Maria stiffened. "What's that supposed to mean?" she snapped.

"Nothin', nothin'," Smith said, chuckling. "Now, what about that guy, Dunn, you talked to? He's a professional lion hunter. Get O'Connor to tell him I want to talk to him."

"What about keeping him quiet?" Sam asked.

The smile on T. L. Smith's face broadened. "Leave that to me." He stood up and slung his jacket over his shoulder. "I'm gonna get me something to eat, make a few phone calls." He crossed the room and went out, shutting the door behind him.

Anna Maria's eyes flashed with anger. "Do you tell your *boss* everything you do?"

"No," Sam said, "but the man ain't stupid."

"Puercos."

"Huh?"

"That's Spanish for pigs. Men are pigs."

"Now, now, is that any way to talk about the man you love?"

"Don't be ridiculous. That was just lust."

"Whatever works," Sam said, stepping around the desk to stand behind her chair.

In her black world, beset by multiple urges, the bear begins to stir again.

The urge to stay, to provide warmth, to protect . . . to lie with the warmth amid the compelling scents, the wriggling warm bodies . . .

The urge simply to move, to stretch limbs and back, rid them of aches, to be in motion . . .

The urge to avoid the other smell, the watering-eye smell . . . the burning irritation on the pads of her feet . . .

But hunger. Absorbing, overweening hunger. The urge to feed, to gorge on the salty flesh and lick the warm, sticky blood from her snout . . .

So she rises, shakes off the cubs, arches her back, and begins her journey.

Down.

SIXTEEN

When Tracer Dunn woke up that morning, he had awakened to a heartening revelation. He didn't have to do any more mule work on this godforsaken ranch. No more digging fence postholes in the limestone-studded dirt. No more repairing sagging wire. No more of any of that. He was going to go into a new business, a new line of work, a rewarding line of work where he got to call the shots and someone else did the labor. He'd sell the herd. Price of beef was lower than a snake's belly, but who cared? Get rid of 'em. Just run 'em over to the auction grounds, take whatever he could get. Might as well do that today.

He was going to develop a big cavern, that's what he was going to do. Put in those lights, get the shadows right, dream up some fancy names, have all the tourists going in for five dollars a head and buying hot dogs or whatever. Sell videos. Maybe he could get that pretty-boy TV announcer, Tom whatever, to be the voice on his videos. Make a damn fortune.

He arose from his bed—Lucia was long since up and about and Tracer could smell both coffee and bacon—and was brought up short by both the annoying aches of arthritic knees and hands and also the awareness that he didn't know how to make a video or, for that matter, what was involved in any aspect of developing a cavern. He didn't even know, he admitted, how to explore a cavern.

Well, he thought on reflection, he'd just take things one at a time.

165

He'd keep Chico, the pinto, just for old times, midnight rides, and all. And there was that part of the horse corral where the fence had gone to hell and he would have to dig just one more fence posthole in this unforgiving dirt. His last fence posthole. That had a nice sound to it.

Then, when he'd got the hole almost three feet deep, that fellow showed up with the white hairs in a plastic bag, like they were some kind of police evidence. Said he was a new employee over at the Diamond Salt plant, but Tracer didn't believe him. That place had been laying off people for months, especially those high-priced managerial types. It didn't seem likely they'd be hiring one all of a sudden, not when they were down to a skeleton crew, mostly a bunch of wetbacks working under the lash of Jesse Bowles, the fat old tyrant who ran the place. So how come that boy—Blood, Sam Blood, he said—was lying? If he was, which he probably was. And what the hell was it in that bag? Polar bear hairs? Didn't make any sense.

And now Tracer saw another little cloud of dust rising up from the dirt road into his place.

Weeks could go by without anyone coming down his road and here, today, this was his second visitor. He snipped off what was maybe the last strand of fencing wire he would ever have to deal with again, put down his fencing tool, and watched as a white Trooper, a little boxy thing, rounded the rise between the old ranch house and the WIPP road and stopped near the trailer. The world was full of white Troopers, but he was pretty sure he had seen this one before, bouncing out of his canyon the other night. Confirmation came when the driver stepped out into the sunshine—that Whittaker fellow, the caver.

This, he thought, ought to be interesting. He pulled his hat brim a little lower over his forehead and began to stroll down the slight incline. A blond woman was in the passenger seat, and Tracer Dunn watched as she stepped out of the car. Like all men, regardless of age, Tracer's eye was always drawn by ancient racial instinct to the pretty shapes of attractive women, and this one, he thought, was a knockout. Even from a distance of a hundred feet, he could see that the white blouse and flowing tan pants she wore were draped over the right stuff. She wore her hair up in a knot behind her head, and she stood by the car, looking around through dark glasses. He didn't know who she was, but he'd seen her around in town a couple of times. A fancy lady, Tracer concluded, and he also concluded a bit wistfully that you could be both a fancy lady and a mighty fine piece of ass. He'd met one like that twenty years ago when he was taking people out to hunt lions in the Black Mountains, wife of a doctor from Kansas City. Tracer remembered that he'd been pretty well tongue-tied in her presence and hadn't known exactly what to say even when she came on to him one night in camp when her doctor husband got drunk. She was a little drunk herself, called him her "own personal Marlboro man," said she liked the idea of a rangy, soft-spoken cowboy. Well, them days, Tracer thought . . .

The caver spotted him and waved.

"Mr. Dunn?" he called.

Tracer imagined that Lucia was hunkered inside the trailer, keeping out of sight. All these visitors would've spooked her. She didn't have a green card or anything and spent half her time worrying that the Border Patrol was going to track her down and send her back to Guadalajara. As he came abreast of the trailer's north end, he reached out and knocked twice on the aluminum side, a signal to Lucia that everything was okay.

He stopped about fifteen feet from the visitors and stood with his hands hanging down at his sides.

"Mr. Dunn?" the caver said again. "My name is Whittaker. This is Dr. Roberts. From the museum in town." The blond woman smiled and said hello. Tracer Dunn plucked a toothpick from the breast pocket of his worn denim shirt and stuck it between his lips.

"Pleased to meet you," he said.

"We heard that you're going to be selling your place here," the caver said. "And we'd like to talk to you about that."

"You talk to Seth Baker?"

"Uh . . ."

"He's the agent."

"No, we haven't," the caver said.

Tracer nodded and chewed silently on his toothpick, his eyes on the woman.

"And you're interested," he said, "in buying this place?"

"Well," Whittaker said. "We'd be interested in looking around a little, you know, maybe buying it. If we can agree—"

"What for?" Tracer asked. "You developers or something?"

The woman laughed. It was a pretty sound, tinkly, like water running over rock. "No," she said, and had begun to say something else when the caver interrupted.

"We're engaged to be married, Mr. Dunn, and both of us work in the city. We're thinking about getting a place in the country. You know, away from the bustle. Horses. Quiet."

Tracer saw the woman turn her head at that and stare briefly through her dark glasses at Whittaker, as if he had revealed a secret. Whittaker evidently didn't notice. He was looking around, shielding his eyes with one hand. "I know the WIPP site isn't far off in that direction, but it's out of sight, and it doesn't look like there'd be much to bother a man out here."

Except, Tracer thought, those outsized semi rigs rolling through here every day for the next twenty years.

"You'd be runnin' cattle too?"

"Well, we hadn't really thought about that," the caver said, and turned to the woman. "Had we, dear?"

"Two-thirds of this place, about ten thousand acres, is leased to this ranch. From BLM." He gestured behind him with his head. "You don't run cattle, you lose the lease."

"That leaves five thousand acres," Whittaker said. "That's a lot of land. For people like us."

Tracer noticed that the caver was beginning to sweat.

"Hot, ain't it?" he said. The caver smiled, took a red bandanna from his pocket, and wiped his forehead. "Follow me up that rise," Tracer said, and turned toward the corrals. The two walked along behind him, kicking up dust with each step. Stopping by the corral fence, Tracer pointed south toward Texas. "All that out there is

BLM land. The private land is mostly to the west." He pointed. "That way. Little piece of it lies on the other side of the highway."

He turned to face his visitors. "But I expect you knew that already."

"We looked at the plat. In the county records."

Tracer nodded. "You know," he said, "I've been working this land for a little more than ten years now. At one time, I had five hundred head, but it don't support half that anymore. This is a hard land. I'll be perfectly honest with you folks. It's a bad place to make a livin'. And it ain't gonna be all that peaceful here from now on. Those WIPP trucks're comin' through every day now sound like a bunch of thunderstorms."

He turned to face the west again.

"Mr. Whittaker, I saw your picture in the newspaper about a year ago. I know who you are. You're the feller who rescued that woman from the new cave, Lechuguilla. I guess that makes you some kind of local hero. You're a big-time spee-lunker. And there's only one reason in the world that I can imagine why a feller like you'd want to buy a godforsaken piece of land like this." He squatted down on his heels and looked at the discomfort spreading over his visitors' faces. Small vertical lines had appeared on either side of the woman's mouth—what Tracer called bitch lines. And the cave hero's nearly black eyes had somehow darkened.

"You walk on up this rise another twenty yards and out there to the west you can see the Quahada Hills. They don't amount to much, but I myself have always wondered if they wasn't the tail end of that big reef that stretches north and east from the Guadalupes. Maybe it just keeps going, swingin' south out there. You live on the land like I do, you wonder about these things."

Tracer Dunn was enjoying himself immensely. The woman stole a glance at Whittaker and looked out to the west.

"That little piece of my land, the one across the highway. It stretches up into the Quahada Hills a ways. It could be cavin' country up there on my land. If I had to bet on it, I'd say the best place to look would be in Dogleg Canyon. It's called that because it goes off to the right, crooked like a dog's back leg. Wednesday night I was

169

out near where the ground drops down into the canyon. I was lookin' for lion, and I was thinkin' about how there might just be a cave down there in that canyon. In fact, I'll bet you this whole ranch there is a cave down there. What do you think of that? If there isn't, the place is yours."

Damn, Cassie said to herself. Damn, damn, *damn!* This canny old bastard saw us. When we went in or when we went out. He knows about the cave. What do we do now?

Cassie watched the old rancher stand up effortlessly from his squatting position, and she saw amusement in the lines and pouches around the man's nearly colorless eyes. In the shadow cast by his hat brim, the irises were so pale, they seemed to have been bleached out by the desert sun, so bereft of expression, they struck her suddenly as reptilian. Involuntarily she stepped back a pace as one might when suddenly confronted by a rattlesnake.

"And that's the only way you'll get ahold of the place," the rancher was saying. "On a bet. If you'd checked with the real estate agent, you'd've found out this place ain't on the market anymore. If I didn't already know that cave was a big one, I'd know for sure now. Otherwise you wouldn't be interested, would you, Mister Whittaker?"

Cassie glanced over at Jack, who had thrust his fists into his back pockets and was staring out at the Quahada Hills on the horizon. White clouds had begun to materialize in the western part of the sky. She was surprised to see a smile break out on Jack's face—the shit-eating grin.

"You play the cards you're dealt," Jack said. "And I guess you got the better hand, Mr. Dunn."

"That's right."

"No hard feelings?"

"For a little bit of trespassing? No."

Cassie couldn't imagine Jack giving in so easily—giving up his dream practically without a murmur. And she had heard him use that poker-hand bit—it was one of his little tricks, something like an apology but not quite, whenever he got caught with his hand in the cookie jar.

"Let me ask you," Jack said. "When was it you saw us? Going in or coming out?"

"Wednesday. You was comin' out."

"Yeah. That was a pretty dark night. I guess you came back in the morning and found it. Probably it was blowing."

"Like a whale," the rancher said. "Now I do have a sense of what you're driving at here. You're gonna tell me that if you hadn't been trespassin' and found that cave, I never would've known it was there. So I owe you somethin'. That about right?"

The rancher hooked his thumbs in his belt. His hands were huge, the fingers long and flat. Cassie noticed that Jack had adopted the same pose, part of the game he was playing. The two men were now both facing west.

"No, sir, that's not what I was going to say. I *was* making the point that it was me who found that cave. And you *have* been living here for ten years without finding it. But," Jack said hastily, "you don't owe me a thing."

A cloud passed between them, and the sun and the sudden shadow brought with it a slight drop in temperature.

"On the other hand," Jack went on, "maybe the reason I found that cave and you didn't is that I know about caves. My guess is that you figure you'll develop that cave as a private tourist attraction. And my thought here is that maybe you'll need some professional help."

Tracer Dunn's face was impassive. Cassie noticed that the man hardly ever blinked. Like a snake.

"That's a hell of a big cavern down there," Jack continued. "Just exploring it calls for a lot of expertise. I'm suggesting that you might want to think about us being partners."

The rancher burst out laughing, a nasal and mirthless sound.

"Partner?" He snorted. "Partner up with a trespasser who lied about wantin' to buy a little place in the country?"

"I thought you said no hard feelings."

Tracer Dunn stared down at Jack with a look of contempt.

"I don't have any hard feelings about you, sonny. I don't have *any* feelings about you. But I got a sensible notion that you don't partner up with a man who lied to you first time you ever met." He turned to face Cassie. "I don't see no ring on your finger, so I reckon that was a lie too, about you gettin' married. So why don't you two just get on your way. You're wastin' my time."

He turned and began striding on his long legs down the rise toward his trailer, big hands swinging loosely by his sides. Cassie looked at Jack and again was surprised to see him smiling. He winked at her. Now what? she wondered.

"Oh, Mr. Dunn?" Jack called. "There's something else about that cave you ought to know."

What? Cassie asked herself. What else? The rancher stopped and slowly turned to face them.

"We have reason to think there's something living in that cave."

Oh no, Cassie thought. Not that. Goddammit, Jack. She glared at him and shook her head. And the idiot *winked* at her again. If he winks at me one more time, she thought, I'm going to kill him.

"There usually is," the rancher said. "Bats and all."

"This is different. It's a bear. A kind of cave bear." A wave of nausea swept over Cassie. The rancher stood staring at them.

"Ain't any such thing," he said.

"We have physical proof there's a bear living in that cavern. This woman here, Dr. Roberts, is a zoologist at the museum. She says it's a new species—a bear no one's ever seen before."

"I don't believe you," Tracer Dunn said.

"You don't have to," Jack said. "But when Dr. Roberts shows the physical evidence to the Fish and Wildlife people, they'll believe her. And there's no way they won't declare it a threatened or endangered species, declare the area critical habitat, and shut the place down. Most likely, they'll condemn your land. Maybe you'll get half of what that parcel is worth. But there goes your plan to develop the cave."

"When is she going to do that? Talk to Fish and Wildlife."

"When it looks like we can't all make a deal here."

Tracer Dunn stood motionless for a full minute, staring off at the horizon. Cassie floundered in a sea of conflicting emotions. She was furious at Jack for mentioning the bear to this crooked old bastard and for railroading her into some sort of association with such a man. But she was impressed, even amazed at Jack's coolness, at the brazen way he had manipulated the situation—played out his hand, she thought with something akin to humility. It had been exhilarating. She had to admit that. And if things started to go to hell, she could always opt out and talk to the Fish and Wildlife people herself. For now, she'd play along and see where it went.

The rancher blinked—finally!—and turned toward his trailer, saying, "Maybe you better come inside, get out of this heat."

They followed him down the rocky slope. Cassie put her arm through Jack's and leaned toward him mischievously. "Darling," she said in a loud voice. "When *is* Tiffany's going to send that ring? It's been weeks since we ordered it."

SEVENTEEN

"I'm going to save your pretty ass," Sam Blood had said in his quiet, high voice, standing behind her chair.

But Anna Maria barely heard him, and the words made no sense to her; they were just a meaningless murmur. She was suddenly overcome with a sense of despair, immobilized by despair. Her world had become a continuing catastrophe, a tide she had no power to stem. Events had been wrested from her control and were unfolding in ways that were beyond her imagination. The idea that some predatory beast could be loose in the salt caverns of WIPP was too outlandish to believe, too horrible to contemplate. She felt as if she had been slugged from behind, a blow she never could have seen coming, and she reeled inwardly with a pain greater than any physical pain. Men were being attacked. Killed.

Devoured? Had Holmein been *eaten?*

She almost retched at the thought.

All of the attention to safety, the drills, endless drills, the carefully wrought procedures, the technical classes, the elaborate training, the entire systematic approach to rendering this plant safe—safe for the workers, safe for millennia from the monumental geological processes of erosion, tectonics, all that—it was all being destroyed by a presence so unpredictable that it lay beyond reason, outside what Anna Maria had come to believe was the real world.

Despair—gray and cloying—had crept over her like a shroud.

T. L. Smith had stripped her naked—taken away the only justification she possessed for leading the life she led. For she had chosen to leave behind the faith, the superstition, and the proud, penitential poverty of her upbringing. She had turned her back on her heritage, risking her soul for what she had wanted so badly, a life of achievement, accomplishment, power, a life that was possible for a Hispanic woman only in the United States. With calm calculation, she had set aside a marriage made before she had seen the possibility of embracing the wider world that existed beyond the Sangre de Cristo Mountains, the Blood of Christ, beyond the arid, morbid, elegiac confines of life in northern New Mexico, so enveloped in suffocating tradition and ancient animosities. She had become a loner, making the best of loveless, brief unions and taking her true satisfaction from the exercise of ambition. And she had succeeded. She had studied. She had risen from clerk to director of a five-billion-dollar project, the very flagship of the Department of Energy. She had held the notion that she would one day become the secretary of energy.

And now she sensed, she knew, that her world was crumbling around her and she was helpless. She was utterly alone. She had long since given up the right to pray to one or another of the saints, to ask for their blessed succor as her people had done for the centuries they had survived in an unforgiving land. She had lost the right even to apologize to the saints for abandoning them.

When she was eleven years old, three of the boys in her little town in the mountains had cornered her in a field outside the cemetery. The cemetery lay behind a wall lovingly crafted out of stone. The grave markers—some headstones and many crosses bearing the familiar names of the town's families, stretching back centuries—were always attended by colorful flowers and other gifts that danced in the mountain breezes. In the field next to the cemetery, grasses grew high and turned orange in the late afternoon sun, as if lit by angels. Since she had been a little girl, Anna Maria would sit for a while when the light turned magic in front of the cross that marked the grave of her great-grandmother and namesake and think about the old woman who had loved her so much.

On this day, she left the cemetery, vaulting the low stone wall, and had begun to cross the meadow when the boys appeared. They were older than she by several years—one of them was fifteen—and they had noted the two small bulges that had come into being beneath her shirt in recent months and about which she had ambiguous feelings. Now the boys taunted her, saying they could see she was ready now that she had real tits. They grabbed at her, and the fifteen-year-old unzipped his jeans and showed her his penis, an ugly swollen thing, while the others laughed uproariously, telling her to lie down so Jorge could stick it in her. She cursed them and fought them off, and they stoned her as she fled, pegging rocks at her, and each one that struck had caused a sharp but insignificant pain. It was the pain in her heart, the knowledge that the world was nothing at all like what she had been led to believe, that had made her despair and made it impossible even to sit in peace anymore by her great-grandmother's grave.

It wasn't something she could tell her parents about, and not something she could tell the severe and formal padre in the little church with the mud walls where she had, up till then, felt comfortable. So she had sunk into a purgatorial despair. Back then.

As now.

And so, when Sam Blood's hands curled around her breasts, she barely noticed. With empty eyes, she watched him lift her keys from her desk and cross the room to lock the door, and she watched him walk over to the TV monitor that was showing the protesters outside the plant and turn it off. She was aware, as if standing outside herself, of his hands slowly undressing her, lifting up her naked body, lowering her onto the couch under the huge photograph of the mining machine. Still disassociated from herself, she felt her body awaken as they made what is called love, and she knew she was responding, riding the gathering torrent of lust that roared in her ears, her body performing on its own. And after the flood had subsided, she watched herself watching the man, Sam Blood, get dressed, and her despair intensified.

She needed to get dressed, needed to cover her nakedness in

front of this stranger, but she didn't want to move until he was gone.

He unlocked the door and put her keys in his pocket. She heard herself speak.

"What are you doing? Those are my—"

Sam Blood smiled, showing a perfect row of small teeth, like baby teeth. "As I said, I'm going to save your pretty ass." He left, closing the door behind him with a metallic click.

Tracer Dunn sat spraddle legged on a chair in his kitchen, one elbow resting on the plastic top of a table that took up a great deal of room at one end of the trailer's kitchen. The back of his chair touched the trailer wall behind him, and his boots almost reached the opposite wall. Above his head was a modestly framed print on black velvet of Jesus praying in the desert. His visitors sat with their backs against the wall, hemmed in by Tracer's long legs. The living room could have accommodated everyone in less cramped fashion, but Tracer had explained that he "did business" around the kitchen table. In fact, he didn't want his visitors, these new "partners," to get too comfortable. Keep 'em off balance, he thought.

Tracer knew that these two had the upper hand for now, blackmailing him into accepting them with the threat of ruining the whole enterprise by talking to the feds. But he knew a few things— at least one thing anyway—that they didn't know, and he had a plan forming in his mind. And he figured that he could use the talents of these people to get him to the point where he could implement his plan. Particularly Whittaker, the caver. After all, Tracer didn't know the first thing about caves and caving. Whittaker could save him a lot of time.

Tracer also didn't know what the woman's interest was in all this. If these two were really getting married, then she would share in anything they were to make off this "partnership." But they hadn't acted like two people who were about to get married when they first showed up. The woman had looked tight, tense, even aloof, and it had struck Tracer at the time that she was turning up her nose at more than just the shabby condition of the Dunn homestead and its proprietor. On the other hand, since they'd started back to the trailer, she'd been leaning toward Whittaker, putting her hand on his arm, looking up at him the way you'd expect of people who were getting married.

Still, Whittaker had said it was her, the woman, who would report the critter down there to the feds. Not both of them, but her. Did that suggest that she had a different take on all this? Probably, as a scientist of some kind, she did. But Tracer knew less about science than he did about caving.

"Well, now," he said, "maybe you can fill me in on this bear you say is livin' in that cavern."

"There's not much to tell you right now," Whittaker said. "We have a footprint. We photographed a footprint. It's definitely a bear, and it's bigger than a grizzly. At least its feet are."

Tracer's eyebrows rose high up on his forehead. He glanced at the woman.

"But you haven't seen this bear, right?"

"Not yet," she said.

"Where'd it come from?"

She shrugged. "Maybe it's always been here."

"Well, ma'am, I don't see how that could be. Someone would've spotted it. There've been white people hereabouts for more than four hundred years and the Indians before that. And sure as hell if anyone saw a bear bigger than a grizzly, they would've talked about it."

"If they lived," Whittaker interjected.

"It could have been a nocturnal animal," the woman said. "It seems to have taken to living in caves, at least this cave. People wouldn't be likely to run across it. They say there are undiscovered caves all around here."

"Thousands, probably," Whittaker said.

"Pretty slim pickin's in a cave," Tracer said.

"That depends, right, dear?" the woman said. "Some caves have huge populations of fish."

Tracer laughed, his nasal and unamused laugh. "Take a hell of a lot of fish to feed a big bear. Anyway, what I hear, the fish in caves are little transparent things, like minnows you can see through. Pupfish or whatever the feds get all excited about."

"There's another possibility," the woman said. "They could have developed an extremely long hibernation period. Like decades long. If their metabolism shut down for long periods—like fifty years—they might be able to live on a lot less. There's an article in the paper about how you and some of the other ranchers have been losing cattle. And evidently there were two similar outbreaks fifty years ago and a hundred years ago. Each time people have assumed it was mountain lions, but what if it's this bear, waking up hungry after a fifty-year snooze?"

Tracer scratched his cheek with a big hand and, with one finger, tipped his hat a little higher on his forehead.

"Fifty years ago," he said. "That's about when those boys up in Roswell say they saw the flyin' saucer. Maybe it's UFOs come down every fifty years to have themselves a banquet." He snorted. "That's just as easy to believe as a bear hibernatin' for fifty years."

A sudden low roaring sound from behind Tracer made the woman jump a bit.

"Lucia!" he called. "The coffee's done."

The short, stout Mexican woman entered the kitchen, poured three white mugs of coffee from the electric coffee machine, and put them on the table. She brought spoons and a blue plastic bowl of sugar and left.

"But the bear does exist," Whittaker said. "I can show you the photographs of its footprint."

"Then I reckon we better go find it."

"That," the woman said, "is exactly what I—what we want to do."

"Get a look at it before anyone else hears about it," Tracer said.

"Anyone else?" Whittaker said. "There's just the three of us."

"Feller named Blood, Sam Blood. Came by here this mornin' with some hairs. Said he found 'em outside his house in Loving. They was bear hairs for sure, but they were white."

Tracer watched the couple glance at each other with evident surprise, and he felt a small surge of satisfaction. "I told him the nearest white bear was a polar bear in the zoo in Albuquerque; maybe someone was playin' a prank on him. But he wasn't tellin' the whole truth. Said he was just hired as a manager over at the Diamond Salt Company, and I just don't believe that. They ain't doin' any hirin'."

"I'm pretty sure he lied to me too," the woman said.

It was Tracer Dunn's turn to look surprised. "The same man?" he said. "Short brown hair, real neat dresser? Thick blond hair on his arms?"

"Yes. He said he was renting a house over near Loving until his family came out from back east, but he didn't know the street name. If you moved into a new area and rented a house, wouldn't you know the address?"

"Some of the people I've met from back east couldn't find their butt with a road map," Tracer said. "What'd you tell him?"

"I said I didn't know; maybe it was a pronghorn—"

Tracer snorted.

"—and I kept a couple of hairs back. They're on their way to Albuquerque. A man there can identify them for us. In a few days. In case you're wondering, I didn't tell him where they came from."

"That makes five people," Whittaker said. "Five who know, or soon will know, that *something* unusual is somewhere around here. I think we better find out who this guy Blood is. Do you suppose he's a fed? Is that his real name?"

"Looked more like a military man to me," Tracer said. "Got eyes on him like a snake." The woman smiled, and Tracer wondered what was so funny about that.

For another hour, the uneasy partnership continued its discussions, each wary to one degree or another of the other two, each revealing only enough to seem forthcoming, trustworthy. They circled around each other like vultures circling in the sky, where each bird gains from the added pairs of eyes and hopes to beat the others to the carcass. It was agreed that Whittaker and the woman would make inquiries, try to find out who Sam Blood was, and maybe get a better idea of where the hairs might have come from, not that it had been established that they were from the same animal haunting the cavern. Tracer himself was tied up for the rest of the day and the next, as he had arranged with the Forbush Land and Cattle Company from Artesia to collect his herd and take them off to the auction block. The days of cattle drives were long over. The herd would be trundled off in large trucks just like chickens or chili peppers or TV sets. After they were gone, it was agreed, would be the time for the three to go down into the cavern.

The she-bear stops in the blackness, puzzled. She knows where she is. The way is familiar now, part of a maplike sense in her brain of where to turn, where there is a rocky descent, or a body of water, or a forest of obstacles unseen but felt: all learned. This is her familiar territory, which she could and did defend against others like her, the other she-bears. What puzzles her is the scent, the presence of the scent that makes her shake her head, makes her eyes water. She knows from a primal sense of geography that the place of the bad smell has grown. The smell should be farther ahead along her route. It is not strong here, barely registering on her olfactory cells, but it is puzzling, and she stands for a while, sniffing the air and growing irritable. Too many new things in her world.

The scent—unpleasant, sharp, sickening—also is associated in her mind with the burning sensation in her feet that is always part of this journey but not this soon. It should be farther off. She could feed in the water back behind her, gorge herself on the tiny fish in the water. Or she could go farther, seeking the larger prey that lay beyond . . . the rich taste of flesh, thick mouthfuls of flesh, and salty blood gushing warm . . . This fills her brain, damping, overcoming all else, even the instinct to remain with her young, to keep the he-bear at bay.

She is at the end of her reserves still, depleted from the long period of sleep and ferociously intent on filling her belly. This is a dangerous time. Without food, she will be unable to feed the suckling mouths. Without her presence, the young ones might fall prey to the he-bear. But without food for her, they have no chance to survive. The calculus of survival, which the bear knows nothing

181

about except in the form of instinctual urges, is not all that complex. Eat the richest food you can get for the least effort and live to breed again.

She makes her way along the familiar route, increasingly irritable, impatient, shaking her head from side to side, gaining single-minded momentum.

Jack Whittaker glanced out the car window at the brine lakes, glittering with a morbid gleam in the sun, the black tatters of mesquite rising from the shores, testimonials to the continuing anti-life propensities of too much salt. An odd thought struck him: the brine lakes were anti-lakes in the same manner that Satan as the anti-Christ. A few dumb waterbirds might be tempted into landing on them in their migrations, but there was nothing there for them. Just a rest stop in the devastation. A few head of cattle browsed hopelessly in the desert surrounding the lakes—maybe those were Tracer Dunn's, off to the executioner.

Jack realized he was being gloomy. He didn't like being gloomy. He knew some people who liked being gloomy. Like Eeyore, the tail-less donkey in the Winnie-the-Pooh stories. He wondered if guys like Eeyore actually liked being gloomy or if they even noticed.

Jack's basic attitude was that if there was even a finger of liquid in the glass, it wasn't empty. So why, he wondered, was he feeling gloomy?

Let me count the ways, he said to himself.

Tracer Dunn, for one. Enough said. The shrewd old bastard wasn't in their pocket. In fact, the whole deal could unravel, probably was unraveling. But . . . it still could come off, his idea, his grand plan. How? Work out the details. Keep your eye on the ball. Keep an eye on Dunn, that was for sure. The thought crossed his mind that if Dunn had an accident on the way into the cave . . . and he felt ashamed.

His ex-wife, for another. Cassie. Sitting in the passenger seat of his Trooper with one knee against the glove compartment, staring straight ahead of her, with the little lines around her mouth. Taut as a string on Earl Scruggs's banjo. It was nice, wasn't it? In fact, beautiful, having her lean into him that way, put her hand on his arm, smile at him like she wanted to get home and get in bed with him. . . .

"That was a hell of an act you put on back there," he said, and wondered why the hell he had said *that.*

She glanced over at him, and he saw a look of pain on her face. Or was it annoyance?

"Oops," he said, and she turned back to staring out the windshield.

After a few minutes, she said, "I never come out here. I hate looking at these lakes. They look so blue, the water, but it's misleading. And all that salt, glittering like snow but so dead."

They drove on, past the last of the brine lakes and into country that undulated with more signs of life. The desert scrub was greener.

"Jack, you know, it wasn't all an act. Our marriage, I mean. But a lot of it was. I saw a shrink after you—after we split. He made me realize that I was playing a lot of roles. And there were some I just couldn't do."

"Did the shrink tell you why you were playing roles instead of just, I don't know, what? Just being yourself?"

"A lot of reasons."

"Stuff we talked about?"

"That too."

She said nothing more, and Jack decided that there was still some tiny thread of hope left if she was talking about all this at all. To him.

EIGHTEEN

Sam Blood had been a subscriber to *Soldier of Fortune* magazine, a monthly, for nearly fifteen years. He read it not to find out the latest in laser-operated gun-sighting equipment or the newest models of serrated bayonets and knives, such as the Cold Steel Company's Carbon V Twist Master or even the latest reports from the training camps of Iranian terrorists or Latin American guerrillas. He read it for amusement, just as some people take *The New Yorker* only for the cartoons. For the notion of all these potbellied former military men or semiliterate cop wanna-bes racing down to the local post office to order by coupons thousands of dollars' worth of high-tech equipment, all bearing guarantees that they made killing bad guys a cinch, moved him to laughter.

Here were guys, as Sam saw it, practically invisible behind the headsets of their cybersights and terrorist ski masks, carrying weapons that looked more complex than the space station, with gimcracks and gadgets attached like barnacles on a whelk, wearing the newest in camouflage and snake-resistant combat boots, laden with battery packs, a kukri (the boomerang-shaped knife of the Ghurkas) and assorted other blades with toothed edges—lumbering through the woods in search of what?

Fulfillment of some kind. If any of them ever ran up against a bad guy out in the national forest, they'd all probably wet their pants and set off a series of electrical shorts (as it were) that would send

184

the whole raggedy-ass brigade up in a sizzling storm of sparks. One of Sam's old buddies in the Rangers regularly advertised a camp (group rates available) where you could go for actual simulated combat conditions. The guy was laughing all the way to the bank— he was the Disneyland of Rambo addicts.

Sam was no hunter of game, but he knew the same wonderful consumer-goods techno-array was employed by hunters. They would go off clattering around the landscape on their noisy little all-terrain vehicles like little four-wheel scooters, laden with high-priced optical equipment, sound detectors and antennae, batteries, radios (which could survive the bite of a grizzly!), and enough automatic firepower to wipe out an entire town from three thousand yards. That they ever actually saw anything alive except one another was a miracle, what with all the noise they had to make lugging all that gear. That they ever killed anything besides the trees they sprayed with hundreds of rounds was simply not likely. Maybe a few cows.

Sam smirked about all this because he knew that when it came to killing, the best advice was to keep it simple, flexible, mobile, and secretive, but mainly simple.

And quick. Generally if you were good, one shot would do it.

For such a job as the one at hand—luring out of the gloom whatever mammal was down there and killing it—Sam preferred to use the standard lever-action Winchester 30.30 with a relatively short barrel that he had owned since he was a kid and brought with him most places he had to go. It was simple, smooth, practically an extension of his hands. Sam was old-fashioned that way.

But not so old-fashioned that he wouldn't take advantage of more lethal ammunition—and it was here that the perfervid imaginations of the arms industry were, he thought, particularly effective. So Sam had loaded his old Winchester with that same company's newest shells, called Fail Safe, which they said "will not fail on the *biggest* North American or safari game." The notched hollow cavity and the lead core protected by double steel inserts meant the bullet would penetrate deeply and expand dramatically on impact. He had found a box of them in a gun shop in Carlsbad, though what anyone in southern New Mexico needed such ammunition for was beyond him. Hit a pronghorn or a mountain lion with a bullet like that, and it's bye-bye, trophy. Nothing left but mush and a few tufts of fur.

For this hunt, Sam had eschewed the steel-toed boots and hard hat that were de rigueur for anyone venturing underground at WIPP. He passed up the goggles and the respirator that would give him a wholly inadequate fifteen minutes of breathing if the salt collapsed on him, sealing him in like a drum of transuranic gloves and tools and preserving him mummylike for ten thousand years. Instead he went bareheaded and wore a pair of running shoes, blue jeans, and a sweatshirt. In his right hand, he held an eight-cell flashlight, heavier than a billy stick. On his belt, by way of backup, a leather holster hugged his right hip, in which sat a small Colt .45. On his other hip, Anna Maria's master keys hung from a brass key chain next to a leather sheathe that housed a handcrafted hunting knife with a Randall blade.

One of the keys activated the elevator in which Sam plummeted down into the earth, walls of salt racing past just inches outside the cage, a dead white blur that gave him the panicky sensation of being in free fall. It was four-thirty, and the shift was over, the workers gone from the great cavern of WIPP, their brasses turned in, each man accounted for. There would be no one underground but Sam and his prey . . . if it showed up.

Another of the keys activated any of the little electric carts that hauled people around the underground tunnels if they had the proper authorization (a blue badge as opposed to the yellow ones that the plebeians wore). A number of these carts, maybe twenty in all, sat parked in precise rows to the left of the elevator when Sam stepped out of it after coming to a stomach-churning stop. A little fleet of orange carts, Humvees for hobbits. He decided to go on foot. He was in a large open area, with what were clearly rooms, maybe offices, around it, places where tools were kept, whatever. With doors that were securely locked. From the large open area, tunnels led off in four directions. Very rectangular. Very regular. All white or whitish and dark, the occasional light on the ceiling making a dull bruise of yellow on the floors and the walls of the tunnels. Overhead, fifteen feet up, chain-link fencing appeared to be bolted to the salt ceiling. Holding it up? A half mile of salt and rock and God knows what, being held up by a chain-link fence?

From studying a map of the underground tunnels, Sam knew which of the tunnels to take. He would have to pass three cross tunnels, take a right, and pass another six cross tunnels. The seventh would be S10249. Underfoot, his running shoes crunched with a soft sound on the salt. Otherwise the place was quiet. No, not quiet. The place was utterly silent. Maybe, Sam thought, this is what they mean when they say, "A deathly silence fell . . ."

The silence was a good thing. He would hear anything that moved, especially anything big enough to scare a man half to death. Like a white bear? A white whatever. A whitish animal might be hard to see in these poorly lit, whitish tunnels. At each crossing, he stopped, listened to the silence, and peered into the gloom.

He had never been in a place so lifeless, so inert. Nothing moved. The air was still and so dry, he could almost sense it sucking moisture from him. The idea that he was two thousand feet under the surface of the earth began to sink in. The immensity of salt and rock poised over his head became a nearly palpable weight. He had a fleeting vision of himself half a mile down in an escape-proof maze—the only human left alive on a planet that had died. He felt the hairs on his arms stand erect as if in a sudden chill, and he began to think that maybe it wasn't so smart, going freelancing like this. If he succeeded . . . okay. If he fucked up, his ass was grass.

Under one of the overhead lights, he noticed that the electric carts appeared to leave very faint tracks in the salt floor, maybe the ones loaded with salt to be conveyed to the elevator dedicated to hauling the stuff out of the mine. He turned and saw that he left no tracks in the salt. What did bears weigh? Three, four hundred pounds, maybe. Probably a bear would leave no footprint discernible on the salt floors of these tunnels. The damn thing could be anywhere in here by now, Sam thought.

Five minutes after leaving the elevator, Sam reached a T and took a right. So far, so good. He came to the first cross tunnel, five more to go, and then . . . But the stillness, the silence, was shattered. The sound had come from the cross tunnel. A thump like something falling and a scraping noise. Sam was already in a crouch, the Winchester in his right hand, pointing down the tunnel. There was no overhead light in this tunnel, and Sam's eyes strained to see motion. He flicked on the flashlight, and its beam played around the walls and floor of the tunnel, lighting up the whorls in the walls like ghostly fingerprints left by a giant. A rank smell assaulted his nostrils, and he realized it was him. Sweat had erupted in his armpits and from his forehead and from his chest. He shivered as the sweat immediately began to evaporate in the dry air.

Seeing nothing move, no unexpected shape lurking, he stood and began slowly pacing into the tunnel, keeping the flashlight beam hurrying back and forth over the walls and the floor ahead. Then he saw it. Something out of order, something white, something hunched in the center of the tunnel about fifty feet away. He stopped, shone the light on it, and mouthed a word: *Shee-it.*

It was a small pile of salt. He walked up to it, looked up, and saw a shallow depression in the salt of the ceiling above the chain-link fencing. Some of the salt had simply come loose and fallen. He reached down and stuck a finger into the rough salt crystals. They were dry to the touch. He stood up, retraced his steps, and proceeded on toward S10249, concentrating on the job of listening and trying to shut out the vision that had recurred that he was in an escape-proof maze that was closing in on him, falling apart. The walls of the tunnel seemed to be growing closer together, the ceiling growing lower.

Sam swore to himself. He stopped and took ten deep breaths. He would not let this place get to him. This awful place. How could anyone work here five days a week? He would rather be slogging through a swamp, up to his hips in muck. He longed to have the sky overhead. This, he guessed, was what they called claustrophobia.

He had no phobias. Heights, spiders, none of that bothered him at all. But this godforsaken, dead salt mine . . .

But not lifeless, he reminded himself.

Two minutes later he stood at the entrance of the tunnel called S10249. It was barricaded with Jersey Barriers like on the highways, and a sign in large red letters announced that by order of the director, no personnel were permitted to go any farther. The sign offered no explanation. Sam vaulted disobediently over the cement barrier and looked down the tunnel. It looked like all the others he had passed through and looked down. Lights in the ceiling, spaced about two hundred feet apart, created ugly yellow glows that punctuated the gloom. But, Sam noted, the chain-link fencing in S10249 stopped partway down the tunnel, and in the almost total dark of the tunnel's far end, light reflected dimly off something metal—no doubt one of those big mining machines like the one in the photograph in the director's office that had presided over their recent coupling on the couch, a giant voyeuristic boast.

This tunnel under construction had been closed since Monday, and the big machine that scraped away at the far end of the tunnel with its huge, spinning cylinder had been idled. In the meantime, two guys had disappeared from this place, leaving behind a damaged radio and a smear of blood. Fred Fontaine, who wasn't exactly a fainthearted wuss, had been scared half to death and was in something like a coma, with his safety suit torn by a claw, and the hairs of some large mammal found near the machine and on the far wall. But nobody, not even T. L. Smith, who had eyes like a hawk and a sixth sense about security, had spotted any way some creature with claws and long, white, coarse hair like a bear's could get in—or out.

Sam Blood didn't believe in magic. And he didn't believe this was some kind of prank, as the rancher-hunter Tracer Dunn had suggested—or sabotage. He smirked at the image of a saboteur sneaking around down here in a polar bear suit. No, there was something like a bear down here, and there was only one way something like a bear could get in and out. It seemed impossible,

189

but it had to be. He set off down the tunnel, and the hair on his arms tingled in the sudden chill that returned like an icy finger tapping him on the shoulder.

Head moving side to side, assessing the darkness, she makes her way through the eye-burning stench, the pain in her footpads raising irritation to anger. Through the stench, carried on the faint breeze that blows toward her, another smell reaches her nose and registers in her brain.

The rank smell of the old he-bear.

She stops and stands still on the damp ground, burning her feet. He is ahead of her, somewhere ahead of her in the passage, between her and the satisfaction of her raging hunger. She screams out in anger and frustration and turns around, not wishing to confront the larger and always irascible male. The sound of her voice rumbles in echoes through the passageway.

Over the generations, her kind has come to avoid this most dangerous violence except when it is necessary to keep the he-bear from devouring her young. She has in her brain now the urge to go to the place that teems with fish, and she hastens through the dark back the way she came.

Below, the great male makes his way through the invisible mist that burns his eyes and his nostrils and fills his stomach with nausea. And anger. But through the foul odor, he is tracking the faint, seductive scent of old blood that still clings to the rocky floor.

The machine loomed up in front of Sam, bigger than he had reckoned from the photograph in Anna Maria's office. Above its broad base that squatted on the floor like an enormous crab, a housing held the operator's chair and an array of gearshifts like those on a bulldozer. Two huge metal arms, bent at the elbow, held high the cylinder with its lethal teeth, sharp, conical teeth that gleamed in the beam of Sam Blood's flashlight. The cylinder was poised only a foot or two from the ceiling. The faint odor of machine oil was in the air.

Sam climbed up into the housing and sat in the operator's chair.

He spent a few minutes examining the gearshifts, locating the ignition, finding the ignition key from among the bunch hanging on his hip. It didn't look much more complicated than a backhoe. The base of the wall of salt at the end of the tunnel was only some ten feet ahead of the machine, and a lot of loose salt was on the floor. The wall glistened, sparkled, in the flashlight's beam. It slanted up from the floor at an angle. At the ceiling it was farther off, maybe fifteen feet away. The sides of the tunnel were, like all the others he had seen, vertical. The whorls on the sides of the tunnel gleamed too but had a duller sheen than on the wall in front of him.

He climbed down from the machine and walked around it to the angled wall of salt, shining his light up from the base to the ceiling. It wasn't smooth, but rough. There were ridges, like vertical folds. He couldn't picture how the toothed cylinder, now poised some six feet above his head, could have left the wall with vertical ridges. It should have been flat. He became aware of another odor, a faint smell of rot.

He set the Winchester and the flashlight down on the machine behind him and stepped closer to the wall, stretching out a hand. With his forefinger, he poked the salt at about chest level. It was soft. His finger went in up to the first knuckle. He pulled out his finger and a few small bits of salt, tiny chunks, spilled out and rolled downward a few inches.

It struck him like a clap of thunder. This wall was soft, like a pile of sand. He pinched some off the wall and held it in his hand.

It was damp! It glistened because it was damp. How could those guys have missed that? The forensics, that engineer, the big Navajo mine safety guy—how had they missed that? They couldn't have. There was only one explanation. It was dry when they were here, and it was damp now. Water had begun to seep into this wall, softening the salt, and it was slowly collapsing from above. Just like a steep sand pile. If you disturb the bottom, sand pours down from the top. And obscures the disturbance.

What disturbance? Sam asked himself rhetorically.

Something burrowing through it.

The fucking bear.

Was that possible? Sam drew his hunting knife from its sheathe and began to probe the salt at waist level. Carefully he dug out a depression in the wall about six inches deep. He widened it, and it held. Then he deepened it another two inches, and salt began to trickle down from its upper edge. The smell of something rotten grew stronger. Sam dug deeper, jamming the knife blade into the salt and twisting it, then scooping out the loose salt with his other hand. The upper edge began to collapse, salt fragments beginning to slide down the wall onto his arms. He had the sense that he had somehow set off a chain reaction with his little hole in the wall: salt was cascading down the wall. He stood back and gaped. Before his eyes, the wall was trembling, pulsing.

Just as it dawned on him what was happening, an explosive burst of foul air and salt struck Sam in the face and he reeled backward, his upper back slamming into the base of the mining machine. He heard the Winchester clatter onto the floor as the monstrous head appeared before him, an enormous white face emerging from the salt, red eyes blinking furiously, a gaping red mouth, huge fangs. The world filled with a horrendous sound, a vast cataract of sound, and Sam heard his own voice screaming. Long black claws reached out as the bear emerged from the wall, and Sam rolled to his left and scrambled around the big machine. The bear was white, almost as tall at the shoulder as Sam himself. It filled the air with a putrid stink, and Sam felt a terror he had never experienced take hold, as if his body had been drained of all its organs.

Instinct screamed, "Run, *run!*" but his legs wouldn't move, and then adrenaline exploded into his bloodstream. He glanced over his shoulder—the bear's head swung back and forth on a long neck. It was gigantic, a monstrosity. An oddly flat face, with huge teeth set in what looked like a hideous grin. He saw it lift its forelegs off the ground, standing up. It towered up, the massive head only a few feet from the ceiling, and roared again. Running was no use.

Sam pulled the Colt .45 from its holster and leapt up onto the machine, grabbing hold of the housing and swinging into the operator's chair. He fired a shot at the bear, and blood erupted from its shoulder. The huge mouth opened wide, and the cave was filled with its deafening roar of surprise and pain and fury.

Sam tore the key chain from his belt loop, fumbled infuriatingly for what seemed an aeon, found the right key, and thrust it into the ignition of the machine. The engine caught, and Sam thrust a lever forward. Overhead, the enormous cylinder with its dragon teeth began to turn, spinning faster and faster. Sam fought with other levers: Which one? Which one lowered the goddamned cylinder that was now a blur of metal in the light cast by the flashlight down on the machine's base, a lethal weapon now spinning only a few feet from the monstrous carnivore's face? It roared again, and Sam struggled with another gear lever. He felt it slide home and the spinning cylinder began to descend, but suddenly the grotesque face dropped out of sight and in an instant appeared at the side of the machine, rearing up, its great maw agape, and the monster lunged upward. Sam fired the Colt again, the sound almost drowned out by the horrid voice, and he saw a fountain spray of red before he felt the agonizing pain and saw his left arm flop wildly before him and fall lifeless. He was sprawled on his side. His shoulder was crushed. A huge paw with talons longer than fingers raked across his face and neck, and he screamed until he choked as his own blood filled his throat. Huge teeth were coming at him and, as the world went black around him, Sam Blood was relieved to die.

The pain is new, strong. It sears through his shoulder, down his back. He can only move his foreleg with a leaping of the pain, so intense, it makes him see red lights in his eyes. Still leaning against the unfamiliar, cold thing, he turns and licks the place and tastes blood. He has never tasted his own blood. He snatches at his prey and wrenches it back and forth in his jaws.

The pain shoots through his leg as he drags the body down and across the floor. He growls around the food in his mouth, a sound of fury replacing puzzlement.

NINETEEN

About twenty protesters still stood in the parking lot outside the WIPP plant. It was five o'clock, and the WIPP workers had all departed, a huge caravan of cars and pickups all roaring off at ridiculously high speed down the access road, racing across the desert in the twice daily running of the WIPP 500. The sun burned down from the west, and the light was beginning to take on a spun-gold cast. In the parking lot, only a few cars remained. A trim white Chrysler sat in the spot earmarked for the director. Next to it was a nondescript sedan, also white. Derby Catlin recognized Chryslers, but midsized, midpriced cars all looked the same to him. The other vehicles in the lot were mostly those of the protesters.

Derby had decided to do a human-interest story on these die-hards. Why were they standing around in the heat, standing around even after the day's work had ended and the big semis had steamed off northward with empty canisters? The plant was open for business now, and nuclear waste was accumulating in the deep salt beds. The matter was settled, wasn't it?

Derby's notion of a human-interest story for a weekly newspaper supported solely by advertising revenue from businesses, all of which were members in excellent standing of the Carlsbad Chamber of Commerce, ran to the satirical. He had hoped to find at least one of these protesters who would say something utterly loony. Instead they had all told him that they were here simply making a statement against the day—maybe thousands of years from today and maybe much sooner than that, like tomorrow—when someone died of radiation poisoning. It was a matter of conscience, and they were merely bearing witness. Hearing that, Derby had thought to make these people out as religious fanatics, harebrained Quakers or something, but that evidently wasn't the case. He hadn't gotten a single absurd quote, only the sense that these people, mostly women, intended to keep up this vigil forever. They would take turns.

So he gave up and was about to set out to where his pickup was parked at the far end of the lot some hundred yards from the WIPP entrance when he saw a four-wheel-drive vehicle approaching the plant. The remaining protesters formed two lines as the vehicle approached, what they called a moral gauntlet that every DOE vehicle would have to go through. Derby stopped to watch. Through the windshield he could see the rectangular head of the driver, that fellow O'Connor, the onetime marine who was in charge of security at the plant. And in the passenger seat, if he were not mistaken, was none other than Tracer Dunn, sitting there, staring straight ahead from under the brim of his battered and stained Stetson hat.

Derby felt a surge, an adrenaline rush.

This was news.

Everybody, and especially everybody who frequented Ma's and got to talk to the gaunt old rancher for five minutes, knew he hated feds, hated any and all feds with an icy passion and on sheer principle. Then what was the old guy doing in a government-issue vehicle being driven by a government security chief into a government facility?

The rancher stared straight ahead as the car came to a halt before the gate. A rent-a-cop stepped out of the guardhouse and bent over on the driver's side of the vehicle, nodded, and went around the nose of the vehicle to open the gate. Derby pushed through the silent gauntlet, saying, "Excuse me, excuse me," and approached the passenger side of the vehicle. Tracer Dunn stared straight ahead, unseeing, with an expression on his face that looked like he smelled something awful, and Derby got a glimpse of the top four

195

inches of the blue-black business end of a Winchester 30.30 lying next to Tracer Dunn's chest.

Son of a bitch, Derby intoned to himself, utterly bewildered and utterly fascinated.

Smelling Pulitzer.

At five minutes before five, Marjory Blenhem, registered nurse, was tidying up the nurses' station on the third floor at the Carlsbad hospital and keeping her eye on the clock with its glacially slow minute hand inching toward quitting time. Marjory Blenhem was an efficient and well-trained nurse who worked hard and with care when on duty. In a decade and a half of nursing, she had suffered the foolishness of numerous young doctors and had earned wages that started low and barely kept up with inflation. As a result, her early Mother Teresan idealism had long gone. It was just a job. One member of the next shift had already arrived, and they had exchanged a few pleasantries and routine medical updating on the patients on their ward. One-oh-two (which was to say the patient in room 102 who had had the heart attack) was unchanged and doing fine. One-oh-four, the mystery patient who had been brought in from WIPP, was also unchanged, all vital signs okay, but still in his comalike state. And so forth, around the ward.

At last, at last, the minute hand achieved verticality. Five o'clock. End of shift. Nurse Blenhem said, "Good night," and proceeded down the corridor. She peeked in at one-oh-four and noticed through the window that the patient's lips were moving. She stepped inside the room and approached the bed, hearing him murmur and seeing his head moving slightly, side to side. She leaned over the bed and listened, like a robin cocking its head to listen for a worm in the lawn.

"Fucking bear," the patient named Fred Fontaine said in a hoarse whisper. "Gigantic fucking bear." Then the whisper turned into a whine. "No. No. Oh, God, no." His eyes popped open, then closed. Nurse Blenhem would have bet that the eyes saw nothing. She stood motionlessly, watching the patient, but he said no more. She left the room, went back to the nurses' station, and told the nurse that one-oh-four had begun to babble. Then she left the hospital and drove home.

While Nurse Blenhem was a good nurse, given to believing in the value of routine in medical situations, once off-duty, Marjory Blenhem was something of a free spirit. She was thirty-eight years old, single, and currently without a boyfriend. This was not a situation that she relished and so, as she made her way to her little house on the eastern edge of Carlsbad, she decided it was a good night to go to Ma's and see if she could scare up some amusement.

"Mr. Dunn, I am aware that you have a complete and utter disrespect for the federal government, and I'm sure that if I were in your boots, I'd feel pretty much the same."

T. L. Smith strode back and forth before the couch in Anna Maria Gonzales's office. Tracer Dunn sat on the couch, feeling uncomfortable, one big brown hand on each knee. Chuck O'Connor had introduced him to this man in the dark gray suit, white shirt, maroon tie, and shoulder holster, saying he was director of security for the Department of Energy from Washington, D.C. And while Tracer Dunn did hate feds on general principle and thought anyone from Washington, D.C., had to be dumb as a rock, he had never met a fed who was so exalted a big shot as this man. He exuded power. Tracer felt a bit underdressed in his dusty old cowboy boots and worn jeans. He took off his battered cowboy hat and set it down next to him on the couch and ran his hand over his hair.

"But," Smith continued, "I am also sure that you love your country, that you are a patriot."

Tracer reflected that he probably was a patriot and probably did love his country, but only so far as it let people like him live their lives in peace and without regulation. And this was exactly what was going wrong with his country. But he didn't need to be flattered by the slick feller from Washington. O'Connor had told him that the people at WIPP needed some help and would pay him five thousand dollars for what would probably be a night's work. That was enough to get Tracer into the car and over to WIPP and into this office. Tracer hated feds, yes, indeed, but he wasn't bone stupid.

Five thousand dollars was a hell of a big sum of money for a man like Tracer Dunn, and as long as he didn't have to do anything that was too illegal to get it, he would happily take on an assignment from even the feds. He was also extremely curious about what the assignment could be. O'Connor had told him to bring along a hunting rifle. What would he be hunting around WIPP? There wasn't anything in the vicinity but cows and coyotes. And maybe a mountain lion.

Tracer had also been introduced to the director of WIPP, the pretty Hispanic woman named Gonzales, a little chunky, maybe, but a good piece. She was now standing before the window to his right, with her arms folded beneath her breasts. Black eyebrows almost touched over her nose and gave her a bit of a stormy look. She was watching him carefully, the way someone might size up a horse they were thinking of buying.

Smith was going on about how he didn't want to exaggerate the importance of what they had in mind, but that it could be considered a matter of national security. The nation's scientists had determined that nuclear wastes had to be buried in a safe place; otherwise, as they accumulated, they put people at risk, grave risk. So it was a matter of the nation's health and safety that the Waste Isolation Pilot Program proceed without a hitch and show the world that placing these lethal wastes underground in such places was safe and intelligent.

"Of course," Smith said, "I'm sure you know that there's a whole lot of people who are plain ignorant about such things and scared half to death by the very word *nuclear*. Those Sierra Club type of people, same ones that think cattle are the spawn of the devil and a cow pod in the wilderness is some kind of damn sacrilege. You know who I mean."

Tracer smiled minimally. "I've had my set-tos with them folks."

Smith nodded. "Well, if those people hear there's the slightest glitch in the operation of this plant, they figure the world is going to end in the next ten minutes from a nuclear explosion, and they start calling their congressmen and senators, and *those* people . . ." T. L. Smith shrugged and walked around behind the desk and sat down.

"Well, Mr. Dunn, we do have a glitch here in this plant. And we have reason to believe you are the best man around here to help us take care of it. See, they're still digging more tunnels down there in the salt. And it seems like some kind of critter has been showing up in one of the new tunnels. We haven't figured out where it comes from or how it gets in or out—I mean that tunnel is half a mile down—but we want you to help us kill it. Before anyone hears about it and the rumors start flyin' and . . ."

It struck Tracer Dunn like a thunderbolt. His eyes blinked rapidly, and all at once he saw the whole thing in sharp relief. What was that feller's name? Gore? Blood. Sam Blood. The one who wasn't really from the salt company, the one with the white hairs like a bear's. He was from here, WIPP. That had to be it. So some critter like a bear was getting into WIPP, and some critter like a bear was leaving footprints in his cavern. So the two—WIPP and his cavern—were connected somewhere. And if he, Tracer Dunn, got rid of the bear in WIPP, part of his own problem was solved.

Shoot, shovel, and shut up. The feds were going to *pay* him five thousand dollars to kill what was sure as hell an endangered species. He loved it.

Obviously there was more than one of those critters, had to be, but if he got rid of the one prowling WIPP, then he could get rid of the others in his cave, and those two, Whittaker and the Roberts woman, wouldn't have any leverage over him anymore. He'd be free and clear to kick their asses out of his life and get on with making a fortune developing his cave. "Does that seem fair to you, Mr. Dunn? Five thousand dollars?"

"It's a good fee for a hunt, yessir."

"Of course, we expect you not to say anything about it. Not to anyone."

"I reckon not."

"Not even to Lucia, your—uh—wife, who forgot about getting a green card."

Tracer Dunn bristled inwardly while retaining a bland expression on his face. He bristled not because he thought it would be the greatest tragedy in his life if the Border Patrol ran Lucia out, but because this big-shot fed could so easily find out about her status—and his—and use it as a club.

"I understand what you're sayin,' Mr. Smith. I got no problem with keepin' secrets. I've always been a private man."

"Good. Then it's settled."

"Yep. When does the bear hunt begin?" Tracer said. T. L. Smith's head jerked sharply, and the Spanish woman seemed to have started. "It's got to be some kind of bear down there."

"What makes you think so?" Smith said. His eyes had narrowed slightly.

"Feller named Blood, Sam Blood, came by, said he was from one of the salt companies. That was just this morning. Showed me some hair. Bear hair for sure, but white. I reckon this Blood feller works for you people. I figure you got some kind of underground bear down there. Critters that live underground sometimes lose color. That's what I've been told."

Smith and the woman were silent. These big-shot city-bred feds, Tracer thought, they make a mistake thinking that everyone who lives out in the country, out on the land, is an ignorant rube.

Smith turned to the woman. "Where is Sam? Do you know?"

The woman's face, which was about the color of coffee with cream in it, seemed to get paler. She looked at her watch.

"He left about three hours ago. He didn't say where he was going."

Smith reddened. "Goddamn it, don't lie to me. Sam doesn't just go off without letting someone know where he's going. What did you two cook up while you were—?"

"He said he was going to save—to solve the problem himself," Anna Maria blurted out, and her face darkened, red creeping up her neck to her cheeks. Like some kind of chameleon, Tracer thought, taking note that these two—and that Blood feller—were all evidently working at cross-purposes. And that might give him, Tracer Dunn, an advantage somewhere down the road.

"Oh, Christ," T. L. Smith said, glaring at the Spanish woman as if he was going to attack her. "He's gone down on his own, the damn fool."

Tracer stood up and put his hat on his head.

"I reckon the bear hunt'd best start right now," he said.

TWENTY

At a table near the bar at Ma's, Jack Whittaker and Cassie Roberts were about halfway through their bottles of a golden-colored Mexican beer called Corona. Outside, the sun still shone brightly, casting long, late-afternoon shadows in the street. Inside, it was cool, the light dim, coming mostly from red glass bracket lights here and there on the walls. Ma's—the Stand Pipe Saloon—was windowless.

"Okay," Cassie said. "I'll tell you. What difference does it make now anyway? The shrink helped me understand why we didn't work out. It was because we were the wrong people for each other. I can't take uncertainty, surprises. And you thrive on that kind of thing."

"You paid this guy to tell you that?" Jack said.

"No, no, he helped me understand why I was like that. Why I tend to pull back from people, from—well—relationships."

"Why?"

"Remember me telling you about my grandmother? My mother's mother. I adored her. And I told you how hard it was for me when she died when her little sailboat capsized in the bay?"

"Yeah, I remember."

Cassie looked straight ahead, her eyes focusing on some other place and time. The words began to pour forth.

"Well, I never told you the whole story. I was never even able to think about what really happened. I was there. On the boat. I was ten. The boom smacked my grandmother on the head when the boat went over. Knocked her out. She just sank. And I couldn't find her. I dove down and dove down, but the water was all dark. Green and murky. I couldn't find her. Between dives I was calling for help, but there was no one. Finally I swam to the shore and ran home, crying so hard, I could barely see. It was in the late afternoon, and my father was already drunk. He began yelling at me, how it was my fault she had drowned . . ."

"Shit. What a—"

"I must have believed him. I couldn't ever think about it without thinking that somehow it had been my fault. It put the really private part of me into a shell. I couldn't even tell you about it when we . . . when you were my husband. The shrink said that losing someone like that and taking the blame—well, it just made me fearful. Fearful of a lot of things, needing someone to lean on, to trust. I mean, I'd killed the only person I ever had really trusted and loved, see what I mean? I was always looking for someone to take care of me. And you . . . Well, it didn't work. You weren't . . . And so I went back in my shell. I had to." She looked at him with eyes that glistened. "It's so sad."

"And I was always barging in on the shell?" Jack said.

"Something like that."

"As well as being unpredictable."

She nodded. They fell silent, each off in a private world, but they became aware of some loud voices at the bar. The regulars were getting revved up. Relieved to find a distraction from sad old events and sad memories, Cassie smiled and listened. It had been a long time since she had simply sat in a bar and listened to the locals talk nonsense.

"What I hear is one of them Sandia people was down in a new drift they was diggin' and the damn fool operator of one of the big machines, you know, with all the teeth on 'em, he hit an electrical cable and the Sandia guy was electrocuted. That's what I heard."

The man swigged his Bud Light long neck with an air of self-importance.

"Oh, sure, Ollie," said his neighbor on the next stool. "And his body just went up in smoke, cremated the sonofagun on the spot, so they buried his ashes right there in WIPP."

Laughter rippled down the bar. In all, five men in western shirts and jeans sat at the bar and one woman. She was dressed in an orange tank top, a pair of shiny black cowboy boots, and a pair of black Wrangler jeans that were at least one size too small, and she sat at the far end, where she had been talking quietly to Ma.

"What I heard," Ollie's neighbor said, "was that the guy from Sandia just got fed up and took off. Left work. Left town. Guy named Holmein."

"Nah," said a third man at the bar. "The Sandia guy was secretly a member of the Sierra Club, and when they found out, they transferred his ass to Russia to help those dumb commies at that Chernobyl place. Hell, if it was me, I'd let those Russkies fry."

The door to Ma's opened behind the men at the bar, and Derby Catlin came through it.

"Hey, Derby," said the man called Ollie. "Get your butt over here. We're gettin' the skinny on all the troubles over at WIPP."

"What troubles?" Derby said, walking toward the bar and peering at the table where Jack and Cassie sat. The editor raised his left eyebrow, then waved. Jack lifted two fingers and smiled.

"Well, hell, Derby," a man at the bar said, "they had two men disappear on 'em and right after that another guy, EPA inspector, had a stroke down there and died in the hospital."

One of Ma's sons uncapped a cold bottle of Bud Light and put it down on the bar in a space between the men and the woman in the orange tank top. Derby hoisted himself onto the bar stool and grasped the bottle. "Mysterious doings," he said. "Very mysterious."

He recognized the woman in orange and black but couldn't remember her name. He had seen her from time to time here at Ma's. She'd always been with a guy who looked ten years younger than her. But now she was alone, packed tight in her tank top and black jeans that looked like they'd split at the seams if she squeaked. Must be out looking, Derby decided. Well, don't look any further, darlin,' he said to himself. She had mouse-colored hair that she wore short, curling slightly behind small ears, and a wide mouth in a face that was just a tad long. Her nipples made little bumps in her shirt, and Derby thought, Oh, my, oh, my.

She turned and caught him looking at her.

"Hi, there," he said with a friendly smile. He put out his hand. "I'm Derby Catlin. You're almost a regular here, huh?"

She shook his hand briefly. "You do the little newspaper. Oops. I mean . . ."

Derby laughed cheerfully. "Good things come in little packages is what I always say. And you?"

"I'm Marjory Blenhem. I work at the hospital. I'm a nurse."

Derby noticed that she was drinking bourbon on the rocks. He called Ma's son over and told him to give his Bud Light to one of the other guys. He would prefer to have a bourbon on the rocks, like his friend Marjory. He was thinking it wouldn't do any harm to have a source in the hospital, even if it never amounted to more than that.

At their table, Jack leaned over and whispered, "Watch this. Pickup in process."

"I'll bet you the next round that she touches him first," Cassie said.

Derby bent closer to the nurse and laid on what he thought of as the full Derby Catlin charm. They chatted and drank, and ordered two more bourbons, and chatted some more, turning on the stools to face each other more directly while the other patrons at the bar continued to speculate about WIPP. She laughed easily and often, and their eyes held each other. In response to some whispered item, she threw back her head and laughed loudly, and put her hand for a brief interval on Derby Catlin's forearm.

Jack Whittaker signaled Ma's son behind the bar, holding up two fingers, and then dug out his wallet.

"How'd you know that would happen?" he asked.

"Science. They've watched people at singles bars, and people do the same thing as chimpanzees. The females are the real aggressors. Subtler, but they're the ones that really get things going. A lot of eye contact and soft voices, and then the female touches the male."

"And then?"

"Then the male gets his swagger going. Watch."

Ma's son put the third round of bourbons in front of Derby and his conquest, and he turned his head to listen to Ollie, who was now braying about the fact that the new tunnel they were digging had been shut down, off-limits, for three days. Now, wasn't that just strange as hell?

And Derby smiled and said, "You boys want to know something really strange at WIPP? Something there's an unimpeachable witness to instead of all this speculation and rumormongering you're doing?"

"Who's the witness?"

"Me," he said, taking a healthy swallow of his bourbon. "Guess who I saw driving into the WIPP plant this afternoon? In a government vehicle. Driven by that guy O'Connor, the security man."

"John Wayne, back from the dead."

"Geronimo."

"Derby, we don't want to play no guessing games with you. Who?"

"Tracer Dunn," Derby said. He turned back to Marjory and said, "You know him?"

She shook her head.

"He's a rancher out near WIPP. Used to be a professional mountain lion hunter over in Arizona. Nobody in Eddy County hates the feds more than Tracer Dunn. So," he said, turning triumphantly back to the men, "what the hell would bring Tracer Dunn to WIPP?" He paused. "Carrying a rifle."

The men at the bar were silent. This was real, this was major news. But what did it mean? Marjory Blenhem took a belt from her glass and looked at Derby with her eyes gleaming with admiration. She had her hand firmly on his forearm.

"What do they need a hunter for in WIPP?" Derby said. "Place is as dead as a tomb."

Marjory, feeling the thrill of being part of something like a conspiracy and feeling warm and loose from six ounces of bourbon already consumed, said, "I know."

All heads at the bar swiveled toward her.

"The guy with the stroke," she said. "He didn't die at the hospital. He's still there. He began muttering about a bear. A big bear.

And it wasn't a stroke. The doctors say it was some kind of shock. And he started coming to, talking about a bear."

At their table, Jack and Cassie stared at each other, eyebrows raised. They heard Ollie laugh loudly, a braying sound.

"A bear?" he said in a loud voice. "Now that's just about the wildest damn notion I ever heard. How the hell could a bear get down there? It's half a damn mile down."

"Yeah, that don't make no sense at all."

"A bear. Shee-it."

The men at the bar began to laugh, and Marjory stiffened. Derby leaned toward her and whispered something in her ear. She squeezed his arm and let go. He put his arm around her back, and she relaxed.

At their table near the bar, Jack Whittaker said, "Holy shit. Did you hear that?"

Cassie nodded.

"Let's get out of here," Jack said. "Go someplace where we can think, talk." He put six one-dollar bills on the table, added two more, and stood up.

Long before they reached S10249, they heard the high-pitched whine, a steady, piercing sound.

"What the hell is that?" T. L. Smith demanded. He had exchanged his dark suit for a set of white overalls. Helmetless, he held his Walther in his left hand. Chuck O'Connor was leading the way, armed with a twenty-gauge shotgun and wearing the regulation overalls and a hard hat. Tracer Dunn, a head taller than the other two, walked unhurriedly behind them in denim shirt and jeans, his Winchester grasped firmly in one large hand.

"Only one thing it could be," O'Connor said, and was interrupted by Tracer Dunn.

"Something's dead down here, rotten," the rancher said. "Smell it? Like rotten eggs."

"Christ," T. L. Smith said.

"Someone, I guess your man, turned on the mining machine," O'Connor said.

"Why do that?"

"Maybe we'll ask him," O'Connor said.

They moved on down the poorly lit corridor, Tracer's eyes devouring the look of the place, the details, the fencing on the ceiling, the cables strung along the walls, the occasional sensor. It was the worst place he'd ever been, he concluded. Not even his days as a miner had ever led him into such a godforsaken, tomblike place. The whine grew louder and the rotten smell stronger as they continued down the tunnel.

"What *is* that smell?" Tracer asked. "Sulfur?"

"If it's sulfur," O'Connor said, "we got a disaster on our hands. And we won't want to spend a whole lot of time down here. Here. This is the one." The men stopped and looked down the tunnel that opened off to their right. It looked like every other tunnel. O'Connor shone a powerful flashlight down it, but its end still wasn't visible. The whine now filled the cavern and pained their ears.

"Well, I reckon I'll have a look," Tracer said. "One of you fellers might want to stay back a ways, cover our rear." He set off down the tunnel.

"What do you mean, a disaster?" T. L. Smith asked.

"If sulfur in some form, like gas or whatever, is in here, it's coming from outside," O'Connor said. "It means the salt is breached. It means the plant is kaput. The whole damn plant."

T. L. Smith turned to follow the rancher. For once in his career, he didn't have anything to say.

Aboveground, in the room outside her office, Anna Maria anxiously watched the console, the little green lights marking the progress of the hunters through the underground tunnels. They had reached S10249. She was unable to shake the iron blanket of despair that had settled over her again. Nothing good was going to come of all this. Of that she was certain.

Tracer Dunn walked toward the screaming machine, the whirling cylinder held on huge metal arms, thrust out toward the end of the tunnel. It was immense, this machine, bigger than he had been prepared for by seeing it in the photograph up above. It seemed to quiver with the violence of its spinning. Whoever ran these things either wore earplugs or was stone deaf. It hurt his ears. As he drew within fifteen feet of it, in the dim light that came from behind him, he saw the dark stains on the floor and on the machine itself. He stopped and stared and listened but could hear nothing but the shriek of the machine. He couldn't think with all that damn shrieking.

He ran the final five yards to the machine, set his Winchester down, and climbed up into the operator's housing. He peered at the levers and controls and, dimly, he made out a bunch of keys hanging. The ignition. He turned the key, and the shriek immediately began to subside, turning to a loud whir, and then to a hum, and then there was silence.

Tracer climbed down and found T. L. Smith standing near the rear of the machine, hands hanging down at this sides, the mean-looking pistol held loosely in his hand.

"Shit," Smith said. "Sam." The man was stunned.

Tracer eyed the blood spattered on the machine and on the ground at his feet. He had Sam's blood on his shirt, his jeans, his hand. Off to the right, on the ground near the base of the machine, was a small Colt .45. He picked it up, sniffed it, and removed the clip. He wasn't familiar with this type of weapon—never had used sidearms—but it appeared that it had been fired. He moved toward the front of the machine and saw the rifle on the floor, a match for his own. The sulfuric stench, mixed with the smell of blood, was making him nauseous, and his eyes were stinging. He couldn't believe what he was now seeing.

"Mr. Smith," he said quietly. "I think maybe you better come over here."

Smith stepped over and stood beside Tracer Dunn, his head down, bowed. He looked at the smear of blood on the floor, stretching from the side of the machine to the crumbling wall of salt, and—

"Oh, God! Oh, Jesus!"

T. L. Smith saw the hand, the wrist, extending out of the red-stained salt. The bloody fingers were curled almost into a fist. Thick blond hairs covered the wrist.

"No, no, this can't be," T. L. Smith said, his voice almost a whisper. "This can't be."

He reached out with his right hand and grasped the wrist of his onetime assistant.

Still holding it, he turned to face Tracer Dunn and said, "This can't be."

Tracer backed away in horror as the forearm appeared, emerging from the bloody salt, then the elbow, the bicep, and then the end—the shoulder—torn off, a ragged mass of congealed blood, tendons, and flesh. Smith stood, eyes wide and unseeing, holding Sam Blood's arm by the wrist. It dangled down, the smashed and bloody shoulder touching the floor.

"Mother of God!"

It was O'Connor. Tracer spun and saw the ex-marine's eyes go wide. He had come around the edge of the mining machine and stood, transfixed. Staring. Staring not at the arm T. L. Smith held dangling by his side, but over Smith's head.

"It's moving!" O'Connor shouted. "The fucking place is caving in!"

Tracer Dunn turned back to the wall of salt and saw it sway and belly out like a sail, salt crumbling and falling in large chunks. The stench of sulfur was overwhelming. He backed away, bumping into O'Connor, who lunged forward, passed him, and grabbed the still stunned T. L. Smith by the collar.

"Move! Move!" O'Connor shouted. "Drop that and move, goddammit!"

He pulled Smith away from the wall as more salt crumbled and fell. Tracer Dunn backed away and saw a huge white paw with long black claws reach out from the cascading salt, then another, and the snout full of fangs, and the end of the tunnel was suddenly filled with the enormous bear lunging out from the salt, shattering the world with a horrific roar that shook Tracer like a gale wind. The gigantic animal was standing on its hind legs, its enormous mouth agape, roaring, red eyes burning. It towered above them, bellowing in its ferocity, and Tracer saw O'Connor drop back and lift his shotgun as the bear struck out with its paw, a huge roundhouse blow.

A fountain of blood erupted as T. L. Smith's body was thrown to the side, his head hitting the mining machine's dragon-toothed cylinder with a sickening clunk. Impaled on its metal teeth, he hung there for an instant, then slipped off and fell to the ground, blood gushing from his head and his torn, ragged neck as O'Connor's shotgun exploded and a large round patch of red mushroomed in the white fur of the giant's chest.

The bear screamed and lashed out at O'Connor with its claws. Tracer leveled his Winchester at the bear, and his foot went out from under him, sliding in the blood, and as he fell he saw O'Connor duck away, turning—and he saw that part of the man's cheek had been torn away, a bloody flap of skin hanging from his jaw, teeth showing like a skull. The bear screamed and roared, and behind it, above it, the top of the tunnel caved in, salt cascading down around the beast. O'Connor scrambled away, and Tracer scrabbled to his feet and began to run. The ground shook under him as more of the ceiling gave way and he ran, hearing the tunnel collapsing behind him with a deafening crash, a continuing roar that replaced the outraged roaring of the bear.

Tracer looked back over his shoulder—the mining machine, the bear, all were gone, buried, as the tunnel continued falling in, countless tons of salt collapsing, raining down, and O'Connor was stumbling toward him just ahead of the thundering moving cataract of salt, his mouth a huge gash extending to his ear, shouting:

"Go! Go!"

More salt fell, and O'Connor disappeared under the avalanche.

Around Tracer Dunn, behind him, the tunnel was imploding, water now too, water gushing from the ceiling. He ran. Above him, the chain-link fencing bolted to the ceiling sagged and began to give way with a metallic screeching. More salt crashed down, and the dim yellow lights up ahead winked out. Cables snapped, sparks showering, electricity crackling around him like blue lightning— now the only source of illumination in the dark.

Tracer Dunn ran, his chest bursting with pain.

PART THREE

TWENTY-ONE

The lights went off for only a moment before the plant's emergency generators kicked in and power was restored to the offices aboveground, the air filtration system, and the elevators. But even before the thirty-second interval of darkness ended at seven-twelve and a siron bogan wailing, Anna Maria Gonzales, alone in the room outside her office, knew that something catastrophic had happened, something fatal. In a premonitory flash, she understood that the twenty-year-long effort called the Waste Isolation Pilot Project might well be over.

Five billion dollars down the drain. A million and a half manhours without a day missed from accidents, and now . . .

On her watch.

She picked up the phone and punched the emergency number. Albert Yazzie, duty man in the Mine Safety Department, answered.

"Yazzie here."

"This is the director. What the hell happened?"

"I'm on my way down."

"There are men down there, four. A special inspection. Use the waste shaft elevator. The other is already down below."

"Roger."

Anna Maria hung up and made three other calls, summoning the WIPP management team from Carlsbad and informing the duty officer in the energy secretary's office in Washington, D.C., that there was a code red at WIPP; details would follow. Ten minutes passed, seemingly an eternity, and the radio's red light went on. She flicked on the machine before it got a chance to buzz.

"Yes," she said.

"It's real bad. Real bad. That drift, S10249? It's gone. Caved in."

"Oh, God."

"Yeah, all but the first hundred, hundred and fifty feet. The fencing is down, just a wall of salt down here. And there's a real bad smell."

"Do you have a mask? A gas mask?"

"No."

"Damn! You better come up."

"Well, ma'am, see . . ."

"What, what?"

"There's water leaking down. From the ceiling, it looks like."

"Water? Oh, my God. What about the men down there?"

"I don't see nobody. I didn't see nobody. But I came straight here from the waste shaft."

"They were there, in that drift. At the end. Oh, God almighty. Yazzie, get out of there. Now. Come up." She clicked off the radio as the phone rang. She snatched it to her ear.

"Gonzales."

"This is Secretary Engels. What—"

"We're breached, sir. A drift has collapsed. One of the new ones. Water is seeping."

"Good Christ! This is . . . this is a catastrophe! Can it be sealed off?"

"I don't know, sir. There is apparently some water. We may be totally compromised. And I'm afraid we've lost some personnel."

"Oh no. How many?"

"I don't know for sure yet. It could be as many as four."

"Is Smith still there?"

"He may be one of the missing, sir."

"Jesus. Get the Sandia people down there. I'll send . . . Oh, hell, I'll be there in the morning. God, think of the damned investigations we'll have over this."

The secretary hung up. Anna Maria put the phone down and looked up to see the hunter, Tracer Dunn, standing in the doorway. A yellow pallor underlay his tanned face. His jeans and his shirt were smeared with blood. She stood up and took three steps toward him.

"Are you . . . ?" she began. She was trembling.

"I'm okay. The others," Dunn said, "the tunnel caved in on 'em. Smith and O'Connor."

"And the other man, Sam Blood? Did you find him?"

"Well, yes, ma'am. We did." He paused and looked down at his feet. "He was pretty badly chewed up."

Anna Maria felt like she might throw up. "Oh, God. The animal? Did you . . . ?"

"No, ma'am. I don't know how it happened, but it looked to me like that feller got himself tangled up with that big machine. Like that one," he said, pointing to the photograph over the couch. Anna Maria watched the man's nearly colorless eyes, her attempt at a truth check, but the eyes were as expressionless as the rest of his face. "The machine was runnin' when we got there."

Anna Maria had the sense that this gaunt old rancher was lying. About something. And the thought crossed her mind that it might be a useful lie.

"You better sit down, Mr. Dunn, and give me the details of what happened down there."

"I don't understand," Cassie Roberts said. "How could one of them get from that cavern into WIPP? It's almost a half mile down to those tunnels in the salt and miles—how many?—between the two."

They were seated on the steps to Cassie's front porch. Leaving Ma's, they had stopped at Estella's for takeout green chili stew, and the empty plastic containers and the white plastic spoons were now on the bottom step. Dusk had filled the quiet residential street as they ate, the western sky staying pink until quite suddenly it was night. Behind them, a few moths were harassing the screen door, trying to reach the light inside the house. The sound of traffic from

215

Canal Street was diminishing, Carlsbad going to bed. The temperature had dropped ten degrees in a half hour—down into the mid-eighties—and a light breeze had begun to blow from the west. It made a quiet rustling sound in the huge old trees that had lined the street since the turn of the century.

Jack was leaning back on his elbows, holding a half-full bottle of Negro Modela beer in his hand. On the top step, her knees drawn up, Cassie leaned forward. "Maybe," she said, "that guy in the hospital was just having hallucinations or bad dreams or something."

"In other words, if it isn't theoretically possible, it didn't happen. Right?"

"Right. I don't see any sense in speculating about what's going on if nothing *is* going on."

"Don't you think it'd be a hell of big coincidence, us finding that a bear of some kind is living in a cavern over there, and a few miles away, a guy in WIPP has a stroke and wakes up talking about a bear?"

"No," Cassie said. "Bears are big, scary animals. And they're part of everybody's tribal memory. Their mental landscape. Even little kids in cities hear about them, you know, 'Goldilocks and the Three Bears.' Lots of people have dreams about bears."

Jack shook his head. "You scientists never have any fun. Okay, try this." He sat up, took a drink of beer, and put the bottle on the step beside him. "You remember I asked you if you smelled something funny down in the cavern? I've smelled something like rotten eggs down there. Especially near that pool where we found the footprint. Just a whiff, you know? I think that's the answer.

"They've got a cave down in Mexico that's still actively happening. Growing. It's a sulfur cave. Apparently hydrogen sulfide is leaking sideways through the earth from some oil fields about fifty miles away, and when it hits limestone—like our reef—where there's water, it turns to sulfuric acid and eats away at the rock. And they've found that the place is full of bacteria, like the ones in the oceans that live in those hot vents. The bacteria live on sulfur, and they make more sulfuric acid. They live right in the rocks, like part of the rocks, turning them mushy. They call those formations snotites."

"That's disgusting." She shuddered.

"Yeah. Well, there are bugs, like flies or whatever, that live on the bacteria, and fish that live on the bugs. I mean, lots of fish, zillions. So suppose we've got one of those caverns happening here too. The hydrogen sulfide is leaking in from all the old oil fields around here, and it's been eating out a cavern between WIPP in the salt beds and our cavern in the reef. It's been getting more and more concentrated, going faster. I mean I'm talking a long, long time here. Faster is a relative term. First the sulfur cave breeches our cavern a long time ago, maybe ten thousand years ago, more than that. Then suppose all that stuff—the bacteria, the bugs, fish—gets in down there. I don't know how they get there, but they do. And the bears have been eating the fish all these years, along with bison and now some cows. Suddenly, like only yesterday, people are digging what amounts to another cavern—the WIPP plant—and it gets closer and closer to where there's all this sulfuric acid. Then suddenly the acid breaches into the salt, starts destroying it. One of the bears finds its way through all that crap into WIPP and voilà, a new food source: DOE employees. See how that works?" Jack smiled happily. It made perfectly good sense to him.

Cassie sat quietly for a minute. She had changed into a pair of cutoff blue jean shorts, running shoes, and a large and loose-fitting black T-shirt. Her hair was down, hanging beside her face. Jack watched her, hunched over, and he admired her legs, long and smooth, visible in the light from inside the house. Each knee still bore the scabs from their trip into the cavern. He could also make out her eyebrows, pinched together, skeptical, pondering what he had just said. Sitting in judgment, he thought with a flickering of an old but still familiar sense of irritation. He finished off his beer.

"Yeah, I guess," she said finally.

"Well, thanks."

She glanced over at him. "Hey, don't get huffy. I'm just thinking about it. And I think it could work. Okay?"

"Yeah, okay. Can I get another beer?"

She stood up. "I'll get it." She went into the house, the screen door slamming lightly behind her.

She doesn't want me in her house, Jack thought. Keep the tradesmen out of the house. Shit. Then he thought, Why am I getting so edgy?

She returned with two beers, handed one to Jack, and settled down on the upper step again.

"Okay," she said. "So one of the short-faced bears in the cavern has been getting into WIPP, scaring a guy half to death—"

"And eating another."

"—and the WIPP people find the hairs," she continued, "and somehow put two and two together, and they bring in this hunter. Obviously to kill the bear. Probably DOE wanted to keep it all quiet, the way they do everything." She paused, sipping her beer. "Because if a bear can get in, so can other stuff."

"Like sulfuric acid, water, and—"

"And radioactive wastes can get out, and that's the end of WIPP."

They were silent for a moment. Each had lived through years of the noisy controversy over WIPP. Large and powerful national citizens' groups had warred with the government. Senators and governors and presidents had all gotten involved, along with several gigantic corporations, the whole nuclear industry. Now the whole thing, billions of dollars and millions of man-hours, could be brought crashing down by the totally unpredictable presence of a relict population of Ice Age bears.

"Jesus," Jack said. "Think of it. They couldn't keep that kind of thing secret."

"Who knows? They could try."

"You mean that members of the holy brotherhood and sisterhood of science would allow that?" Jack said, realizing that he shouldn't have said it. "That was a joke."

"No, it wasn't. It's just ignorant cynicism."

They had been in this place before, but Jack went on anyway. "It isn't ignorant cynicism to point out that it was scientists who got us on this nuclear roller coaster in the first place. Gonna make electricity too cheap to meter. Sure. And oh, sorry, friends, we forgot about all the radioactive waste. Drat."

"I don't want to have this discussion with you, Jack." Cassie's voice was calm, measured, and as cold as ice. They sat silently on the steps, each in a separate cubicle, the walls raised instantly, walls made of old habits, old angers, old failures. At length Cassie stood up and said, "We have a practical problem to deal with."

"What's that?"

"If this guy Tracer Dunn is down in WIPP killing one of the bears, there's no reason why he won't go down into the cavern and kill the others. If he wasn't thinking about that before, he must be now. Shoot, shovel, and shut up. All those old ranchers think that way. So he kills the rest, and then he's free to do whatever he wants with the damn cave. We have no leverage."

"Unless we stop him," Jack said.

"How would we do that? It's on his property."

Jack shrugged. He thought again of a convenient cave accident. Easy to arrange. Then he decided that wasn't thinkable. He took a long swallow of beer.

Cassie sat down again, resuming her seat on the upper step. A police cruiser rolled slowly along the street and stopped at the stop sign. The cop looked through the window long and pointedly at them, and Jack wondered if the cop had read his shameful thoughts. Then he drove off.

"There is a way we can stop him," Cassie said. "Only one." Her voice was quiet, almost a monotone. The night was now still, the breeze gone. The temperature had dropped another few degrees.

"How?" Jack asked, knowing he wouldn't like the answer.

"I'm going to talk to the people at Fish and Wildlife."

"Goddamn it, Cassie—" Jack leapt to his feet and turned to face her.

"It's the only way to ensure—"

"You think *you* are gonna just unilaterally decide what to do about this? Where do you get off thinking you can do that? *I* discovered the cave, *I* discovered the footprint, *I* was the one who—"

Cassie's entire body went taut, like she was tensing for a blow. Or tensing to deliver one.

"You know," Jack said. "Up there on your high horse, you might consider this. What if I agree with Dunn?"

"Do you?"

"If it wasn't for those goddamn bears, I might . . ."

"Get rich?" Cassie said. "At the expense of a living species that's managed to survive in hiding for ten thousand years? You'd put your pathetic little dream of money, of ripping off a bunch of ignorant tourists, you'd put that ahead of them? Living things. One of the most important scientific discoveries of the century. Jesus, Jack, you're no better than that creepy old rancher. Worse! I can't believe I ever—"

"Ever what? Shared a bed with me?"

"Ever thought you were a decent, whole person."

"Oh, bullshit."

Cassie stood up. "Anyway, I am going to Fish and Wildlife. Tomorrow." She turned toward her front door.

"They won't believe you. You're wasting your time."

"I'm a scientist, Jack. They'll believe me. I'll give them more evidence. They'll shut the place down. You and Tracer Dunn can go pull some other con. Partners in sleaze."

Jack spun around, looked at the street, and spun to face his ex-wife. "Great! Great! This is all the thanks I get. You hard-assed, holier-than-thou . . ."

"Bitch?"

"You said it, Cassie. You said it." He put the beer bottle, half empty, down on the step, turned, and stormed down the path to the street. He heard the screen door slam lightly and bounce against the doorjamb.

"No, no," he said, and waved his hand back and forth at the proffered Bud Light. "Bourbon. Rocks." As Jack took a position on a bar stool, Ma's son put the brown bottle back in the cooler, plucked a glass from a rack above his head, scooped some ice into it from the other cooler, sloshed two jiggers plus of Evan Williams bourbon into the ice, and set the drink on the bar in front of Jack. Some woman with an adenoid problem was singing a song about love, lies, and New Orleans on the sound track.

"Four dollars," the bartender said.

"Very generous," Jack said, fishing a twenty-dollar bill out of his wallet. He placed it on the bar, and Ma's son waddled off to the other end of the bar. Jack took a long pull at the bourbon, swallowed, and shuddered.

That's it, he said to himself. That's it. She's a holier-than-thou bitch. Always was. He took another drink from the glass. All that BS about her private self needing to hide in a shell. My God. And now the holier-than-thou bitch has totally bitched up my cave. My discovery. My plan.

My dream.

He finished off the bourbon and put the glass down with a loud clack. Ma's son began waddling over, and the man to Jack's left looked at him from under a straw cowboy hat. It was the man called Ollie, still here from earlier.

"You're that caver feller," Ollie said.

"Right." Ma's son took the glass away and began to fix another.

"I'm Ollie. You was in here before, weren't you?" Ollie's face was a deep red, and his eyelids had drooped half closed.

"Yeah." Jack picked up his new drink and took a swallow.

"That was a mighty fine-lookin' woman you was with. What we used to call a classy piece of ass. Till the women's libbers got all up in arms."

"That was no piece of ass," Jack said. He took another swallow, and he was beginning to feel the heat in his stomach and the buzz in his brain. "That was my ex-wife."

"Oh, man," Ollie said. "That's why you're settin' out to drunk, ain't it? Exes do that to a man."

"Ollie? That's your name? Ollie, I don't want to talk to you. I'm busy, see?" He tapped his forehead with his forefinger. "Leave me alone."

"Well, shee-it," Ollie said, sliding off his stool and heaving himself unsteadily onto the stool beyond. He leaned over toward the man next to him and pointed at Jack with a thumb. "Antisocial sumbitch. Put a piece of coal up his ass and in two weeks you'd have a diamond."

Jack thought about his cave. Sure, his. That beautiful chamber with the helictites like chandeliers. Cassie's Ballroom, that's what he was going to call it.

I wouldn't name a toilet after that woman. Or maybe I will. Serve her right.

Well, that's all down the tubes now. Flushed. Flushed by Fish and Wildlife and flushed by Dr. Cassandra Bitch Roberts, wouldn't even change her name to mine—oh, it's a professional name, right. La-de-da. Professional pain in the ass.

Jack finished off his second bourbon and signaled for a third. From her perch at the far end of the bar, Ma looked closely at him for a moment, but he didn't notice. Her son set the drink down in front of him and took the empty glass away.

Greatest caver in the United States, Jack was saying to himself. Rescue expert. Fuckin' hero. Found the cavern of caverns, the dream of a lifetime. And what've I got? A trailer to live in, about four hundred dollars in the bank, and an ex-fucking wife who's sold me right down the goddamn river in the name of science, the purity of science. All the goddamn scientists in New Mexico never found that cave, but I did. Now it's flushed. How many times in a lifetime do you find a cave like that?

Shortly afterward, when Jack had finished his third bourbon, he put his head down on the bar. He was unaware of the arms that lifted him off the stool and carried him out to the parking lot. He was unaware of the hands expertly fishing his keys out of his pocket and placing him on the backseat of his Trooper. And he was, therefore, of course unaware of the state trooper who arrived at Ma's a half hour later when his shift was over.

He brought the news to those regulars at Ma's who were still capable of listening that a major cave-in had occurred at the WIPP site. A catastrophe. Three people dead, buried in the salt . . . Yessirree bob, the shit has really hit the fan. . . . Yeah, I understand they're flyin' some DOE big shots in from D.C. to do a damage assessment. . . . They might have to close the place. . . . Well, there goes the Carlsbad economy. . . .

TWENTY-TWO

Cassie Roberts was up by seven in the morning. She had a slight headache that had accompanied her through the night. The argument with Jack had haunted her sleep and gave her a grubby feeling that even a long, hot shower couldn't wash away. Those arguments—they had always come on like that, out of nowhere, sudden, like electrical storms. One minute they'd be talking like normal people and then—bam!—they were yelling at each other, digging in the knives, savaging each other from some raging, despairing core.

Well, no more. There was no longer any imaginable need for them to ever see each other again. Cassie was going to call in the feds, and they would close down that cavern and that would be an end to it. Or the beginning of something wonderful in science. And Jack? What would he do?

She didn't give a damn. He was completely unprincipled.

Hard-assed? Holier-than-thou? That had hurt. He knew how to hurt her, always had. Why did people hurt each other like that?

She tried to put it all out of mind. She had work to do. But the epithets, the argument, the sound of their voices, hard-edged, flat with anger—it haunted her still, like something lurking on the periphery of her vision.

First she would call Ferrell O'Hara, the feathers and fur expert. Get confirmation that the whitish hairs were from a bear of an unknown species. Then call Fish and Wildlife.

She got dressed—in jeans, running shoes, and a loose-fitting pink shirt—ate a bowl of cold cereal and drank a glass of orange juice that seemed to curdle the milk in her stomach, and set off to the museum, feeling a bit nauseous. But free. Free of uncertainty. She knew what she needed to do about this bear thing and knew she could then get back to her own work.

She remembered that Ferrell O'Hara tended to be something of an early bird, so at five after eight, she dialed his number at the Museum of Natural History in Albuquerque. It rang five times, and she despaired, but then O'Hara picked up.

"O'Hara."

"Ferrell, this is Cassie Roberts."

"Hey, good morning, Cassie. How ya doing? What's up?"

"I FedExed you a package yesterday. You should have it this morning."

"A package from you? I don't do bones, remember? Of course, I'd be happy to do your bones—as in jump them."

"Har-har. Ferrell the smooth talker. Look, it's some hair, mammal hair, and I think it's real important. Like a major thing. Do you think—?"

"Shit, Cassie. I'm out of business here."

Her heart sinking, Cassie asked, "What do you mean?"

"My fifty-thousand-dollar equipment, made in Germany and paid for by the FAA and the National Science Foundation, is down. Kaput. The Krauts are sending a man. Evidently no one except their man knows how to put Humpty-Dumpty together again. It'll be a week anyway."

"Damn."

"That's one of the things I said."

"Look, Ferrell. What I sent is what we think is bear hairs. Whitish hairs."

"Polar bear? What are you doing with polar bears?"

"That's the point. We don't think it is a polar bear."

"I never heard of an albino bear. What's going on, Cassie?"

"We think it might be something new."

"Come on."

"I was hoping you could confirm that it is a bear but not any known species."

"Wow. Well, as I say, in a week. I'll eyeball 'em for you, but that's not what I'd call confirmation."

"That'd be great, Ferrell. Thanks."

"And then maybe you'll tell me what the hell this is really all about."

"I'll try. Bye, Ferrell."

Cassie hung up the phone and bowed her head in a moment of despair. Damn! A week! Well, she'd just have to go with what she had, which wasn't much. A photograph of a footprint. And her own account of a human femur recently gnawed. And, as Jack had said what seemed months ago when they emerged from the cavern, both bits of "evidence" arose from a place where she had been trespassing. But . . . she was a respected scientist, and that carried some weight. And, she also supposed, the Fish and Wildlife people were probably accustomed to a bit of the clandestine.

She left her office and walked down to the reception area, where Martha kept a pot of good Costa Rican coffee going for most of the morning.

Martha, a short, round widow of about fifty and a full-time volunteer at the museum, was just bustling through the front entrance.

"Cassie," she said, clearly excited. "Did you hear?"

"Hear what?"

"About the cave-in? Last night. At WIPP. One of the tunnels caved in. Apparently three DOE people were down there when it happened. They were buried alive. In all that salt. Isn't that horrible?"

"Good God," Cassie said. "That's awful. Where did you—?"

"It was on the TV this morning. I, uh, I watch it while I'm eating breakfast. It breaks the silence."

"It was DOE people?" Cassie asked.

Martha looked puzzled. "Yes. They said it was two people from Washington and one local man, I forget the name, but he was chief of security at the plant. An Irish name, I think. Why?"

"How horrible," Cassie said.

Martha busied herself with the coffeepot. "And they had a man on from that group in Santa Fe, the one that's always been fighting WIPP? He was positively *gloating,* saying it proved his point, that WIPP should be closed and all. Imagine, playing politics with a tragedy like that. I mean, within hours. . . . Some people!"

Ten minutes later, Cassie returned to her office with a mug of Costa Rican coffee, wondering if she could confirm what Martha had said—that it was three DOE people in the cave-in. And not Tracer Dunn, who was down there last night with a rifle, according to that little editor, Derby Catlin, in the bar last night.

Maybe Catlin could confirm it. He was sort of a newsman. She looked up his number in the phone book and dialed it. It rang four times, and a voice came on: "This is Derby Catlin's number and that of *The Intelligencer.* Please leave a message at the beep, and I'll get back to you as—"

Cassie hung up.

She needed to sit quietly and think it out as coldly and calmly as possible. The report was that it was DOE people, but if Tracer Dunn was in fact one of the men in the cave-in and was dead, then obviously the bears in the cavern were safe. For now. But someone would buy the ranch at some point, so they weren't safe in the long run. But at least she could wait a week for Ferrell O'Hara's report. Then again, if the news reports were true—and probably DOE wouldn't try to cover up the death of a local rancher in their plant—then the bears were in imminent danger.

And that meant she'd have to call Fish and Wildlife right away. There was no point in waiting even until later this morning to hear from Ferrell's eyeball analysis—because, she realized, she couldn't honestly say where those hairs had come from. They could, for all she knew, be from some antelope skin from Africa, used as a covering for a footstool. Or whatever.

From her desk, she fished out a directory of state and federal government offices and found the number for the director of the New Mexico Ecological Services Office in Albuquerque. Of the twenty-odd offices listed under Fish and Wildlife, that sounded like the one concerned with endangered species. She dialed the number, thinking that this was going to be complicated. Would she be dealing with a scientist-administrator or just a bureaucrat?

She dialed the number and a woman answered, a cheerful young woman who listened as Cassie identified herself as a biologist at the Carlsbad Museum who needed to speak to the director about a new and certainly endangered species that had come to her attention. She was put on hold and drummed her fingers in irritation as she waited for almost an entire minute.

The cheerful young woman returned, explaining that the director (it was a woman with a double last name and no "Doctor" in front, so probably not a scientist) was not available, but an assistant would pick up the phone in just a moment. A Mr. Flowers. Again Cassie drummed her fingers on the desk.

"Hi, this is Jim Flowers. What can I do to help you?"

"Mr. Flowers? I'm Dr. Cassandra Roberts at the Carlsbad Museum. I'm a biologist, a paleontologist, to be exact. I want to talk with someone about an endangered species—a new species—we've come across down here. I believe it urgently needs the attention of you people."

"You have my ear, Dr. Roberts."

"This is going to sound bizarre, so stay with me, please. I have a series of photographs that were made of a footprint. I have also seen this footprint. It's a bear. But it's larger than a grizzly footprint by half."

"Uh, okay. Where did you see this footprint?"

"In a cavern east of Carlsbad."

"In a cavern."

"Yes. A fresh footprint, down quite far in a cavern."

"Um, what cavern is that, Dr. Roberts?"

"It's one that's just been discovered. No one knows about it except for two or three people. And one of them, the owner of the land where the entrance is located—he is very likely to get rid of the animal. Animals."

"Oh, there's more than one?"

"Obviously. There has to be. That's sort of basic."

"And you've seen this one footprint."

227

"Yes, and I'd like to fax you a photograph of it."

"Well, that's fine. Of course. And what are you—um—suggesting should happen?"

"Mr. Flowers, I have what I, as a scientist, am satisfied is evidence of a hitherto unknown species of bear living in at least one cavern here in southern New Mexico. I know that sounds, well, as I said, bizarre. But it's there. And if its habitat is not protected immediately, I am quite confident that the owner of the property will exterminate it so that he can develop the cavern for commercial use. So I am suggesting that you, the Fish and Wildlife Service, send someone here and close down this cavern until a complete investigation has been made. . . . Mr. Flowers?"

"I'm afraid it's not that simple, Dr., uh, Roberts. There are certain procedures, documents. . . . We can't, I'm afraid, simply on the word of a citizen and on the basis of a photograph of a footprint . . . We can't on that basis intrude on private property or declare it potentially critical habitat. Also, it takes rather a long time to have a species declared threatened or endangered."

"But . . ."

"I mean, it would take a good deal of time, Dr. Roberts. By all means, fax us the photograph, and we'll take it from there."

"But there isn't time, don't you understand?"

"Yes, ma'am, I'm sure. But really we need more evidence than a photograph of a footprint that might have come from a given place even to demand entry to it. Anyone could fake a footprint, after all. You know, Bigfoot, and all that."

"Okay, okay. Thanks."

Cassie hung up and said, "Shit! The runaround."

She knew what she had to do, and it made her sick to think about it. She never wanted to see the inside of another cavern for the rest of her life.

"A *bear?* That's just preposterous! A bear a half mile down in a salt deposit?"

The secretary of energy, Lawrence F. Engels, was turning red. Dangerously red, Anna Maria thought.

"Insane," the secretary continued. "Had T. L. Smith lost his mind? Snapped? Good God."

The secretary had arrived three hours earlier with a small phalanx of assistants and the departmental director of external affairs—which is to say, a politically astute PR man. The secretary was still wearing the dinner jacket he'd had on when he first heard about the catastrophe, during the intermission after the second act of *La Bohème* playing in the plush red opera house at the Kennedy Center. Upon arrival, he listened intently to Anna Maria's assessment of the damage, asked a number of not wholly irrelevant questions of a semitechnical nature, and descended the elevator to observe the cave-in firsthand. One of the Sandia Laboratories engineers who had been flown in in the middle of the night explained that the acidic water that was visible as a slight trickle here and there on the edge of the massive volume of salt that had collapsed into the tunnel was surely the culprit. A wholly unforeseen leak from some unknown source that had not previously shown up on any seismic or other scans of the area. It was a relatively weak sulfuric acid solution but amply strong to wreak havoc with sodium chloride. If it wasn't stopped, sealed off somehow, more of the plant would be eroded. No, there was no current understanding of how to stop it, but a Sandia team was working on it, here and on the computer models in Albuquerque.

The secretary had stood silently for a long time only a few feet from the cave-in, as if in prayer. He was a large, florid man with graying hair, a balding head, and thick glasses. Now in his early sixties, he had been, until two years ago, a member of the Pennsylvania delegation to the U.S. House of Representatives and chairman of its committee on science and technology.

Now, in Anna Maria's office, the secretary asked again if the department's director of security, a man who would assume nearly omnipotent powers in the event of a terrorist attack on any nonmilitary nuclear installation, had lost his mind.

"T. L. Smith was a brave and brilliant man. I want to know what happened to him." He peered closely at Anna Maria. "You must be

229

exhausted, Ms. Gonzales. If we can talk for just a while longer, you can get some rest."

Earlier, Anna Maria had glanced at herself in the mirror in the ladies' room and was depressed to see how haggard she looked. Dark, almost black pouches hung below her eyes, beyond the aid of makeup. I'm a hag, she had thought, and looked away. Now she shifted in the chair she had brought up in front of the couch.

"We lost two men in that tunnel, sir. Last Monday. They disappeared, leaving only some blood. That's why Mr. Smith came out here, and of course he was, by regulation, in charge of the plant. He brought his forensic people out, and they discovered a few strange hairs down there. Mammal hairs. Then one of the forensic team, Mr. Fontaine, had a stroke of some sort, and he is still in the hospital in Carlsbad."

"'Troubles come not as single spies,'" the secretary said.

"Sir?"

"Shakespeare. Please go on."

"Mr. Blood then attempted to find out what the hairs were from and seemed to have concluded that they were the hair of a bear. He and Mr. Smith then concluded that some such creature could be loose underground and went down, with Mr. O'Connor, our chief of security here at the plant, to investigate further. I believe they hoped to locate the creature and kill it."

"Insane," the secretary said.

"If you'll forgive me, sir, I thought it was pretty far-fetched. We had checked and rechecked every conceivable entrance into the underground, and there is simply no way a creature bigger than a rat could get in. And, of course, we have no rats either."

"Who was aware of this? That they thought there was a bear loose in here." The secretary shook his head.

"Just the three who were—who are down there. And me. And now you as well, sir."

"Ah." The secretary looked off in the distance. "Well, we don't know, do we, just how bad things are. If the plant can be saved or not. But however it turns out, there will obviously be investigations. News stories, God, what stories those vultures will put out.

Congress will surely have its own investigation as well. All of it a terrible embarrassment to—to everyone involved. I think it would be a good idea if we kept this strange, aberrant notion of Smith's to ourselves. I believe we can agree to that, can't we?"

"Yes, sir," Anna Maria said.

"Good. So now, I suppose, we simply have to wait for the engineers. They'll report to me this afternoon. If I were you, young lady, I'd get some rest. We're going to be very busy here later on today. Obviously this is an extremely delicate matter—for all of us. For the entire administration. I will be discussing it with the president shortly."

"There's one thing, Mr. Secretary. At some point we'll have to explain what those men were doing down there after hours."

The secretary raised his eyebrows. "Indeed," he said, and became silent, thinking. Then he smiled. "Has this plant received any bomb threats?" he asked. "I'd be very surprised if some lunatic fringe Earth Firster hadn't called in with some cock-and-bull threat that, of course, had to be investigated." The secretary beamed and stood up, and crossed to the window. Anna Maria understood that she was dismissed.

TWENTY-THREE

When the three elephants he had been herding through the river turned back on him, bellowing, and he began to sink into the muddy water, Derby Catlin woke up gratefully to see the sunlight pouring in—but through a totally unfamiliar window. He blinked, lifted his head from the pillow, and looked around the totally unfamiliar room. It was peach with white trim, and near the bed he was lying in was a dresser, painted white like the trim. He turned over, and on the opposite wall was a white table with a kidney-shaped top covered with hairbrushes and cosmetics. A woman's room, clearly. What woman? Derby's brain was lost in the fog of deep sleep and mild hangover. Yes, he'd had plenty to drink. Bourbon. Enough so he couldn't quite remember . . .

The nurse. That's it. At Ma's. And . . . yes, her place. Yes, a lot of splendid athleticism here on this very bed. He squinted at the floor around the bed and saw clothes, his and hers, strewn here and there. They'd been in a great hurry, hadn't they? Where was she? It was all coming back now, short little thing, chunky, with wide, welcoming hips, *mucho* soft tissue to roll around on, delightful, yes. He couldn't remember her face. But her eyes—she had eyes full of mischief. He could see them now.

He smelled coffee.

Sitting up carefully, he looked around the room again, then snagged his shorts from the floor and stepped into them. At the door, his ears picked up the sound of a television announcer. He walked across a hall and peered into what was the living room, also peach with white trim. There was a brick red sofa under a window that looked out on the street—what street? Derby had no idea where this house was—and two large recliner chairs side by–side, facing the television set at the far end of the room. Over the back of one of them, he could see the top of a head with mouse-colored hair. He coughed, and the head spun around, popping up, grinning.

"Hi," she said. "I hope the TV didn't wake you up."

"No, it was the smell of coffee."

"Come and sit down. There's a news bulletin coming on. See, there's our mayor. Out at WIPP. Something happened."

A familiar face filled the screen, the popular newscaster of KOB TV. He looked extremely upset. Derby came around the recliner and jumped when he saw that his consort of the night past was sitting in her chair naked as a jaybird, grinning at him. Her face looked different, well, yes, plainer than he had begun to remember it. It was a very wide, possessive grin. He sat down as the voice on the television mentioned the word *catastrophe*.

"It occurred last night at approximately seven-thirty. Three men are known to have been in the tunnel and are presumed dead, buried under countless tons of salt that fell from the ceiling. Spokesmen for the Department of Energy have informed me that the cause or causes of the collapse are unknown, but that engineers and scientists from Sandia Laboratories in Albuquerque have arrived to make an inspection. We have with us Mayor Harry Jenkins of Carlsbad. Sir, I wonder if you have any further details that could shed a bit more light on—"

"No, Tom, I don't at this point in time. But I do have a thought I'd like to pass on to your viewers. There is an element—not in Carlsbad, but elsewhere in the state—who have already, this early, come forth to claim that this vindicates their continued but failed efforts to close this WIPP plant down. Not only do I consider such remarks unseemly, given the tragedy we've had here, lost lives . . . but surely wrong. We in Carlsbad have been pleased and honored to be part of the solution to the nation's efforts to contain nuclear wastes. We are

233

well informed here about such matters, unlike the nervous nellies, and we have every confidence that once things have been sorted out here, WIPP will continue as the nation's first repository for these substances. They will be safe down in those salt beds, I can assure you."

"Thank you, Mayor Jenkins. This is KOB TV with this news bulletin. We will return as soon as more details come to light."

The nurse flicked her remote, and the picture disappeared.

"Isn't that just horrible?" she said, wide-eyed. "Three men buried in all that salt." She turned to face him and jiggled.

Suddenly Derby felt overwhelmed, as if the ceiling had fallen in on him as well. Here was news of the worst kind of calamity that could befall WIPP and Carlsbad, the biggest news out of this town in ten years at least, and here he was—a newsman—in a house located he knew not where, in his shorts, sitting next to a nurse he had been making love to the night before when he should have been on the story—here he was, Derby Catlin, editor and publisher of Carlsbad's second newspaper, in a recliner next to a stark-naked woman whose name he couldn't remember.

"Do you want some breakfast?" she asked, still grinning, even leering. "Or maybe—"

Derby jumped to his feet. "Ah, no, no. I have to run. I'm a newsman, and this is of course . . ." He fled into the bedroom and scrabbled around, collecting his clothes from the floor.

Like a dagger, the rays of the sun sliced into Jack's right eye and beyond into his brain. He closed his eye and felt the pain reverberating around in his skull, returning to sit throbbing just behind his eyes. He had no idea where he was. He didn't want to open his eye again. He wanted to throw up. He put a hand out gingerly and felt the edge of the sofa or whatever it was he was lying on. He stretched the hand down to where a floor might be expected and felt the rough carpeting and some sticky cardboard. The thought crept into his mind that he should know where it was that he was going to throw up, so ever so slowly he moved his head to the edge of the sofa and looked down at the floor. A Wendy's hamburger box.

Scrunched-up paper napkins. A large Coke container. A plastic straw. An unopened direct-mail envelope addressed to Jack Whittaker. It was his car.

What the hell was he doing lying on the backseat of his car? How had he gotten here? Where, for that matter, had he been? He didn't want to throw up in his own car. He'd been at Ma's. Sitting in the bar. Drinking bourbon. Oh, God. The thought of it, that murky, mawkish, thick taste of bourbon . . . He reached up, opened the door, thrust his head out, and retched.

I hate this, I hate this, I hate this.

But he felt a little bit better.

He sat up, fetched his handkerchief from his pocket, and wiped his mouth. He looked at his watch. It was almost eleven. His eyes burned, and the ache that squatted behind them was growing more intense. He hadn't had a hangover this bad since the binge-drinking college days in Boulder. His forehead was clammy, and he was shivering in spite of the ninety-five-degree heat.

Stepping slowly out of the Trooper, he moved around to the passenger side, opened the door, and fetched his dark glasses from the glove compartment. Better. The killer glare was gone. His keys weren't in his pocket, and he remembered the custom at Ma's and set off across the parking lot. Inside the front door of Ma's was a dark entryway and to the right, along the wall about seven feet from the floor, was a row of brass cup hooks. There he found his keys, noting that either he was the only patron who had spent the night in the parking lot or possibly he was merely the last to leave. He stood in the dark hallway, relieved of the sun's glare, and listened. Ma's was silent, dead.

It was coming back—the argument that had broken out like a pack of wild dogs, the fury at Cassie for wrecking the possibility of . . . of what? His dream. Screw his dream. It seemed pretty far-fetched this morning with his head throbbing, his mouth feeling like it was full of dead moths, and his self-esteem in the toilet. Time to go home. Back in the sunlight, he stopped, remembered another custom at Ma's, and went around the far side of the building, where there was a spigot and a bucket. He splashed some water on his face and filled the bucket. He crossed the lot with the bucket, dumped it on the scene of his shame next to the Trooper, and took back the bucket.

Once seated in the Trooper, he put his hands on the wheel. They were shaking, and he wondered if he might get arrested for DWI if he ventured out of the lot.

The hell with it.

He pulled out onto Canal Street and headed north, his mind drifting back to the argument the night before. Man alive, they had said some ugly things to each other. Like always. Well, at least like the last year of their marriage. He didn't want to think about it. But something she said kept nagging at him. If only he could remember what it was.

Sitting in traffic at a stoplight, lost in thought, Jack Whittaker failed to notice his ex-wife's Jeep Cherokee pull out from the Texaco station onto Canal and pass by him ten feet away, headed south.

Cassie Roberts opened the glass door of Guadalupe Mountain Outfitters, a long, cavernous room crowded with a maze of shelves and display cases filled with the esoteric arrays of equipment favored by mountain climbers, cavers, and other outdoors people. Above the shelves, along the one wall, hung an army of backpacks, fanny packs, and other packs. Pegboard displays were festooned with an infinite variety of tools and hardware. Tents and sleeping bags in primary colors, thick woolen socks, various types of outdoor boots, coils of yellow and orange ropes, helmets, compasses, a glass case of black rubber watches, another case given over to topographical maps—Cassie experienced a kind of vertigo, a sensory overload. Where did one begin?

The store appeared to be deserted. No one was at the glass counter where the cash register sat along with piles of pamphlets and books. Cassie had made a mental list while driving to the store, but it was scattered like leaves in the wind in the presence of this chaos of choice.

Okay, she thought. A helmet. She saw an array of helmets on top of some shelves in the approximate middle of the store, red, black, royal blue, gleaming in the fluorescent lights that hung from the ceiling. She picked her way through the maze toward the helmets and started with a slight gasp when, on turning a corner, she found herself towering over a small, brown-haired woman with very dark brown eyes and a pleasant smile.

"Can I help you?" the woman asked in a voice that was barely audible.

"Oh. Um, yes. Yes, I'm sure you can." Cassie smiled back. "I'm completely lost in here."

"Aren't you . . . ?" the little woman began. "You're Dr. Roberts from the museum. I heard you lecture last month. It was fascinating."

"Well, thank you."

"I'm Becky." They shook hands. "What can I help you with?"

"It looks like I'm going to be doing a bit of caving, and I need to get myself outfitted. I know some of the things I'll need, but . . ."

"Boots and a helmet are most important," Becky said, looking down at Cassie's feet. She was wearing a pair of thick-soled hiking boots. "Actually," Becky went on, "those are fine. Now, you'll want a rock climber's helmet. They're a bit expensive, but they're the safest . . . and most comfortable."

For five minutes, the two women moved around the store, plucking things from racks and shelves.

"You've done some caving before?" Becky asked at one point.

"A couple of times."

"It gets to you, doesn't it?" Becky said. "I'm a caver, my husband and I. We used to live in Tennessee. But this is the mecca, so we moved our store here last year. Where are you going to go?"

"Excuse me?"

"Caving."

"Oh." A nervous smile flickered on Cassie's face. "I don't know, exactly. It's up to my friends. They're the ones who do a lot of this stuff."

"Locals?"

"No, no. Some friends from Albuquerque," Cassie said.

A few minutes later, a small mountain of equipment was piled on the counter by the cash register. Cassie looked at it, and then her eyes widened.

"Rope," she said. "I'll need a hundred feet of rope. That braided stuff that doesn't spin."

"Gee, Dr. Roberts," Becky said in her tiny voice. "Do you really need that? I mean, all this here is going to cost plenty, and I'd think your friends'd have rope. It's not like I'm trying to discourage sales or anything . . . but good caver's rope is expensive."

Cassie looked at the little woman and smiled. "I guess I'd rather have my own. You know. Self-sufficient."

Becky nodded and went to the rear of the store to fetch a coil of rope. Returning with it, she sorted through the pile of caver's matériel, punching numbers into the cash register, and gave the total to Cassie, who wrote a check. Becky put the receipt in one of the plastic bags that was filled with carabiners, a brake bar rig, a first aid kit, and a few other things and added a brochure.

"It's a brochure on caving safety," she said. "My husband and I are real bears about safety." Cassie was anxious to leave now, but the little woman kept talking. "So much can go wrong underground. It's always good to review the safety principles and to be ready. You heard about the cave-in at WIPP? Horrible. But you know, they had a wonderful safety record, won awards from the mining industry. You just don't know what's going on in Mother Earth's mind, do you? So Danny, that's my husband, Danny and I are real bears on safety, like I said. Here, let me help you carry some of that."

With the gear stowed in the back, Cassie drove south and then east. Along with the newly purchased equipment, she had—on the backseat—a new and, regrettably, heavy Nikon camera and a special rifle. She smiled now at how easy it had been to talk Troy Duggins out of the weapon that morning.

Troy Duggins was an associate curator at the Desert Museum and Gardens just outside of town. He was a master-degree zoologist, a fine naturalist, who had taken a relatively low-paying job with the Desert Museum because it put him in the perfect position to exercise all his interests without requiring him to do much of anything he didn't want to do. There he looked after the few desert animals on exhibit—tortoises, rattlers, jackrabbits, coyotes, and one old male mountain lion—and the xeric gardens full of cacti and other attractive plants that could get along without much by way of water. And management let him go out on call whenever necessary.

Troy was the one who people from miles around called if they found a rattler in their bedroom or a mountain lion prowling around their yard. He was the ex-officio wildlife rescue department of Eddy County and had a little zoo behind his house outside Carlsbad that was always filled with hawks with broken wings, rabbits that had been hit by cars and survived—the lame and the halt of Mother Nature as locally configured.

On those rare occasions when a mountain lion or another big animal like a pronghorn was in the wrong place, Troy would be summoned, and he would bring along his rifle specially designed to fire not bullets but darts. The darts were a bit like small hypodermic needles that, on impact, injected a fast-acting anesthetic into the errant beast, putting it soundly to sleep for—ideally—up to three hours, during which time Troy would place it in the back of his pickup after tagging it and take it off into the wilderness of the Guadalupes, where it would wake up shortly afterward, groggy and probably confused, but alive.

Troy wasn't exactly licensed to do all this, and there were those in the state's various interest groups and government departments who felt that Troy wasn't really sufficiently versed in exotic veterinary practices to be running around with a dart gun full of anesthesia—dose being a crucial and tricky matter. The wrong dose could lead to a dead animal or a dead biologist. But Troy had almost unanimous local favor and appreciation for his activities, and Cassie Roberts was among the most distinguished people in Carlsbad to have lent him written and vocal support against state bureaucrats and overly fussy do-gooders.

So when Cassie had called him that morning at the Desert Museum and Gardens and asked if she could borrow his dart gun, some darts, and some particularly powerful anesthetic—one made from the same chemicals as heroin, in fact—Troy had not only agreed, no questions asked, but had volunteered to drive the weapon to her house.

Driving east now, Cassie wondered how she was going to lug all this stuff. She had been in the earliest throes of panicky second thoughts when Troy arrived at her house, grinning conspiratorially, and she had considered asking if he would like to come with her on a caving expedition, but she thought better of it. She remembered hearing him explain once that there was only one place he would never go if an animal rescue was called for and that was "one of those damn caves." Troy was admittedly a hopeless claustrophobic and cheerfully explained that he'd been in a cavern once and "seized up so bad, if I'd been an engine, I'd've thrown a rod."

Cassie tried not to think of what lay immediately ahead—the descent into hell.

TWENTY-FOUR

It had been years, decades, since Tracer Dunn had slept past dawn. But when he had gotten back to his trailer, past midnight, he fell into bed and slept for eight hours so soundly that Lucia wondered if he was sick.

He awoke wondering if he hadn't made a big mistake, not telling the Gonzales woman about that bear. Even in the state of near shock he'd been in during the endless elevator ride up, it had struck him that it was best if the WIPP people didn't know for sure that the bear existed. Because the bear had to have come from somewhere, and Tracer knew where that had to be—his cavern. Somehow, somewhere down there, that tunnel down in WIPP and his cavern were connected. Or at least they had been. And if the feds found out about that, it was curtains for any plan he cooked up for the cavern.

So he lied, and the Gonzales woman bought it. And once she got over the shakes, she told him straight out that it would be better for him to say nothing about being there—to anyone. Same as T. L. Smith had done, threatening to bring in the Border Patrol if he didn't keep it under his hat. That was fine with him. He was happy to keep it quiet.

But now, thinking about it in the light of day and after a good sleep, he began to have some doubts. Would they want to excavate the cave-in to recover the bodies? If so, they'd sure as hell run into the carcass of that giant bear as well. And the arm of Sam Blood, but not the rest of him, which Tracer reckoned was mostly inside the bear. If they found all that, the Gonzales woman's tits'd be in the wringer and she might need to finger Tracer, tell whoever that he'd been there and lied to her about what had gone on down there. But no, it'd be too late for her to do that. She would just say she didn't know what had happened. She wasn't there, after all. How could she know?

Well, Tracer decided, it was too much for him. His old brain just wasn't up to figuring out how people like that—government people—thought. And he had urgent and practical things to do. He was going to need more powerful ammunition than he had to kill anything the size of that humongous damned bear. The thought of it rising up on its hind legs—must've been ten, eleven feet tall—made him shudder. And he needed some rope. The sooner he got down in that cavern and shot the rest of the bears down there, the better.

He wondered how many there were. Well, he'd find out soon enough. He loaded up his pickup with what gear he could muster for climbing around in the dark and drove into town, reaching Dan's Gun and Ammo just after it opened at ten o'clock.

Dan himself was sitting on a stool behind the counter, leafing through a catalog. He was a diminutive man with a pencil-thin mustache, a two- or three-day growth of whiskers, and little by way of a chin.

"Well, hey," he said. "It's Tracer Dunn. Howdy, Tracer." He held up the catalog, which had about twenty pictures of women on one page. "It says here that all these beautiful, educated Russian ladies are lookin' to get married to a sincere American man. I'm just havin' a terrible time pickin' one out. Look at 'em. All that nookie just waitin' for us to call."

Tracer stared at the man until he put the catalog down.

"What can I do for you, Tracer?"

"I need some of that high-powered ammunition for my carbine. They call it something like Fail Safe."

Dan scuttled around the counter and went to the back of the store, where he picked out a box. "Here you go," he said. "Last box. Funny, we don't have much call for this, but there was a feller

242

in here just the other day askin' for it. What're you goin' after, Tracer? Elephants?"

Tracer took the box without comment, paid for it, and left. Dan shook his head and muttered to himself, "That other feller wouldn't say, neither."

The air flows gently past the bear as he prowls. It carries a new scent to his nose, something he—in his young life—has never smelled before. It is a bear scent, but not one he knows. He is puzzled by it, and excited. He follows the scent through the dark, his head moving back and forth, gauging the scent's strength. It leads him to a place where he has not been, and so he must slow down, even though the scent draws him more urgently now. He must pick his way past unknown obstacles in this unfamiliar place.

He pauses from time to time to listen, hearing only the distant *drip-dip-drip* of water somewhere. But then, pausing again with the scent strong in his nostrils, he hears another sound, a high-pitched sound. It is unfamiliar too, and he stands still, listening until it stops, then moves on.

Underfoot, it is damp, but the ground dries out as he climbs, led upward by the scent over huge boulders to a flat place. The high-pitched sound begins, louder now, and he knows what it is. He sniffs, pads closer. Two whining sounds now, louder, and he reaches his nose toward the warmth and touches the fur of one of the cubs. It shrieks, then both shriek, and he opens his jaws.

His ears are assaulted by the roar behind him as a clawed paw rakes his haunch, the massive blow knocking him sideways. He spins around to confront this attack and roars in pain when the claws strike again, raking his snout. Fangs sink into his shoulder, and he surges backward, falling, crashing into rock. Immediately he is up on his feet, pain screaming into his brain, and he runs, panicked, crashing into obstacles, stumbling, desperate to escape this unfamiliar place of fury.

This looks like the place, Cassie said to herself. She slowed and pulled off the road. The Cherokee bounced over limestone chunks, and she heard something metal fall off the backseat onto the floor. She slowed further and bumped along for about a hundred yards into the scrub until she realized that she had turned off the road at the wrong place. She should have reached the mouth of that canyon by now.

She stopped. The land rose gently ahead of her. She looked south, then north, and chose north. The Cherokee crept over the ground, rockier now, and after a quarter of a mile she saw a break in the high ground to her left and found the canyon.

She plunged into it and in moments found the side canyon and drove even more slowly over the dry streambed until she saw the ledge. She stopped the car, turned off the engine, and sat in the heat and the silence. Soon she became aware of a sound, a continuous buzz like an insect somewhere far off, a locust maybe, or maybe it was just her ears. Her chest felt tight, and she took a deep breath, letting it out slowly, and watched a raven arrow across the sky, disappearing beyond the canyon wall. She looked up at the ledge and visualized herself backing over the edge.

It took Cassie five or ten minutes and three trips to haul all her gear up to the cavern entrance on the ledge. Methodically she laid it all out on the ground and proceeded to assemble herself into a properly decked out caver.

First the sweater, then off with the jeans and on with the overalls. Then wind the ten-foot length of tubular nylon webbing around and around as a belt and hook it together with a carabiner. Fill the backpack—camera, film, first aid kit, food bars, water bottles, carabiners, Jumar, flashlight, extra batteries, candles, waterproof matchbox, darts. Leave one dart out.

Snap the electric lamp onto the helmet, run the cord through the overalls to the battery pack, and hook that onto the belt.

Loop more tubular nylon webbing around the big boulder, the rock of Gibraltar. Assemble the brake bars and run the line through and tie the line to webbing. Remember how to make a bowline knot—a tree with a hole at the bottom and the snake comes up through the hole, goes around the tree and back down the hole. Yes!

Toss the coil into the entrance hole and watch it disappear into the gloom. Pay no attention to the enormous insect flopping around in your stomach, telling you to throw up. Put on the seat harness—more webbing—and tighten it up.

Wish Jack Whittaker wasn't such an asshole. Do not think about that. Do not wish he were here.

Load the dart into the rifle with fingers that feel like Jell-O.

But first wonder why those pebbles just rattled down the canyon wall . . .

Cassie looked up the canyon wall that slanted up from the ledge. It was ten, maybe fifteen feet to the top. Looking back at her was Tracer Dunn. His face was in complete shadow from his hat, and a Winchester carbine hung in his hand, pointed at her.

"Oh no," she said.

"Oh yeah," he said. "Boy howdy if this ain't convenient." He smiled at her. She had never seen him smile. He was missing one of his canine teeth. It was an ugly smile. "I been watching you, missy. That's a lot of nice gear you got there."

"How long have you been up there?"

" 'Bout ten minutes. You got real pretty legs. I've always been a sucker for pretty legs."

"Wow. A dirty old man," Cassie said.

"You just stay right there, missy. I'm comin' down." Casually keeping the carbine pointed at her, he walked a bit farther along the edge to a fissure in the rock. "I saw your vehicle go down into the canyon back there," he said, climbing down amid a clattering cascade of pebbles and dirt and sliding the last few feet. On the ledge, he dusted himself off elaborately and stepped toward her. "I'm thinkin' we can do a little spee-lunkin,' just the two of us. I reckon you can save me some time down there, lead me to them bears."

"Not on your life," Cassie said.

"Now I see you brought your camera along. Goin' down there to photograph the bears, ain't that right? Now why do you need to do somethin' dangerous like that?"

Cassie said nothing.

"Evidence, is what I figure. Those boys at Fish and Wildlife're gonna need more than just a photograph of a footprint. Ain't that right?"

Again Cassie said nothing.

"So they don't know they're there. And you and me, we're gonna go down there and I'm gonna shoot every last one of 'em. One of 'em's already dead."

"What do you mean?" Cassie said.

"One of 'em was in the tunnel at WIPP, the one that caved in. He was buried in all that salt. Big son of a bitch."

Cassie's stomach lurched. "You saw it."

"Yeah, I did. Never seen such a big animal, except a circus elephant. Must've stood ten, eleven feet on its hind legs. Big white thing, eyes like red fire. And teeth—those big old canines must've been four inches long. Yeah, it'd eaten one man down there, all we found was the man's arm, and it was comin' after us when the whole damn place started cavin' in." Tracer smiled his ugly smile again. "I was the only one got out."

"What makes you think I'll help you find the bears?"

"Well, for one thing, missy—"

"You know my name," Cassie snapped.

"For one thing, *Doctor* Roberts, I'm better armed than you. That's one of them dart guns, ain't it? They use 'em to immobilize critters. And I just happen to notice that you haven't put the dart in it yet. So it ain't much good, is it?"

Cassie smiled. "Well," she said, putting the dart gun down on the ground, "you play whatever hand you've got, right? Maybe we can make a deal, Mr. Dunn." She let her shoulders slump, her posture soften. She took a tentative step toward him.

"Seems to me I've heard that someplace—"

Cassie lunged at him, swinging the dart, and felt it strike his arm. He lashed back and his hand caught her hard on the side of her jaw, spinning her sideways, and she fell to her knees. The rancher stood staring at her. She tasted blood in her mouth and put her hand to her jaw. It hurt, but it didn't seem to be broken.

"You'll be out in about ten seconds, old man," she said, and got to her feet. "There's enough anesthetic in that dart to put a tiger down for hours. You'll probably survive, but you won't be going anywhere for a couple of days."

The old man said, "You damn bitch, I'll . . .," and he dropped the Winchester on the rocks with a clatter. His knees sagged, and he slumped to the ground. Cassie stepped over to him and kicked his arm with her boot. Inert. She picked up the Winchester, unloaded it, and threw the bullets over the edge of the ledge, then the rifle. She collected the dart gun, loaded the dart into it, and walked over to the cave entrance. Without hesitation, she picked up the brake bars, tightened them on the rope, and backed down into the abyss.

TWENTY-FIVE

The phone rang in Jack Whittaker's trailer shortly after twelve noon. The second ring woke him up, the third got him off the bed, and by the fifth he had crossed the trailer into the kitchen and snatched up the receiver, noting that his head still ached and the dead insects were still lodged in his mouth.

"Hello," he said groggily.

"Is this Jack Whittaker?"

"Yeah."

"This is Becky. From the outfitters?"

"Yeah, Becky, how are you?"

"I'm fine, but there's something I've been, well, fretting about for an hour. It's not really any of my business, but you know how Danny and I focus on caving safety."

"Yeah, you do a good job."

"Well, there was a woman in here about an hour ago, bought a whole caving rig. She said she was going caving with some people from Albuquerque, but I got the feeling she was going off by herself."

"What made you think that?"

"She bought a hundred feet of line, braided line. I said I thought she didn't need to buy it because her caver friends would surely have some. But she said she wanted to be self-sufficient."

"Did she say where she was going?"

"No. She said her friends would decide."

"That doesn't sound so good, Becky, but what—"

"Well, see, Jack, it's none of my business really, but I thought maybe you'd want to know. See, it was your ex-wife . . . Jack? You there?"

"Yeah, yeah. I . . ."

"I thought maybe you'd know where she could be going and—"

"Okay, thanks for calling, Becky. I'll see what I can do. Thanks."

"Okay, bye, Jack."

Jack hung up the phone and stared at the wall for a full minute. "Shit!" he said, and went over to the sink. He took a bottle of Advil out of the cupboard, fumbled with the adult-proof cap, stuffed four of the pills into his mouth, and drank cold water from the tap.

"Stupid, stupid, stupid," he said. "Damn fool is gonna kill herself." Well, he thought, that's her problem. I'm sick. No, I'm not sick. I'm hung over. I'm hung over because she was a flaming absolute ball-busting bitch. Wrecking my life. So it's her damn problem.

Jack sighed. "Shit," he said. He marched into the living room and began collecting his gear.

Tracer Dunn lay prone on the ground, motionless. Listening.

It had struck him instantly when the dart hit his sleeve but not the flesh of his arm that it would be easier to follow the woman than to make her lead him, which she plainly wasn't going to do. So he collapsed and played possum when she kicked his arm. He heard her empty the Winchester and heard the bullets and the rifle clatter down below the ledge. And he heard her descend into the cave. Okay. So now he rose from the ground and jumped down off the ledge to fetch his carbine.

Back on the ledge, he scrambled up the canyon wall and picked up his pack full of the gear he had assembled—some line, a flashlight, extra batteries, matches, more ammunition, a couple of water bottles, and some apples.

Three minutes later, Tracer Dunn had rigged some clever knots and loops that hitched him by the belt onto the nice orange line that she had rigged. With the Winchester slung over his shoulder, he backed out over the hole and began to let himself down, slowly, silently. Except in the most general sense, he didn't know what to expect in this cavern, but he didn't doubt for a minute that he could track the woman. She had about a seven-minute lead on him, he reckoned. He'd catch up when he needed to, but now he could just lay back, out of hearing.

He was beginning to think that this business of walking backward down the rock was simple enough when suddenly, terrifyingly, the rock was gone. He kicked but couldn't find the rock, and his body swung forward and hit the wall painfully. Above him, the sky was a deep blue through the entrance hole. He looked down for the first time and saw that he was dangling over a widening black abyss.

The chief engineer from Sandia Laboratories' division of mining science and technology was a large man with the reassuringly solid, even stolid, look of a banker or a successful businessman. In his fifties, balding with graying blond hair neatly barbered, he wore an old-fashioned pair of horn-rimmed glasses and, under his white overalls, a white shirt with a starched collar and a narrow necktie with red and blue stripes. His name was McIntyre, and he spoke with the hard-edged twang of rural Indiana. A man who had earned high self-esteem from several decades of successful labor in the vineyards of federal science and technology, the last few years being spent chiefly as an administrator, he was not visibly or otherwise awed by reporting to so august a figure as the secretary of energy. On the contrary, he was quite sure that the secretary did not—and probably could not—grasp the basic principles of geology and engineering upon which the entire WIPP site was constructed. He was equally sure that the secretary's primary concern would be political. The president and his heir apparent, the vice president, would not relish having to explain to the electorate, not to mention the opposition, why, after the expenditure of some five billion dollars, WIPP had failed.

But, in the engineer's opinion, it probably had.

He had spent the past few minutes in the director's office, explaining geological and engineering matters to Secretary Engels, along with some basic chemistry.

"So," he was saying, "we'll have to probe the tunnel to find out what caused it to collapse. If that smell is in fact hydrogen sulfide— and we'll know that within the hour—then there is a truly serious breach. Probably fatal."

"It can't be walled off?" the secretary said. "There must be a way to close that section—what do you call it? That panel of tunnels. Impregnate the salt with something."

"That is something we could look into. I'm dubious, however."

"How are you going to probe the tunnel?" Anna Maria asked.

"Mechanically, I should think. Sensors on probes."

"I'm concerned," she said, "about recovering the bodies of those men."

"In my judgment," the engineer said, "from examining the nature of the cave-in, I would suggest that a rescue effort would be quite dangerous. For the rescuers. We have no idea yet of the extent of the instability."

"I've spoken with our mine safety people, of course," Anna Maria said. "They seem to think we could at least try it."

The engineer opened his hands, palms upward, a Jovian shrug. "I suppose there are other considerations besides the purely technical. It's your decision to make, of course."

"Of course," Anna Maria snapped.

"I think we should definitely make the effort to recover the bodies," the secretary said. "The public would expect nothing less. And I want a report on the possibilities of sealing off that part of the plant in such a way that the rest will be secure."

"That's a tall order, sir," the engineer said. "It's for ten thousand years. But . . ."

"That's exactly why we need a thorough-going study. I want a complete examination of all the possibilities. I think we can hold off—I think we can explain that this is not as serious as it might sound—except of course for the tragic loss of three men, but that sort of thing happens in mining situations. And that we are exploring all of the available solutions. This will, of course, take time, several months at least. We should aim for a full report on our options in six months."

"December," the engineer said, a knowing smile creeping around his eyes. After the election, he thought.

It was a crock, of course. There simply was no way to seal off an area of salt if it was being breached by water or, God help us, sulfuric acid, no matter how dilute. But . . . they could have meetings about it, endless meetings. They could blue-sky the project. Maybe some genius *would* hit on a solution. Who knew? And, if need be, they could hold up any report till it was convenient. So, the engineer calculated, he could go along with this charade without suffering any real professional shame. He hadn't gotten this far along in his career by telling his superiors how stupid they were.

When Cassie Roberts reached the clamshell-shaped chamber at the bottom of the entrance shaft, she realized that she hadn't had to give full attention to managing the brake bars and the rope. It had seemed almost routine. Nor had she experienced even a whiff of the terrors. Instead, for much of the way down, she found herself thinking about the possibility that these bears had a superlong hibernation period. Fifty years, maybe, given that newspaper article about the attacks on livestock. That meant an individual bear could live for hundreds of years—most of it unaware, of course—but think of the changes it would experience each time it came out of hibernation and ventured out of the cavern!

The climate would be different, at least somewhat different, each time you woke up. Outside the cavern, new prey would show up. It would be like waking up every day for most of a week and, each day, finding the occasional pronghorn herd to hunt. Then on Friday you wake up and the pronghorns are gone and there are all these other creatures—cattle—out there. Much easier to catch. Then on Sunday you wake up and you find there's a new kind of prey—people—right there in part of your cavern. And outside, the landscape is very different than last time. Roads, cars, lots of fences. And the cattle are fewer and farther between. It would be, Cassie thought, like living with the fast-forward button on all the time.

The only constant in their lives would be this cavern, and even that changed a little over time—and now a lot.

And one of the bears was now dead, a victim of the collapse in the man-made cavern.

She wondered if it was the one that had left the footprint by the pool—and the femur. The man-eater. But, she thought, any carnivore that's big enough will become a man-eater if a man is easily available. It was people, shoving their way into short-faced bear habitat, who were responsible for whatever problems these bears caused, not the other way around.

As she stooped over and made her way into the horizontal crevice where the first tunnel was, Cassie smiled to herself. Here I am, she thought, coming to the defense of the most ferocious predator ever to inhabit this continent, a bunch of animals that would just as soon eat me or anyone else that comes into their cavern—and have done just that.

And of course, she was in a cavern. She hated caverns, and she'd be in this damned cavern for hours. But she was on her own, with a clear purpose, properly equipped and armed. She had disarmed that grubby rancher, put him out like a light and for a good long time. She had taken a hit and bounced right back. She was doing the right thing. This was her show. It was a rush, a major rush.

Her plan was simple, and the only one possible: Go to the little pond where the footprint was and probe from there. The ropes that Jack had rigged were still in place, and the route was marked wherever there was a choice to make. And she had brought along her own markers—Day-Glo stickers—to keep track of her own exploration of new territory in this Minotaur's maze. She was in no rush—there was plenty of time to be cautious, careful, methodical.

She crawled into the first wormhole of her journey, slithered through the low, narrow part, pushing the dart gun ahead of her and dragging her pack from a foot, then crawled out onto a rocky balcony, a ledge overlooking an immense chamber most of which lay beyond the power of her headlamp. She remembered this place. Down past the huge boulders were columns where the tites and mites had joined. At the far end, out of sight, was some brownish flowstone like thick draperies and another tunnel about ten feet above the floor—the tunnel that Jack called the Alimentary Canal. It was in the large chambers that she needed to be completely alert. In the narrow tunnels, she was safe.

For a full minute she stood on the rocky balcony, listening and hearing nothing but the sound of her own breathing. She made her way down, climbing over and among the great chunks of rock and then winding through the huge fluted columns toward the far end of the room, pausing every now and then to listen and to look behind her. This wasn't only for fear that one of the bears might be behind her but also to get a picture in her mind of what the way out looked like. She could recall much of what the way in had looked like, but their retreat—their escape—was so fraught with terror and so exhausting that she could remember very little of it. She had just plodded along, trying to keep up with Jack. For a moment now, in the open in this large chamber, a slightly panicky feeling returned and she felt goose bumps erupt on her arms.

Presently she came to the far wall of the room and saw the brown flowstone, a frozen cascade, and above it the black hole of the tunnel. An orange rope hung down the brown drapery. Moments later, her torso was in the tunnel, her legs dangling out. She pulled herself forward and stood, stooped, in the Alimentary Canal, catching her breath. She remembered that it curved around, descending, and that it had seemed forever that they were in it, but in all it was a ten-minute leg, beyond which was another huge room with white soda straws and a phalanx of gray stalagmites that had reminded her of the Confederate army.

She set off down the tunnel, feeling confident. It was here that she had checked out her sense of direction, finding that it was accurate. The west-running tunnel curved south at some point up ahead. She came to a place where the ceiling grew low enough to force a crawl. She didn't remember that but continued on hands and knees for about twenty yards until the ceiling rose and she could walk almost erect. Soon her light picked up what looked like the end of the tunnel. She emerged into a chamber, but not the one she remembered. It was small, maybe twenty-five feet across, and the walls were sheer, vertical. She stepped out into the room and tipped back her head. The light revealed whitish gray walls that extended upward into total blackness. She was lost.

Somewhere she had made a wrong turn. How could that be? Her heart was pounding in her chest like a trip-hammer, and sweat erupted from her forehead. She was suddenly cold.

Okay, okay, she thought. Calm down. Retrace your steps.

She turned and saw the entrance to the tunnel she had come through, stepped toward it, and gasped.

"Oh no," she said out loud, and her voice echoed in the room. Two tunnels gaped in the rock wall, three feet apart. Which one had she come through?

She shivered violently.

TWENTY-SIX

Cassie Roberts took ten deep breaths, exhaling slowly after each one. She knew that if whichever tunnel she chose didn't soon become too cramped to walk nearly erect in, it was the wrong one. It wasn't much to go on. She hadn't timed anything, and both tunnels could narrow down. But it was all she had to go on, so she chose the tunnel to her right and stepped into it, crouching slightly. The dart gun and the pack were getting heavy. This was a stupid idea, she thought, really stupid. *Nobody has any business alone in one of these caverns, especially me.*

She took heart when the tunnel's ceiling did close in on her, forcing her to crawl for a ways. Then she found it opened again to where she could stoop-walk. Was she back in the Alimentary Canal? It seemed so, and in another five minutes she was peering out into the big chamber she had crossed earlier, the orange rope hanging down over the caramel-colored flowstone she had scaled. She lay on her stomach, peering out into the gloom beyond the reach of her headlamp, and heard a slight rattle. Pebbles falling? A natural mini-rockfall? Or a bear? Her throat closed up, and she shuddered. *Oh, God, not a bear. I'm not ready for that.* Her heart was pounding again, and she struggled to breathe and to get control of her terror. She listened but heard nothing more, so she turned and checked her watch. She'd been underground for a little more than three hours now. The place was already getting to her. She swallowed hard and headed back down the Alimentary Canal.

Tracking the bitch through the rocky places was proving to be more difficult, more time-consuming, than Tracer Dunn had imagined it would be. He had started out about seven minutes behind her, he reckoned, but thought he had probably lost another ten minutes or so following the minimal sign of her across that big room. But then he spied the smooth, almost shiny curtainlike brown wall with an orange rope hanging from a hole about ten feet up. He had turned off his flashlight, put it in his pack, and taken the rope in his hands to scale the wall when he thought he saw a slight glow of light from the hole above. It grew brighter, and Tracer ducked down and crept to his right where he had seen a particularly deep fold in the curtain. Slipping around it, he squatted down and heard the rattle of a few pebbles dislodged by his feet. Damn, he thought, and stayed perfectly still. He heard the bitch above him, moving away. Standing up, he peered around the fold of rock and saw that the light was gone from the hole. There was nothing now but utter darkness all around him. He scrabbled around till his hand felt the orange rope.

Ten minutes after setting out for the second time down the Alimentary Canal, Cassie emerged into a large chamber with reddish brown walls, the ceiling nearby festooned with hundreds of thin white soda straws. At the far end, out of sight, was the Confederate army, she was sure. She was relieved. But she was also spooked. On her way through the tunnel this time she hadn't seen how she went astray earlier, no place where she could have taken a wrong turn. That was eerie, scary.

Best not to think about it.

She pressed on, hearing water dripping, and passed among the stubby gray army to the end of the chamber. There she found one of Jack's tinfoil markers at the entrance of a tunnel, one of what looked like three such entrances within thirty feet of each other. She went in. A half hour later, she stood above a familiar kidney-shaped body of green water. Big white lily pads extended out over the water. And off to her right was the rope Jack had rigged, with belaying ropes at intervals, for getting through this place without going in the water. That had been arduous and time-consuming.

Cassie thought briefly about shucking her clothes and swimming it: so what if the damn pool got a little human sweat and grime in it? But she couldn't think of a way to get all her gear across. It was far too much to carry in one hand over her head while she paddled through the water with the other. She sat down on a nearby boulder, dug into her pack, and opted for a chocolate-flavored Power-Bar Harvest rather than something called a Zanzibar. She turned off her light and sat in the all-enveloping dark as she hungrily devoured her minimal meal. She had been in this cavern almost three hours now, and she had a long way to go.

It was paramount to conserve her resources—food and batteries. And equanimity. She was still spooked by getting lost back there and then, almost worse, not finding out how she had gotten lost. One thing was for sure. Her sense of direction had abandoned her. She had no feeling at all for what direction she was facing. And the sense of exhilaration, the rush she had felt at the beginning of this lunatic mission so long ago—that had abandoned her too.

She felt the first light breath of panic stir the back of her neck, and she reached up and flicked on her headlamp.

"Look out, for chrissake!"

A rumbling was followed by a roar and the ceiling gave way, white chunks cascading down. Albert Yazzie leapt backward, still grasping the shovel with which he had been slowly digging the beginnings of a passageway through the fallen salt that plugged three-quarters of the tunnel called S10249. He had gotten only five feet in and his crew had already wedged one of the steel beams over the entranceway, held there by two upright beams. But to no avail. The salt collapsed and the steel beams were shoved aside, one of them striking Yazzie on the back of his calf as he leapt out of the way. It knocked him onto his knees and two of the crew grabbed him, one by the arm, the other by the collar of his overalls, and hauled him out of harm's way.

Twenty feet back, Anna Maria Gonzales emitted a small shriek from behind the hand she had clamped to her mouth and was deeply relieved. She had insisted on being present at the attempt to rescue the bodies from the cave-in. Now she walked toward the men and bent over Albert Yazzie, who was seated on the salt floor, holding his leg in both hands.

"Are you all right?" she asked.

Yazzie nodded. "Yeah. It's like a charley horse. I'll be okay."

Anna Maria stood up and put her hands on her hips. Dressed in a white hard hat and white overalls like the others, she nonetheless had the posture, the bearing, of authority.

"We tried," she said. "Thank you, men, for making a good effort. But this is not something that can be safely undertaken. I don't intend to lose anyone else. Seal it off. The entire drift."

She turned and strode out of the tunnel, comfortable that now no one would ever know exactly what had happened to the men who died in this tunnel. Not even her.

Cassie Roberts guessed she was about halfway across the cavern, some ten feet above the water. She had just passed one of the belaying ropes that disappeared into the gloom above, lashed there to some outcrop or stalagmite. The process was tedious, removing one carabiner from the line, hooking back on the line past the belaying rope, then repeating the action with the second carabiner. She was thinking that she would have to do this another three times when a loud crack shattered the darkness above her and she was falling. Her feet hit rock and went out from under her and she hit the ground hard on her side, sliding down the rocky slope, aware of a monstrous shadow, a huge shape, flying over her head, a crash as it hit the slope below her, and a titanic splash. She felt water spray her face and then her feet landed on something hard. One of the lily pads. It cracked and gave way, and she was up to her thighs in the green water, suspended there by the rope that was now taut as a violin string, putting added pressure on the remaining belaying ropes. Cassie was too stunned to move, and the old, horrid memory of green water closing over her head as she clutched at the wooden gunwale flashed through her mind. She saw her grandmother's body slipping down, farther and farther into the darkening sea.

She stared at the dark object sinking away, and it came to her that it was a long, columnar piece of rock, not her grandmother. It had broken off and fallen, evidently bouncing high over her head before it plunged into the water. The rope had sagged, and she was in the water. It was cold water. The dart gun was still strapped over her shoulder, the butt well under water. She needed to get out and get moving. Hypothermia, she knew, could occur even at temperatures in the fifties. The big chunk of rock had now sunk out of sight. She pulled herself up onto the remaining half of the lily pad and slowly, carefully, stood up, taking some of the pressure off the rope. The battery pack hadn't gotten wet, and she wondered if it held enough juice to fry her if it had been in the water with her, like a radio falling into a bath.

Gingerly she pulled herself along the rock wall, hoping the rope would hold. And she knew finally, deep in the core of her being, that her father had been wrong. She couldn't have saved her.

Two and a half hours later, she stood on the edge of the hole—some fifty feet across—where the small pool lay in the stillness and, a few feet from its edge, the footprint of *Arctodus simus*. Behind her was the immense room, the size of five football fields, its entire ceiling beyond the power of her headlamp to illuminate.

She had passed through the room full of ragged scree where she had fallen and jammed her ankle and where Jack had been so concerned. Later she had hurriedly gone through the brilliant ballroom with its glittering chandelier helictites, Jack's Taj Mahal. She was trying not to think about Jack, trying not to wish he were with her. She'd gotten lost once and had fallen into that damn lake and, on a scale of one to ten, her confidence in her caving prowess had reached zero. She regained some of it when she easily rappelled the three hundred feet down the red flowstone into this monster cavern, but now—here at this little pool ten feet below her, the water deceptively deep and still as death—she was definitely in bear territory. She figured she had a fifty-fifty chance of dying in this cavern that Jack had found. Dying from exposure, lost in some dark hole, or worse. And she was exhausted. Her back had one muscle in spasm from lugging both her pack and the dart gun for how long? Six hours, about. Her feet were sore and her legs ached and at the same time felt like they were made of rubber. The air was clammy. And she thought she smelled something rotten, like rotten eggs. Maybe it was just suggestion. Jack had said . . .

Screw Jack.

She needed to rest. Needed to eat, to drink. She would do all that, sit here and revive herself.

In bear territory.

Should she sit up here on the edge of the hole, with the vastness of this dark cavern behind her? Or down there where she knew for a certainty that a bear had been at least once? She looked down at the edge of the pool, where the footprint was. It seemed different. Disturbed, maybe?

Oh, Christ.

She remembered her camera, the snappy little point-and-shoot she had dropped. It had fallen onto one of those lily pads, and she had left it there, fleeing

It wasn't there now. Gone.

She decided to stay where she was while she gathered her strength and searched her soul for courage. She was in no rush.

For starters in the courage department, she decided she would not keep looking back over her shoulder. There was a great deal of open ground—maybe a hundred yards—covered with loose rock and pebbles between her and a small forest of huge stalagmites. No animal weighing fifteen hundred pounds could get across that without making noise. She clutched her dart gun and looked steadfastly forward.

Had Cassie turned and looked over her shoulder at exactly the right moment, she might have seen a light glowing three hundred feet above, where the red flowstone issued forth from the wall and where the rope she had just descended hung.

Tracer Dunn approached the opening and realized it was an entrance to yet another cavern. He doused his flashlight and crept slowly toward the edge, one hand stretched out in front as far as he could reach. He felt the rope and peered out. Far off, way down in the oceanic darkness, he saw a small glow of light. It was the bitch.

He watched the light unblinkingly, scared that if he blinked, he would lose it. It didn't move. She was resting, probably. His eyes began to sting, and he blinked. The distant light was still there. He decided to stay put and watch.

TWENTY-SEVEN

At six-thirty the light was turning gold and long shadows were lengthening across the desert.

Derby Catlin loved this time of day, the world turning saffron.

He had spent the remainder of the morning and the afternoon handling important matters in his office—mainly, laying out the ads for the next issue of *The Intelligencer*. Often as not, it was something of a juggling act, since so many advertisers wanted to appear on a particular page or at a special place on the page. It took some ingenuity to accommodate all these competing requests, and it was a task that took Derby's complete attention. But this afternoon, his mind had drifted off in two directions. One, to the possessively grinning buck-naked nurse whose name had finally come to him—Marjory Blenhem. She was indeed a good deal plainer than the bourbon at Ma's had led him to think, but she was certainly an accomplished lover and . . . In any event, Derby had called her in the middle of the afternoon—she had told him it was her day off today. He apologized for running off so abruptly this morning and said he'd like to get together with her again, but not tonight since he had so much work still to do on the newspaper. He would call tomorrow.

The other direction in which Derby's mind strayed while he laid out the ads was to Tracer Dunn and his visit to WIPP the day before. What on earth had he been doing there? Marjory had said some nonsense about a bear. A WIPP man had come out of a coma or something, raving about a bear. Of course, everyone at Ma's had ridiculed the idea, hurting Marjory's feelings, and he had comforted her with polished kindness and understanding, which of course had paved the path to the rambunctious hours at her place and all that. . . .

But what was that anti-fed rancher doing at WIPP?

So once the ads were laid out, Derby got in his three-year-old Plymouth Neon and headed out toward WIPP. He was, after all, a reporter as well as editor and publisher. He would go to Dunn's ranch and confront him with the question. It was what was called investigative journalism.

He pulled off the WIPP road where the wrought-iron gates to Dunn's place sat back from the road about twenty feet. They still said Harwell among the crude decorations, and Derby wondered what kind of a man would let someone else's name welcome people to a place he had owned for a decade. A poor man, he concluded, and this conclusion was amply born out by the status of the ranch house, an old building made of local stone with the windows rotted out and the roof fallen in. Beyond the ruined house was a trailer and some corrals. Despite the trimness of the clothesline hung from one end of the trailer to a post, and despite a small array of geraniums growing in the ground next to the trailer door, this was obviously another little slice of rural poverty. He stopped the car about thirty feet from the trailer and got out into the heat. The sound of a wheezing window air conditioner reached his ears from somewhere around back.

Derby considered his appearance again. He wore a light blue polo shirt and khaki-colored slacks over a pair of well-worn and reasonably well polished cowboy boots—Tony Lamas. Not too official looking, but not overly casual either. He approached the trailer and knocked politely on the door.

He had the sense that from one of the windows, he was observed. Then, after a few moments, the door opened a crack and a Mexican woman of indeterminate age peered out a bit myopically and said, "Yes."

"Señora," Derby said, "I am looking for Tracer Dunn. Is this where he lives?"

"*Sí,* yes."

He took a card from the pocket of his blue polo shirt and held it out to the woman.

"My name is Catlin. As you can see from my card, I'm the editor of *The Intelligencer.*"

The woman stared at him, uncomprehending, from her large and nearly black eyes.

"That's a newspaper, señora. Would you tell Mr. Dunn that I would like to have a word with him? Give him my card?"

"Not here," the woman said. "Left."

"Left? You mean left for good?"

"No, no. Left to work."

"I see," Derby said. "When was that?"

"When?" the woman asked.

"Yes, when."

"This morning he left."

"Ah," Derby said. "Well. Would you give him this card when he returns?"

The woman snaked out a hand and took the card. It was, Derby noticed, a hand that had seen much labor.

"*Sí,*" the woman said, and closed the door.

"*Gracias,*" Derby said anyway, and got back into his car. So, he thought as the Neon bounced and rattled over the dirt track, Tracer Dunn went to WIPP and returned at some point. That's something. Not much, but something. Derby believed that he was definitely on to something here. A scoop.

For days now Lucia had suffered an increasing uneasiness about her life. She was quite convinced her man was going crazy. Running around the countryside with his rifle, talking about poachers, rustlers, and now bears. This morning he'd said he was going bear hunting and might be gone for a couple of days. So when he dumped a pack in the back of his pickup, Lucia had pointed out that she needed the truck to go to the supermarket in Carlsbad. The old man had grumbled and then had her drive him to the piece of his land that sat across the road and drop him off. Surely he was mad, loco.

Whatever he was doing, it certainly was attracting a great deal of attention. Four visitors in fewer days. Normally weeks would go by without anyone coming to the ranch—which was how Lucia liked it, being what the gringos called a wetback. First the blond man, then that couple who sat around part of one afternoon talking about some sort of partnership, and then the man from WIPP. Now this man who said he was with a newspaper. She didn't believe them, especially this last one, and was increasingly convinced that the Border Patrol was on to her.

So Lucia put her few possessions—clothes, a wooden carving of Our Lady of Guadalupe, and a painting on black felt of the Ascension—into a battered old suitcase, took seventy-five dollars from the drawer in the kitchen, and got into the pickup. Three and half hours later, having driven some two hundred miles, Lucia drove across the bridge from El Paso, Texas, into Ciudad Juarez.

On familiar ground again after being attacked and driven off by the enraged mother bear, the young male slept and now wakes up hungry. There is pain in his face and on his back where her claws slashed him. He is puzzled and irritable. Heaving himself to his feet, he steps out of the large niche in the wall that he uses as a den. Irresistibly he is drawn to the place where the scent of the cubs had led him. New ground. His native curiosity is aroused. And after he has come some distance, he receives yet another scent, carried ever so faintly on the gentle wind that moves through the darkness.

A new scent. Prey. He picks up the pace, walking quickly now, confidently, along the familiar route.

Cassie Roberts rigged a rope over the edge and shinnied down the ten feet to the pool. She had eaten, drunk, and rested and found herself getting drowsy, so it was time to get going. A rank smell assaulted her nose—not the smell of rotten eggs, but something else. She picked her way around the pool to the footprint, thinking this was where it had all begun. The footprint was still there, but another had been superimposed on it, heading in the opposite direction. The original one had pointed toward the overhanging rock where Cassie had bumped her head. The new print faced out. She squatted down and looked back under the overhang in the light of her headlamp. It continued back into a tunnel.

She peered over the edge of the pool, and through the almost totally transparent water she saw her Rollei Prego camera resting on a limestone ledge. So, a bear had been through in the meanwhile and evidently knocked her camera off the lily pad where it had fallen. She slung her pack off her back, rummaged in it, and pulled out the Nikon and one of her plastic bottles of water, which she placed beside the palimpsest of footprints. She ran off three shots from slightly different angles, the film advancing automatically with a loud buzz, the flash filling the world with silent bolts of lightning, blinding her.

She waited for the purple and green dazzles to leave her eyes. Then, her gear stowed, she took a deep breath, ducked down under the overhang, and stoop-walked toward the entrance of the tunnel, the dart gun clutched firmly in one hand. The ground fell away near the entrance, which was large enough to permit Cassie to walk in erect. An unexplored, unknown tunnel. She was presumably the first human being to tread this ground. What did the cavers call it? Scooping beauty. Ridiculous phrase.

There was nothing beautiful about this place. The tunnel consisted of rough, grayish rock walls and rough, grayish rock floor. Ugly rock. It stank. The rank odor that she guessed was the smell of bear mixed nauseously with the smell of rotten eggs. If it got any worse, she might have to turn back. As she came around a curve in the tunnel, her headlamp picked up an object on the floor. Not a rock. More like a section of a large branch. As she drew closer, she saw that it was broken in pieces about six inches long. She knew what it was. A monstrous bear scat. She wondered if that was the remains of the man whose femur she had . . . and the grisly thought made her gorge rise. She tightened her stomach muscles and swallowed hard and narrowly avoided retching.

The tunnel descended at a fairly steep angle, narrowing, widening, curving, and Cassie followed it down with increasing apprehension. It was getting hard to breathe, and she didn't know if it was the foul air getting fouler or simply her body telling her to go home, get out of here. She fought off the waves of claustrophobic panic that lapped at her mind.

This isn't claustrophobia, she said to herself. It's a logical, legitimate fear.

She stopped and listened. Ahead of her the top of the tunnel gleamed with moisture, and water slickened the floor. She heard water drip from somewhere up ahead but didn't see it falling. Behind her, there was only the silence she had been walking through. For a moment she thought she might burst into tears. She bit her lip. Logic suggested that the most intelligent thing she could do— besides fleeing—was to get out of this tunnel. She pressed on, taking care not to lose her footing on the slick floor.

Another thirty yards and, with a profound sense of relief, she stepped into what appeared to be a large chamber. She stopped and moved her head slowly up and down, back and forth, peering into the light as it moved. She was standing at eye level with the bottoms of a forest of stalactites hanging from the ceiling, which was only twenty feet or so above her head. The ground at her feet fell away sharply to what looked like a wide ledge, almost a balcony, below which was an inky void. On the balcony below, she saw more bear scat, glistening with moisture. Obviously fresh, but how fresh?

She extracted a Day-Glo sticker from the outside pocket of her pack, affixing it to the rock wall at the entrance of the tunnel, and picked her way down the slope. Reaching the balconylike ledge, she looked over the edge into the void. Her light lit up a bit of the floor of this cavern some thirty or forty feet down, a forest of stalagmites matching their counterparts above. Water dripped in the dark. The stink of bear and sulfur seemed abated here, perhaps simply because there was a bigger space for it to dissipate in than back in that awful tunnel. Off to her right, what resembled a trail led down the slope, and she followed it down, realizing that it was indeed a trail, a pathway rendered slightly smoother, slightly more rock- and pebble-free by the passage of generations of bears. They had created a switchback trail up and down this steep place.

Cassie was suddenly struck with an overwhelming sense of awe. Here, in the pitch dark deep in the earth, the short-faced bear had managed to survive for more than ten thousand years, evolving into exactly what she could only guess, but still much the same— big, carnivorous, with amazing talents not the least of which was finding their way around this lightless place, creating traditional routes, probably particular territories. She marveled at the tenacity of this species that had somehow managed to take on an entirely new and extremely arduous habitat rather than whimper off into extinction like so many of its then contemporary species had done when the world changed around them. A Pleistocene bear, still with us. The fear, the claustrophobia, the discomfort, the obvious peril of being here—it would all be worth it to see this astounding creature. It would be an unimaginable thrill, the sort of thing a paleontologist could only dream about.

She followed the path downslope to the damp, rocky floor of the cavern. She would realize that dream. All she had to do now was follow the bears' own route, their path.

And hope the dream didn't become a nightmare.

She walked across a damp floor, a region of large stalagmites, the ground sloping slightly upward. The visible path petered out at the edge of a field of large boulders, rockfall from the ceiling, she supposed. She clambered between and over them and stopped to listen. From above, somewhere ahead in the gloom, came an odd, high-pitched sound. Cassie froze.

TWENTY-EIGHT

The high-pitched sound came again, a prolonged squeak, but not a small sound. Then silence but for the occasional drip of water on rock. And then, to her right, far off, a dull clunk and the rattle of pebbles falling. All around her was an immense darkness. Only the narrow cone of light cast by her headlamp anchored her to the real world. The dripping of water, the rattle of pebbles dislodged by water—these were disembodied sounds. All that was real lay ahead in the light, and beyond the light. Cassie crept forward.

Every detail of the white and gray rocks stood out in sharp relief, as if she were seeing them close up, enlarged. Tiny pricks of light glittered on the rock. Crystals of some sort, tiny crystals embedded in the rock.

The squeak came again, and Cassie knew what lay ahead. She let out her breath, realizing that she had been holding it in for almost a minute.

Ahead were two large boulders about four feet apart, creating a natural gateway. Cassie crept between them and peered into an open area behind which a wall of reddish brown flowstone soared straight up into the gloom. She saw them, lying together at the base of the wall. They were white, soft looking, with black noses, curled up with each other. One slender white foreleg stood up out of the tangle of legs, bodies, and fur, the foot dangling limply. One of them was on its back, head lolling to the side. Its eyes were closed.

They were like puppies . . . maybe two feet long, the fragile progeny of giants. Living, breathing relics of a time long gone. Short-faced bears. Their snouts were indeed short, stubby, their mouths wide. Something like cats. Clearly different than any other bear.

Cassie watched them, transfixed, a feeling of elation filling her chest, reverberating there. Tears filled her eyes. My God, she said to herself over and over. My God. How beautiful.

But part of her mind nagged, like the insistent ring of a telephone. Finally she heeded the alert. Cubs mean a protective mother. Somewhere around. Better get busy.

She put the rifle down on the ground beside her, fetched the Nikon from her pack, and peered at the cubs through it. She twisted the zoom until the cubs filled the entire frame and hit the button, an instant of white light filling her vision.

From the balcony, off in the dark, Tracer Dunn saw the flash of white light. He had followed the bitch down the long descending tunnel, laying back a hundred yards, moving with practiced stealth. From where the tunnel exited into this chamber, he saw the yellow cone of light from her headlamp moving down below among those big columns. He picked his way down the slope until he reached a flat place, a ledge. He stood there and watched the yellow light moving, now looking erratic. Climbing over rocks, he reckoned. Going up. Stopped. He unslung his carbine from his shoulder and turned, his foot dislodging a rock that fell over the side, raising a little bit of a clatter. He reached out with his free hand and felt rock at about waist level. On the edge of the ledge. He stepped behind it.

The bitch's light moved forward again. He lifted the carbine, the eyepiece of the nightscope against his eye. He could see her now. She was standing between two big boulders, staring straight ahead. He swung the carbine slightly to the right and saw the bears. Two of 'em, it looked like, all wrapped up together. Young'uns. Cubs, right in his sights. Like fish in a barrel. He saw the flash of light, bleaching out his view for an instant.

The bitch's flash went off again and again. The cubs seemed to

271

recoil. His finger closed over the trigger. One of the cubs was now sitting up, separating itself from the other. Its head was rounder than a bear's should be. He zeroed in on the round head, just behind the closed eye.

Two shots, he thought, and two dead cubs. Then just sit here till the mother shows up. Three dead bears. A good night's work. He pulled the trigger, the carbine jolted with the explosion, he levered another round into the chamber, and . . . something slammed into his back, jerking his head back, the carbine up. He saw the explosion of flame, heard the loud report, felt the recoil as his body crashed into the rock in front of him. The trip-hammer blow exploded his breath from his body, his lungs were suddenly on fire, and he fell to the ground, chest heaving, trying to breathe, knowing he couldn't.

Jack Whittaker was nearly knocked unconscious by the hurtling, diving tackle. Red and yellow light flashed in his eyes, a terrible explosion seemingly in his head, and he felt Dunn collapse. He had a vicious pain in his knee and was struggling to get to his feet when he heard a loud cracking and sensed that part of the ceiling was falling. From below, a great roaring sound reverberated. Rock on rock. Dunn's second shot had gone astray, jolting a stalactite loose to plummet to the ground. Jack pulled himself up and looked over the side of the ledge.

Cassie had spun around toward him, toward all the noise. Her headlamp was a bright single eye shining at him through the gloom. He knew she couldn't see him. Too far away. In the dim glow that the headlamp cast around her, Jack saw something white move behind her, saw it rise up, immense behind her. Christ!

"Cassie!" he shrieked, knowing it was too late. "Behind you!"

An enormous rumbling roar grew in the cavern.

Cassie heard a shot, terrifically loud in the cavern, and saw the sitting cub's little white head disappear in an explosion of blood, its headless body thrown against the wall, falling lifeless and inert. She spun to the right and saw one of the stalactites falling through the gloom, landing with a roar, and the roar continued and a voice called her name. The roar was . . . She spun around and the animal loomed up, towered up over her, its mouth wide, two great ranks of teeth, red eyes burning, an immense roar of sheer fury, deafening. . . . Reflexively she held the camera out in front of her and pressed down on the button and the lightning flashed again and again. The mammoth bear screamed and reared backward, eyes shut, and Cassie turned and ran toward the gateway, thinking to stoop down and snatch up her rifle. She turned, pointed the rifle at the bear looming up only a few yards from her, and pulled the trigger. She didn't hear anything over the bear's roar and saw no reaction. *Missed!* Shit. She leapt through the gateway, cracking her shins, the camera smacking painfully on her ribs, and stumbled through the boulders in her path. She was aware of light up above in front of her and a horrendous snarling roar behind her, and she ran through the stalagmites, thinking that those huge fangs would snatch her off the ground any moment and puncture her body and blood would spurt. . . .

Jack stood helpless on the ledge, his headlamp on but not powerful enough, seeing Cassie's headlamp jerking through the dark, his eyes boring in for the sight of a white form behind her, and just as he saw it, he saw light moving behind him. He turned and saw Tracer Dunn getting to his feet, swinging out with a knife, a hunting knife, a big flashlight in his other hand. Jack raised his arm and ducked his head, and the knife sliced his shoulder with a searing pain. Dunn's eyes were wide, maniacal, and he lunged forward clumsily. Jack was shoved against the rock on the edge of the balcony and grabbed the crazed, flailing old man by the hair, pulled his head back sharply, and drove his fist into the man's abdomen with all the force he could muster.

Air escaped in a loud whoosh as Tracer Dunn doubled over and struggled to stay on his feet. The knife clattered on the rocks. He lurched sideways and tried to take a step, and his foot slipped on the edge of the rocky ledge. Jack watched as the old rancher waved his arms, desperate to get his balance, and then—as if realizing it was no use—sagged, went limp, gave up, and disappeared over the side. Jack caught a glimpse of the man's eyes. Life had left them already.

Cassie's chest was going to burst. She ran, legs pumping, leaping over the ground, headed for the path that led up to the ledge. She didn't dare look behind, look into the maw of the monster. Oh, God, oh, God, oh, God. Sound flooded her ears, deafening sound, closer. Someone had shouted her name. What? Who? She reached the place where the path began its ascent. She didn't think her legs could carry her up the switchbacks. Something big hit the ground next to her with a sickening thunk and she screeched and ran on. Not a rock. What? What's that light? Oh, God, go, go, go.

Jack saw it all at once, Cassie churning up the slope under the ledge, the rancher's body striking the ground in a tangle, the immense bear closing the distance but slowing, stopping, rearing up over Dunn's crumpled body, roaring, Jesus Christ what an enormous . . . The bear, back on all fours, reaching down, snatching Dunn up, jaws clamped on the man's abdomen, rising up again, the body being hurled back and forth, its head snapping, arms and legs flapping, a broken rag doll spouting blood.

Jack leapt from the ledge and skittered down the slope toward Cassie, shouting, "It's okay, it's okay, it's me!"

No, no, this is a bad dream, I'll wake up when my heart explodes in my chest; who's this? Who's this? I can't breathe anymore. I can't run anymore.

Jack? Here?

"Jack?" she shrieked.

He grabbed her arm and pulled her up the slope.

"C'mon, c'mon! Run!"

"I can't," she gasped. "I can't."

"You have to." He pulled, and she pumped her legs. They reached the ledge.

"The bear," she said. "Where . . ."

"It's down below," he said, panting. "Distracted. For now. Come on. We gotta get out of here. Now."

They scrambled up the slope and into the tunnel. Cassie felt like someone had plunged a knife into her side. This was no wormhole where they'd be safe. This was the *bears'* tunnel.

"Jack," she gasped, clutching her side. "I've got to stop. I need to . . . You're bleeding! Your shoulder's all bloody."

"It's not that bad," Jack said, holding it tight with his other hand. "Not deep. We can fix it later. But we better get out of this tunnel. What's that rifle?"

"A dart gun. Anesthetic."

"Why didn't you use it back there?"

"I did." She hated to admit it. "I missed."

"Load it," Jack said. "You won't miss the next time."

Next time? Cassie didn't want to think about any next time. It took a minute to get the darts from her pack and load one, putting two others in a pocket of her overalls. "What are you . . . ? How did you . . . ?" she asked, still trying to get her breath. The stitch in her side had gone.

"Long story. I'll tell you later. I came another way, was waiting for you up there, by the pool. That's the only place you knew to go. But I saw a light behind you, up on the flowstone, you know? So I stayed out of sight. It was Dunn. He followed you into this tunnel, and I followed him. Now, let's go."

My God, Cassie thought. Dunn had been somewhere behind her the whole time. He had to have faked getting hit with the anesthetic by the entrance. "He shot one of the cubs, the bastard," Cassie said as they began ascending through the tunnel. "Killed it. What distracted that bear back there? Him?"

"I guess old Tracer Dunn is dinner by now."

Cassie's stomach lurched violently. It could so easily have been her. "Can we go a little faster?" The nauseating stink in the tunnel was growing stronger. She felt the tears well up in her eyes, and she began to sob uncontrollably. She was stumbling along behind Jack, crying, tears streaming down her cheeks, just like a little girl.

TWENTY-NINE

The female bear's rage subsides as she feeds on her prey, her snout, her whole face, covered with warm blood from the torn abdomen and the organs within. She turns, leaving the remainder on the ground, and pads through the columns of rock and over the boulders to her den. Through the blood on her snout, she smells more. One is squealing there. She presses her nose toward them, touching one of them. It moves toward her stomach. She reaches her nose out for the other, touches it. It doesn't move. She pushes it. Still it doesn't move.

One of her cubs is nuzzling her hungrily. The other is still. From deep within her chest there arises a long, low moaning sound that fills the darkness and reverberates from the rock.

They had reached the cascade of red flowstone when they heard, distantly, a sound like the wind blowing, a long, low moaning sound. They stopped and listened. The moan continued.

"Jesus, what's that?" Jack said. "It sounds like it's coming from back there."

"Grief, I'd guess," Cassie said. "The mother found her dead cub. That bastard Dunn."

From somewhere else, they heard a deeper growling sound, faint. And what seemed like coughing. There was no way to tell where it came from, but it meant there was another bear somewhere. Jack insisted that Cassie precede him up the flowstone. She would be safe on the way up and, once there, she would still be safe since the tunnel leading away from the edge narrowed down at one point to where you had to crawl on your stomach to get through. No way a bear could do it. He would be right along after her, and they could rest, eat, gather themselves. He would keep the dart gun with him and bring it up.

"How are you going to do that?" Cassie asked. "You've only got one good arm."

"I'll do it with my one good arm," Jack said. "Now go." He watched her disappear upward into the dark beyond the reach of his lamp. He realized he was getting a bit light-headed, and he fetched a food bar from his pack and ate it. The bleeding had stopped on his shoulder, but he imagined it would start again when he began climbing. He sat down, his back against the wall, waiting for Cassie's call and reflecting on the disaster taking place in what he had thought of as "his" cavern. There were at least two bears active, probably more. Surely more. He calculated that the odds of both him and Cassie getting out of here alive were about fifty-fifty. Was the glass half full or half empty?

An hour later, the two of them were safe in the tunnel a few feet back from the precipice. The climb had become an agony, his shoulder throbbing, his legs weakening. He'd had to stop at decreasing intervals to keep his calves from cramping up and to get his strength back. He guessed he'd lost more blood than he thought. His pack grew heavier and heavier, a dead weight, and the rifle kept hanging on his back, the strap raising hell with his shoulder wound. At the top, only his head above the edge, he'd seen that Cassie had an expression on her face somewhere between concern and outright fear. She had grabbed him by the collar and helped haul him over the edge. Now she was strapping his shoulder with white tape from the first aid kit. Her fingers felt warm on his skin, gentle. His helmet sat on the ground, casting light on his shoulder.

"We're in trouble, aren't we?" she said.

"We'll get out."

"You need to eat."

"Yeah."

They ate and drank, and Jack felt drowsy.

"We don't need to go anywhere right now, do we?" she said.

"No. We can rest."

She rearranged herself into a sitting position and pointed at her lap. Jack put his head on her thigh and went immediately to sleep. Cassie reached out and turned off his lamp, then turned off hers and listened to him breathe in the dark. Every now and then she thought she heard a far-off coughing sound, but the distant moaning had either stopped or they'd gotten out of its range.

The young male bear is increasingly irritated. He has lost the enticing new scent that was drawing him, and he has himself become confused, lost. He stands in a place full of obstacles in the dark. It is damp underfoot. He is puzzled, angry. He growls again, snaps his jaws. Coughs. These are the sounds of anger or threat. He threatens this unfamiliar part of the world he has become lost in and presses on.

Cassie awoke with her chin on her chest and a sore neck. She needed to use her hand to push up her head. She flicked on her headlamp and looked at her watch. Just past midnight. What difference does that make? she asked herself. Midnight, noon, all the same in this awful hole. She didn't hear the coughing noise. Her leg, the one Jack's head rested on, had gone to sleep. She noticed he had put his hand on her thigh beside his head. She reached down and pushed some errant black hair back toward his temple, and his eyes opened.

"I could happily stay right here," he said.

"How do you feel?"

"Terrible."

"Me too," she said.

"So, we're off."

They geared up, and Cassie shook off the pins and needles in her leg. "I hate this," she said. "It feels like your foot's got dropsy or whatever. You go first." It wasn't just her leg that was numb. She was numb to the core, all the conflicting emotions of the past hours having exhausted her. Awe at seeing the cubs, anger, terror, disgust, dread, a deep-seated sadness, a hopelessness akin to grief—but for whom? The cub? All these creatures? Herself? She thought she was going to cry again. In the light of her lamp, she saw Jack crawling ahead of her through the tunnel, humping along like a three-legged dog, keeping his shoulder as free of motion as he could. He had saved her life back there. Was he—were they—strong enough to get out of here? It was all so sad.

It was an eternity of walking, crawling, slithering through tight spots, climbing, scrambling over too many rocks, stopping to listen, to sniff for the rank bear smell, heart leaping whenever water dripped or pebbles fell. Were they being stalked? Again as before when they were fleeing this place a thousand years ago, Cassie's feet were sore, ankles sore, legs aching, rubbery. Jack plodded along in front of her, an exhausted slump to his shoulders She carried the dart gun, which had begun to weigh a ton. From time to time, they stopped to drink, to rest. She would look at her watch, but the hands on the dial, the numbers, time itself, had lost meaning. She was too tired to be fearful. Just numb, making their way through vaguely familiar territory.

"We're almost there," Jack said as they crossed a large cavern littered with huge boulders and graced at the far end with vast, fluted columns. They had let themselves down ten feet from a tunnel, down the smooth caramel flowstone to the floor, and were amid the columns when they heard a low growl.

"Oh, shit," Jack said. He reached back, winced, and grabbed Cassie's hand. "Run! Run, for chrissakes!"

They dodged among the columns, reached the far wall, and began scrambling up the loose rock. Over the sound of rock falling and pebbles rattling, the growl grew louder. Jack reached the top of the loose rock, a ledge, and yanked Cassie up, almost flinging her into the black maw of a tunnel, shouting, "Head down, head down!" She raced along on her knees, scraping them on the rock, and felt Jack behind her, scrabbling, and the tunnel was filled with a thick smell of musk, with deafening sound. It had to be an earthquake, a cave-in. Cassie's ears were shot with pain. The bear, jammed in the tunnel only a few yards behind them, unable to move farther, roared in frustration, its wide jaws snapping.

"Don't look back! Just go! Go!" Jack shouted, and Cassie crawled on until the tunnel narrowed and removed her pack, lashed it to her foot, and began inching her way through. The horrible roaring had subsided, and now Cassie heard the thunderous drumbeat of her heart pounding in her chest. But they were safe.

The tunnel opened up somewhat, permitting her to crawl again. It was widening. They were nearly at the clamshell-shaped room only seventy-odd feet beneath the entrance hole. As the tremendous infusion of adrenaline subsided in her blood, she suddenly felt tired. Her arms gave way, and she pitched forward, painfully landing on her chest on the rock.

"You okay?" Jack said from behind her.

"Yeah, yeah. Just slipped." She pushed herself up and crawled on and in moments realized that the tunnel had ended; she was in the clamshell and could stand up. She rose to her feet, bumped her helmet lightly on the overhang, and ducked down again as Jack came up bedside her and stepped forward. Just then she was aware of a sickening smell and looked up.

Her lamp and Jack's, who was a pace ahead of her, lit up the bear. He stood between them and the orange rope that was their last, their final passage to safety. He was enormous in the yellow light, reddish lips pulled back in a snarl, massive teeth gleaming in the light, slobber dripping from his mouth, and the room was filled with an unholy growl that grew louder and louder like an onrushing tornado. Jack stepped between her and the bear, its immense head as high as his, only a few steps away. She pulled the dart gun off her back and aimed at the bear, but Jack was in the way, crouched.

"Jack! Get down! Get down!"

She saw the bear's huge paw flash through the light, and Jack ducked. The bear roared, eyes burning red. Cassie fired over Jack's head, aiming for the place where the long white neck met the thick chest. Yes! A hit. The bear screamed, swatted at its chest with one paw, lashed out with another as it lunged forward, and Jack screamed and toppled, his legs knocked out from under him, falling on his back. The bear stood over Jack's body, mouth snapping slowly, and then sagged and fell sideways. Its massive paw lay on one of Jack's spraddled legs.

"Jack!" she screamed. "Oh no, Jack!" She leapt over to him, the bear stench filling her head, and saw that one of the claws was stuck in through Jack's overalls and into his thigh. There was a large tear in the white cloth, and it was now turning red. He was looking at her wide-eyed but blinking. Oh, thank God, he's blinking. She squatted over his body and grabbed the paw in both hands. It was almost a foot across, the claws a half a foot long, black, ugly. She yanked at the paw, her stomach churning, and it didn't move. She leaned forward to get more leverage, and pulled again, and saw the horrid black claw emerge from Jack's leg with a sickening oozing sound.

"Can you move?" she shouted around the bile that had risen in her throat. "Can you move your leg?"

His legs closed, and she let the massive paw drop to the ground. She stood up, turned to face him, and reached for his arm. "Not that one," he said. She grabbed the other and pulled, and he managed to get to his feet, the weight on his remaining good leg. He was wincing.

"Okay," he said groggily. "Okay. You're gonna have to go up and get help. I can't climb that rope. This leg doesn't work, and this arm doesn't work. You go, and I'll stay here. Leave me with the dart gun in case he wakes up before you get back."

"No way, Jack Whittaker. No fucking way. You're coming with me."

"But—"

"Shuck your pack, all that junk around your waist. Give me that webbing you use as a belt. Take off your boots. Right, I'm the Chinese general now. I'm organizing this orderly retreat." She helped him off with the boots, and he shucked all his gear.

"Now the overalls," she said. "I've got to do something about that wound."

He stood in his sweater and shorts, and she squeezed the bleeding gash together with tape and wrapped the leg with gauze, sealing off the puncture until later, when it could be induced to bleed. She led him, hopping on one leg, over to the rope and turned her back. "You're good with knots. Tie yourself to me." She handed him the webbing and began fitting herself with the rope-walking rig.

"Cassie, you can't haul me up that rope. I'm too heavy."

"You're gonna do some of the work. You got one good arm."

Five minutes later, Jack was strapped to Cassie's body with a multitude of knots and carabiners and to the ratchet device called a Jumar in such a way that some of his weight would be transferred to the rope. "Okay," Cassie said. "Let's go." She reached up with her left leg and pushed down. She pushed the ratchet up the rope and stepped down with her right leg. They ascended. Six inches with each step. As she took each step, Jack pulled with his good arm.

It took almost an hour. They stopped so many times, they lost count. Her muscles screamed with pain. All she could do was stare at the rope, the straps, the ratchets, and push with one leg, then the other. When she dared to think she was getting close, she looked up and saw the night sky above them, a ragged circle of blue-black sky with a handful of tiny diamonds. She was crying, tears streaming down her face again.

"We're going to make it, Jack. We're going to make it."

She had no idea how they got over the edge of the hole and onto the ground. Her legs, by then, barely worked. It must have been Jack, hauling them over the edge with his good arm, maybe both. He rolled them over on their side, and his hands began undoing all the straps, all the gear. They were out. They were free. Lying on the open ground, underneath the grand canopy of the sky, they were free. Safe.

"You saved my life back there," Jack said. "Thanks."

"We're even, then."

Jack rolled over on his back, his arms spread out. "Ahhh!" he said. "Do you know what, Cassie?"

"What?"

"What you did was stupid. And selfish. I discovered that cave, and I shared it with you. Then you decide its future without any regard for me. That's selfish. Then you go down there alone—anyway, you thought you were alone. And that's just plain stupid. I love you, you know that, but you just can't go treating the world that way. Look at the result. We came damn close to dying down there, and one guy did."

"A mess," Cassie said, almost a whisper. "Oh, Jack, I'm so sorry."

"I don't give a shit about that cave anymore," Jack went on. "I found it. Probably the most amazing damn cave ever. I discovered it, the Holy Grail. And that's enough for me. I need a new dream. That's not *my* cave. It's the bears' cave, as a matter of fact."

Cassie rolled toward him and put her head on his shoulder.

"Do you mind?" she said.

"Why would I?"

"I stink."

"You're beautiful when you stink."

They looked up at the sky for a few minutes as the pink of dawn crept into it. A pair of ravens arrowed overhead, wheeled, and disappeared beyond the canyon wall.

"I better get you to the hospital," Cassie said. "Get you stitched up."

"Stitches? Nah. They're just cosmetic. I'd rather not have to explain how I got these cuts. They'll heal by themselves."

"We better go anyway. If there's another entrance to the cave, one of those bears could be . . ." She shuddered at the thought.

Grunting with aches and pains, they stood up and made their way down from the ledge to Cassie's Jeep, which sat in the shadows. Next to it was Jack's Trooper.

"We'll come back for yours later," Cassie said. "You're too woozy to drive."

Five minutes later, Cassie steered the Jeep onto the highway.

"Jack, you're right. I was stupid. And selfish. Tight-assed and holier-than-thou. I'm really sorry." They drove on another mile before Jack said anything.

"What do we do about all this now?" His head was lolling on the headrest, and he looked like he was half asleep. "Call in Fish and Wildlife?"

Cassie smiled. "They didn't believe me when I called them about it. Who knows about those bears? No one but us, right? Maybe it'd be best if no one knows about them."

"What about Dunn? Don't we have to report to the police or something? Then everyone will know about the bears."

"That son of a bitch," Cassie said vehemently. "He killed a cub—God, its head just disappeared—and he tried to kill you. Probably would have killed me too after he got all the bears. We don't owe him a thing. And I don't guess anyone'll ever find much of him."

"And so he's just a missing person. Vanished," Jack said. "A missing person who won't be making the payments on his ranch."

"It goes on the block and we buy it," Cassie said.

"And?"

"And then the bears will be left alone, at least till next time."

"What about science?" Jack asked.

"There'll be a time for that. They hibernate a long time."

"We'll have to run some cattle," Jack said. "Keep the grazing license. Probably lose a few head till the bears hibernate." He closed his eyes and felt sleep coming on.

"Where are we going?" he asked.

Cassie looked over at him. His face was covered with grime, even his eyelids. He looked terrible.

"My place," she said.

EPILOGUE

At a press conference held in Carlsbad a few days after the cave-in, a spokesperson for the Department of Energy announced that shipments of transuranic wastes to the Waste Isolation Pilot Plant had been halted until an internal report was completed. The report was due in December, and it would provide the secretary of energy with a thorough analysis of the causes of the cave-in and the options available for WIPP.

The spokesperson also announced that the director of WIPP, Anna Maria Gonzales, was transferring to Washington, D.C., where she would take up the position of assistant secretary of energy for administration, reporting directly to the secretary. This position, of course, called for confirmation by the United States Senate, which, the spokesperson said, was virtually assured. He announced the name of the next director of WIPP.

Two days later, Derby Catlin's newspaper, *The Intelligencer,* was graced with its first banner headline. Derby realized that the little fact that he knew was probably his only chance to loft the paper out of triviality and low circulation. He decided to risk it all, even the wrath of the Carlsbad boosters, and if it didn't work, he would abandon the paper and move elsewhere. The headline read:

DOE TELLS ONLY PART OF CAVE-IN STORY

The article below the headline was brief (there wasn't that much to say). It merely pointed out that "this reporter" had seen local rancher, Tracer Dunn, being escorted into the WIPP site by its director of security only hours before the cave-in was said to have occurred. It described the rancher as a man "with little affection for the federal government" but who nonetheless apparently had taken on some assignment that called for him to be carrying a Winchester carbine. "This reporter" also had determined that Dunn had returned home late the night of the cave-in. All of this had taken place only days after Dunn had put his ranch (which was adjacent to the WIPP site) on the market and then taken it off the market. In the meantime, Dunn had disappeared, along with his common-law wife, leaving behind all his belongings, including a pinto horse and his cattle.

Derby's report was noticed by the editors of *The Albuquerque Tribune* and carried verbatim, along with a cautious editorial chiding DOE for playing things so close to its chest, creating the kind of public mistrust that made its important work more difficult to achieve. The *Tribune'*s piece was picked up by the wires and then the television networks, and soon all the anti-nuclear groups were aswarm, and a United States senator from New Hampshire called for a thorough-going congressional investigation of this tragedy at WIPP that was now enshrouded in murk. Senate confirmation of Anna Maria Gonzales as assistant secretary for administration would, of course, be delayed until the investigation was complete.

Derby Catlin thoroughly enjoyed his fifteen *days,* not minutes, of fame and looked forward to its renewal when the Senate investigation got under way and he, obviously, would be a star witness, if not *the* star witness.

Later, in the early autumn, Winnie Anne Macklin, age eleven, won the barrel-racing event at the children's rodeo on a pinto horse named Chico. The Eddy County Livestock Committee had agreed to take possession of the abandoned animal and promptly gave it to Winnie Anne as a reward for the bravery she displayed when she rescued a four-year-old boy and a dog from the Pecos River.

On the same day Winnie Anne won the barrel racing, the bank held a closing in which Dr. Cassandra Roberts received the deed to the ranch of the missing Tracer Dunn in return for making the payments he had failed to make and assuming the remaining debt on the place (at a half point higher interest rate). The following day, Jack Whittaker took up residence in the abandoned trailer and began making repairs to the old ranch house. A herd of fifty head of cattle was delivered by truck to replace the cattle Dunn left behind, which had been sold by the Eddy County Livestock Committee.

One of the Roberts herd disappeared within a week of arrival. Another vanished the following month. There were no losses thereafter.